THE READER'S RESORT

THE READER'S RESORT

E. M. JONES

LAMPPOST PUBLISHING

Published 2026

Hardcover ISBN: 979-8-9910106-3-4

Paperback ISBN: 979-8-9910106-4-1

E-ISBN: 979-8-9910106-5-8

Logo design by Kim Taylor Creative

Cover design by Stuart Bache

The story, all names, characters, and incidents portrayed in this production are fictitious. No identification with actual persons (living or deceased), places, buildings, and products is intended or should be inferred.

ALSO BY E. M. JONES

THE DARLING KILLER

GOODNIGHT LYDIA

For Aaron Bogan

For not all books are written with words

Chapter 1

Florence had never desecrated a grave before, but then, this could be the least dangerous thing she'd have to do today.

She parked beside the country road and lowered her foggy window. Light rain sprinkled on her face, mixing with the cool autumn air. The woods were quiet. No cars coming down the street or birds singing in the trees, only raindrops on the forest floor.

Across the street, the cemetery gates were closed and locked. It was six in the morning, leaving Florence roughly fifty minutes before the caretaker showed up. Plenty of time, if she hurried.

She raised the window and shut off the engine. Slinging her old, battered purse over one shoulder, she stood outside her car and listened for oncoming traffic. Florence zipped up her black rain jacket and tucked her hair inside the hood. No umbrella; she needed her hands free.

She jogged across the road. A black gate loomed ahead of her, supported by a stone arch and secured with a thick chain and padlock. A medieval sign hung from the arch that read, BALOR CEMETERY.

A wrought-iron fence surrounded the property, waist-high and topped with small spikes. Florence wasn't very tall, but she knew she could jump the fence and avoid impalement. Her next option was to climb a tree along the fence line, shimmy to the edge of a branch, and drop down on the other side.

No. This was the fastest way to get inside.

Gripping the fence with both hands, Florence gingerly hopped up and wedged one shoe between two spikes while her other foot dangled behind her. So far so good.

Behind her, the road echoed with heavy tires on wet pavement, coming around the bend.

Florence jumped and cleared the fence, instantly slipping on the wet grass. She fell on her back, knocking the air from her lungs right as a pickup truck sped by the cemetery.

Despite the dew soaking into her jeans, she didn't move at first. She stared at the towering archway, the medieval sign gently swaying in the wind. The branches of a tall oak tree stretched far above her, shuddering like wings in flight.

How long had it been since she'd last visited this place? Three years? Four? Far too long. And always during the day, with flowers. Not like this.

Rolling to her feet, Florence fixed her hood and adjusted her purse, thankful she didn't land on it the wrong way and accidentally join the dead.

She stared at the long sloping hill in front of her and the gravestones shrouded in fog. She knew the way, didn't she? Three years hadn't damaged her memory. She could find Chloe's grave in her sleep. Florence closed her eyes, breathed in, and started to walk. How often did this cemetery appear in her nightmares? How often did she feel guilty for rarely coming here?

As she walked deeper into the cemetery, Florence looked over her shoulder, convinced someone would arrive and ruin her plan—the caretaker running ahead of schedule, a passing jogger, or a spouse too haunted to sleep. But on a bleak Wednesday morning, who wanted to be among the dead? No normal person would grieve like this.

Florence made it halfway up the hill and stepped to the right, stopping at a gray oval headstone.

Chloe Lang. 2000—2017.

Florence's heart ached, trying to picture what Chloe would look like now, at twenty-six years old. Engraved on the headstone was the last thing Chloe had said to her mom: *I love you, goodnight.*

Before the funeral, Chloe's mom had asked Florence if those words were good enough for the epitaph. As if Florence, Chloe's best friend, had any say in the matter. As if, after everything that happened, she still had a place in their family.

Florence knelt beside Chloe's grave and opened her purse. She dug to the bottom, removing a small hand-held shovel, and held it up in the dim light. The black rubber handle fit perfectly inside her palm.

It was one thing to buy a shovel at the hardware store, knowing what she wanted it for, but another thing entirely to sit in front of her best friend's grave and intend to use it.

In the early morning mist, the shovel looked like a knife. Florence raised it above her head, gripping the handle with both hands. It wouldn't take much; the rain had softened the ground. She struck the earth, pushing the little shovel down as far as it would go. Leaning over the grave, she pressed one hand against the grass and pulled the shovel out. She stabbed the ground to break up the soil and scooped out chunks of mud and rock to form a dirt mound beside her.

The short, erratic shoveling stole her breath, but she didn't stop. She knew if she stopped, she would give up and run away.

And she was tired of running.

Florence dug deeper, thinking about the casket; about Chloe's bony hands folded, her skull grinning up at Florence with pride. The cold, soggy earth wormed beneath her nails. In her head, she thought this would be neat, like gardening, but she felt like an animal digging for a dead thing.

"I'm sorry I took so long," she told Chloe. "I'm sorry I never came by." Only three visits in nine years, and each one harder to stomach than the last, each trip through the cemetery like a penance, a purgatory nightmare.

Dropping the shovel, Florence wiped her grimy hands on her jeans and rifled through her purse, removing a battered paperback copy of *Jane Eyre*. With a deeply cracked spine, a torn front cover, and dog-eared, stained pages, the book wore the scars of a hard but fulfilling life.

Florence opened the book to the title page and the handwritten note: *I think you should read this. -Chloe*

Florence remembered meeting Chloe at a park. They were both turning eleven and playing with their friends, and after their birthday parties merged on that windy spring night, they did everything together. On their thirteenth birthday, Chloe gave her a book. *Jane Eyre*. Straight from Chloe's personal library. And despite the personalized note in *Jane Eyre*, Florence had never wanted to keep it. She knew it was Chloe's favorite book and always intended to give it back, believing she had all the time in the world to do so. They'd spent hours talking about the book, watching every TV and movie adaptation, rating the scariness of the mad wife upstairs and the romantic appeal of every Mr. Rochester. If most friendships have a no-going-back moment, theirs was on the couch, with snacks, eyes glued to the television with the copy of *Jane Eyre* open and face-down beside them, deepening that cracked and broken spine.

"You told me you wanted to be buried with your books," Florence said, placing *Jane Eyre* in the freshly dug hole. "Do you remember that? I thought it was a wonderful idea. I'm just sorry I waited so long to give this back to you."

She pushed the dirt mound over the hole, burying the book with Chloe, thinking that if Charlotte Brontë were present, she would grimly approve.

Florence leveled the ground, tapped it with the shovel, and ripped up grass nearby, sprinkling it over the disturbed earth.

She made it look as normal as possible, then placed the shovel inside an empty grocery bag and stuck it back inside her purse. She would need it again later for something much riskier than disturbing a grave.

"I'm going to the resort," she told Chloe, pain forming in her chest. "We should be going together, since it was your dream."

Steady there, Flo, just breathe.

"I never got the chance to apologize, so I want to find you and make sure you're okay, and finally tell you how sorry I am."

She stood up, wiped her eyes, and touched the cold headstone. "Can you meet me at the resort? Or are you already there?"

She looked around, praying for someone to answer her questions, but there were no ghosts in the cemetery.

"I think you're already there, so I'm going to try and contact you." She smiled, hoping Chloe was somehow listening. "Every single day, I wish that I could change what happened and get you back. So this is how I can see you again."

Again, no answer.

Florence shouldered her purse and walked down the hill, looking back at Chloe's grave and hoping for *something* to happen. But it never did.

She climbed over the fence, crossed the road, and started her car. In the cemetery, the fog was lifting. She could almost see Chloe's headstone up on the hill and the brown patch of broken earth in front of it.

She had never done something like that before, and while it scared her, it was a necessary step for what came next.

The resort was a forty-five-minute drive through the countryside; she needed to leave now to beat traffic. She'd expected more relief after returning the book, but this was only the start. Heading to The Reader's Resort and performing a dangerous ritual at Ohio's most notorious haunted site—that would be the true test.

After nine years of regret, Florence would make things right.

She was going to find her friend.

Chapter 2

Florence *had* to be close.

She'd come to a dead stop in the countryside, blurry red brake lights stretching half a mile up the road. She checked the location on her phone. If her position was accurate, The Reader's Resort was up ahead, hidden behind a towering grassy hill with a crooked tree at the top. The October air had turned its leaves into a thousand little sunsets. With the gentle patter of rain, it was all so dreary and drab and perfect.

Traffic hardly moved, promising at least another half hour before Florence could park. Unlike other resorts, where you could check in and out when you wanted, The Reader's Resort required the same designated stay for everyone. Like a cruise. Five days and four nights, Wednesday through Sunday. The founders believed that if everyone stayed and read together, it would build a genuine community around books. Who wouldn't want to be part of something like that?

What the hell, Florence thought, turning her car halfway into the ditch. She put her hazard lights on and threw her rain jacket hood over her head. Stepping out of the car, she felt the beady, judgmental eyes of everyone nearby and decided she didn't care what they thought.

Your hands and jeans are filthy; you already look like a lunatic.

She smiled at that. *What can I say? I'm impatient.*

Someone honked, and she ignored them. She trudged up the steep hill, slipping on the wet grass. She placed her palms against the ground to balance herself, her fingernails lined with dirt from Chloe's grave. Eyes on the hilltop, she climbed and thought about how stupid she probably looked. Imagine waiting in line like a normal human, only to see a mud-covered woman scamper up a hill like an animal? Oh God, what if she fell? How embarrassing would that be? She'd slide all the way into the road. Into someone's *car*.

But she still didn't look back, and she didn't fall. After a few more slips, she reached the summit. The wind knocked her hood back, and she left it, unbothered. The dark green countryside churned like a stormy ocean. After a lifetime of walking the busy streets of Sharonville and watching the graffiti-stained trains slither past like great metal worms, this isolated part of southern Ohio was another world. It promised endless adventures—the old-fashioned kind, the kind that didn't seem to exist anymore.

Florence brushed the raindrops from her eyelashes and looked at the field below, at The Reader's Resort. Of course, the pictures online didn't capture the best of it. Not even close.

The resort looked like a sprawling Victorian mansion. The main structure stood four stories high, with dark windows and Gothic arches, balconies, and ornate railings. It looked like a castle, a fairy tale.

It rested on the edge of a cliff. The rest of the resort, the expansions and added wings, the many rooms and reading nooks, extended behind the main building and followed the curve of the ridge. If the rumors were true, they had also built enormous rooms beneath the resort for storage and employee-only spaces.

A light fog clung to the resort and drifted over the cliff, shrouding the valley beneath them and the hills in the distance.

Florence couldn't stop staring at it. People claimed The Reader's Resort changed their lives. After they left, they didn't see the world the same way. The books and rooms changed them. They believed in magic again.

She also finally understood its reputation for ghost sightings. It was creepy in a brooding, mysterious way, like how she imagined Thornfield in her head.

Florence slid down the hill and back to her car. Traffic hadn't moved much, and since people had nothing better to do, they watched her stumble through the rain.

She didn't care. The world had disappeared. She was half a mile away from the place she and Chloe had dreamed about.

Half a mile from finding her best friend.

She moved faster because walking felt too slow. For once, she had something to embrace. Something ahead of her, as real as the rain and the wind in her face.

Back in her car, she waited impatiently for traffic to move. Finally, she parked in the lot behind the resort and followed the winding sidewalk to the front entrance.

Dragging her suitcase behind her, Florence stared at the tall glass doors. A resort employee, wearing the traditional purple button-up and black vest uniform, extended one white-gloved hand like a magician ushering her onstage. She lost her breath; she couldn't help it. Despite her true intentions for coming here, she was still a reader, with a reader's soft, bleeding heart.

Smiling, the man opened the door for her. "Welcome... to The Reader's Resort."

Florence thanked him, stepped inside the breezeway, and a pair of automatic doors opened to let her through. She wore her purse and backpack over her shoulders, pulling her suitcase along, the little wheels silent on the thin mat beneath her.

She entered the lobby, a place she'd seen a thousand pictures of. Unlike in the themed rooms, the resort management encouraged taking pictures in the lobby and posting them online.

On her left side, the reception crew waited behind a long, polished wooden counter. They also wore purple shirts with black vests, their winning smiles and white gloves bathed in the warm magic-hour glow of antique lamps.

Straight ahead, two glass-walled side-by-side elevators moved between the resort's four floors. Two women walked into the left elevator. As the doors closed, the women looked at the packed lobby through the glass walls, their faces pinched with excitement. The elevator took off, and Florence felt her stomach lift with it

No. Don't trust the elevators.

She'd read that online somewhere, but it could've been another exaggerated tale from a paranoid guest.

On the lobby's right side, guests lounged on couches and chairs. Against the wall, a small staircase led to a round balcony, the kind you might see inside an old stage theater. The balcony featured a thick wooden railing with a detailed floral design carved into the wood. Behind the balcony, a built-in bookcase was filled with rare editions, signed collections, and out-of-print books. They were organized by color, from the deepest maroon to the brightest yellow. Above the bookcase was a round stained-glass window of a woman sitting beside a stream, her long dark hair flowing into the water. She held an open book in her lap, surrounded by green hills and a purple sunset sky.

A tank of water was behind the stained-glass window. When the water moved, the image rippled, projecting light across the lobby. Florence looked up at the mix of purple and green on the ceiling, swirling like an ocean, the color of the northern lights.

She'd seen pictures of the balcony, the bookcase, and the stained-glass window before. But nothing captured what it *felt* like to stand in the center of it all; to hear the chatter of excited readers, the soothing voices in reception, and the occasional laughter.

A woman stood on the balcony and posed for a picture, one hand on her hip, the bookcase and window behind her.

Influencers waited years for this shot. Posing on the balcony at The Reader's Resort was pure status. If not pictures, they made reels with clever sayings or celebratory dances, doing all the cute stuff Florence never figured out how to do.

I made it, the picture would tell their followers. *I made it to paradise.*

Men and women stood in line for their balcony picture, their languages mixing. The resort attracted people from around the world because there was nothing else like it. Even if themed hotels or lodges could compete aesthetically, no one matched the resort's highly praised curating team. Without them, this place would be a gimmick.

"Welcome, welcome," a voice echoed. Halfway down the reception counter, a young man, barely out of high school, waved and passed his fellow co-workers to greet her. "How are you today, miss?"

Florence had been standing in everyone's way, gawking. She moved to the counter, shifting her backpack to relieve her shoulders. "Hi, I'm good, you?"

"Never been better! Name and ID, please."

"Florence Noelle." She set her driver's license on the counter.

The young man paused. He stared at the computer screen and bit his lower lip, as if he had bad news.

Florence stopped breathing. She'd checked the confirmation email a million times. She *was* a guest at The Reader's Resort on this day and at this time. Everything was supposed to be in order.

He smiled. "Perfect. Your room is ready."

Returning her license, he gave her a thin card with a black stripe along the back. "This has your name, room, and account on it. You'll use it for the unlimited meals and drinks package." Then he reached under the counter, opened a drawer, and straightened. "And here's your room key."

He held an old skeleton key with a tag attached, the room number printed on both sides.

Florence took the key, running her fingers over the metal edges.

"We pride ourselves on our unique physical keys. Please remember to manually lock your door. It will *not* lock on its own. We also have spares, of course, if you need them."

The key was heavier than it looked. "Thank you so much."

He handed her a folded map of the resort. The front picture showed a woman reading a novel and laughing, showing off impossibly white teeth. The map came with a packet stuffed full of schedules and additional information.

She thanked him again and pretended to show interest in the resort's amenities. As if she had any intention of sunbathing on a pool float.

He instructed her to set the suitcase and backpack on a cart beside the counter, where someone would tag them and drop them off in her room.

Florence left the suitcase but kept her backpack and purse. The last thing she needed was someone looking inside her bags and calling security. She thanked him once more and walked toward the elevators. When she looked back, the young man stood off to the side, texting. He looked up, noticed her staring, and smiled with a blush.

Something in his eyes bothered her, as if he knew her from somewhere. It was likely just her imagination. She moved behind the elevators, leaving his sight.

She went to press the UP button when the elevator doors suddenly opened, unprompted.

Maybe they *were* haunted after all.

Florence walked inside the elevator, and the doors closed, swallowing her.

Checking her room number again, she pushed the button for the third floor. The elevator jolted upward, perfectly ordinary.

Through the glass walls, Florence looked at the crowded lobby, the endless line for the balcony, and for a brief second, she felt like a guest. Part of her longed to see the room they chose for her, the curated bookshelf, the view from her windows.

Her room could be *anything*. Readers talked about the themed rooms online even though they weren't supposed to, so the resort changed them often, sometimes weekly. It was impossible to know what they had in rotation. Florence imagined her room as a cozy murder-mystery cabin with a roaring fire and paintings on the walls. Or a pirate hideout, or a medieval royal bed chamber.

Her expectations were too high; she knew that, but how could she avoid it? Chloe used to tell Florence about the resort and their magical rooms. Whenever they stayed up too late on a Friday night, half-asleep on the couch while the TV played, Chloe would whisper stories about the resort. Her words built a fantasy world inside Florence's head, and now here she was, living a dream they once shared.

The elevator dinged, and the doors opened to the third floor.

Despite the hope of seeing Chloe again, this could go wrong in a million different ways.

Florence took a deep breath. She'd come too far to run away now, and with everything in place, she had to finish what she started.

There was only one thing left to do.

Chapter 3

Florence stepped onto the third floor and checked her room number again.

Room 350 could be *anything*. Any theme, any time period. Even though it didn't truly matter, Florence still wanted to invite Chloe into a room they would both love, a room capable of fixing what was broken.

The hallway walls were cream-colored and decorated with dull yellow light bulbs behind thin wire fixtures. The plush carpet was the color of blood, and as Florence walked, she left a trail of dark footprints behind.

Along with the themed rooms, the doors also varied in style. Some looked ancient and required a skeleton key like hers. Others didn't have keyholes or even door handles. One looked like the entrance to a medieval dungeon. Another was entirely a screen with clips of deep space nebulae on repeat. What could possibly be in that room? A space station? Then Florence remembered Gravity by Tess Gerritsen, and her heart jumped. She envied the people who worked here, who knew every theme. Every little secret. And they weren't allowed to talk about it.

Although most themes rotated, some rooms had been used for decades and were legendary to hardcore fans: Dracula's castle, the Halloween Forest, and the Hobbit Hole.

Florence took the skeleton key from her pocket and cradled it in her palm. When she had filled out the resort's application, she kept Chloe in mind. Sadly, they didn't have a *Jane Eyre* room (and if they did, it *would* be terrifying, wouldn't it?). Instead, Florence targeted the next best thing:

the Sherlock Holmes flat. Chloe had read the complete works of Sir Arthur Conan Doyle because she was a nerd, and Florence absolutely loved her for it (Florence had made it halfway through the completed works herself before getting ruthlessly distracted by Poe's entire collection). Old books had been commonplace at Chloe's house—it was like living in a library museum—and always made Florence feel self-conscious about her mom's bland little apartment.

You should be here, Florence thought. *You would be here if I hadn't gone to your house that night.*

She reached the end of the hallway, on the garden side of the resort, and stopped in front of her door. Room 350. This room seemed almost set apart from the others, although Florence couldn't pinpoint why. Maybe because there wasn't a room across the hall from hers.

Either way, this was the right place; the mystical room she'd waited a year and a half for.

It had an ordinary door with an old-timey keyhole. She inserted the skeleton key and turned it, hearing a deep, satisfying *click*.

Florence closed her eyes and slipped inside the room, shutting the door behind her and leaning against it. There would be no rushing this.

Finally, she cracked open her eyes.

The floor was made of old, creaky wood. The queen bed featured a floral-pattern comforter and two pillows as white as the pamphlet lady's front teeth. The headboard was short, stumpy, and slightly crooked. The nightstand, dresser, and desk were a matching set of mud-stained wood and worn brass handles. The desk had an oval mirror above it, and inside, a dull reflection of Florence.

A gramophone sat atop a little table with curved legs, with a pile of old records stacked beneath it: Dean Martin, Frank Sinatra, and Sam Cooke. The right wall was made of wood panels, and pushed against it, between the doors for the bathroom and closet, was an old piano. Above the piano, a tall, narrow bookcase was attached to the wall, holding the fifteen hallowed, curated books.

The glass balcony door let some light in, a natural rival to the ceiling's crystal chandelier. The nightstand held an old lamp with a gleaming milky-white glass shade.

It was a 1940s-style room.

Florence clutched the skeleton key, disappointment digging its teeth into her like a thousand splinters.

This was it?

She *loved* old things. She loved antique stores, old books, and typewriters. They were windows into the past, but...

It looked like an antique store had vomited everywhere.

Florence dropped her purse and backpack on the floor, ungrateful and annoyed at herself for screwing up somewhere on the application. She'd expected so much more than this.

The piano was the only redeeming quality because Chloe loved to play, even though she complained about her piano teacher's annoying habit of snacking during lessons.

Chloe would imitate the teacher by smacking her lips and mumbling, "Now from the top, Chloe-dear," like a Shakespearean actor.

Florence sat on the piano bench, smiling at the memory. *I miss you so much it hurts.*

She examined the bookcase in front of her. Out of the fifteen books, she recognized six of them. She'd already read four, which was typical. The curators couldn't possibly know about every book she'd ever read, and they allowed up to five replacements for that reason.

On the resort's application, she selected Mystery as her top genre, followed by Thrillers and Romance. If the guests didn't have time to read everything, they were allowed to take five books home at the end of their stay. Since she wouldn't do much reading here, Florence hoped her curator had thrown in a few gems she could keep.

But none of the titles caught her eye. Nothing in her wanted to touch the lifeless spines and see the covers. Not when this room was clearly meant for someone else.

It wasn't fair, and she knew that. But Chloe deserved better.

She flopped on the bed, which they must've also snatched from the 1940s, because it was hard and uncomfortable. She half-expected to find a chamber pot in the bathroom and a barrel to wash herself in.

Now she really wasn't being fair.

She opened her phone and tapped on the resort's app. It held everything: e-book and audiobook versions of the titles on her shelf, so she could consume books in her preferred format and seamlessly alternate between them. Readers could also track their reading progress, earn rewards, and, of course, feed the data monster the resort used to improve the guest experience. She logged in with her room number and saw the titles populate, along with a prompt: *Good morning, Florence! Which book would you like to read first?*

Rolling off the bed, she set her phone down and looked at herself in the mirror. She still wore her black rain jacket and muddy jeans. Her eyes looked like the sky before a good rain.

"I'm sorry about this room," she said out loud. "But we'll make it work."

Someone knocked on the door. Florence opened it, letting a resort employee bring her suitcase in and set it on the floor, then make a swift exit.

Florence shut the door and locked it, counting on no more interruptions.

She knelt and opened her backpack. Sure, she had nothing *explicitly* dangerous inside. Only some road flares, crystals, a lighter, lighter fluid, and of course, a book of incantations.

She set everything on the wood floor.

"Okay, Chloe. Come talk to me, girl." Florence withdrew a silver chain with a black raven hanging from it. The necklace had been Chloe's and was wonderfully gothic at that time in their young lives. Florence wore it the night Chloe died and hadn't touched it until she packed for the trip. It spent the last nine years in her dresser, out of sight.

"I know, I never returned this either, like *Jane Eyre*." She placed the necklace on the floor beside the book of incantations and had the same sinking feeling as earlier: that planning something like this and *actually* doing it were two very different things.

She was about to pry open an invisible door she didn't understand and hope that whatever waited on the other side was Chloe. *Just* Chloe.

Florence organized her research on the floor and set out the various methods of summoning spirits:

A Ouija board, a crystal pendulum, white candles, sage, and a pen and paper for automatic writing. Typical stuff, and maybe all fake, but if Florence was going to play the game, she might as well learn the rules.

Next, a stack of printed news articles detailing the tragic past of The Reader's Resort. If someone other than Chloe showed up, she could hopefully identify them.

She stood up, content with the placement of everything, and drew the curtains over the balcony door. She switched the chandelier off and let the room settle into darkness—the old furniture looking broken, weathered, and a little creepy in the low light.

Everything online warned her: *never summon a spirit alone*. Make it a group activity because it's dangerous. But also... have fun with it! Most websites couldn't pick a lane. Was summoning a spirit a harrowing Pandora's Box, or a great way to connect with lost loved ones?

Most people didn't know what they were talking about. They laid out séance rules like it was a banana bread recipe. If it were that simple, everyone would be summoning their dead grandmother for a friendly chat.

One blog was the closest thing to feeling real—enough to give Florence goosebumps when she first started reading. The author posted monthly articles detailing the intricacy of the spiritual realm. *How* did the author know so much? They weren't very forthcoming about that, and Florence didn't care. She read every post they'd published over the last ten years.

The author kept it brief: the spirit world was layered over the natural world. The two worlds were intertwined and commonly bridged, usually where the membrane separating the worlds was extremely frayed.

These were known as thin spots.

The Reader's Resort was likely a thin spot; places with high paranormal activity often were. The author went into extreme detail on the nature of thin spots and how they were affected by high winds. Most of it was quite dense and made Florence wonder if this author did anything else with their life outside of scientific experiments on the supernatural realm.

Probably not.

Either way, the articles were extremely helpful, especially with making contact.

The author offered an easy way to start communicating with the dead: just reach out. Make it as fancy or as simple as you want. If that doesn't work, try the boards, the books, and the crystals.

Just reach out.

The author wrote, "The human soul is the strongest natural bridge to the spiritual world. No other method can replicate its divine power to cross space and time. YOU, reader, are a walking, living thin spot. Humans are doorways between worlds, hence why possession comes from the simple act of opening your inner door and letting something in."

The author barely touched on famous summoning practices. Just reach, and your soul will do the rest.

It almost sounded more far-fetched and New Age than the popular methods, but something about its simplicity gave Florence hope. Of course, she didn't tell a single soul she was doing this. She knew it was unlikely to work. She knew she shouldn't trust a random blogger online. She *knew* these things, but her heart persevered.

She had to try *something*.

And even though she had no clue if Chloe was haunting The Reader's Resort or not, she did have a little faith, and according to that blog, if you could reach through a thin spot, you could generate an echo. Chloe's spirit didn't *have* to be physically close, but it certainly helped.

Florence withdrew the hand shovel from her purse, unwrapped it from the grocery bag, and set it gently on the floor. She wasn't positive the dirt from Chloe's grave would hold any power, but why waste it?

She carefully brushed the dirt into a small pile on the floor and dropped the shovel back inside her purse. Taking a white candle, she lit the wick with a lighter and placed the candle beside the dirt.

What if Chloe showed up exactly how she died? Or partly decomposed?

She stared at the flame, suddenly finding it hard to breathe. Florence couldn't stop her imagination. She pictured Chloe in the corner, her pale flesh decaying, her mouth caked in spit and vomit, hair falling in troubled waves. But Florence couldn't assume anything. For all she knew, Chloe would show up dressed like a goddess, a book in one hand and a spear in the other, a golden halo behind her.

Florence smiled. She took Chloe's necklace and put it around her neck, the raven resting gently against her collarbone.

Just reach out.

Okay, Chloe. Let's do this.

She removed a handwritten letter from her purse and unfolded it. Inside, it contained things she'd never said out loud before. And at the top, she'd written two words:

My Confession.

Chapter 4

Florence stared at the letter in her hands. The candle flickered. Footsteps padded on the floor above her. She looked up as the chandelier swayed like a ship at sea.

Okay, focus. Don't worry about anyone else.

Voices echoed in the hallway, someone called their friend's name, and laughter rang out. So much joy outside her door, and yet in here, Florence's throat burned as she tried not to cry.

Come on, Flo. No stalling. You came all this way.

Focus.

Just reach out.

Florence glanced at the messy handwriting, the smeared ink, and the tear-shaped ripples in the paper. She cleared her throat. "Chloe."

She sighed and started again, struggling to hold the letter still. "Dear Chloe. I'm going to get this wrong, and I'm sorry for that. I'm sorry about more things than I can count. I don't know where you are, but if you can hear me somehow, please talk to me."

She paused, looking around the dark room. But it wouldn't be that easy.

She kept reading. "Nine years ago, I went to your funeral, and I've thought about you every day since. I still wear one of your old T-shirts when I go to sleep, and it makes me dream of when we were young and playing in your backyard. I haven't worn the necklace until now because your mom gave it to you, and..."

She froze, pinching the paper between her fingers. She couldn't breathe again, couldn't say this next part out loud. She felt as if she were standing before God, confessing every sin in her life. Tears blurred her eyes, making it hard to read, but she pushed on. She had to reach.

"I wore it that night, if you remember, because I liked the raven. I was wearing it when I woke up next to you. Your mom probably looked around and never found it."

She shivered, checking the corners of the room. "I should've given it back to her because she would've loved to have it. I'm sorry I kept it in my drawer all these years. I'm sorry I never told your family how much I loved them. After you died, I didn't go see them, which probably hurts you to think about."

Just reach out.

Deep breath, one two three.

"I'm sorry I brought those pills over." There, she said it. And she'd say it again, if Chloe appeared. "I'm sorry I gave them to you. Every day, I think about how you'd still be alive if I hadn't come over that night."

One part left, the part that made her sick to her stomach. "And I'm sorry I left you there and ran away. Please, please forgive me."

It happened on a school night, nine years ago.

Florence and Chloe lived in the same neighborhood and had made a habit of sneaking into each other's houses after dark.

That night, Florence climbed through Chloe's bedroom window, carrying pills they'd tried earlier in the summer. Chloe had already taken something she got from a school friend, and she mixed them when Florence wasn't paying attention. They'd turned seventeen in the spring and spent the summer experimenting with things they didn't understand. They got drunk together, smoked weed together, and tried those pills together.

Florence wished they had died together.

Sometimes she prayed she'd die in her sleep. Sometimes she thought about buying pills again and taking them all. It tempted her, especially at night, in that no-man's-land between sleeplessness and dreaming.

The memory of waking up beside Chloe's cold body, covered in puke, haunted Florence every day. But nothing compared to the raw shame she carried. She wasn't supposed to be at Chloe's that night. And after sobbing into Chloe's pillow, after realizing her best friend had overdosed, Florence climbed back through the window and vanished like a coward. Chloe's necklace dangled from her neck, and her clothes were stained with vomit, but she made it home and never told her mom the truth. When Stephanie and Tyler Lang found their daughter in the morning, they had no idea Florence had been with Chloe that night. Florence could've softened the blow; she could've warned them and begged for forgiveness.

They treated her like their own daughter, but her relationship with them ended the day Chloe died because Florence couldn't look them in the eyes. How could she stand in front of Stephanie and say, *Your daughter is dead because of me. I got her messing with things we didn't understand because I was young and stupid and invincible.*

Florence opened her eyes to the dark room. She could've helped Stephanie through the tragedy, and instead she let nine years pass, wasted.

How different would Stephanie's life have been had she known the truth about that night?

Florence dropped the letter and hugged her knees to her chest. "I'm here for the week, Chloe. If you're mad at me, I understand. But... I'm here. I'm trying to make things right again, if you could come hug me and show me that you're okay."

She *reached*, her soul aching like deep, growing pains. "Please be okay."

Everything went dark.

She blinked, confused. Did she black out? She looked at the corners of the room, the shadows playing tricks on her eyes. The room *felt* different, but maybe she imagined it.

God, I hope you're okay, she thought. *I love you, girl*. She blew out the candle.

Smoke trailed like a gray river through the darkness. She would try again tomorrow and every day until Chloe appeared, or until Florence found a way to forgive herself.

She stood up and turned around.

A woman sat on her bed, hands resting in her lap.

She had long black hair that parted around her face. Her shiny eyes were wet with tears. She smiled at Florence, showing black teeth.

No, not black, but bloody. Blood trailed down the woman's chin, dripping onto her dirty nightgown.

Stuck in place, Florence waited for the hallucination to pass.

But then the woman smiled a little wider, reached out with her broken fingernails, and held Florence's hand.

Chapter 5

Florence held the woman's warm, scarred hand and fought the urge to scream. Part of her had been going through the motions. Yes, she believed in ghosts and that contacting Chloe was *possible*. But seeing this woman here still shocked her. The ritual actually worked! Sort of.

The woman sensed Florence's panic and dropped her hand. She smacked her lips, smearing the blood on her mouth, and stood up.

She wore a long-sleeved, cream-colored nightgown that ended just above her bare, dirty feet. The nightgown had a square neck opening, secured by an old-fashioned ribbon tied just below her throat. The thin material barely hid her bruised and skinny frame.

Neither of them spoke. Florence wanted to, but she couldn't mask the fear in her voice.

The woman suddenly rushed forward, her hair spilling over her eyes, and vanished from the dark room.

Florence felt a warm breath of air on her face. She flung open the curtain and squinted at the lighted room.

Nothing. No ghost.

She looked at the smoking candle, the necklace, and the dirt from Chloe's grave. *It worked*, she thought. *But that wasn't Chloe.*

Florence sank to her knees and fumbled through the printed stack of news articles and pictures. Compiling this list had taken some time—the resort did not eagerly promote the many (and sometimes bizarre) deaths that had occurred over the years.

She'd created a profile for each individual. Now, she flipped through the pages one at a time.

Raul Cortez, a resort supervisor, fell to his death while fixing a stuck window on the third floor.

Anne Borough died of a seizure inside her room. Found the next day by housekeeping.

Leon Stevens died of a heart attack in the elevator. Discovered by a guest in the middle of the night.

Taylor Livingston fell off a fourth-floor balcony, died on impact. Alcohol found in system, declared an accident.

Brody Anderson was found dead inside his room from an apparent suicide. They also found not only drugs in his system but chewed-up pages in his stomach.

Florence looked at the fifteen curated titles on her bookshelf. What would possess someone to eat their books?

The last two profiles were famously connected.

John Walter, co-founder of The Reader's Resort, launched the resort in 1985 with his wife, Lori. Three years later, John jumped off the roof and landed in the gardens. He died on impact.

Alyssa Larkin was John and Lori's secretary. At age twenty-three, she knew the resort as thoroughly as the founders and often interceded with them on behalf of employees. She disappeared sometime during 1988.

Sometime? Florence checked the article. She'd just copied and pasted the general facts, and it didn't go into more detail.

"Holy shit." She stood up, letting the other papers flutter to the floor.

Alyssa Larkin disappeared *sometime* in 1988, and later that same year, John Walter killed himself. Her disappearance and his suicide were widely assumed to be connected, though no link between them was ever publicly acknowledged.

Florence raised Alyssa's profile into the light. The picture was pulled from the resort's website, and showed a small group of young people posing on the roof. She recognized Lori and John Walter, their arms around each other. Alyssa Larkin sat on the stone battlement, her knee almost touching John's side. Her bright eyes were caught between waves of black hair, her toothy smile innocent and youthful.

Florence dropped the final page and ran out of her room. She wove through clumps of readers excitedly pointing and chatting about each other's rooms. Their voices made her squirm. How could they be so innocent? Did they have any idea what this place was? She ran into the stairwell, nearly crashing into another reader, a girl her age, who was walking with an open book in her hands. Florence needed air, a place to breathe. She jogged up the stairs and barreled onto the fourth floor, finding the same cream-colored walls, old-timey light fixtures, and fluffy maroon carpet.

Following the signs, she fast-walked toward the rooftop bar and lounge.

It felt like her heart was pounding inside her skull. Her stomach convulsed. The necklace shifted against her skin, dragging her back to that sleepover.

She burst onto the roof, her vision swirling in a nauseating sea of spots until she settled on her shoes and the small stains of dirt from Chloe's grave.

The dead are not all dead.

Florence lost control of her body. Her chin dropped to her chest.

Then she fell.

Chapter 6

Logan Yates had a long-standing belief that people in Human Resources were all clones. They all looked the same, talked the same, and had this secretive I-know-something-you-don't gleam in their eyes, like they were connected to a corporate hive mind. And he always found them attractive—how was that possible?

Lisa Bachman, the HR rep for The Reader's Resort, was no exception to this rule. Makeup in place, smile intact, she rattled away like someone was feeding her lines through an earpiece.

Far-fetched, but not impossible.

Lisa, who looked to be in her mid-thirties, sat behind a clean, polished desk. She held a steaming mug of coffee in one hand that said, DREAM BIG. GET SH*T DONE. HAVE FUN.

Despite having a decade on him, Logan might've asked her out to coffee if not for the extravagant engagement ring on her finger, which she kept *clinking* against her mug. Selling his car wouldn't cover the cost of that thing. Besides, he had the bet to think about; that stupid, childish bet he wished he hadn't made.

"So, Logan, how was your drive in?" Lisa asked.

Logan shifted in his chair. "It was cool. I never come out this way, so I love the view. And sorry I'm a few minutes late. The rain slowed me down." The tires on his car were so bald, wet roads were like black ice. He had been in such a hurry to get inside the resort, he parked in the grass beside the parking lot *and* managed to lock his phone, wallet, and keys inside his car, along with his lunch: two very thin peanut butter and jelly sandwiches. He'd wasted precious time making those, which made his morning, like most of his life, a colossal failure.

Lisa waved a hand. "Oh, don't worry about it. It even happens to me sometimes. I know we interviewed you on Zoom, and I think you did the virtual tour, right?"

"Yes. This is my first time actually here."

"Okay, awesome. That's exciting." Lisa smiled for a beat too long. That meant bad news for Logan. Or someone forgot to give her the next line.

She cleared her throat. "So, before we get started, I wanted to go over something with you. We had a position recently open up. It's a little different from working on the dock, but we'd like to offer it to you. We'll pay you the same as a dockworker; we'd just rather fill this spot."

"Oh." Logan thought about the stupid bet again. His hands were tied. "Would I still start today?"

Lisa nodded. "Yes, we'd love for you to start now."

"What's the job?"

"You'll be working in the stacks." A cell phone buzzed on her desk, and she started typing away. "Sorry, I'm confirming Mike's able to take over. He'll give you a tour."

"I'm open to anything. What are the stacks?"

Lisa stood up. "Let's go find Mike. He'll give you the rundown."

He stood up to follow her.

"Is that?" Lisa paused, squinting. "Sorry. Is that a phone number on your arm?"

Logan raised his left arm, where a tattooed owl was perched on his bicep, named Poppy. Below his owl, written in Sharpie across his forearm in comically large fashion, was a fading phone number.

"Yes." He didn't want to explain it and now wished he'd worn long-sleeves.

Lisa nodded, clearly thrown off her script. "Right this way." She smiled, bringing her face back into a friendly shape.

She led him through a series of short hallways and then into a stairwell. They went down, her tall black heels clicking on the concrete steps.

"As you saw in the virtual tour, Logan, we're going down to the lower level. The stairs all have signs, so you shouldn't have trouble getting around."

Logan *did* technically watch the virtual tour… while also playing *Call of Duty* and listening to his favorite YouTuber. Weirdly, he could not drum up a single fact about the resort, other than that it catered to readers. The lower level could be a government lab for all he knew.

They walked down one level, just beneath the main floor, and he followed her through a long, empty hallway. Other hallways and doors branched off on either side, marked with gold-plated numbers and badge scanners. His theory about the government lab felt more plausible now.

A door to Logan's right had a plaque above it. In loopy, hand-painted, bold maroon lettering, it read: *The Stacks.*

Who would make a handmade sign for their place of work?

Logan passed the door, almost speaking up, but Lisa's heels clicked steadily down the hallway. No time for interruptions. Keep up or get left behind.

He patted his pocket with a flash of panic. Oh, right, he'd locked his phone inside his car like a stupid idiot. Not that he needed it now anyway.

Finally, they reached the dock. Positioned at the rear of the resort, the charm ended here. No magic on the dock, not even a little leftover residue. Trucks backed in and out, depositing supplies. Multiple bay doors had been left open to let in fresh air. Forklifts moved; dockworkers operated without talking. Everyone had a job to do, and they knew how to do it. A cool breeze blew in from the cloudy, rainy morning.

Lisa led him into a small office where a man sat in a beat-up chair at a desk covered in papers, dust, and circular coffee stains.

"Hey Mike." Lisa leaned inside the office. "Got Logan Yates here. First day."

Built like a lumberjack, Mike stood up and towered over them both. He ran a massive hand over his bald head and grinned. "Logan? Good to meet you."

They shook hands. Mike's handshake was gentle, but his fingers felt like sandpaper.

"He's open to working in the stacks," Lisa said. She turned to Logan. "If you really don't like the looks of it, you can still work on the dock. Just come find me after the tour and we'll talk."

This would all be a lot easier if someone explained the stacks to him.

Mike sat back down at his desk. He wore a small holster with a yellow box cutter inside, which looked perfectly badass.

"How much you know about this place, Logan?"

"Not much."

"So nothing. That's fine. Makes my job more fun." Mike signed a few papers, grabbed his half-full, plain white coffee mug, and made for the door. "This'll be an exciting tour, Logan. We'll start with the 'core' mission of this company." He used air quotes even while holding the mug. "First, we'll meet the resort's curators."

They walked to a set of doors.

"And what do they do?"

Mike paused, hand on the doorknob, and grinned. "Oh Logan, they're God's gift to mankind." He opened the door, throwing his head back with laughter.

Logan smiled. Mike seemed like his kind of people.

"They're a bunch of prissy librarians." Mike wiped his eyes. "Oh man. I'll tell you about them on the way. We gotta hoof it to the other end of this place, 'cause the curators wanted to be as far away from the dockworkers as possible. That's my theory, anyway. So now, we get to walk."

And with that, Mike took off, never slowing down, not even to sip his coffee.

In a speed walking competition, Logan would lose to everyone here. He tried to keep up, still thinking about that homemade sign and what it meant.

The Stacks.

He'd find out soon enough. He didn't have to like it; he just had to keep his head down and work hard. Thanks to the bet, this could be the most important job of his life.

Chapter 7

While Dean Winsky reclined behind his desk, texting on his phone, Robert Hauser sat in the "guest chair," AKA "the electric chair," and reminisced about the hundreds of times he'd been brought into this office.

Robert's entire career at The Reader's Resort had been carefully monitored by Dean, the Restaurant and Dining General Manager. Dean hadn't been promoted in twenty years, which didn't surprise Robert. Complacent people were everywhere at the resort. Once they latched onto the job they wanted, they sat on their prize like a lazy dragon in a dark cave.

Having spent many depressing hours in this prison cell of an office, Robert knew it well. Dean claimed to be a minimalist. Robert (and anyone with a shred of observation skills) knew that was bullshit.

Dean left the walls blank and the desk empty (devoid of creativity). No pictures of the wife or kids (they left him years ago—shocker). His desk had a thin layer of dust (sloppy) and a few leftover crumbs from his usual morning drive-thru breakfast sandwich. The smell of sausage still lingered in the air.

Minimalist, as if.

"Okay." Dean set his phone down. "How's everything going, Robert? How are the chefs? Are they *getting* it?" He smiled with all his teeth, even the deep yellow ones that never saw the sun. Dean was *not* the grinning type. He looked like a wolf who'd gotten away with something terrible and was itching to tell his wolf buddies about it.

"I think so, yeah." Robert's stomach started sinking, slow and heavy. Dean treated small talk like seasoning before the barbecue. If he jumped right in and ridiculed you, at least it would be over soon. A small-talk windup meant trouble. It meant Dean was about to deliver a home run.

Dean nodded a few times, as if hearing a song in his head. "Since the changeover, I've been impressed with the difference in... quality. You've done a good job, catching them up to speed. And I can't say I miss the old kitchen crew. We really did ourselves a favor." Dean chuckled, hands folded over his belly. "I mean, you and I both know we had some deadbeats in there. I'm glad most of them quit. Now I don't have to see them scrubbing my toilet."

I liked them, Robert thought. *You told them they could resign or transfer to housekeeping. Not much of a choice for a line cook.*

"But anyway, point is, you've done good." Dean smiled.

Robert cringed, clutching the armrests of his chair. Was this about the folder? Is that why Dean brought him in here? Did someone find it?

Dean coughed. "Listen, I know we've been making a lot of changes and recycling old systems, and it's been a long time coming. It was very necessary, believe me. This place needs to modernize, and revamping the kitchen proved it can be done. As you know, the owners are just getting started with this stuff. But now that we've fixed the cooks and the menu, we need to fix management."

Robert knew this was coming. He fucking knew it.

"We're offering you the same deal as the others. We have a new position you can take, which *is* still part of the kitchen crew." Dean opened a desk drawer, withdrew a single sheet of paper, and slid it across the desk. "Or you can resign."

Dean's sweaty, oily face glowed in the white light. The small dents on his cheeks stood out. Battle scars from his youth when the acne wouldn't leave him alone. Robert stared at Dean's face with rigid intensity. Somehow, he managed to stay in his chair instead of climbing over the desk and painting the bare white walls with Dean's blood.

Dean hadn't always been *this* petty. The switch flipped two years ago when Robert applied for another job at the resort and didn't get it. Dean found out, and while most bosses would encourage internal promotions, Dean took it personally. Robert *clearly* didn't appreciate his lofty position in the kitchen hierarchy.

Now, Dean had the resort behind him. No one could prove malicious intent. Robert had no way of fighting back except to stay and execute his plan. In a matter of days, Robert wouldn't be working for Dean anymore. Not if his gamble paid off. And it would. It had to.

I'll show him, Robert thought, biting his lip to keep from giggling. *I'll shove my promotion down his throat.*

Dean patiently waited. He knew Robert couldn't afford to quit. He knew exactly what he was doing.

Robert used his middle finger to scoot the paper across the desk. "What's my new job?"

Dean snorted and stood up; this day was getting sweeter and sweeter for him. "I'll show you."

"Who's replacing me? A *professional* kitchen supervisor?"

"It's called an executive chef, and he's got twenty years between culinary school and fine dining experience."

He's everything you're not, Dean was trying to say.

Dean left the office, and Robert followed him to the kitchen. A few chefs were already slicing up lettuce, veggies, and fruit. They looked at Robert and said nothing. They knew better than to pick sides.

Robert's phone buzzed with a text from John, the new guy in reception.

Florence is here, just checked in.

Robert smiled and instantly felt better. If only he could see her reactions. Did she like the lobby? Was it everything she had imagined?

Dean opened the basement door and beckoned down the wooden stairs.

"What's in the basement?" Robert kept thinking about the folder hidden down there and how Dean would go ballistic if he found it.

"Your new position," Dean said, keeping a straight face. "We created it for *you*, Robert."

They descended into Robert's least favorite place in the resort. And no, not because of the cracked concrete floor, or the massive rodent traps, or the hellish spiders, but the *air* felt like the inside of a coffin. That was why he hid the folder down here; nobody would poke around.

The basement was cold, dark, and matched the size and shape of the kitchen above. Shelving racks lined the walls, overflowing with kitchen supplies and random knickknacks that everyone forgot about.

"Your pay will stay the same," Dean said. "Obviously. Even though you'll be grossly overpaid for this work, we wouldn't cut back on what you're getting." He waited a beat. "I know how much you need it."

Robert didn't take the bait. The ceiling creaked above him as the chefs prepped and whispered rumors about Robert's demotion.

"We need someone to do inventory full-time." Dean gestured to the shelves.

But that's not full-time work, Robert thought. "Will my hours be the same?"

"They will."

"What exactly do you want me to do?"

"You'll need to reorganize the way it's set up down here. It's chaotic and makes me want to blow my brains out. You'll also assist the chefs."

"Assist?"

"Yes." Dean blinked, as if talking to a child. "You'll run them up what they need when they need it. They shouldn't have to come down here unless you're on the shitter. You'll essentially work for them."

Robert shook his head, biting back the words he desperately wanted to scream. Ten years at the hotel just to get bullied by a man with a chip on his shoulder.

"There's something else," Dean said, reaching inside his pocket. His face gave him away. He couldn't hide his excitement. "In reality, this won't keep you busy full-time. There's another uh... *responsibility* we'll need you to stay on top of."

Dean withdrew a small metal object and handed it to Robert.

It was a nutcracker. Shaped like a V, you would place the shelled nut between the sharp metal teeth. When you squeezed it, the teeth bit down and cracked the shell open. It was an old device that worked perfectly. They used it all the time for sprinkling nuts on salads.

"*What* are you saying?"

Dean rolled his eyes. "We're ramping up the operation, and we go through so many nuts every day, we need them to be ready beforehand. It'll slow the chefs down."

"You want me to sit down here, by myself, and *crack nuts*?"

Dean shrugged. "You can refuse the new job and resign. No hard feelings. It's been a good few years, bub."

"You're serious?"

"About the nuts, or resigning?"

Robert stared at the nutcracker in his palm. He clenched the sides together, the teeth clamping on air.

"Since I assume you aren't quitting, let's start training," Dean said.

"Training for what?"

"Start with the walnuts."

"I know how to do this, Dean."

"I need to be sure." Dean shrugged. "New job, new training. It's out of my hands."

Dean found a wooden chair with a round seat. He set it in the middle of the room, grabbed a small trash can, and placed it beside the chair. "Go on. Show me."

Robert walked to the shelf and removed a bag of walnuts. He sat in the chair, his vision blurring. He couldn't speak. He'd get himself fired if he opened his mouth.

Hands shaking, Robert opened the bag. He pulled out a walnut and dropped it. Dean stood in front of the trash can, arms crossed, breathing heavily.

Robert found the walnut and positioned it between the nutcracker's teeth. Using both hands, he pushed the metal handles together, crunching the nut between them. Walnuts required a little muscle, but he squashed them, and the shells exploded in his hands, obliterating the nuts inside. Pieces scattered in his palm, but most of them shot in every direction and missed the trash can.

"Try again." Dean lifted one shiny, black dress shoe and brushed off powdery crumbs with a grunt. "If you crush the whole thing right away, you'll lose the good stuff."

Robert dropped the ruined walnut in the trash and tried a new one.

Crack. The walnut broke apart in his palm, intact.

"Just work on this for today. Walnut, almond, and pecan." He pronounced it *pee-can*, which made Robert temporarily blind with rage. "Bags are on the shelf. I'll be down later to check on you. I'd like to hear about how you plan on organizing everything." He walked away, pausing at the foot of the stairs.

"And take that apron off."

Robert looked down at the gray apron, his former symbol of authority. He considered making a snide comment, but Dean was already leaving.

If Robert hurried, he could bring Dean back down the stairs and make up something about seeing cockroaches. While Dean was busy stressing,

Robert could drive a screwdriver through the back of his neck. Would it be hard to scream with a ten-inch stainless-steel flathead in his throat? Probably!

And what about the body? There were a million places to hide it, and a million ways to clean up, because Robert already worked alone in a horror-movie basement and had nothing but time and resources at his fingertips. What luck!

But Dean sauntered away, and Robert let him, his imagination in need of a reality check. Robert grabbed two large plastic bowls and set them by the trash can, one for walnuts and the other for *pee-cans*. He slipped the nutcracker inside his pocket and walked to the corner of the basement where he'd stashed the folder between tall, white cardboard boxes full of napkins.

He carefully removed the folder, brushed the thin layer of dust from its cover, and opened it.

A picture of Florence Noelle was taped to one side. He'd pulled it from Instagram.

Seeing her again in this folder, and knowing she walked the main floor above him, filled Robert with something he'd never experienced before. Not even with his long-time ex-girlfriend. It wasn't butterflies, but something more powerful. He felt *intoxicated*.

Giggling, Robert closed the folder, slid it between the boxes, and rushed to his little wooden chair. He plucked the nutcracker from his pocket and held it up to the weak, yellow light. He'd better get started with his new job.

It was going to be a *very* busy day.

Chapter 8

Florence opened her eyes to a small crowd standing over her. When they gasped at her stirring awake, she thought, *This is what an animal in a zoo must feel like.*

"You just fell over," a middle-aged woman said, helping Florence to her feet. Her wiry hands were firm, warm, and reminded Florence of the ghost woman. "You're not bleeding," the woman said, briefly touching Florence's hair. "That's a relief."

"I'm fine. I haven't eaten today," she said. This satisfied a few, and the group downsized. "Really, I'm fine. I'm fine." Florence wiggled out of the woman's grip and smiled. "Thank you, thanks everyone, I'm so sorry I... I don't know what happened."

"You just fell over," the woman said again. "Do you need a snack? I have granola bars?"

"I know. I..." Florence hated the way they gawked at her. A woman wearing a white ball cap was talking on her cell phone. She abruptly pressed it against her stomach and addressed Florence with severe authority.

"Do you need an ambulance?"

"No, I'm fine, thank you."

The woman nodded suspiciously, then exchanged a brief goodbye with the dispatcher on the other line.

"Thank you again, everyone." Florence wanted to sprint back to her room, but the first woman tapped her arm a few times.

"You need fresh air, and you should sit down," she said, reading Florence's mind. "Do you need help? Where would you like to sit?"

Florence gave up, exhausted. She felt like she'd been awake for days. "Anywhere."

What happened in my room? She thought. *What did it do to me?*

The woman led Florence to the edge of the roof and eased her down onto the battlement. Florence sat with her back to the iron railing. "Thank you. I'm really fine."

"I know," the woman said, pressing a granola bar into Florence's hand. It seemed to have materialized out of nowhere. "Yell if you need me."

Florence tilted her head back against the cold railing. She made the mistake of looking down, where the dark green grass rippled like the ocean, and the wind heaved against the resort as if to push it over the cliff.

Slow down, Florence, breathe.

"I'm good," Florence whispered, taking a deep breath. She focused on the roof—the resort's most idyllic reading spot.

Large medieval lanterns lined the perimeter. It had to be stunning up here at night, swallowed by a comfy lounge chair and reading in lantern light; stone fire pits to warm yourself against and extra blankets for when the wind howled through the eaves; nothing between you and the starry sky but the book in your hands.

On Florence's right was a bar with a chalkboard drink menu. Three bartenders worked the counter, making anything from coffees to cocktails to smoothies. They'd make whatever you wanted if you bought an unlimited food and drinks package.

On the ground, cars filled the single country road as far as she could see, the latecomers impatiently inching forward. Florence recognized the tall hill she'd climbed earlier. The giant tree shivered in the breeze, dropping those massive red leaves.

Straight across from her, the roof overlooked the resort's famous gardens: the spot where John Walter jumped from the battlement. Legends said you could see his bloodstains on the walkway during a full moon; the blood wet and glistening like it had never dried. He took his life sometime after his secretary, Alyssa, disappeared.

She didn't disappear, Florence thought, *I've seen her ghost. She died.*

Florence could be the only person alive who had seen Alyssa Larkin since she vanished; the only person who could confirm Alyssa hadn't aged a day.

But was any of it real? After all, Florence lived with a host of traumatic memories, all easily brought to the forefront by innocuous triggers. Was it a stretch to question the validity of what she saw?

Absolutely not. Florence wasn't the most stable person for this job. She came in desperately searching for ghosts, and the bone-tired exhaustion and fainting spell didn't help her case. She could've had an episodic breakdown, a complete split from reality. Unresolved trauma can do that. On the beautiful roof among ordinary people, breathing ordinary air, the events in her room felt like a nightmare and nothing more.

Nothing real.

Still, what did she believe? Did she trust herself or not? While it felt silly to resist the very reason she came to the resort, accepting the reality of it would still require a leap of faith.

Florence didn't always believe in ghosts. It was Chloe who came up with the most impossible questions. Lying in the dark after a late summer night of milkshakes and classic movies, Chloe would roll over and say stuff like, "What if dying feels like waking up?"

There was never a precursor; without warning, she'd hit Florence over the head with the hardest question her tired, mysterious brain could conjure.

Is that how I ended up here? Florence thought, glancing at the roof with a soft, teary blink. *Nobody's asking me hard questions?*

The one Florence remembered the best had to do with Florence's dad, who passed away in a car crash when she was a baby.

"If you could see your dad's ghost, would you?" Chloe asked.

Florence didn't hate the question. In truth, she'd never thought of it before. "That's not possible."

"But what if?"

"Then no."

"Why not?"

"Because I wouldn't recognize him."

Before Florence could expand on how her dad died, and the state of his broken body, she told Chloe she didn't believe in ghosts, so it didn't matter.

"You don't?" Chloe stared at the dark ceiling. "I do. I want to be buried with my books. That way my ghost will have something to read when I'm not slaying dragons or whatever I'll be doing."

Florence laughed. "You make it sound like an adventure."

Chloe was quiet for a while. "It is," she said finally. "It has to be."

On the roof, Florence recalled those words. *It has to be.* And they never left her, all these years they taunted her from afar, daring her to try something bold—something Chloe would cheer for. *She'd love to see me trying,* Florence had thought endlessly. *Whether ghosts are real or not, she'd love to see me try.* It became a lingering question, year after year, that Florence decided she needed to answer. She had to try and contact Chloe. After years of hating herself, she'd found a way forward.

Now, Florence left the roof because people wouldn't stop staring at her, and she had to decide about what she saw in her room.

The fourth floor was bustling with readers. Move-In Day was always popular on social media, and as Florence wove through the crowd, she passed readers taking selfies or filming reaction reels.

"I'm about to see my room for the *first time,*" one young girl said, holding her phone up. She opened her door, gasping.

Florence walked by, catching a glimpse of blood-splattered curtains, black walls, and a white chalk outline of a human on the floor. A whodunnit room.

Everything flashed through her mind: John Walter jumping off the roof, Alyssa Larkin sitting on the battlement, smiling next to John and Lori, the *happy* couple, the founders; Alyssa on Florence's bed, blood spilling from her mouth.

It came in a rush. The chalk outline on the floor; the young girl screaming with joy; the nearby readers closing in, comparing rooms.

Florence ducked into the stairwell and ran down the steps, fighting to stay on her feet. She hadn't been ready for this. Real or not, she couldn't deal with ghosts, murders, and cold cases.

She did her part. She read her letter to Chloe, and she tried to reach out. But the woman on her bed had been too real and too dangerous for Florence to mentally handle.

Should she leave the resort altogether? A rational person would say *yes* because she never should've come in the first place. *Look* at what it had done to her already.

Florence unlocked her room, opened her door, and immediately saw it.

The message.

Blood smeared across the oval mirror; two words written with an unsteady hand.

HELP ME.

Chapter 9

Logan followed Mike through a maze of plain hallways. Each hallway was numbered and led to a set of four doors: two on the left, two on the right. Each door had a letter, and some were decorated with art, signs, and welcome mats.

"What's all this for?" Logan asked.

"Employee apartments."

"You can live here?"

"A lot of us do." Mike kept pulling his yellow box cutter from its holster and snapping the blade in and out. He did it without thinking, like clicking a pen. Logan stayed out of his way to avoid an accidental shanking.

"Do *you* live here?"

"Sure do." Mike turned left and started up a stairwell. "Went through a nasty divorce last year, and moving here saved my ass. It's not bad. The apartments are kinda small, but you get used to them. They rent them out super cheap, so that's a plus."

"Why go through the trouble of housing employees at all?"

Mike shrugged. "Back in the day, the founders gambled on this place, I mean, they went all in on something that might've backfired horribly. They went from renting out a Victorian mansion like a bed and breakfast to building a full-scale resort. They were so set on the idea of building a community that they included the staff, not just the readers. But it was a win-win. As you've noticed, this place is in the middle of nowhere, and living here means no commute, beautiful hiking, and cheap living."

"Did it work? Building a community?"

"Hell yeah, it worked. The culture here is hard to explain, but you'll see what I mean. Our first stop will tell you a lot. Now, I should warn you. You gotta take these guys and gals with a grain of salt."

"The curators?"

"Oh yeah." They left the stairwell, passed through a door, and turned down a hallway. "The head honcho curator is Charlie Walter, the son of Lori Walter. Lori and her husband, John, founded this place."

"Oh boy."

"Exactly. It's a family business, and Charlie's the worst because he grew up here, you know? And it's really gone to his head."

Logan smiled. "So he's got a complex?"

"It's bad, man, you'll see. He's so uptight, too. He smokes like a freight train. Take it all with a grain of salt, okay? Charlie's the kind of guy who buddies up to you one day and fires you the next."

"Why are the curators part of the tour anyways? What do they do?"

"According to them, they make the *magic* happen," Mike snorted. "And here we are. I'm leaving you, 'cause if I stay, I'll throw Charlie through a window."

"Feeding me to the wolves, huh?"

Mike scratched his neck beard. "You'll be all right. Just don't talk about anything other than books, or they'll look at you like you're stupid. Remember, they're the resort's *finest*."

"Got it."

Mike stopped in front of an unmarked door and scanned his badge. The badge reader changed from red to green, the door unlocked, and they walked inside.

Logan did a cartoon double-take. They'd gone from a cozy resort to a modern office. Corporate America, baby! Logan's worst nightmare. He almost backed out of the room, hands raised in surrender. He had a long-standing theory about office workers that he didn't have time to ponder, because as soon as they entered the room, the curators gave them hostile, *get-off-my-turf* looks. These people were not wolves, but hyenas. Their conversations died on their glossy lips as a door to a private office opened and a man waltzed out.

"Hey Mike."

"Hey Charlie." Mike's dock uniform, box cutter, and grease-stained hands stood out in the clean, bright office. Logan felt a bond form between them. They weren't office bros, but grungy blue-collar working stiffs. Logan envisioned it all going south in his head. *Say the word, Mike, and I'll fight these Barbie-looking motherfuckers for you.*

Charlie smiled. He extended a hand to Logan. "Charlie Walter, Curating Manager, nice to meet you."

"You too."

He fiddled with an expensive watch, as if that handshake had twisted it. "Just doing a tour? First day?"

Logan nodded. "Yes sir."

"All right, glad to have you." Charlie was in his thirties, clean-shaven, with a paper-thin comb-over. His shoes squeaked with every step. "Good to see you, Mike, as always. I'll give you a holler once we're done here."

"Appreciate it." Mike nodded at Logan and left the room.

Once the door shut, Charlie cleared his throat. "So what did Mike say about me?"

Logan gave him the most awkward smile of his life. "Oh. Uh. Nothing?"

Charlie huffed. "Mike and I go way back. I know what he thinks, and that's fine! He drives a forklift. He's good at his job, and we're good at ours. And somehow, he can't understand that."

Logan nodded, embarrassed and confused.

Charlie grinned like it was all a joke, but Logan knew better.

"Anyways, welcome to the tower. Come meet the team."

"The tower?"

"Merlin's."

Logan pretended like he understood.

Charlie rattled off everyone's names—about two dozen men and women who sat at their desks, surrounded by books, papers, and personal items. Each desk had a name plate on the outside, but Logan still struggled to keep track.

Charlie shushed the room. "Logan, what do you know about this hotel and what we do here?"

Logan wished he'd actually paid attention to the virtual tour. "Not much, to be honest."

"That's fine, that's fine." Charlie waved his hands. "We can describe it better than anyone, because this room, right here, is the reason this hotel has the reputation it does."

Everyone nodded along. They'd heard this before, but clearly, they believed it.

Charlie circled the group, one hand in his pocket. "When the guest, the *reader*, comes to this resort, they stay for five days. When they come, they are assigned a room. Have you seen the rooms yet?"

Logan shook his head.

Charlie checked his watch. "You might be able to see a few before the readers move in. I'll check with Layla. You have to see the rooms—they, are, magic. And they're all different. Every single one. They all have a theme that's important to the reader. Themes can be specific, like *Sleepy Hollow* or *Nightmare Before Christmas*, or generalized, like a tropical beach or a northern island. Due to copyright, we sometimes have to capture the aesthetic of a room, without having actual props or characters being displayed. The rooms are also based on real life, everything from the Bible to World War II. We then create a booklist that matches the theme, and the historical time, or location of the room. We go as far as to capture concept themes, like zombies, mountaineering, or space exploration. Whatever it is, the themes always come back to what will inspire the reader."

"How do you know what theme will fit the reader?" Logan asked.

"Good question." Charlie's eyes burned brightly. He lifted a finger. "Every guest, to secure their spot at The Reader's Resort, must *apply*. I know, it's weird. People get annoyed when they realize they have to fill out an application to stay somewhere. Those are the kind of people we don't want here. The application does two things: it filters out the people too lazy or unorganized to finish applying, and it gives us, the curators, all the insight we need to plan a reader's stay. The application isn't terribly long, but it covers enough to give us a glimpse at what sort of person we're dealing with. Room assignments are based on that. We give them the base model and then personalize the room if we can."

"That's impressive."

Charlie circled the room, drawing from his vape pen and blowing a cloud of white smoke behind him. Other curators vaped as well, and the air smelled of mint, fruit, and chemicals.

"So, the readers show up and they're given a room that best fits their personality. But that's not all. That's not even the best. Each room comes with a personal bookshelf. When the reader shows up, they are given fifteen books. Books that are handpicked, curated, by us, for *them*. Books we believe will change their lives. We base it all on the application, social media, anything we can find on the reader."

"So, this really is a resort for readers?" Logan didn't think it was this straightforward. "People pay to come here and just read?"

"No." Charlie smiled. "They pay to come here because they want to be changed. And the books we provide will do that."

Logan was about to say he didn't know how a book could change someone's life, but given the present company, he hesitated. He needed a cleaner approach.

"Does it actually work?" He wasn't trying to provoke them; he wanted the truth without the charades.

"You tell me," Charlie said. "The wait list for this place is almost two years. Do you think it works?"

Fair enough, Logan thought. *Damn, he's good.*

"Now, I hope that explains a lot," Charlie said. "What do you like to read?"

"Oh, I don't read much." Logan cringed. "I play video games if I have free time. But I do have a question. How do you know someone hasn't already read the books you've picked out for them?"

"Anyone want to answer that?"

A woman spoke up. "We give each reader fifteen books, but we allow them to exchange up to five of them. This helps account for books they might've read already, or books they immediately don't like the look of. So, although the reader gets fifteen, we pick out twenty titles for them. We have them submit their Goodreads profiles or personal book tracking system, that way we can give them fresh new books, especially the A-Readers, which is what we call people who read a book or two a day."

"Good Lord." Logan couldn't fathom recommending more than one book to someone. Should he be reading more?

"You were trying to solve something earlier, weren't you?" Charlie asked the group. "Pull it up, let's show Logan how we operate."

After a few clicks, a TV on the far wall came to life. It showed a profile of a young woman with her picture, basic info, resort application, and social media links.

"Sarah Porter." Charlie pointed at the screen. "She's twenty-seven. She works as a physical therapist's assistant, and she's been reading since she was a little girl." He looked at Logan. "Part of the application is listing the top twenty books you love, fiction or nonfiction, we do both here."

The screen moved down, and Sarah's list of twenty books came into view.

"So, what's the problem?" Charlie inhaled from his vape pen and blew a white cloud over his polished dress shoes.

One curator spoke up. "We can't figure out what she wants. Based on everything in her socials and reading list, it's all over the place. Does she read to learn? Does she want to escape? Does she want romance? Or a fantasy world? We can't pin down where to start. There's no pattern."

Charlie squinted at the screen, grinning in one corner of his mouth. "Come on, there's always a pattern. Everyone reads for a reason. Any ideas?"

Nothing.

"All right then." Charlie walked up to the screen. "Remember, Sarah's *looking* for something. A reader is always looking for something, whether you know what that thing is or not. You are not reading to passively waste time. This isn't Netflix. You're reading because you're hoping to *find* something. Now, Sarah's a professional. She's finished school. She's in a challenging field. She could be on the hunt for more knowledge because, after all, that's her career, right? Practical, hands-on, holistic knowledge."

He paused, taking another draw. The group waited for him to explain.

"Look again at her top twenty. Narrow it down. She loves Jane Austen, and who doesn't? Ignore that. Look again. What's the theme coming through? All these books resonated with her. Why? Why did *Lord of the Flies* resonate? And what does it have to do with *All the Light We Cannot See*? That's newer. And that's number three on her list; that's a big deal."

"Survival?"

Charlie snapped his fingers. "Why is Sarah struggling to survive? Why do books about society breaking down, falling apart, and that human, grueling need to survive, why does that story, that theme, set her heart on fire?"

The team went quiet again.

"I want answers to this." Charlie checked the time. "Ten minutes. Everyone, write down an answer. Nothing vague, it has to be personal to Sarah. Let's go."

The team started talking, exchanging ideas. Charlie knew how to make them listen, how to kick-start their brains. It was skillful, even if Charlie *was* the arrogant asshole Mike had described. In fact, the curators didn't look as plastic now as they first did. And no, Logan wasn't warming up to that office life, but their jobs were unique, and that intrigued him.

"I hope we taught you something," Charlie said, coming to Logan's side, eyes twinkling. "And I hope this place treats you well. What department will you be in?"

"I guess they need my help in the stacks."

"Ah." Charlie smiled. "The stacks. I used to play there when I was a kid."

"Is it a good place to work?"

"That depends."

"On what?"

"On what you're looking for." Charlie nodded at the screen. "Why does Sarah dream about survival?"

Logan waited a beat. "Because life's been too easy. She's smart. I mean, she's twenty-seven and she's living her dream job. I bet she wishes the world would fall apart so things could be hard again."

Charlie smiled. "Sometimes comfort does more harm than good. Don't tell the team, yeah? They'll figure it out. How'd you know?"

Logan shrugged. "I'm twenty-seven, and I keep making life hard for myself."

"You'd hate it if things were easy. Is that why you've got a phone number written on your arm?"

Logan smiled. "Pretty much. I have a bet with my brother. And if I lose, I gotta call this number."

Charlie moved to a nearby desk, plucked a Sharpie from a curator's cup of pens, and tossed it to Logan.

"Better retrace it then, let it motivate you. I hope you find what you're looking for, Logan, and I hope I'll see you around. I *am* hiring. Just a thought. For now, go out that door, hang a right, and follow the hallway to the main lobby. I'll text Mike."

Logan thanked everyone for their time. Half the group waved and said goodbye. Charlie said nothing. He watched Logan leave, the vape pen raised to his lips, looking very pleased.

Logan shut the door behind him, finding it hard to believe he'd impressed the head curator.

Not bad for a guy who didn't read. See, who needed books anyway?

Logan uncapped the Sharpie and retraced the phone number on his arm. He had to remind himself why he made the bet in the first place. Working here didn't seem so bad, but that really depended on two unanswered questions:

What are the stacks?

And why does everyone avoid talking about it?

Chapter 10

How long had he been here?

Robert stared at the bowl of freshly cracked walnuts with no memory of how they'd gotten there. He'd been thinking about Florence again. He would sometimes daydream about her and wake up minutes or hours later with a headache and an empty stomach and little recollection of what he'd been doing. It wasn't like that at first. He had to be more careful now.

The nutcracker slipped through his fingers and clattered on the concrete floor.

Scratch, scratch.

Was that a rat? Robert had never seen one at the resort, but the old-timers talked about them like they were mythical creatures.

He stood up and scanned the basement. Where was it coming from?

Scratch scratch. More insistent this time. Directly in front of him. He approached the shelves, thinking, *If I were a big fat rat, where would I be?*

The scratching increased; it wanted Robert to come closer.

Robert then noticed something he'd never seen before. The wall behind the shelves didn't match the other stone walls in the basement. The original wall had been covered by a thin wooden sheet and painted gray.

Robert pushed aside cans of beans. He reached through the shelf and ran his fingers along where the wooden sheet ended.

He pushed on the flimsy wood, feeling it shift. It wasn't even nailed down on all sides. The shelves mostly kept it in place; the wall was only nailed along the top.

Robert grabbed the shelves with both hands, threw his weight backward, and managed to drag them a foot.

Progress.

He tried again, repeatedly yanking, until the space behind the shelves was wide enough to fit through. He slipped behind it, grabbed the false wall, and pulled. He expected resistance, but the wooden sheet fell and hit the concrete. The nails had been there for years, possibly decades, and had grown soft. Robert glanced over his shoulder, waiting for a nosy chef to investigate the commotion he'd made.

No one ventured down.

He *should* stop wasting time and get back to the nuts, but why not finish what he started? He carried the wall out from behind the shelves and set it aside. The scratching had stopped, and that bothered him a little.

Going back to where the wall had been, Robert took his phone out and turned on the flashlight. He took a step back. The stone wall was covered in dirt, with defined ridges running up and down. He ran his palm over the wall, knocking away loose stone and cobwebs. An outline appeared above his head, going down to his shoes.

He brushed away the debris, blackening his hands with grime and dust.

The outline was unmistakable.

It looked like a door.

The rat resumed scratching on the other side. It was cornered and needed a way out.

Maybe the door led to a smaller basement, a cellar, or an old underground tunnel. In a place this old, it could be anything. He believed it was something important because *someone* had tried to hide it.

The door had a standard handle and deadbolt; an odd choice if it didn't lead outdoors. Why put a deadbolt on this side unless you wanted to lock something out?

Or lock something in.

The deadbolt gave Robert a bad feeling—though not *all* bad. Part of him hoped to find something horrible on the other side of the door, like observing a car accident.

Robert bent down, noticing a smaller outline on the lower half of the door. Brushing the grime away, it took a second to register in his brain.

"A pet door?" He laughed, checking the stairs. "What the hell?"

A sealed door in the basement was already suspicious, but something about the pet door sent chills down his spine. He tapped on the old, worn rubber and the dried glue around the edges, where someone had attempted to keep the door from opening ever again.

Sitting with both feet forward, he braced himself and kicked the pet door. It bulged, the left side breaking away from the glue. He kicked it again and watched it shift. Another kick, and his shoe went right through it, his foot propping the little door open.

A gust of air escaped the pet door, as if the room on the other side had heaved a great tired sigh, and with it, the distinct smell of freshly dug earth. He heard scampering, tiny echoes.

The rat.

Jerking his foot back, he lifted the pet door and waved his phone's flashlight inside.

It *was* a cellar, a small version of the basement. It had a dirt floor, four stone walls, and at least one rodent. He rotated the flashlight back and forth, adjusted his position, and still couldn't see the corners closest to him. He wasn't about to stick his whole head in there.

He stood up, letting the pet door swing shut, and considered this new problem. The critter might've been trapped with the door sealed. Now, thanks to Robert, it had a way out.

He moved the shelving rack back so the pet door was visible just above the bottom shelf. He carried the wooden wall across the basement and slid it between two tables, then stacked the cans on the shelf in front of the door to prevent anyone from noticing. He left the bottom shelf empty, leaving the pet door accessible. His little secret.

He reached through the shelf and tested the deadbolt. It was stuck and would need a hammer to turn, but Robert wasn't in a hurry to get inside the cellar anyway—not with the giant rodent on the loose and the likelihood of mold.

Then he set his trash can close, but not too close, to the shelf. He moved his chair and sat down, positioning himself directly in front of the pet door. Front row seat and plenty of work to do. He could simply wait it out until lunch when his Florence plan would really begin.

Crack.

Back to cracking nuts. They'd need almonds soon, and *pee-cans.*

"I didn't do anything wrong," Robert said. He set the walnut between the nutcracker's teeth and gripped the handles. "Neither did you, little buddy. I'm sorry."

Crack.

Another one bites the dust, he thought, laughing to himself.

"*What are you hiding from me?*" He slipped into a singsong voice when he got bored, a habit that used to drive his father crazy. The old man killed himself when Robert was thirteen. He jumped in front of a semi-truck, and since then, Robert's singsong voice came with a pinch of guilt.

He eyed the pet door, but nothing had changed. No scratching on the wall, no rustling behind the door. Was the animal afraid of him? Or did it find another way to leave its enclosure?

He set another walnut. His sweaty palm held the nutcracker, and with practiced precision, he gave it the right amount of squeeze.

The shell split into flying shards. The walnut popped out like a tiny wooden brain, all ridges and lumps.

He laughed at the absurdity of it all. His professional career had boiled down to this: a subterranean nutcracker. And the worst part? No one could stop Dean. The bigwigs wouldn't lift a finger to help Robert or scrutinize Dean because the system protected him.

He checked the time on his phone; it was 11:30 a.m. Almost there.

Then a text from his sister: **Good luck today! You'll do great.**

Margo really wanted this to work out for him. That was sweet of her.

In less than forty-five minutes, he would make the pitch of a lifetime. Unlike most of his peers, Robert had the heart, resolve, and tenacity to chase after his dreams, and didn't life typically reward the risk-takers?

However, for his plan to work, Florence needed to play her part. She carried some baggage, yes. But she wanted to better herself, and he admired that. She had seen her room by now. Did she realize the significance of it? Of course not.

Only Robert knew, and it made his stomach flutter.

He tried to picture what Florence was currently doing. In a dark basement by himself, what else was he going to do?

Was she reading? Was she gushing to a friend about her room? If the weather had improved, she might've gone out on the balcony with a drink and curled up in a blanket. Florence was a quiet reader, a girl who wouldn't turn everything into an aesthetic like the countless fake readers online. But he wanted to see it for himself: the comfortable way she lounged in the sun, the way she held a book in her hands.

Soon, so soon, be patient.

Robert looked at the pet door, still waiting for the trapped critter to appear. Only this time, the pet door was ajar. Did something sneak out?

No. He would've seen or heard it.

Scooting his chair back, Robert crouched for a cleaner view.

The pet door swung closed, swaying a little before settling.

Maybe it got stuck somehow. Disappointed, Robert resumed cracking walnuts. They split, one by one, the shells partially falling into the trash can, with the rest flying away in broken pieces he'd need to sweep up later.

A commotion came from upstairs. Raised voices, pounding footsteps. Robert looked up. The footsteps rattled the support beams, causing dust to fall on him like snow. He wanted to take a break, but he had to wait for lunch, when his plan would truly begin.

Once started, it wouldn't stop. He rehearsed the words he would say—the speech that would ooze charisma and professionalism.

His life would change forever.

Crack.

Wasn't that the resort's mission? Changing lives?

Crack.

The pet door was ajar again. It hung back slightly, as if held open. Robert shifted, and the pet door swung shut. The creature was watching him. It was smart. Smarter than he'd originally thought.

Then he saw it happen—the pet door slowly lifting back, a pair of eyes in that sliver of darkness.

"Hello," Robert said, waving.

The pet door shut again. But the animal was getting bolder and would try again soon.

Maybe it would see that Robert was harmless and finally leave the cellar.

Robert found a stack of Styrofoam bowls on a nearby shelf. He brought one back to his chair, set it on the floor, and cracked a few walnuts into it, grinding the chunks into crumbles. He then crawled under the shelf and pushed the bowl against the pet door.

The animal scurried away on the other side, still afraid of him.

He set the bowl down inside the door and pulled his arm back, closing the pet door. "Eat up, little friend." He brushed his hands against his pants and went back to work.

He checked the time. *Soon, very soon.*

Crack.

He smiled at the ceiling, the falling dust sticking to his forehead and teeth. Very soon, everyone at the resort would see him for what he was.

And all because of sweet, lovely Florence. She held his future in her palm, and she didn't even know it.

He paused and listened, hearing a sound. A rapid crunching.

Quietly, he crawled to the pet door and pressed his ear against it. The creature urgently gobbled the walnuts.

It was hungry. So, so hungry.

Chapter 11

Logan followed the hallway until he reached the lobby. He assumed Mike would find him, so he took a seat near the elevators to make himself visible.

He patted his pocket for his phone, remembering he'd locked it inside his car.

Cool, now he could observe people like a weirdo. He wasn't *addicted* to his phone or anything, but he wished he could hold it, keep it close, and never let it leave his sight. You know, in case of an *emergency*.

He almost laughed, thinking, *When was the last time I sat somewhere and looked around?* He watched the elevators move, the spotless glass walls reflecting the crowded lobby. Guests rode the elevators in pairs, sometimes holding books or pointing at unfurled maps. Some wore bathing suits, some held drinks.

But the flood of readers died out, and the elevators were left empty and waiting. The right elevator sat directly in front of him. The left elevator waited on the fourth floor. Both had their doors open like a warm invitation.

Then their doors closed simultaneously.

Weird.

The elevators moved, one going up, one going down. They switched spots.

"Well, that's not normal," Logan whispered. *Do they move on their own?*

They switched again. The left elevator moved to the second floor and opened its doors. A full minute passed before a woman stepped inside and rode the elevator to the main floor. The right elevator did the same thing on the third floor. It was like they were anticipating the readers.

He looked around to see if anyone noticed or cared, but no one did. A long line of people waited for the balcony with the stained-glass window above it. Apparently, it was a *thing* to take a picture up there. Logan looked back at the elevators on the main floor, side-by-side, as if they knew he was watching.

"Yo! New guy!" Mike waved by the stairwell.

Logan jumped to his feet and hustled over, afraid Mike would walk away without him.

"You need a break?" Mike asked.

"Nah, I'm good." He was starting to get hungry, but he had no food and didn't feel like calling someone to unlock his car right now. "Where are we headed?"

"Time for the stacks, brother, Angel and Mia are ready for ya."

"Only two people work there?"

Mike sauntered down the stairwell, grunting in acknowledgment. "There was a third, but he quit last week. He didn't last long."

"Why not?"

Mike pushed through a door, and they were back on the lower level. "Because it's really not for everyone."

Logan liked ominous jobs as much as the next guy, but even he was getting sick of everyone avoiding his questions. He just hoped the job was physically active. He'd rather do almost anything than be stuck in an office, bored out of his mind.

They faced a short hallway with double doors at the far end, a sign hanging above them:

The Stacks.

The sign was homemade, with the same loopy font as the other sign on the other side of this maze.

"Almost forgot." Mike dug into his pockets, removing a badge with a small clip. "The key to the kingdom, Logan. Don't lose it."

Logan clipped the badge to his jeans pocket. "And this gives me access to…?"

"Employee-only rooms. The back entrance, side entrance, the dock, the stacks." Mike pointed at the badge scanner on the wall. "Give it a shot. Make sure it works."

Logan held his badge to the scanner. The light went from red to green with a *beep*, and the doors unlocked.

"Hot damn, we're in business." Mike opened the door. "Remember, this is a trial. If you really don't like it, you can stick to working the dock. Then I can bug you all day."

"Is there a reason why I wouldn't like it?"

"Not really. Like I said, it's not for everyone. That's all. Angel and Mia are good people, but they do things a certain way," he said, offering a, *You have no idea* look, "and you either love it or you really, really hate it. A lot of people hate it, let me tell you."

Logan looked through the doorway at the strangely dark room beyond. The shadows played tricks on his eyes. He had yet to back down from an adventure, and this time, he didn't have much of a choice.

He had a bet to win.

"Let's do this." Logan walked through the door.

His eyes slowly adjusted to the strange lighting. The room was far bigger than he first thought. It looked like a warehouse with a low ceiling—a warehouse full of tall shelves laden with books.

Now it made sense. If they outfitted each reader with fifteen books every week, then they had to reuse them and store them somewhere. This place was their literary well. A home for thousands of books.

Closed stacks for employees only.
An underground library.

Chapter 12

Florence stared at the bloody words on the mirror. HELP ME.

"Okay. I'm starting to believe," she said to her empty room. Alyssa Larkin wasn't a hallucination after all. Unless Florence was the victim of an elaborate and cruel prank, this actually happened.

Alyssa needed help, apparently, but why make an appearance after thirty-eight years? Had she been dormant? Despite the resort's famous hauntings, Florence didn't believe Alyssa had been showing up on readers' beds for thirty-eight years. No, something changed.

I woke her up, Florence thought. *I brought her back.*

She came here to find Chloe, not to involve herself in the complicated mysteries surrounding this place. But maybe helping Alyssa could lead her to Chloe. Alyssa's presence confirmed not only the existence of ghosts but the true possibility of contact. Florence was now much closer to finding Chloe than she had been this morning. What if Alyssa knew Chloe? What insight could she give Florence into the afterlife?

The choice was obvious.

"I'm coming, girl," Florence whispered.

She examined the mirror. What did Alyssa expect her to do? Either Alyssa suffered a fatal accident where no one would find her, or someone murdered and buried her.

Until Alyssa explained what happened, Florence would assume the worst.

"But I don't know how to help you," Florence said. She looked around, hoping for another visit. "What am I supposed to do?"

If Alyssa was murdered back in 1988, the killer was either dead or quite old. Maybe exposing the killer wasn't an option anymore, and Alyssa wanted someone to find her body and give her family closure.

Florence noticed both the nightstand and the bed had been pulled away from the wall, leaving a gap barely large enough for her to squeeze through.

Florence knelt by the bed and checked beneath it. Nothing there except a bloody smear on the metal frame, where Alyssa must've pulled the bed away from the wall. There was a bloody fingerprint on the corner where the mattress rested against the frame.

Shifting to her feet, Florence moved back in front of the mirror, where the blood was fresher compared to the spots on the bed. Florence waved her hand in front of the mirror, writing HELP ME in the air.

"Then you go to the bed," Florence said to herself, kneeling, pretending to pull the frame away from the wall. "And you bring it out just enough to access the wall." She mimicked the pattern, hand over hand, pretending to turn the bed. She rolled to her side and checked the wall. Sure enough, there was a faint red mark on the trim. The blood on Alyssa's finger had almost run out.

Florence climbed onto the edge of the bed and inspected the wall. The nightstand would've been in Alyssa's way, so she set it aside and stood between the wall and the bed. Why?

She slumped down against the wall and examined Alyssa's last trace, her bloody smudge on the trim, where the floor and wall connected. There were two thin cracks in the trim, about two inches apart, as if someone had replaced a small section of it, and now it wasn't entirely flush with the rest. Why would Alyssa point to this spot?

Florence pressed on the trim, feeling it wiggle and sink beneath her fingers. She pushed until something *clicked*.

A ticking followed; a clock came to life inside the walls. Wood groaned and shifted. Behind the piano, the wood paneling opened, and a dark doorway appeared.

A secret passageway.

Oh, Alyssa, Florence thought. *What the hell are you getting me into?*

Climbing out from behind the bed, Florence tiptoed over to the piano and turned on her phone's flashlight. Inside the doorway, narrow wooden stairs rose up to the fourth floor, vanishing behind a low ceiling.

This can't be good, she thought, half-scared, half-giddy with adrenaline. *This is so very not good.*

Florence pulled the piano bench out, stood on it, and stepped on top of the piano. She slid to her butt and jumped down on the other side.

The bookshelf was attached to the secret door and had moved with it, forcing her to maneuver around. Those fifteen books had *nothing* on this.

She entered the dark passageway and tried not to make a sound on the wooden steps, although she couldn't explain why.

The stairs led to a short, dark corridor with high vaulted ceilings. Ten feet from where Florence stood, the corridor ended in a wall. On either side of her, wooden beams arched into the ceiling and vanished among the cobwebs and shadows.

One step at a time, Florence crossed the corridor and stopped at the opposite wall. Did the passageway work on both sides? Did this lead to another room? And not just a room, but considering the route she took, this was a bridge between the third and fourth floors.

Something about this small space reminded her of Chloe and the summer before their sophomore year of high school, when they set up a borrowed tent in Florence's small, square backyard and slept in it for days, free of all responsibilities. It saved Florence from the embarrassment of her childhood home, where her mom rarely cleaned (and neither did her mom's boyfriends), and Florence's older brothers were too busy to care about what their little sister did. It was the antithesis of Chloe's home, and their little tent in that little backyard seemed to prove it. Florence and Chloe had never camped before and had to use YouTube directions to set up the tent. It was at least a week before Chloe returned home. Florence stayed in the tent for another few nights, often waking up alone in the middle of the night to the sound of drunk voices on the sidewalk and red and blue cruiser lights flickering on the tent's polyester sides

This corridor felt like that tent. A waiting place. An escape from reality.

Why does this exist? Florence wondered. *What's the connection between my room and whatever's on the other side of this wall?*

She leaned against the wood and listened. To her surprise, a voice drifted through from the other side; a string of rambling sentences too quiet to understand. The mutterings came closer, sometimes with a hitch, a sharp cry. It was a woman's voice, and she was growing agitated.

Was it Alyssa? Florence had no way of knowing, and she didn't feel confident enough to call out and ask. For now, she'd assume it was a real person who lived on the fourth floor; someone whose room secretly connected with Florence's.

Something moved on the other side of the wall. Was the woman leaning against it? Who was she?

Florence quietly stepped away from the wall. Her shoe slipped on the wooden steps, and she caught herself, dropping her phone on the dusty floor. It landed with a loud thump, and the opposite wall creaked again.

Florence held her breath. She couldn't take her eyes off the wall, waiting, praying it wouldn't turn into an opening door. She leaned down, carefully picked up her phone, and turned off the flashlight.

The wall, now hidden by shadows, seemed to be moving. Florence knew her eyes were playing tricks on her, but she could swear a sliver of darkness opened and pale fingers curled around a hidden door.

"I know you're there," came a whisper in the dark.

Florence flew down the steps and jumped on top of the piano, grabbing the little bookshelf with both hands and pulling the secret door shut. It latched and blended into the paneled wall. She slid off the piano, clipping the keys on the way down and sending a jarring echo through her room.

"Oh God," she said, "what do I do?"

The hidden door stayed closed. Above her, the chandelier gently rattled. Florence braced herself, allowing the chills to pass. Okay, she could do this. But she had to be smarter.

Alyssa wanted her to find that passageway. After thirty-eight years of silence, Alyssa needed someone to tell her story, and she chose Florence.

The passageway was a start, but it wasn't enough.

Florence had to find out who lived on the other side.

Chapter 13

12:15 p.m. Time to go.

Robert slipped the nutcracker inside his pocket and scooped a handful of almonds. He knelt on the bottom shelf, pushed his hand through the pet door, and dumped the nuts inside the Styrofoam bowl.

"I'll be back soon, little guy. I promise."

No sign of the critter.

He removed his gray apron and placed it on a shelf. Taking the folder from its hiding spot, Robert opened it once more to reassure himself. He had everything perfectly covered. All his hard work was about to pay off.

Robert jogged up the stairs with the folder under his arm and shut the basement door. He hoped the animal would stay in the cellar. Warning others about it seemed wise, but he didn't know what to say.

Hey chefs, there's a rat in a secret, sealed-off cellar, and I've been feeding it nuts.

No, he'd deal with it later. He checked his phone for notifications, but the screen remained blank. That was good. He couldn't afford distractions today.

He cut through the kitchen. The chefs were behind on lunch. Servers waited for food, frustrated and confused about what was taking so long.

Robert left the kitchen with a smile on his face. He checked the time.

12:19 p.m. Perfect.

He ran down to the employee apartments on the lower level and unlocked Layla's door.

Her studio apartment was stuck in a perpetual state of catastrophe. Clothes, purses, and blankets littered the floor, making it impossible to distinguish the clean from the dirty. Ironically, she was the supervisor of room changeover, which required meticulous planning and attention to detail. You'd never know she lived like a slob.

Robert trampled her clothes to reach the dresser, where he kept a small stash of personal items, including a brand-new pack of Marlboro Reds.

He pocketed the cigarettes, a lighter, and left the apartment. The quickest way outside was the employee side entrance. He stepped out into a warm breeze under an overcast sky, the clouds swollen with light. Maybe the sun would break through later, although he wouldn't see it. Not much to see from the basement.

A walking path encircled the entire resort, including a breathtaking view of the cliff.

Charlie Walter walked the loop every single day for forty-five minutes, starting at 12:15 p.m.

Keeping the folder tucked under his arm, Robert opened the pack of cigarettes and put one between his teeth. He didn't smoke anymore, but he missed it. Charlie missed it, too.

Robert walked to the smoke shack near the parking lot, which was quieter than the one behind the resort, where all the dockworkers and housekeeping smoked. He leaned against the shack, lit his cigarette, and patiently waited.

He mentally ran through his pitch, trying to find a weakness. Yes, this was a gamble, but taking risks separated the strong from the weak. This was the stuff of legends, and the resort staff would talk about it for a long time to come: the way Robert forged his own path, defied the odds, and chased his dreams.

His thoughts ran away with that, and he let them run. His imagination always got the better of him.

Charlie came marching around the bend, sucking on his vape like he hungered for it. He looked extra shaken, extra in need of a real smoke.

"Hey Charlie," Robert said, blowing a puff of smoke in Charlie's direction. "You all right?"

Charlie stopped, his armpits sweaty after a single lap, and it wasn't even hot out. Something was eating away at him. "Sorry, it's Robert, right?"

"Yeah." Robert shook his clammy hand. "You smoke? I tried vaping, but I couldn't stick with it."

Charlie licked the sweat from his upper lip, staring at the open pack of Reds. "Fine. I need to calm down anyways."

He lit one up and shifted to the other side of the shack. They smoked in silence.

"You okay, man?"

Charlie laughed. "Just been a day."

"Something happen?"

"Same shit, Robert, different day. I'm still doing reviews on readers coming *next week*. We should be further ahead at this point, not playing catch-up."

"You down a few people?"

"Couple of vacations." Charlie nodded, clearing his throat. "But that's how it goes."

"Can I walk with you?" Robert asked. "Do you mind?"

Charlie shrugged, stamping out his cigarette and switching to the vape.

Robert followed him along the path, shifting the folder from one hand to the other.

"I'd like to ask you something," Robert said. "If that's okay."

"Sure."

"You hire all the curators, right? Is there anything you look for in the applicants? Any specific degrees, or work experience, or anything like that?"

Charlie hiked up his pants, tucking his belt buckle below his stomach. "Not really. I like people who have backgrounds in marketing, psychology, and library science. But there's no single route. Their work experience varies. Some used to be marketers, some used to be literary agents, librarians, you name it. Nali worked for the Peace Corps in Africa. I hired her because she knows the culture better than I ever could. Like I said, there are a few ways to get in."

Charlie took a hit from his vape and opened his mouth, letting white smoke drift out. "Why do you ask? I'm guessing you're interested, right? Otherwise, we wouldn't be doing this."

"I actually set up a profile." Robert held the folder out. "I'd be grateful if you took a look and let me know how I did."

Charlie's eyes widened. "Is this a fake guest, or a real one?"

"Real. She's here today."

"How'd you know she was coming?"

"Hashtags," Robert said, still holding the folder out. "It's easy to search what people are talking about on social media."

This was a lie, but a convincing one. Charlie didn't need to know the backdoor methods Robert used to access information.

"Huh. Resourceful." Charlie cracked open the folder. "You put some work into this. How long did this take you?"

"One month." Another lie, he'd spent three months on it, but how would Charlie know?

Charlie huffed. "My curators make folders like this multiple times a week."

"I know, Charlie, I had a lot on my plate, I went as fast as I could without rushing the quality."

"Fair enough, it's still impressive how thorough you were."

Robert's heart swelled with pride. "Thank you. I've been studying you and the other curators for a long time."

Charlie smiled. "I know, Robert. I rejected your application two years ago. You thought I forgot about that?"

I had been hoping, Robert thought grimly. *I also know you told Dean, and Dean hates traitors, so thanks for making my life miserable.*

"To be honest," Robert started, reading from the script in his mind, "I think you dismissed me too quickly. I didn't even get an interview. I know I didn't have much experience, but you just said there are a lot of ways to get in."

"I said a few ways."

"Everything in this folder shows you what I can do. If you still don't want me, I'll leave it alone."

Charlie flipped through the folder. Maybe he was mildly impressed and didn't want to admit it.

"Well, you got the research down, I'll give you that. Of course, research and drawing the correct conclusions from said research are two very, very different skills." Charlie grimaced. "Let's cut through the field here. I always skip the gardens."

Robert understood why. John Walter's legacy hung over Charlie like a rain cloud. Nothing worse than growing up where your dad killed himself, not to mention the endless theories and urban legends about how he haunted the place.

They trudged through the wet grass. Robert had a million things on his mind but didn't trust himself to speak. He'd talk himself into a corner.

Charlie studied the pages. "I remember Florence Noelle. I think I remember her books, too. I reviewed her profile last week."

"I'm sure some of my picks will be different from what your team decided on, but I can back them up."

"I bet you can." Charlie looked at the list of twenty recommended novels. Fifteen on Florence's personal shelf, five for backup. It was all that mattered—matching the right book to the right reader. At the end of the day, despite education, background, and their ability to research, the *right* recommendations made the resort's reputation.

Robert read at least two books a week. Although he read widely to better prepare for this role, his guilty pleasure was horror. He knew all the popular books, trends, and social-media-made-me-buy-it fads. But most importantly, he knew what Florence needed. He knew what books would unlock her potential. Of course, he only started reading aggressively two years ago, which made him a little inexperienced, but Charlie didn't need to know that, either.

Charlie read the bookshelf list for an agonizing minute. "Huh. Interesting."

"How'd I do?"

"I'd have to look at her profile to be sure. Some of these I don't recognize, which is hopefully a good sign."

"Book summaries are behind that page. Very detailed. I give an analysis of how each book will change her life."

They reconnected with the path on the other side of the gardens. Robert looked up at the roof, wondering how John, or anyone, could make a jump like that. However, if Charlie handed the folder back and told him to try another career path, Robert might jump off the roof himself. He would not work in that basement for the rest of his life.

"These aren't bad," Charlie said, not smiling, but not frowning either. "Can I keep this list of books? I'd like to compare it with what we came up with."

"Of course," Robert said, desperately containing his excitement. "Keep the folder if you want."

Charlie stopped walking. "What book changed your life and why?"

Robert had answered this question a million times in his head, and always pictured himself on a late-night talk show, cameras rolling, the audience hanging on his every word. In his fantasy, he delivered a poignant, clever response. But now, staring into Charlie's eyes, his script felt cheesy.

Fake.

So he changed it. He improvised. "*Fight Club.* Because I'll never forget it for as long as I live. A good book does that, I think. It infects your memories first, and something in you starts to change, even though you don't know it yet."

Charlie threw his head back and laughed—an action so unlike him, Robert retreated a few steps.

His stomach convulsed. Did he just screw this up?

Wiping his eyes, Charlie inhaled his vape and talked the smoke out of his mouth. "We'll be in touch, Robert. Now for the love of God, let me enjoy my walk."

"Of course, sir, not a problem. You need my number?"

Charlie shook his head. "If I'm interested, I'll find you."

"I understand."

"Good. Thanks for the smoke." Charlie followed the path along the cliff, eventually disappearing around the corner.

Robert stood completely still, his lungs filling with fresh air. That had gone *far* better than he had imagined. Everyone knew Charlie was hard to work with, but he had been pleasant today. Charlie had liked Robert's gutsy approach, and he liked Robert's work ethic. Sure, that weird horse laugh at the end kind of scared Robert, but Charlie had an eccentric side and wasn't known for being predictable.

The best part? Charlie had asked the question: *What book changed your life and why?*

Apparently, Charlie asked that question in every single interview, and it was rumored that he made his decision to hire you or not based on your answer. This wasn't just a pitch, but an *actual* interview, something Robert didn't get last time because he'd played it safe and followed the rules. Look at him now! He even improvised his answer and still made a good impression. He couldn't really explain the last-minute change. Something about using *American Psycho* as his choice didn't sit right. That book *did* change him significantly, but not in ways Charlie would understand.

Robert made the right call.

He smiled up at the sky, the sun finally breaking through the clouds like a good omen.

His plan was working beautifully.

Chapter 14

Logan had seen stunning and unique libraries before, mostly in Europe (and one in Bar Harbor, Maine), but he'd never seen anything close to this.

The stacks had long aisles with towering shelves. Bare, vintage-style light bulbs hung from the ceiling, casting warm golden light across the room. Ladders were installed on both sides of every aisle. Made of dark, polished wood, the ladders had wheels on the bottom legs, with the top portion secured to a steel bar three-fourths up on the shelves. The ladder's range allowed you to reach any book. Like a child, Logan wondered how fast the ladders could go. He'd seen similar ladders in old libraries and bookshops, but this was on another level. It was somehow both quaint and industrial at the same time.

Mike walked down one aisle, flicking his box cutter blade. "Pretty cool, huh?"

Logan stared at the countless books. "This would be paradise for a reader."

"Oh dude, you should've met the people who put this thing together." Mike shook his head. "Craziest bunch of book junkies you ever saw. They dumped their own cash into all this shit, like the fancy lights and the weird decorations they got hanging around. None of the original crew still works here, but all this stuff belonged to them."

Logan nudged one of the ladders. It rolled smoothly on the steel bars. "These ladders go pretty high."

"Yeah, it's a safety hazard. They gave each employee this silly harness that clips onto the rungs, but I doubt they use it. It just slows 'em down." Mike walked to the edge of the aisle and looked around. "Angel and Mia are here somewhere. Hey, Angel!"

Mike immediately backpedaled as something approached. A red two-seater golf cart swung into view, hardly making a sound. The driver, presumably Angel, leaned over the steering wheel.

"Yo, is this the new guy?" Angel spoke quietly, looking over his shoulder.

Mike shook his head. "Logan, meet Angel."

"Nice to meet you," Angel whispered. He was near Logan's age and had a mop of curly black hair and wore a black T-shirt with a gray bandanna tied around his neck. He wore a wristwatch on one hand and a chainmail bracelet on the other. He kept looking behind him, as if worried about being followed. In an underground warehouse, the golf cart looked about as natural as a spaceship.

Logan had so, so many questions.

"Show him the ropes." Mike patted Angel's shoulder. "Call me if you got questions. You good, Logan? Angel will give you the tour. I'll be back around a little later."

"Sounds good."

"See ya," Angel said, still quiet, still looking around.

Mike shook his head with a chuckle and walked out. The doors swung shut, clanging loudly in the silent library.

Angel beckoned Logan to come closer. "Hurry. Come on, hop in. Are you good with your hands?"

"*What*?"

"Are you fast? Are you good with your hands, or should you drive?"

Flustered, Logan gawked. "I don't know what you're talking about!" A sound came from a few aisles down, a small *skrrt* of wheels on concrete.

"We don't have time, dude." Angel paused. "Hear that?"

Another, much louder noise echoed through the stacks. It sounded like a printer spitting out a receipt.

"Get in, get in, get in!" Angel slapped the seat beside him and hit the accelerator.

Logan caught the golf cart as it took off. He grabbed the roof and jumped in, swinging his legs inside and colliding with Angel. The golf cart jerked, narrowly missing the shelves.

Logan clung to his seat, the walls around him a blur of books and ladders.

"There's a printer on the other end of the center aisle," Angel said, cutting left, maneuvering the golf cart wide enough to keep it from flipping. Even still, the cart shifted, its left wheels wanting to lift from the ground. Angel leaned against the tilt, one hand on the wheel.

The cart stabilized, and Angel floored the pedal. He pointed ahead. "See that station? It's the table with the receipt printer. The receipt hangs down toward us. See it?"

"Yeah!" Logan barely saw the flash of white paper hanging from the printer.

Forty feet left.

"When we go by, I need you to grab it."

"Okay. I can do that." Logan leaned out of the cart, extending his right hand.

"I'm not slowing down."

"What? Are you serious!"

"Come on, man!"

Twenty feet.

Tires screeched behind them. Another golf cart emerged from an aisle, ink-black and decked out with colorful stickers.

"Holy shit!" Angel slapped the wheel. "We got this, Logan, we got this!"

Logan *had* to grab that receipt. He was certain his life depended on it.

He leaned out, Angel swerving to block the cart behind them. Logan flexed his fingers. The white paper hung from the printer. Easy enough, right?

Just grab the stupid paper!

They sped past, and Logan lunged for the receipt. He grabbed the white slip and felt it fall through his fingers. It dislodged from the printer and spiraled behind them, sweeping over the other cart.

Logan sat back down, nothing to show Angel but his empty, no-good hands.

Angel's smile vanished. He slowed down and turned, but the other cart had already pulled over. The driver was a young woman with long black hair. She plucked the receipt from the ground and waved it at them.

"Son of a bitch!" Angel jumped from his cart. "We had that."

"Sorry," Logan said. "I thought I had it."

Angel walked over to the woman and looked at the receipt. "No worries, Logan, we'll get the next one."

On cue, the printer sputtered to life and ejected another receipt. Angel ripped it away and held it above his head. "Too slow, huh?"

The woman smiled, ignoring him. "Nice to meet you, Logan. They said we'd get a replacement, but I thought it would be forever." Despite her thick Korean accent, she spoke perfect English. She looked to be in her early twenties and wore a billowing sweater weighed down by a silver fox necklace.

"I'm Mia." She fluttered a few fingers, as if a full wave would've been overkill. Between both hands, she wore at least six rings.

"I like your fox necklace," Logan said.

Mia ran a thumb over her necklace and nodded at his arm. "I like your owl."

"You got tattoos?"

Mia rolled up one sleeve. A watercolor fox trotted across her forearm, surrounded by clumps of tall grass with a black tree and full moon in the background.

Angel gasped. "What the hell? You never told me you had tattoos!"

"You never asked." Mia dropped her sleeve.

"I love it." Logan smiled. "I originally thought my owl should be clutching a dead mouse, but I was talked out of it."

Mia laughed, sitting back in her golf cart. "Smart choice."

"Whoa, whoa, okay, hold on." Angel stood between them. "I can't be the only one without an animal tattoo."

"You hate needles."

"No, I don't hate them, I hate the idea of getting stabbed over and over again, for hours!"

"I'll give you a tattoo, any animal you want, free," Mia said.

Angel shuddered. "Any animal?"

"Even a dead mouse."

"I really hate needles."

"It's not that bad," Logan chimed in. "I'll hold your hand."

"Oh, like you held the receipt? No thanks." Angel grinned. "I'm kidding, it's your first day, butterfingers. Come on, we'll discuss this back-alley tattoo while we get back to work."

Mia waved. "Have fun, Logan. Angel scares everyone away with his tours."

"If it helps, I'm already scared."

Angel handed Logan the new receipt, bristling. "I do not *scare* people." He slipped behind the wheel and brought his cart around. "Come on, Logan, time for a leisurely drive. Unless we get another order, then you gotta grab the receipt this time." He chuckled and started to drive off.

Logan jumped into the passenger seat, his heart still soaring from the excitement a few minutes ago. Now, what would the HR hive mind think if they'd seen Angel tearing through the stacks like it was the Fury Road? Then Angel read his thoughts.

"Obviously, we play this game where we race to grab the orders first. And yes, it's a little sketchy, so we definitely don't do it when the higher-ups are down here. That's a golden rule."

"Is there a prize or something for getting it first?"

"Nah, man, just passes the time, you know?" Angel pointed in Mia's direction. "She came up with it. She looks safe, but she's a daredevil behind the wheel. If you thought my driving was bad, wait until she takes you for a drive."

"This thing goes faster than normal, right?" Logan asked, realizing these carts were electric. "Or was I imagining that due to stress?"

Angel laughed. "Welcome to the stacks, Logan!" He reached out a hand, and Logan shook it. "This place is the wild west, my friend. Our carts are fast, we're mostly unsupervised, and we get the job done, so no one looks at us twice, you feel?"

"I feel."

"You know, you really went for that receipt. That says a lot about you. All right, let's start this tour." Angel lifted his bandanna and dabbed his sweaty forehead. "This isn't a normal job. I think you can see that, but you'll do all right."

"So, what do you do, shelve books?"

"Mostly." Angel came to the other end of the stacks and slowed down. He turned the cart around and faced the aisles. "You see the back of this thing yet?"

Logan looked behind them. The backside of golf carts normally had a bench facing outward, but this cart had been modified. Instead of a bench, the back was a bookcase. It extended from the footrest to the cart's roof. Each shelf had a tall ridge along the outward edge to keep books secure during transit.

"So when the personal bookshelves in the rooms need to be changed out, you load up these carts with the new orders," Logan said.

"Exactly." Angel pointed to the opposite wall. "We run the carts over there and send the books up the floors by using a dumbwaiter. Then people take the books and stock the bookshelves in each room."

"A dumbwaiter?"

"Yeah man, old-fashioned. It's quicker than sending books up the elevators." Angel gestured at the stacks. "You ready for the tour? We'll get the books on that receipt too, so you can see how it's done."

So this was *the stacks*. The perfect anti-office job. You worked with your hands, always on the move; you lived in a town made of books, drove down aisles like narrow streets, and risked your life for a receipt. Logan tried to calm the giddiness in his stomach. How long had it been since he'd looked forward to a job? "I'm ready when you are, buddy."

Angel grinned. "Let's go."

Chapter 15

Gazing at the ceiling, Florence wondered how she could arrange an inconspicuous way to meet her upstairs neighbor.

The answer came instantly with a high-pitched shriek from the room above her, followed by footsteps that rattled the chandelier hard enough to make the finial glass beads clink together.

"Don't touch me, don't you dare touch me!" a woman screamed, possibly the same one Florence had heard in the corridor. Was someone attacking her?

The chandelier swayed back and forth. Glass shattered upstairs, followed by more yelling, this time too faint to make out the words.

Florence ran out of her room, not bothering to lock the door, and hurried up the stairwell. On the fourth floor, she nearly collided with a fellow reader.

The young man dropped his book in surprise. He bent down to pick it up, jerking his head back and forth. "You scared me. I thought I heard someone yelling."

Voices echoed through the hallway. Doors opened and closed. The elevator *dinged*, and more guests spilled out.

Florence hesitated, unsure of what to say to the young man. All the people around made it hard to think straight. Quickly turning away from him, she moved closer to the roof entrance, stepping aside for guests juggling drinks and books, their loud, cheerful conversations filling the air.

Florence stared at the carpet and waited for them to pass, trying to picture the resort's blueprints.

The rooftop bar *wasn't* above her room, because the fourth floor had a slightly different layout from the third floor.

A small hallway branched to her right, concealed by a pair of floor-length, blood-red curtains. If she was picturing things correctly, this hallway was partially above her room.

It looked like a janitor's hideout, like a backstage entrance to a restaurant. It had no markings, so readers wouldn't give it a second thought.

Florence slipped past the curtains, holding her breath until she was sure an employee or a nosy guest wouldn't follow her through. The curtains gently rippled as people shuffled by.

She stood in a small, plain hallway with an unmarked brown door at the other end. She waited for the door to open, for someone to start accusing her of something, but it stayed closed.

All she could think was, *I'm not supposed to be here.*

But that didn't stop her from inching closer to the door. The peephole glared at her like a glass eye. Was someone watching her from the other side?

She paused, seeing something small on the floor.

Resting on the plush maroon carpet, beside the unmarked door, was a little brass handbell. Like a Victorian relic, something you'd ring to usher the maids in.

Florence stepped around the bell, reached the door, and pressed her ear against it. Was it her adrenaline-fueled imagination, or could she hear heavy breathing on the other side?

Too many books, Flo, you've read too many books.

True, but Florence couldn't shake the feeling of being watched. Who lived in a room without a number?

It could be a family member. The resort was still owned by the Walter family: Lori, the only living founder, and her son, Charlie. No one saw Lori anymore. She'd amassed quite a reputation over the last twenty years.

In old interviews, Lori had been poised, elegant, and thoughtful. Since she stopped public appearances, rumors started to spread. Anything from a developed deformity to agoraphobia to early dementia. Everything circled the same narrative: something was wrong with Lori Walter.

Through the unmarked door, Florence heard the same woman's voice again, but calmer and quieter. Florence almost knocked. After all, she'd overheard a heated conversation. No one would blame her for checking in. Plus, she *wanted* to know the woman's identity.

"You're not real," the voice came again. "I know you're not real." Her words dissolved into giddy laughter.

Was the woman talking to a *ghost*? What if Alyssa was appearing to other people? Lori Walter had known Alyssa better than anyone.

All questions and no answers. Florence had to find this woman's identity, and she raised her hand to the door, holding it there, battling herself. She hadn't crossed a line yet. This was something she could walk away from. This plain door felt like the West Wing in all the stories; the dragon's lair, the fire-lit room with the high-backed armchair, where Uncle Andrew waited and rubbed his long fingers together.

She shouldn't be here.

This didn't involve her, and she'd made a mistake by coming here. The dread was in her throat now, making it hard to breathe. She turned to leave, accidentally kicked the little bell on the floor, and sent it flying against the wall with a loud *ding!*

The door unlocked, the deadbolt snapping like a cocked shotgun. Florence ducked through the curtains and turned the corner, hearing the door fling open.

Would the woman follow her?

Florence looked at the dark tracks her shoes left on the maroon carpet, picturing the woman tiptoeing through the hallway, not making a sound. The door with no number did not close; otherwise, Florence would've heard it. Whoever lived there was still in the doorway, looking at the tracks in the carpet, at the parted curtains, wondering why someone would come up and kick the bell like that.

Florence quietly slipped inside the stairwell and rushed back to her room. She slammed the door, leaned against it, and looked at the ceiling. The woman upstairs paced back and forth, making the chandelier sway again.

Was that truly Lori Walter?

Who was she talking to?

Florence looked around her room, taking in her printed articles, backpack, laptop, and notebooks.

Too much had happened in the last hour. She needed to write everything down and try to understand Alyssa's connection with John and Lori Walter. If Alyssa showed herself again, Florence would be prepared.

Since the internet had limited information regarding the resort's early years, Florence had to try a new angle. Luckily, this was The Reader's Resort, where you could read about anything.

Florence opened her door and felt the curated books giving her death stares. "I'll get to you," she told them. "But I have to find another book first."

Chapter 16

After his brief interaction with fresh air and sunshine, Robert returned to the basement feeling higher than when his old line-cook buddy fed him special gummies without disclosing their contents. The kitchen struggled that day.

Roberts's pitch had been nearly perfect. Now he had to wait for Charlie's call.

Back in the basement, he had assumed the critter would've crawled through the pet door to find more nuts, but the bowls and open bags were untouched.

He knelt and glanced through the pet door. Nothing ran away this time. Robert started to wonder if the animal had escaped, but then he heard it breathing.

Buried in the murky darkness, the creature breathed deeply, as if meditating, purring. It was still in there and apparently had no plans of leaving.

Robert grabbed a handful of walnuts, shuffled back to the pet door, and paused, about to put his hand through.

What if the animal was too big to fit through the pet door?

He jerked his hand back. What kind of animal would be too large for a pet door? And how would it get stuck in a cellar? Part of him wanted to unlock it and go inside, but he had no clue what lived in there.

The pet door shifted and cracked open. Dark eyes watched him. It sniffed, still hungry, pupils shrinking in the light.

The poor thing didn't deserve to starve. Robert pushed against the pet door, and the creature crawled away.

The Styrofoam bowl was just out of reach. The damn thing had trampled it.

Robert rolled to his stomach and reached for the bowl, his entire arm inside the cellar. The bowl was too far, so he dumped the walnuts in a neat pile on the ground and felt warm breath on his wrist. He didn't want to yank his arm back and startle the animal, but he didn't want to get eaten either. Robert edged backward, easing his arm out a few inches at a time. When the creature sniffed his wrist again, he thought about all the walnut dust coating his arm and how delicious he must smell.

Then something clamped down—a human hand tightened around his wrist.

He refused to scream or strike out. For a moment, he remained still.

"Who are you?" The voice drifted through the pet door, warbled and broken; a voice that hadn't been used in a long, long time. It gagged when it spoke, as if in immense pain. It took several tries before Robert understood its words.

"Rob—Robert."

Silence. The thing, the human, wasn't used to conversation.

"Help me," the voice slurred.

"Let me go, right now, and I'll help you, I swear to God."

"Help me." This time, a whisper, a struggle. The creature could barely talk. If it wasn't holding Robert's wrist like a manacle, he'd almost feel sorry for it. Robert tried to pull away, but the hand yanked him back.

"Let go, seriously. Let go right now." Robert kept his voice low. As ridiculous as it sounded, he didn't want the chefs running down and finding him arm-deep through a pet door, fighting something inhuman, shutting down the resort, and sending Florence home... no, that was not an option, no matter the suffering.

It mumbled words he couldn't interpret. The voice made his skin crawl. He tried to free his arm, but it held firm.

"I said let go." Robert thrashed his arms, hoping to dislodge its grip. It worked! The hand slipped. It held on with its fingertips now. Another pull and—

Sharp teeth sank into his arm like a thousand needles digging for the bone. Robert froze, his brain and body numbing, shivering. The teeth withdrew with a wet sucking sound, and the creature smacked its lips.

Shaking, Robert braced his feet against the wall and pushed. His arm came free, sliding through the pet door, leaving bloody streaks behind.

He held back a scream. His throat ignited; his arm burned like fire. He started crawling away when the hand reached through the pet door and snatched his ankle.

It slowly pulled him back toward the door. He reached with his good arm and knocked over the wooden chair and bags of nuts. He had nothing to grab on to. Then he remembered the nutcracker, and he fished it from his pocket. He whipped around, brandishing the nutcracker like a weapon. A pale, thin arm hung through the pet door, with the hand still wrapped around his ankle. The fingernails were jagged and rotted. The nutcracker would snap those fingers like twigs.

Robert waved the nutcracker, and the hand quickly let go and retreated. The pet door swung shut. The human didn't say anything. Neither did Robert. He crawled out of reach, touching his warm forehead to the cold concrete, unable to breathe, unable to stay awake.

Robert blinked at the ceiling as laughter rang from the kitchen. Everything drifted down the basement steps—music, conversations, sizzling grease and metal spatulas scraping against grills. Dust fell from the ceiling, coating Robert in a fine powder.

He was sitting on the wooden chair, loosely holding the nutcracker in his right hand. He'd fallen asleep with his head up, his neck out.

When he looked down, his arm was completely fine. Not a scratch. Sliding off the chair, he crawled to the bottom shelf, his neck aching.

He studied the pet door, tipping it open, seeing nothing but darkness and the Styrofoam bowl turned over.

The eyes, the hand on his wrist, the raspy voice, had all been a dream. There was no bite on his arm.

However...

Was it his imagination, or did his arm itch where the teeth marks would've been?

"*It's this place*," he sang. "This dreadful, horrible place."

The basement was working on him, stretching his mind like fresh dough. Robert smiled, tasting blood in his mouth. *That was a mean trick,* he thought. *A very mean trick.*

"Robert, you down here?" Dean's voice echoed down the stairs, followed by heavy footsteps.

Robert quickly stood, his head swimming.

Dean turned the corner and frowned. "You look rough. You sick?"

Robert shook his head. "What can I do for you, Dean?"

Dean was never a good liar, and he didn't preamble when he was flustered. If he reeled you into his office, that meant official resort business. If he found you at your station, that meant *unofficial* business.

Dean rolled his head from side to side like a fighter in the ring. He held up his phone.

"Charlie texted me."

Robert didn't think Charlie would consult anyone. Why would he? He alone hired new curators.

"He asked me if I've had any problems with you." Dean chuckled, plain tickled by the irony of it all. "Now, why is he asking me that? What the hell did you do?"

"I didn't do anything."

Dean shrugged. "Fine. Don't tell me." He typed on his phone, and the text message swooshed away. "I just asked him why. He can tell me himself what you've screwed up." Dean walked closer, putting his hands inside his pockets, puffing his chest out. "You could've told me first and come out ahead of whatever shit you're stirring up. But if this is about your new position..." he trailed off, his chin shaking. "If you went to Charlie-fucking-Walter about your new job down here, I swear you'll be gone tomorrow."

"I didn't tell anyone about my new position."

Dean couldn't hide the disgust on his face. "If I find out—"

"Besides," Robert cut in, "I was under the impression that these changes were all above board. If that's the case, why do you care if Charlie Walter knows you put a ten-year employee in the basement to crack nuts? Why would he care? And why would I complain to the *family* about something like that?"

Dean shook his head. "You didn't... good God, Robert. This isn't about him rejecting your application, is it?"

Charlie would spoil it when he responded to Dean's text, so Robert said nothing. It was an in-house promotion and none of Dean's business.

Hands on his hips, Dean grinned. "I can't believe you. The guy turns you down once, and you harass him about it *two years later*." Laughter crept into his voice. High, squeaky giggles. "Um, hello, Robert. You were rejected, okay? Move on, buddy. If you didn't have the stuff to get the job last time, you think he's gonna give you a second chance?"

Robert itched his arm, not trusting himself to speak.

"Charlie Walter is a scientist, not a bleeding heart. Did he tell you he'd give you another shot? *And did you believe him?*" Dean walked away, his mood very much improved. "You should know better, Robert. And here I thought you were a smart guy." Dean walked up the basement steps, his pale lips pinched together to keep from laughing.

Robert stood there, a useless scarecrow.

No, Dean had it wrong. Charlie *was* impressed with Robert's pitch. Once Charlie hired Robert, Dean would have no choice but to swallow his words. What a glorious day that would be.

Robert decided to take a quick break, then come back and clean up and waste time before clocking out. He'd accomplished very little today—something Dean would've noticed if his head wasn't so far up his own ass.

It wouldn't hurt to check on Florence. She played a crucial part in his plan, and he wanted to see her settled in comfortably.

Months ago, after Layla logged him into the resort's management system, Robert scrolled through the upcoming applicants. He'd lied to Charlie about using social media to determine Florence's stay at the resort, because if anyone knew Robert had been given access to the reader profiles, he would've been fired. He spent a week trying to find the perfect reader, and he couldn't say what drew him to Florence over anyone else.

He'd never met her before, but something in her eyes spoke to him. She harbored a lot of pain, probably from losing her best friend at the tender age of seventeen. That pain, paired with her natural beauty, set her apart from most women. On her application, she'd admitted to feeling survivor's guilt after her friend passed away. No one else had been so honest and real about their past.

This girl was different.

Overnight, he'd gone from anxiously searching for the right reader to following her using fake social media accounts. She didn't post very much, which made it harder to understand her, but the internet gave Robert plenty of context about her life. After a month of working on her profile, he drove to Sharonville. Looking at pictures of her made his midsection hurt, as if the butterflies inside his stomach had sharp, unforgiving wings. But pictures had limits. If Robert wanted to be the best curator she could've asked for, he had to know everything about her. Where she lived, how she commuted, and what she did for fun after work.

He'd known following her around Sharonville was above and beyond typical curator practice, but Robert didn't care to be like the other curators.

He had to be better than them.

Could he see her again, somehow? She was probably in her room, and wandering the resort looking for her would be a waste of time, but Robert needed to get his mind off Dean and far away from this God-forsaken basement. One look at that young, pretty face, and those old-soul eyes, and he would be well again.

Chapter 17

Logan sat in the passenger seat while Angel drove the golf cart through the stacks, using his best tour guide voice.

"At this end, we have non-fiction, which is split into categories like history, memoir, and health. Everything is organized by topic, not by the author's name, like fiction is. And the topics range from world politics to Ohio history. And the Ohio books are either about the Wright brothers or haunted stuff 'cause people eat that up."

"What?"

"You know, they say this place is haunted."

"That wasn't in the job description," Logan said, as if he even read the whole thing. It actually could've been in there.

Angel chuckled. "We keep all the fiction lumped together in one big section, that way you don't have to wonder what genre a book falls into. As you can see, we have ladders to help us reach the top shelves. We were given harnesses with clips to prevent falls. But there are only two of us. Three, if you stick around. You can use one if you want, but we don't, and no one enforces it."

Logan smiled. "The wild west."

"Exactly!" Angel shook his head. "For real, though, be careful on those ladders. I oil those wheels myself."

"Is everything in here designed for maximum speed?"

Angel cackled with laughter. "You're really starting to get it. We stock books all day, every day, baby. We gotta be fast."

Logan realized the ladders weren't confined to a single aisle. The steel bar made a loop, so you could roll a ladder from one aisle, around the bend, and over to the other side, inevitably crashing into the ladder in that aisle. The two ladders could run laps all day.

"So, what are we working on now?" Logan asked, staring at the receipt in his hands.

"See that list?" Angel pointed at the thin paper. "Each reader gets five replacements, available to them any time during their stay. Most people hit the replacement button within the first few hours of getting their room, which is why we're so busy right now. Our job is to collect these five new books, send them up to the appropriate level, and the room team will take it from there. They'll collect all the discarded books from the rooms and send them back down, where we gotta re-shelve them."

"The list is alphabetical," Logan said. "*The Midnight Library* by Matt Haig is at the top. We should be close to H, right?"

Angel whistled. "That's a good book." After pulling into an aisle and parking, he jumped out, adjusted the ladder, and climbed the rungs. Halfway up the ladder, he pushed off the shelf, rolling down the aisle like a stowaway on a train. He climbed another two rungs, his fingers dancing along the spines, and plucked a book from the shelf. Hopping down, he put the book in the golf cart's bookcase and slid behind the wheel.

They started driving again. Angel looped around the far side of the stacks and circled back around. Logan held the receipt tightly in his hands, watching it ripple in the wind. "That was fast."

"Lots of practice. If we don't go fast, the books stack up, orders get behind, and the readers get pissed. Last thing we need is Crusty leaving her lair to come yell at us."

"Did you say Crusty?"

Angel smiled. "There's no way to sugarcoat this, Logan. Our supervisor's a real bitch. Her name's Amanda, but down here we call her Crusty. She works in a broom closet two doors down. She orders new books and keeps inventory, yada yada. I honestly don't know what she does, except watch Netflix. All I know is she leaves us alone unless we screw something up."

"Got it. No screw up, no Crusty."

Angel grimaced. "Exactly. Anyways, let's grab these suckers. You take *Five Decembers* by James Kestrel and I'll get the rest."

"Oh, so you think you can get three books in the time it takes me to get one?"

"Let's find out, Logan!" Angel slowed the cart down, pointing at an aisle. "That's it! That's your spot! Go go go!"

"Aren't you going to stop?"

"You're gonna miss it!"

Shit.

Logan jumped from the moving cart, almost tripping over the lower steel bar that held the ladder. Angel revved the cart and took off, tires spinning.

If this was some sort of hazing ritual, Logan was all in. Although he didn't have a firm opinion on this job yet, he certainly wasn't *bored*. He thought back to Charlie's limp job offer. Yeah right. Like he was going to sell his soul to a tidy office when he could be pushing twenty miles per hour through a paper jungle.

The aisles were named, not numbered. A neat but horribly inefficient system. Each aisle had a plaque on it, labeled with a famous fictional place.

The Shire.

Hogwarts.

Derry.

Tatooine.

Arrakis.

And on it went.

Logan was in the Overlook aisle. Very appropriate. Thanks to the power of cinema, he knew that reference. Who needs books, right? He jogged down the aisle, finding a placard for K sticking out from the spines. Okay, progress. K... E... S...

Five Decembers! It was up there, just out of reach. Logan bolted to the nearest ladder and ran with it. The ladder nearly slipped from his hands—it sailed on the steel bars in a perfect glide. Angel was right, these babies rolled.

He jumped on the ladder and climbed three rungs, pushing off the shelf, accidentally knocking a book off. He'd grab that later.

The ladder nearly rolled past *Five Decembers*, so he had to grab the shelf to stop himself. He plucked the book from the shelf and jumped off the ladder (the least dangerous thing he'd done yet on this job).

Angel waited at the end of the aisle, in his golf cart, texting. The other three titles were stowed in the cart's bookcase.

Logan sighed. He picked up the fallen book and re-shelved it.

"You'll get the hang of it," Angel said.

"I thought I was going fast."

"You did good. You'll get faster."

Logan shelved *Five Decembers* and hopped in the cart.

They drove past the double doors Logan first came through, to the right corner of the room, where the wall turned into a small sliding door with a chipped, silver handle.

Angel slid the outer door open, then pushed aside a squeaky, black metal gate. Inside the wall, the dumbwaiter held piles of books. They moved the books to a nearby table.

"We leave re-shelve books here," Angel explained. "We can shelve them later, or do it now, if no orders are in. Mia's been killing it on the re-shelves. This table's almost empty."

Across the room, the printer sputtered to life. Mia flew by them, swerved around the corner, and swiped the receipt without slowing.

Angel clapped for her, smiling like a kid. He collected the five books from their cart and handed them to Logan. "Set these in the elevator, *por favor.*"

Logan placed the stack neatly in the center of the dumbwaiter, next to a plaque that read LOAD NOT TO EXCEED 200 LBS. Angel handed Logan the receipt, which he stuck between the top two books.

"The receipt tells you what floor it goes to." Angel shut the metal gate, the outer door, and pressed the number 4 button. A silver panel on the wall had buttons starting with S, then 1 through 4. The dumbwaiter rumbled inside the wall, rattling all the way to the fourth floor.

On the same table as the re-shelve books, a handheld radio was docked into a charging station. Angel picked it up. "Delivery on four." The radio beeped, and he set it back on the charger.

"So." He wiped his forehead. "You gotta have some questions, right?"

Logan shook his head. "Just trying to take it all in."

"It's a lot."

"Yes, it is."

Angel pointed at Logan's arm. "Where'd you get that?"

"The owl or the phone number?"

"The owl. I wasn't gonna even ask about the phone number."

"I actually got this done in Amsterdam."

"That's badass. How long were you there?"

"Only two years."

Angel snorted. "*Only* two years. You must have some stories, man. Tell you what, let's shelve these books, and you can tell me about Amsterdam. I've heard it's crazy there."

Logan thought about Nina. About coffee dates and late nights and drunken skinny dipping, fighting through crowds and kissing on bridges.

He thought about red wine, broken English, and screaming matches. Passionate hugs and bruises and make-up sex.

Yes, he had stories, but not the good kind. Stumbling through the red-light district, high as a kite, bumping into strangers, was not as glamorous as some would think.

"Amsterdam can be a little wild. How do you think I got my tattoo?" Logan said.

Angel pumped his fist. "I knew it, I knew it, my man's got *stories*! Woo! Let's get to work, and spare no details, please."

The printer echoed through the stacks. The receipt flashed in the gold light. Farther down the aisles, Mia turned the corner, jerking her golf cart to a stop. They made eye contact, and Logan busted out his telepathic skills by thinking, *I'm new, go easy on me*.

"Logan," Angel whispered, edging toward his golf cart. "*Logan*."

Logan didn't take his eyes off Mia. He felt like a hiker seeing a bear for the first (and last) time. He pointed at the printer, hoping she'd cut him some slack.

It didn't work. Mia looked like a sugar-high kid on a go-kart track. Ride or die, baby.

"Logan!" Angel jumped behind the wheel. "Let's go!"

Mia kicked her accelerator, spun around, and disappeared behind an aisle. Logan ran after Angel, and for the third time that day, jumped inside a moving golf cart. He leaned out of his seat, his hands and feet better placed this time.

"You got this!" Angel swerved down the aisle, swinging left, giving Logan no time for adjustment. The printer was right there.

He crouched and steadied his right hand. Angel whooped and hollered as Mia's cart fell in behind them, betting on another slip-up.

Logan reached for the receipt, his heart soaring, and he wondered how anyone could ever call this work.

Chapter 18

Contrary to a misguided curator, Florence did not want to live in the 1940s. It isolated her, like her own little *red-room*, and for once she wanted a comfortable proximity to strangers. If she was going to spend hours researching the resort's dark history, she'd do it someplace livelier.

Florence took the stairs to avoid the elevators.

The stairwell kept winding down, marked with EMPLOYEE ONLY signs, but she took the exit for the main floor. She walked to the front desk, secretly pleased that the young man from earlier wasn't around.

"Can I help you?" an older woman asked, half-moon glasses on the edge of her nose.

Florence fake smiled. After seeing a very real ghost earlier, she felt an even stronger need to hide herself. No one needed to know what she knew, or what she was trying to do. Not until she gathered enough evidence about Alyssa's death to get the police involved.

"I'm looking for a book on the history of this resort," Florence said, pretending to be the dopey, slightly aloof girl strangers always assumed her to be. "Do you have any books on that?"

"Well." The old woman typed into her computer. "Well, let's see. We have at least a dozen titles on Ohio history. Some of those mention this resort."

"But you have nothing just about the resort?"

"Well." The old woman squinted at her screen. "How about I put a request in, and someone can get back with you very shortly?"

"Oh, no need to bother," Florence said. "Is there someone I can talk to? Or a place I can go to see more books?"

The woman shook her head. "We only have closed stacks, I'm afraid. What's your name? I know we can find what you need."

"That's all right, thank you though."

"You sure?"

"Yes, thank you," Florence said with a forceful smile. She had a hunch where the stacks would be. Turning away, she headed for the stairwell. Once inside, she ran past the EMPLOYEES ONLY sign, down to the lower level, and tested the door at the bottom.

Unlocked.

She didn't have a strong reason for distrusting the system, but if she kept snooping like this, and someone started to ask questions, she didn't want a trail. Other than, of course, the stairwell camera staring her in the face. Oh well, she wasn't a pro.

She opened the door to the lower level. Hallways branched off in every direction, but straight ahead, two double doors waited for her. Now *these* were locked, and a homemade sign hung above them that read, *The Stacks.*

Despite being easy to locate, she had no way inside. Would it be crazy to knock?

Seeing no one, she jogged to the double doors and tested one, and sure enough, it was locked. Then she knocked three times, scooted back, and waited.

A minute later, the right door cracked open, and a guy with an owl tattooed on his left bicep leaned through the doorway and gave her the blankest look she'd ever seen.

"Hey." She had prepared a question, but his face completely erased her thoughts. Not because he had a pleasant face, though there was that, but the look he gave her was that of a bank teller watching armed thugs open their duffel bags on the lobby floor.

"Is this where you keep the books?" She felt like the dumbest person alive, but the guy seemed to immediately understand.

"Yeah, you came to the right place. Hella books in here. Also, I'm not trying to get you in trouble or anything, but I don't think you're allowed down here."

"I know, I'm sorry. I'm looking for a book on the history of this resort. Do you have something like that?"

"We got everything," he said. "I'm Logan; I'll check for you."

She didn't want to use her real name, but she didn't have a backup, so she awkwardly smiled and was only saved by someone inside the stacks yelling for Logan.

He turned away, letting the door click shut, and yelled in return.

Minutes passed. A few employees crossed the hallway behind her but continued their way, oblivious. After seeing the real thing today, Florence wouldn't dare call herself a ghost, but sometimes she felt like one.

The door finally opened, and Logan handed her a book, his bicep flexing, the owl ruffling its feathers. "My boss wants to know what room you're in so we can check this out in the system."

"I'm not your boss!" someone yelled.

Florence slowly retreated. "Is it okay if I just take it? I promise I'll give it back." That sounded pretty suspect, so she added, "I'll bring it back tomorrow! If it gets checked out in the system, my curator will probably know, and I don't want to hurt anyone's feelings."

Logan relayed that to his boss, or whoever, and the stacks erupted with knee-slapping laughter.

"She is so right! Let her have it!"

Logan tried to suppress a smile and completely failed. "Make sure you bring it back, okay? I'm new here, and it's not a good look if I got readers stealing on my watch."

"I promise." It might've been the most honest thing she'd said all day. "Wait and see."

"I hope I'm right about you," he said with a smirk, as if he knew she was up to something and he couldn't figure out what.

Florence spun around and headed for the stairs, hearing the door quietly shut behind her.

In her hands, she held a short book on Ohio's most haunted sites. The Reader's Resort was on the cover and apparently had the final and largest section of the book dedicated to it.

Now all Florence needed was a place to read, and *that* wouldn't be hard to find.

Chapter 19

Back on the main floor, Florence paused in front of a large, hand-painted map of the resort.

The resort featured four Reader Rooms—communal spaces designed for relaxation, reading, and drinking. Two were on the main floor, one on the second, and another on the fourth: the rooftop lounge. After her last visit, Florence had no plans to return.

She moved with the flow of readers through the hallway, passing the Hemingway Café and the Ballroom, both iconic staples of The Reader's Resort.

Florence briefly glanced into the Ballroom. At the far end was a tall stage with instruments, banners, and a few employees setting up equipment. The resort hosted nightly parties here, and for the readers who liked that sort of thing, the night was filled with drinking, flirting, and dancing (or so Florence had heard). She didn't know much of these wild parties apart from what readers had posted on social media—dimly lit pictures of themselves wearing beautiful dresses or crisp suits, sometimes holding a book or posing with friends.

Florence followed the hallway deeper into the resort until a pair of glass double doors opened in front of her. The floor turned to wet stone, and the air warmed, smelling of chlorine.

Reader Room One: the pool. It looked like any other indoor pool area—reclining chairs with towels draped over them, discarded flip flops, and personal bags overflowing with snacks and dry clothes.

Except at *this* pool, 90 percent of the guests were reading. Many of them had drinks, some floated on inflated rafts, and while there were a few teenagers, no little kids were in sight. The pool had become a place solely for books, and despite Florence's deep love of reading, the eerie silence made her skin crawl.

Across from her, another set of glass doors led to the outdoor pool, which was gaining popularity as the afternoon warmed up and the sun came out. Readers lounged in picture-perfect swimsuits, squeezing the last remnants of summer from Ohio's usual October pattern: warm days, cool nights, and frequent rain.

Florence didn't plan on swimming during her stay, so she left the warm, quiet atmosphere and found Reader Room Two: the bakery.

Located a stone's throw away from the pool, this room had a coffee bar on one end and a pastry table on the other, the space between them filled with massive couches, bowl chairs, and armchairs that could swallow you whole. Stringed lights crisscrossed the ceiling, and a smooth jazz playlist played over the speakers. The room had the right vibe for research, but Florence wasn't done exploring.

Taking the same stairwell to the second floor, she found Reader Room Three: the hangout.

As it turned out, the name was quite literal. The room was full of swings, hammocks, and treehouses. Actual, indoor treehouses.

The hammocks came in various sizes and styles. Same with the swings. While some were swinging benches, others were long rope swings. Then they had bamboo, egg-shaped swings, with a little opening for you to climb inside. You could curl up in a bed of blankets and read your book while the swing drifted in slow, lazy circles.

With a bar in the far corner and low-fi music quietly in the background, Florence could settle here for a while. The room had four treehouses, three of which were on platforms, not trees, and were accessible by ramp. The fourth was perched in a fake tree and had only a short ladder to climb up. Each treehouse was small, but came with a little couch, a table for drinks, and of course, more blankets.

Florence felt nostalgia for a childhood she never had. Growing up in Sharonville, she rarely spent time in nature. Her mom worked at a local factory, and during the summer, an old woman from their apartment complex watched Florence and her two brothers. Jacob and Andrew often played video games, and Florence was rarely included. The old babysitter, Helen, always brought a stack of magazines and spent the entire time thumbing through them, so Florence spent a lot of time watching her brothers play.

She'd never been inside a treehouse, even though Chloe once took her to Sharon Woods, and they played in the creek and talked about finding a treehouse somewhere in that big park. They never did; they outgrew that dream.

With every treehouse occupied, Florence found an empty egg-swing and crawled inside. She liked the comfy blankets beneath her, and the warm privacy of the egg while still hearing the murmur of the bartenders, the whisper of turning pages, and the occasional creaking of the rope swing. Snuggled in blankets, she crossed her legs and opened the book that Logan from the stacks gave her.

It reaffirmed the timeline: In the autumn of 1988, three years after launching the full-scale resort, John Walter tragically ended his own life by jumping from the roof.

In the wake of his death, resort employees questioned the whereabouts of Alyssa Larkin, who hadn't been seen for weeks. Lori Walter, overcome with grief, holed up inside her suite and ignored the growing demand for answers. In a rare interview, years later, Lori claimed she'd heard the gossip about her husband and Alyssa. Rumors of infidelity were damaging enough, but they paled in comparison to the onslaught of accusations that John murdered Alyssa before taking his own life. Lori had no answers for the public. She never understood why John left her, or why Alyssa left. She was left to manage the resort alone, and nine months after John's death, she gave birth to Charlie.

The helpless child was born into a firestorm of controversy and debate. Some publicly accused Lori of infidelity herself, and insisted John couldn't have fathered Charlie, prompting another round of vile rumors and eyewitness testimonies. Lori retreated further into herself, raising Charlie in the controlled confines of the resort. She refused to sell it despite the generous offers. As the resort's infamy grew, so did the business. In 1989, the resort formed a wait list. Three years later, the application process was launched to help mitigate the influx of popularity. Lori, after weathering years of accusations, never returned to her former self. She turned down offers to franchise, sell, or accept new partners. In the end, she never recovered from the events in 1988, and Alyssa Larkin was never seen again.

Alyssa and John were the resort's first casualties, but they were far from the last. Numerous deaths occurred at The Reader's Resort over the years. Legends grew, and stories of apparitions and strange noises increased. The resort became an early internet sensation, attracting paranormal enthusiasts and even a documentary series. Unlike its reclusive founder, the resort never managed to escape controversy or public attention.

Florence set the book down, her heart thumping. She *had* to meet Alyssa again and hear her story. Between John's death, Charlie's birth, and the endless parade of speculation, everyone stopped looking for Alyssa, and she faded into the background.

Later, Florence would attempt to contact her again. She'd do the same thing: reach out, open the door, and hope for the best.

Because if Alyssa was still clinging to the resort, were other spirits doing the same thing? Did that mean Chloe was wandering around somewhere, waiting for the right door to open?

Florence looked up, her primal instincts kicking in. This whole time, the egg-swing had been rotating in slow circles, and now the opening of the swing faced the room's front entrance.

A man stood in the doorway. He was at least a decade older than her and had disheveled brown hair and a clean, red-cheeked face. He was stocky and wore faded jeans. The man scanned the room, clearly looking for something.

Florence sank into the blankets, disliking his wandering eyes. He noticed the movement and looked at her, his face contorting with emotion.

He clearly worked at the resort, but she couldn't read the name on his badge. The egg swing moved, and Florence pretended to read her book while she watched from her peripheral vision. The man couldn't take his eyes off her.

He started moving as the swing rotated around. Now she couldn't see him. The swing was turning toward the back of the room, and Florence held her breath, waiting for him to grab the swing and peer inside.

Her heart fluttered in her chest. Where was he?

The swing slowly rotated back to the front entrance, but the man was gone. She poked her head out and checked the room. No sign of him anywhere.

She'd never seen him before, but the look on his face bothered her. It was like he recognized her.

Chapter 20

Robert returned to the basement in a daze. Somehow, Florence had become more beautiful since he last saw her. He wanted to give her time to settle in, so he didn't approach her, but he would soon. Seeing her again made him dizzy.

And best of all, she was *reading*. Even though he couldn't tell which book she had, the sight of her in that little egg swing with a book in her hands made him almost feverish. He knew no one would understand how he felt. No one except for Florence. He felt the connection when they first met. Did she? Would she recognize him? Maybe not, but that was okay. In time, she would see his devotion to her. He'd never believed in love at first sight, but that was before he met Florence. Before he became her curator and learned everything about her. If she only knew the care he'd taken to study her; to memorize every quirk, every milestone in her life. She flew under everyone's radar. Robert felt like he'd discovered a hidden treasure. He probably knew her better than anyone else. Very soon, she'd realize what she meant to him, and when that happened—no, no more daydreaming. Robert had to finish work.

With renewed optimism, he cracked the remaining walnuts, almonds, and pecans. Time flew by, and when his shift was up, he hurried to the studio apartments in the lower level. Layla was gone, either working overtime or coping in a bar somewhere, which was fine by him. She'd been curt with him all last week, making snide little jabs at his appearance or the type of books he kept leaving on her dresser.

Self-improvement books repelled her like garlic to a vampire, and books written from the perspective of serial killers, like *American Psycho*, 'made her physically ill.' He started leaving them out spitefully—he didn't need this relationship much longer anyway.

Layla wasn't a good fit for him, although he'd known that from the start. After reading *American Psycho*, he'd stumbled down a rabbit hole of books about killers. He found quite a lot online, some good, some terrible. But either way, something about indulging in the deep, primal urges compelled him. Most people didn't live like that. Most people, like Layla, were simply taking up air and slowly dying. Not very inspiring.

He'd never admit *The Devil in the White City* impressed him, but it left a lingering touch on his mind, much like the woman's small footprint left inside H. H. Holmes's hotel of horrors. Robert found himself daydreaming after reading these books. What would it be like to own a hotel designed to trap you? What would Robert do with that sort of power?

He would never forget Layla's face, all red and scrunched with disgust while she waved one of his *filthy* books around. He'd never considered her to be gorgeous, but that was the first time he'd ever thought of her as unattractive. What would her footprint look like on a cellar wall?

Trudging through Layla's clothes on the floor, Robert pulled a long-sleeved shirt from her dresser (he had a small section, right beside her underwear, for his own clothes) and changed shirts to get rid of the basement's moldy stench.

As he collected his car keys and phone, a heavy knock came from the door.

This being her room, Layla wouldn't knock, and she didn't have many friends (the few friends she had *never* knocked—a habit that backfired more than once when she and Robert were intertwined on the floor). A knock meant business. It meant whoever stood on the other side wasn't accustomed to this end of the resort.

Robert checked the peephole and froze. Charlie Walter stood outside.

"Robert?" Charlie called, knocking again. "If you're in there, I need to talk to you."

Things were about to go one of two ways: really great or really, really bad.

Charlie knocked again.

What if he was blown away by Robert's book list for Florence? What if Robert's dreams were about to come true? This would be forever immortalized as the moment Robert's life changed forever.

He forced himself to breathe, his head swimming with delight. All this planning, countless late nights, and sleeping with *Layla*, of all people. It all led right here.

Robert opened the door.

Charlie pushed inside, jabbing a finger in Robert's face. "*What the hell is wrong with you?*"

Robert backed up, tripping over the laundry on the floor, cursing Layla under his breath. "Hi, Charlie, um, what are you talking about?"

"Don't pretend you don't know!" Charlie slammed the door behind him. "How'd you do it?"

"Do what?" Robert would pretend for as long as he could. He thought Charlie wouldn't find out this early.

Charlie lifted his finger again, aiming at Robert's chest. "You changed her books, Robert. Does that ring a fucking bell? How'd you do it?"

Robert shut his mouth. All joy had been sucked out of him, like in the movies, when there's a hole in the spaceship, and everything swoops away in perfect silence.

Charlie paused, hands on his hips, as if something had dawned on him. "Layla? You used Layla to pull this off?"

It didn't matter at this point; Charlie had enough information to bury Robert forever, unless Robert could convince him otherwise.

"How'd you know about Layla and me?" Robert asked.

"Everyone knows about it, now answer the question."

"All right, she made the change." Maybe, somehow, honesty would win him a few points. "I told her my bookshelf was perfect. She knew I'd been studying, and she agreed to help."

Charlie's lip trembled. "So right now, Florence Noelle, your little pet project, has a bookshelf *curated* by you. You? She has that list you showed me earlier?"

"I thought it would impress you! That's the truth. I thought that if she loved her books, it would prove my list was good. I never even interviewed two years ago. I never got the chance to prove anything because I was immediately passed over. I'm not just telling you my work is good. I can show you now. Florence can show you!"

Charlie's face darkened. "You thought you could give a reader your own DIY book list, and you assumed that she'd love it, and that I would beg you to come work for me?"

Robert hadn't pictured the begging, but the rest was accurate. Now that he thought about it, he wouldn't mind a little gratitude for his work.

"How'd you find out?"

Charlie wiped his mouth on his sleeve. "I wanted to take a second look at her bookshelf and compare it with the list you gave me. I noticed a book on there that I probably wouldn't have approved, so I dug deeper. Someone made an edit, right before the order went to the stacks. The edits were made on a different system because room teams and curators don't always overlap, but whatever, I had to look for it, and I found it. Someone changed the entire list to match yours. You know who made the changes? The login showed the edit under the name Bailey, who is currently on medical leave."

"It was Layla's idea, to cover her tracks."

"Oh, so you're throwing Layla under the bus now?"

"No, but she believed in my dream. She knew it was risky. I didn't force her to do anything. But like I told you, I know my stuff. Just wait and see."

Charlie laughed harshly, his face going red. "Wait and see! Wait and see—no, you just screwed with the very mission of this resort, Robert. Without those books, those carefully chosen, life-changing books, this place wouldn't exist. You've ruined the single most important process of this entire goddamn place!"

"Not if she loves the books!"

"She's not reading!" Charlie reached forward, about to push Robert, but stopped himself. His hand curled into a fist. He held it inches from Robert's chest. "She hasn't logged anything in the app yet. Not a single book. Not a single page."

"It's still early."

"I checked the system right before coming here." Spit flew from Charlie's mouth. "Readers love updating their progress. I know for a fact Florence tracks her reading. Why wouldn't she track it here? She's been here since this morning, and she's been doing what, exactly, if not reading? Any ideas? Any excuses? You have my *full* attention right now, Robert, so look me in the fucking eyes, and tell me what she's reading."

Robert felt like vomiting. It *did* concern him that she hadn't logged anything yet. He didn't think anything could get worse than Charlie finding out he had changed the books, but if Florence hated her options, Robert couldn't live with it. He would lose her and his dream job at the same time.

Charlie backed away. "I *was* impressed by what you said earlier. Even though you did ambush my daily walk and flaunt cigarettes in front of me,

I respected the hustle. It took balls to pitch to me like that. That's why I took another look at your list because I saw potential."

Robert waited for the rest. The part that would destroy him.

"But changing those books and giving a reader an unapproved list is crossing the line. A bad list comes back on me. I have to deal with that shit. My entire team has to deal with it. You're a self-righteous prick, not some prodigy." Charlie spat the last word, as if natural talent disgusted him. He opened the door. "You'll be hearing from Dean. He and I go way back, you know."

"Are you firing me?"

Charlie shrugged. "I can't fire you. I guess I'll leave it up to Dean." He walked out and left the door open.

Robert closed it, slowly sliding the lock in place. He expected rage to take over, but he felt exhausted. He sank to the floor, his back against the door, and stared at the clothes on the ground. Layla never picked up her stuff. What was *wrong* with her?

The sheer work that went into swapping the book list had all been for nothing. He'd begun this plan eight months ago, when he started talking to Layla anytime they crossed paths.

Most of the guys in the kitchen made fun of her because she wore baggy cargo pants full of room keys. They called her The Jailer since you could hear her coming from a mile away.

But Robert looked past those details, and he could tell she was interested in him. When he made her a killer omelet for breakfast one day, on the house, he turned on his best charm. And she fell for it. And later that night, she found him in the kitchen after hours, turned the lights off, and offered him a good time. It was not a good time, and the keys in her cargo pants jangled like chains, like old Jacob Marley himself coming to warn them, but for Robert, it was exactly what he needed. As the room supervisor, Layla had access to the system. She knew how to quietly edit a reader's bookshelf.

She could find out what readers were coming to the resort months in advance. Robert told her about his plans to get on the curating team and how she could help him achieve these lofty goals. She agreed to help. She believed he'd buy a house and maybe even marry her when he had the money from his new position. All those late nights seemed worth it.

Did Florence hate her books? Even considering it put dreadful knots in his stomach. No, he couldn't focus on that. Just because she ignored the resort app did not mean she wasn't reading. She'd update it later when she had time.

Florence is reading. She loves her books, he told himself.

Seeing her curled up in the egg swing touched a part of him he didn't know existed. When she looked at him with those deep green eyes, something clicked.

Did she feel it too?

If Dean fired him... that would be the end of it; he'd never know what Florence thought of the books he chose for her. He'd never see her around the resort, a book partially hiding her face, her legs neatly tucked under her. No, he couldn't lose her; he wouldn't let it happen.

And he wasn't about to let Charlie win.

He'd lost the potential curator position, a disappointment that stung, yes, but he would pivot and recover. At this point, losing the promotion paled in comparison to Florence hating her books.

Now, in a cruel twist of fate, he had to *fight* to keep his nutcracking job. Robert smiled a little. He felt like the hero in all the stories, defying the odds.

He just had to convince Dean to keep him on, and how hard could that be? Dean was only the most unreasonable man on Earth.

Chapter 21

After Angel showed Logan how to clock out, they walked to the far end of the stacks, to the last aisle: Narnia.

"No one comes over here," Angel said. "There's nothing on this side of the room except some books and our little secret." He pointed down the aisle. "Ta-da. Check it out!"

The aisle was full of books on both ends, but in the center, a large section of books and shelving had been moved, making a small cave-like opening carved into the wall of spines. A makeshift camp was set up inside, and beside the aisle: a small card table, a few folding chairs, two hammocks strung up between shelving racks, and a stockpile of books, playing cards, comics, and snacks. Across from the shelves, against the wall, was a lone booth and table—a relic from an old diner. Stringed yellow lights crisscrossed overhead.

"This is your break area?"

"*Private* break area. You're welcome to use it. Take a nap, read, watch TV, we don't care. As you can see, it's all the way over here, so no one knows about it. Except the cleaner, but he's chill, so we don't worry about him."

Logan took a closer look at a pile of books beneath the hammocks. "Are those textbooks?"

"Yeah, Mia just started nursing school, mostly pre-recs at this point. Still got a while before clinicals, but that's what this spot is great for. If things are slow, I'll run orders or re-shelve while she studies. It's how we look out for each other."

Logan admired that. "And what about you? What do you do in your free time?"

"What do you think, man?" Angel gestured to the stacks. "I *read*."

"Why does that not surprise me?"

" 'Cause I'm obviously very intelligent." Angel tapped his forehead. "That comes from all the books up here."

Logan chuckled, shaking his head. "Thanks for showing me around today."

"No problem, man. You coming back tomorrow? You better. You totally fit in here. We're both psyched to finally get someone cool for once! You wouldn't believe the number of wet blankets they've tried to send us."

"Yeah, I'll be here tomorrow," Logan said, and almost added: *You see, I made a bet with my big brother. I have to work here. I don't have much of a choice.*

Angel rubbed his hands together. "I hope you like this job. Really. We're gonna make a great team. You need anything, come find me. I got a room here and everything."

Logan thanked Angel again, and they parted ways.

Leaving the stacks felt like waking up after a vivid dream. Logan stared at the elevators, the dull hallways, the fluorescent lights, and reality crashed down on him.

He had no food, no money, no phone, and no car.

He should've called the police's non-emergency line on Angel's phone and waited outside for someone to unlock his car, but something in him didn't care. He wanted to stay here.

Home didn't exist for him.

When he moved back from Amsterdam six months ago, following his explosive breakup with Nina, his options were: move in with his brother, his brother's wife, and their four young children, or stay at Mimi and Papi's house. Considering his brother and family were homesteaders, and Logan wasn't confident in his babysitting skills, he went with the safer option. But after six months with his grandparents, Logan still didn't have his feet under him. For his first job back in the states, he delivered pizza five nights a week. He made decent money but quit after four months because the miles were hell on his car, and he couldn't afford to keep fixing it. He started a job at a clothing store and quit after a month, when the manager kept calling him every day to see if he could pick up extra shifts.

This place is burnin' down, Logan! Get your ass in here!

For a store that sold expensive clothes to preppy white chicks, it was busier than a Starbucks happy hour sale.

No, thanks, Mr. Manager, I quit.

Logan entered the elevator, remembering something he'd read in the initial paperwork (he had, naturally, paid close attention to the Employee Perks section). Something about employees using their badges to buy food in the café, and the cost subtracted from their paycheck. A dangerous system for someone like Logan.

So, he tried it out. The resort had one large cafeteria on the main floor, with a smaller kitchen on the second. The second floor had a twenty-four-hour taco bar, which was the coolest thing Logan had seen in a long time.

He gave the worker his badge, she swiped it, and the taco bar was his to pillage. This place was growing on him. He ate in perfect silence, occasionally patting his pocket for the phone that wasn't there, and thought, *If my phone had a tiny hand, I would hold it right now.*

All this quiet mind-wandering led him back to the phone number on his arm—a mocking reminder that failure was a simple phone call away.

His brother's bet was relatively easy in theory. It had two rules, both doable at first glance, which gave Logan a false sense of accomplishment and led him to accept the terms without much critical thought. The bet would last for one year from today. If he followed the two rules until next October, he'd win. But the year stretched out before him like an impossibly long, winding road.

Rule Number One: Work the same job for twelve months. Big Brother thought Logan had commitment issues, and Logan reluctantly agreed with that diagnosis. Yes, he needed to find something and stick to it. Yes, a whole year wasn't *that* long. No, he didn't want to work at The Reader's Resort forever, but he could manage one year, like it or not.

Because if he didn't hold up his end and walked out before next October, he'd be required (per the terms) to call the number on his arm and ask for a job. His brother ran his own small cybersecurity firm (nerd). And he could get Logan a job at a nice desk, making fine money. A real desk! A real office! Just call the number now!

Glaring at the number on his arm, Logan silently vowed he'd never call it. Working for his brother, in his brother's office, was easily a Top Ten Nightmare. Plus, he wasn't a child anymore; his brother didn't have to keep bailing him out. Logan would prove that in twelve months, when he could efficiently park a golf cart and shelve a book in alphabetical order. Stranger things have happened, big bro.

What about Rule Number Two, Logan? Can you handle that one?

Logan finished his food and headed toward the lobby.

The strangest part of this place was the *silence*. Since most of the guests were reading (shocker), readers were everywhere, quietly turning pages, taking photos of themselves, or looking around with shifty eyes. It unnerved him.

He kept seeing signs and maps placed around the resort promoting nightly parties in a ballroom on the main floor. The party was about to start, and readers were migrating downstairs.

Okay, he *needed* to get back to his grandparents' place. He couldn't avoid reality forever. He could borrow a phone from the front counter, call the police, get his car unlocked, and go back to the drudgery of living with his grandparents.

Brilliant plan. Winning this stupid bet one day at a time.

Logan found the lobby. Music echoed through the hallways, enticing nearby readers to meander toward the ballroom. The lobby had mostly emptied aside from a few stragglers and a lone woman standing on the elaborate balcony.

She wore muddy sneakers, jeans, and a black rain jacket. She shifted her phone from one hand to another, clearly debating something, and she kept looking at the stained-glass window of the woman reading beside the river.

Rule Number Two, that cynical voice in his head sneered. *No relationships.*

Logan's breakup with Nina had rocked his foundation. He thought, after a few years of travel (backpacking and couch-surfing and eventually, Amsterdam), he'd be formidable and experienced. Maybe even wise. He'd naively thought nothing could hurt him, and he was very, very wrong. The first time Nina cheated on him, he forgave her, honest to God, because he loved her in a way that felt eternal, irreversible. The second time she cheated, Logan fell to pieces. He came back to America the same way a shipwreck washes up on shore.

No relationships were part of the bet, because (according to dear Brother), you can't get your shit together if you don't know where your shit ends and her shit begins (a real quote—said over whiskey and fire, after the kids and wife were asleep).

However, Logan knew this woman from somewhere. It took a second to register in his brain. He drifted into the lobby with his hands in his pockets. "Hey! Where's my book at?"

Startled, the woman leaned over the balcony railing, blonde hair falling in her face. "Logan, right?"

He looked up at her, hands on his hips. "Need someone to take a picture of you?"

She stared at him, confused, and then remembered where she stood. "Oh, no. Thanks."

"You sure?"

"Um, yeah." She gave him a weird look. "Could you actually do me a favor?"

Logan smiled. "Depends... I'm an extremely busy man."

"I'm trying to get a picture of the glass window up there." She pointed at the wall behind her. "You're taller than me, and this angle keeps catching the light."

Logan jogged up the stairs, happily ignoring the dumb little voice in his head.

The stained-glass window rippled, sending purple waves of light cascading down the walls, over his skin and clothes, and over the woman as she gathered her things.

She was using the balcony to study. She had an open laptop on the floor, a pen and notebook pushed to the side, and the book about hauntings that Logan had lent her earlier.

Was she studying for school or something? And was the balcony floor really more comfortable than... anywhere else?

An empty glass was on the floor, against the mahogany railing, chunks of ice melting on the bottom.

"Sorry, this was a bad idea." She laughed dryly, closing her laptop and stuffing it inside a black backpack. She slung her purse over her shoulder.

Logan looked for something to stand on. Yeah, he was taller than her, but not enough to get the perfect angle. "I've got an idea." He walked to the railing, stepped one foot on.

"Hey, what are you doing?"

"Getting this shot." He now had both feet on the railing and slowly stood up, holding his arms out.

Baffled, she stared at him.

"Give me your phone before I fall off."

"Get down!"

"Give me your phone!"

She shook her head. "I'm worried you'll drop it."

"Ouch, I see how it is. Now's your chance, you want the shot or what?"

She handed over her phone.

Logan wavered on the railing, afraid that if he looked down, he'd plummet. What a spectacle that would be, and all for the sake of impressing a beautiful stranger.

"Be careful."

Logan nodded. "Can I use your shoulder?"

"Which one?"

"Is there a difference?"

She inched closer. "How's this?"

He placed his fingertips on her right shoulder, noticing a raven necklace against her collarbone, and held the phone above his head, nearly aligned with the stained-glass woman. He snapped a few photos, adjusting the angle each time, then jumped onto the balcony.

She took her phone back, flipping through the images. "Thank you."

Logan stared at the window and the purple ocean of light drifting through it. "You're welcome. I'm really passionate about getting the shot."

"I can see that."

This was the part where Logan would say *have a good night* and walk down the stairs and return to a life he didn't like but was forced to live. The phone number on his arm started to itch, but he didn't want to leave yet.

"What's your name?"

She hesitated. "Florence."

Just Florence, and nothing else. She didn't want to talk or get to know him, and he couldn't blame her. She was clearly in the middle of something.

Everything in him wanted to keep going. He wanted to know more about the girl in the black rain jacket, blinking at him with green eyes washed in purple light.

But she didn't want him to stay, and he had the bet to think about. Why torture himself and talk to this woman when he could barely manage his own emotional baggage? Great, he sounded like his brother now.

He backed away, turning. "Well, it was nice to meet you, Florence. I'll let you get back to it."

"You going to the ballroom?"

"I doubt employees are allowed." He flashed his badge. "You?"

"Not really my thing."

"Is that why you're hanging out up here?"

She looked at the lobby, her face blank. "Sort of."

Cryptic, okay, and intriguing. Just walk away, Logan. Just walk away.

Logan stepped around her backpack and papers, glancing at her notebook. He wasn't trying to snoop. He'd expected a page of boring notes. Instead, the lined paper was split into two sections, labeled Left and Right, with numbers cascading down each column.

Logan had to hurry. She was beautiful, mysterious, and writing secret codes in her notebook. Alarm bells sounded in his head. Evacuate! RUN!

He walked down the stairs, turning one last time. "See ya around, Florence."

"You too, Logan."

Why did she have to say his name? And why did she look so conflicted? Did she want him to stay? Or was she happy to be alone again? He couldn't tell, and he wasn't going to find out. Despite his heart twisting with regret, he kept walking. He had to keep his life in order. Work the job, no relationships. Those were the rules he agreed to. He knew this was the right decision, even though his gut told him he was making a mistake.

You'll regret this, that small, cynical voice said. Two-timing bastard.

Logan hit the bottom step when movement caught his eye. Both glass elevators were empty and *moving*. The left one rumbled up to the fourth floor while the right one stopped on the second. Both elevators opened their doors; no one entered.

Logan spun around.

Florence was watching the elevators, biting her lip.

It felt crazy to even think it, but in his mind, Logan saw the two columns in her notebook, Left and Right. "Sorry, I feel insane for even asking this, but are you... tracking the elevators?"

Her eyes flew open.

" 'Cause they move on their own, right?" He pointed toward them. "I noticed it earlier."

"It's probably nothing."

"No, I mean, it's weird. Elevators shouldn't do that. It's like they're possessed."

She stared at him. "Do you really think that?"

Now this was a fine line to walk. Either she wanted him to say yes because she believed in ghosts, or she wanted him to say no, because she wouldn't want to associate with *those* kinds of people.

Logan went with the truth. "I've never seen a haunted elevator before, or a ghost, but that doesn't mean they aren't real."

Florence nodded as if this confirmed something. She kept staring at him, which normally would've weirded him out by now, but he knew there was more to this story. More to her. And while moments ago she'd been guarded and reserved, now she looked almost sad and defeated.

"Why are you *tracking* them?" Logan took one step up, one step closer to her. "Do you think something's going on?"

A slight nod. It was nearly impossible to decipher her emotions. If he had to guess, she was calculating whether talking to him was a good idea or not.

"I'm looking for patterns," she said carefully. The elevators shifted again, moving in unison, dancing to a song no one could hear.

He took another step up. "Is there a pattern?"

"If I said yes, would you believe me?"

"I'd give you a chance to prove it." One more step. "I just… I don't get how you ended up doing this. But since you wanted that book earlier, are you like a ghost hunter or something?"

Florence sighed, leaning against the railing. The dull yellow elevator lights reflected in her eyes—two golden orbs, changing positions. "So you believe in ghosts?"

"Like I said, I've never seen one, but yeah."

She inhaled slowly, filling her cheeks with air, like a chipmunk, before exhaling. She looked pale, almost sick. "I think I saw a ghost today." The words escaped in a whispered confession, like she was terrified to say it out loud. "It's all I can think about."

"Can I see those numbers?" He rushed up the stairs.

"There's no system. They've been moving randomly all night," Florence said, handing him the notebook and watching the elevators with crossed arms. "I thought a pattern would make sense. Like they rotated spots or something, based on where they were last used. A programming thing. But there's no consistency, they just *move*, incoherently, all the time."

Logan leaned against the railing. "This ghost you saw earlier, where'd you see it?"

"My room."

"You told anyone yet?"

She shook her head. "And tell them what? That ghosts are real?"

"You told me. Your friends won't believe you?"

"I don't have cool enough friends for that."

"Your family cool enough?"

"Nope, same story. Most people don't buy into that stuff."

Logan understood that, he wasn't even sure he believed it. "Fair enough. Well, I got nowhere to be, wanna tell me what happened?"

"Why do you care?"

Good question, Logan. Why DO you care?

"I'm not messing with you," he said, holding her notebook out. "I believe you, and I'm a little jealous."

"*Jealous?*"

"I've always wanted to see a ghost."

She gave him a look.

"I promise I'm not making fun of you. I've always believed in ghosts. I have my reasons."

That seemed to satisfy her. "How much do you know about this resort?"

"I'll tell you what I've told everyone else today: I know basically nothing."

"I'll have to start at the beginning."

"Before you do, can I get you a drink?"

Florence smiled a little. "Yes, but I'll get it."

"Hey, I was offering. I'll buy."

She fished a card from her pocket. A guest ID. "Unlimited drinks. What do you want?"

"Beer, anything."

She jogged down the stairs and disappeared into a long hallway. If she hadn't left her notebook behind, Logan would've thought she wasn't coming back.

She returned a few minutes later with two drinks: a rum and Coke and a frothy pale ale.

Logan cradled his beer with both hands, wondering how his day managed to turn out like this. "Drink package, huh? Not bad."

Florence took a long sip and sat down on the balcony. Logan sat opposite her. When she set her purse to the side, Logan knew they weren't going anywhere anytime soon, and he tried to be cool about it.

"How much do you want to know?"

Logan didn't want this to ever end. "Tell me everything."

Chapter 22

"So, what do you think?" Florence said. She finished her second rum and Coke, which was more than she'd normally drink, but alcohol made her less awkward, and since she'd struck up an unlikely alliance with this random guy, she intended to put her extroverted self to work.

She sat on the balcony with her back to the bookcase. Logan sat against the railing, legs and arms crossed, thinking deeply while the owl tattooed on his arm stared at her. The purple light from the stained-glass window shimmered between them.

Florence set her empty glass beside her notebook, which she'd flipped through to better explain the facts and theories surrounding the Alyssa Larkin case. She'd rambled through the whole thing, and to her surprise, Logan didn't interrupt. She left out the summoning part because that would be tough to explain. In this version of her story, Alyssa just showed up in her room. Finding Chloe was personal, not something Florence would share with a stranger. She also kept the secret passageway to herself. She didn't want Logan telling someone else about this.

Logan was taking forever to respond, and the more she thought about it, the more she regretted saying anything at all. Logan had probably been looking for a chill conversation, not an amateur sleuthfest. His silence bothered her. What was he thinking about? Why did he never once glance at a clock or his phone? Didn't he have somewhere to be?

Florence hadn't dated since high school. She didn't have guy friends. Despite always chatting with customers at the coffee shop, this conversation, this proximity to someone unknown, made her feel a bit reckless. She couldn't afford distractions, and Logan was definitely a distraction.

He finally cleared his throat and drained his beer. "You did all this research *today*?"

"Yes."

"But why? I get that you saw Alyssa, and that's a huge deal, obviously, but you could've moved on, or gone home, or something. I mean, why look into it?"

The question caught her off guard. She knew, deep down, Alyssa was an opening, a potential way for her to find Chloe, but that was none of Logan's business.

"I just want to know what happened. I thought the research might spark some ideas, but I really have nothing. Seeing Alyssa's ghost might prove to me she's dead and not missing, but I can't prove that to the world."

"I'm just impressed you put this together in one afternoon."

"If you're wondering whether I normally get involved in stuff like this, the answer is no. But I've also never seen a ghost before today, so there's that."

He mulled over this for an eternity. "What's the stained-glass window got to do with it?"

She thought of the way he balanced on the railing, his fingertips lightly pressed against her shoulder, and the memory made her smile.

"Look at this picture." She flipped through the book on Ohio's haunted sites and found the resort's old rooftop photo. Apparently, this was the last picture ever taken of Alyssa Larkin. Florence tapped on Lori Walter, slid her finger over to John Walter, and then to Alyssa. "You tell me."

Logan studied the woman in the stained-glass window. "Oh no. She kinda looks like Alyssa."

"Right?"

Logan frowned. "Wonder what Lori thought of that. Yikes."

"*Right!*"

"Okay, okay. Say there is a connection." Logan uncrossed his legs and stretched them out, his shoe tapping against hers. She didn't adjust her foot. The small touch sent warm ripples through her, and she realized how long it had been since another human brushed against her like that. Far too long. "Say Alyssa's death *is* related to John Walter's suicide," he said. "People can't prove there's a connection, but there has to be one. Murder-suicide? An affair? Something! Even the fact that no one can pinpoint when Alyssa vanished is really weird. If you're here for four more days, why not investigate it? Like for real?"

Florence laughed, her vision tilting. "Yes, I'm obviously way too obsessed with this, but Alyssa might not show up again. This case has been combed over for decades, by people way smarter than me. Why would I be any different?"

He clicked his tongue. "Because you *saw* her. That's really something. You might be the only person alive who's seen her. It just seems like if someone was going to take a crack at an old case like this, they wouldn't have a better position than what you have now. You have the time, and you're in the neighborhood. That's more than anyone else is going to get. Look how far you got today!"

He was serious; he really meant it. Although Florence wanted to help Alyssa, she had to be realistic about how far she could take this. She couldn't start a resort-wide investigation on a whim. However, he reminded her of something.

"You know, I haven't even mentioned the woman who lives above me," she said. "I heard yelling, like she might be in trouble or hurt, so I went up one floor and found her room, and it's unmarked."

"Okay?"

"It's a known fact—Lori Walter lives on the fourth floor. She never comes out of her room, people don't see her, and she doesn't make public appearances or do interviews."

Logan's mouth dropped. "And she's right above you? See, this is what I'm talking about!"

"She *might* be right above me. Some people claim she walks around late at night and wanders through the hallways like a zombie, and if you cross her path, she'll start saying weird things to you, like you're a character in a dream she's having."

Logan sat up straighter. "All right, that's actually terrifying, but don't you see it, though? This is the perfect opportunity!"

She rolled her eyes, scooting toward him. "Come on, where would I start? How would I even go about trying to solve it? I'm not... that's not me. I'm not wired like that."

He shrugged. "Look at this research. It seems like you are."

"Are you serious? You just met me."

That stopped him cold, and Florence immediately wished she could reverse time. Her gut told her she'd made a mistake, and Logan's face proved it. Why did she have to ruin a good thing?

"I guess I'm not the best sounding board for this. We *did* just meet." He tried to make it friendly, but silence enveloped them.

Florence didn't know what to say. She wished she had another drink. She wished she could take it back, because it didn't feel like they were meeting for the first time.

Logan's demeanor changed. He suddenly looked tired and indifferent, as if realizing he'd wasted his evening listening to her. But what did he expect? With a little nudge, she'd race through the resort, playing detective? Maybe he was just trying to encourage her, but investigating a cold case was ridiculous, especially when all the evidence so far came from a ghost.

Logan, sensing the rift between them, stood up and offered a hand. Florence took it, annoyed that he had nothing else to say. She quickly realized the drinks had been more effective than she thought. She wavered on her feet, trying to act normal. Whatever *that* looked like.

He handed her the notebook, and she stuffed it inside her backpack.

"So, this place is basically *The Shining*?" He smiled, clearly trying to make up for the awkwardness.

"The book or the movie?"

"Is there a difference?"

"I can't believe you, do you even read?"

He pointed at the color-coded bookshelf in the wall. "I mean, I read in high school. Sort of."

Florence shook her head. "I'll pretend I didn't hear that." She slung her purse and backpack over her shoulders. "You know what sucks about being a reader?"

"You don't want me to answer that."

She thought of something Chloe used to say. "The best thing about being a reader is you'll never run out of books. The worst thing about being a reader is you'll never be able to read them all."

"That actually makes sense."

"Don't sound too surprised."

"No, I mean, you're right, everyone's kinda stuck in the middle of their lives, and we either wish time would speed up or slow down, and so we're never content."

Florence saw the dark cloud hovering over him. Unlike many people, he did little to hide it. Or maybe the alcohol had softened his defenses. He'd been hurt recently and was treading water, talking to a stranger about ghosts instead of going home. And no matter how beautifully impulsive it sounded to abandon her mission and find comfort in this sad stranger, she didn't come here for him. She couldn't be the one holding an umbrella over his head. Not while she battled her own demons.

Logan put his hands in his pockets. "Can I walk you to your room?"

"You act like you're never going home," she said, relying on the railing to get down the stairs in one piece.

He smiled and followed her down. "To be fair, I locked my keys in my car. Along with my phone."

Logan seemed smart enough to know the police would probably come out and unlock his car for him. But considering the time he spent listening to her, no one was waiting up for him.

"What will you do about that?"

"I think I made a friend earlier." He pushed the elevator UP button. "Maybe he'll let me crash on his couch."

The elevator doors opened, and they both stared at it before slowly making eye contact.

"Do we trust it?" he asked, a boyish innocence in his eyes, reflecting that purple carnival light.

Florence made a split-second decision. "I'll risk it, and I think I can take it from here, thank you, though, for offering to walk me back. It was nice meeting you, Logan. Good luck with your new job."

Logan smiled sadly. "Thanks."

Florence hugged her purse to her chest. "I'll see you around."

"Goodbye."

The elevator doors closed. Florence thought she'd feel relief, but the way he said *Goodbye* made her feel lonely. She pressed the button for the third floor.

As the elevator lifted, Florence looked through the glass walls. Logan crossed the lobby, hands still in his pockets. He walked up the balcony stairs, sank to one knee, and collected the empty glasses she'd rudely forgotten about. He didn't look at her. He could've easily seen what floor she stopped at, and the right-or-left direction of her room. Was he being a gentleman, or was this his way of letting her go?

Florence followed the hallway, the maroon carpet swaying beneath her like a sea of blood. She unlocked her room with the skeleton key and stepped inside. The chandelier flickered when she turned it on.

She dropped her backpack and purse on the bed, trying to decipher the feelings roiling inside her. She hadn't expected Logan to encourage *this*. Like he trusted her. Instantly. Without even knowing her true reason for coming to the resort. She'd anticipated a rational discussion or disbelief. She didn't know what to do with someone who believed in her.

It scared her a little.

She only told him about Alyssa because she'd carried this secret all day and sharing it with someone who believed her felt like a weight being lifted. It felt like magic.

She was getting tired and dizzy from the alcohol, but before she passed out, she'd try one last thing. It was safe to assume the secret passageway between this room and the room upstairs was both important to Alyssa personally and potentially critical to the investigation of her death. Since it was also safe to assume no one had professionally combed the passageway for evidence, Florence had a chance of finding something important.

Logan would be insufferably smug if he saw this.

Reaching beneath her bed, Florence activated the secret passageway.

One quick look wouldn't hurt, right?

Chapter 23

It started raining again as Robert walked to his car. Out in the fresh air, his mind felt clearer. There were no dark eyes watching him, no noises, no whispers. The basement had done something to his head, making him see and hear things. But now the creature felt like a hellish nightmare and nothing more.

He called his sister, Margo, and asked her to bring Nathan to the resort. He could tell she wasn't happy about it. As Nathan's primary babysitter, Margo didn't trust the resort or Layla. She said it was no place for a baby, but Robert insisted. He promised only one night, maybe two, while he sorted out this mess with Charlie and Dean.

Margo knew Robert's worst secrets. She found his porn collection on the family computer when he was thirteen. She helped him move on from his abusive high school girlfriend. She was the first to know about Nathan, and she helped Robert fight for custody. She knew about his ex-wife's drug habits and did everything in her power to keep Robert clean.

But Margo could never know about Florence, so Robert hid his true reason for staying at the resort instead of going back to his shitty single-dad apartment: he hated the thought of leaving Florence by herself. Even though she had no idea Robert existed, when she eventually realized his level of commitment to her, she would see he'd been her guardian angel all along.

Robert opened his trunk and removed a pack 'n play for Nathan. He waited in the cold, dark rain, happy to be outside, even in this dreary weather. A light fog clung to the resort, dimming the lanterns on every balcony. Some readers had left their curtains open and could be seen pacing inside their rooms. He could've picked any one of them to profile, and then maybe this wouldn't have happened. He'd be home already, celebrating his job promotion, if he had done one thing differently.

Margo pulled into the lot and parked beside Robert's car. Nathan was fast asleep, but his car seat detached from the base, so Robert gingerly placed a thin blanket over him, gave Margo a goodbye hug, and carried the car seat, pack 'n play, and diaper bag through the parking lot.

He used his badge at the employee entrance, hoping to avoid everyone. He'd never brought Nathan to the resort, and if someone saw Robert with his kid, they would suspect something. Robert didn't officially live at the resort, and his shared room with Layla wasn't as secret as he thought. If Charlie knew, probably many others did, too.

Luckily, the side entrance was next to the stairwell, which he quickly followed down to the lower level. The hallways were clear. Within seconds, he unlocked Layla's apartment. When he flipped on the light, Layla sat up in bed and covered her eyes.

"Sorry." Robert turned the light off. He used his phone's flashlight and navigated the minefield of garbage on the floor.

"Robert, what are you doing?"

"What's it look like?"

"Is that your *kid*?" Layla threw off the covers and climbed out of bed, wearing a T-shirt and ugly zebra-print underwear. "What's he doing here?"

"We need to stay here for a night, maybe more."

"*We* can't keep a *baby* in here."

"Maybe we could if you ever cleaned up." He set the car seat down and scooped an armful of clothes, dumping them in a pile beside the dresser. Layla silently helped.

After forming a walkway through the apartment, Layla sat on the bed, staring at Nathan as if he were a mythical creature. Robert set up the pack 'n play and transferred Nathan into it. He put the baby monitor on the dresser, pointed the camera down at the little man, and checked the app on his phone. The video looked good. For the final touch, Robert plugged in the well-used, beloved sound machine. He turned on Ocean Waves and let it play.

Layla crossed her arms, lips tightly pinched.

She'll get over it, Robert thought.

"Are you coming to bed?" she asked.

"Maybe soon."

"What if he wakes up?"

"Give him his pacifier."

She sighed and rolled over, pulling the covers up to her chin. Robert crept out of the room and quietly locked the door behind him. He rechecked the monitor on his phone. The image focused on the pack 'n play, on Nathan's little chest rising and falling. If Robert angled the camera up, Layla's back came into view, her shoulders moving with deep breaths.

She'd come around. She wasn't the most flexible person in the world, and although her habits were maddening (to put it lightly), he needed her help a little longer.

The resort was asleep. A few guests would be at the twenty-four-hour bar on the main floor. Maybe a few were in the reading rooms, but otherwise, the place was quiet. The ballroom party had dissipated, sending readers off on a drunken trek back to their rooms, their books, or their late-night mistakes with strangers.

Robert took the stairs to the second floor. Unlike his pitch earlier that day, he didn't have time to rehearse this apology. He wasn't sorry about what he did; he was sorry Charlie had caught him. Big difference. He'd have to pretend to be sorry to keep his job.

Charlie, though intelligent, had his soft spots.

Robert followed the hallway down the left side, near the end of the building. Like Lori, Charlie had a unique suite. The Walter family built rooms for themselves, and everyone knew where they lived. Robert had never seen the inside of Charlie's personal world. It was odd to think of him as an individual with his own tastes and preferences. Charlie had always felt like an extension of the resort. It made him dependable, predictable, and easy to find. A healthier man would've moved to the city and commuted to work. But then, with Lori for a mother and this resort for a home, Charlie was exactly who you'd expect him to be.

Robert stopped at the end of the hall, knocked, waited, and forced his shaky hands inside his pockets. He held the nutcracker, running his thumb over the hungry, metal teeth.

The door cracked open, and Charlie stood in the gap, wearing a red and gold kimono. He was barefoot and halfway through painting his toenails a hideous baby blue color. The room radiated enough nail polish to make Robert's eyes water.

"Great to see you again so soon, Robert," Charlie said, sounding more tired than angry. "What do you want?"

"I can't lose my job."

Charlie laughed. "You should have thought of that a long time ago. Are you serious? You try and cheat your way through a promotion, and *now* you're crying about the consequences."

"Please, Charlie. I have a kid."

"So do I. That doesn't make you a hero."

"I'll lose him to my ex. I've been here ten years. I won't make enough money if I go somewhere else!"

Charlie opened the door wider. "Considering the things I've seen from you today, I'm not sure that giving your ex custody is such a bad idea. This is the second time you've ambushed me, and I'm sick of it. You lied, Robert. What do you want me to do?"

"Give me a second chance."

"So you can keep the kid?"

"Yeah, so I can keep the *kid*."

Robert would probably not lose Nathan, job or no job, but Charlie didn't need to know that. Robert couldn't use the real reason for staying, and the keep-the-kid bit seemed effective.

Charlie blinked, his jaw tightening. It was working. If Charlie had a child, maybe he would understand. Maybe they had more in common than either of them realized.

Robert shivered and looked down; he felt the creature staring up at him through the floors.

You're not real, Robert thought, *you never were.*

"Are you okay?" Charlie gave Robert a look-over.

"I just need your word," Robert said. "You won't say anything to Dean, and I'll never talk to you again. I'll never ask you about curating. I'll give it up for good."

Charlie nodded. "Okay, fine, before you shit yourself. Just leave me alone. And hey, buddy? If you want to switch careers, don't take shortcuts, and please find something you're actually good at." He slammed the door in Robert's face.

Robert sighed with relief. It worked! And with minimal begging! Now he could stay at the resort until the end of the weekend, when Florence went home.

The door opened, and Charlie smirked. "To be fair, I already told Dean earlier this evening. I'm sorry I jumped the gun. I was pissed. Anyways, when he calls you in the morning, just know everything I said about you was before this conversation. I didn't know about your kid. I'm not a complete asshole."

No, no, no, please no, Robert thought. "Can you tell him you changed your mind?"

"I didn't tell him what to do with you," Charlie said, neatly sidestepping responsibility. "That's up to him. It's his purview."

The door shut again, with a deadbolt this time. Robert stared at the carpet, thinking. Was he really going to beg all over again? Apparently, yes.

Robert took the stairwell down a level. Dean lived in the management apartments on the main floor. He took the hallway to Dean's apartment, his shoes leaving black trails on the carpet.

He knocked on Dean's door and waited. It was getting late. Dean could be sleeping.

But the door swung open. Dean wore gym shorts and a tank top, hardly concealing his pale, veiny flesh. "Damn, Robert. You look like you're having one hell of a night."

"Did Charlie talk to you?"

Dean nodded, biting his lip to keep from grinning. "There's not much I can do. You did this to yourself. You shouldn't have changed that reader's list."

"Please, my son—"

"I don't want to hear it," Dean said, glancing in the hallway. "*You* did this. Now you expect us to let it slide? What happens when people find out?"

"No one will find out!"

"Layla knows! She made the edits, and we'll probably suspend her, if not fire her because of it. I have a meeting with her boss tomorrow. If we don't deal with both of you, if we don't address this kind of behavior, then it becomes the norm. People like me and Charlie set the standard."

Very cute, Robert thought, because Dean had nothing in common with Charlie. Just a long history of working in the same place.

"I'm sorry, Dean."

Dean shook his head with disgust. "You're way past an apology. Pack your things, you're fired."

"Dean."

"You're done. Goodnight." He tried closing the door, but Robert wedged his shoe in the gap.

"Get out."

Robert pushed his way inside, his hands twitching. "You're not *listening* to me. I'm going to lose my kid if you fire me."

"That's not my problem. Get out, or I'll call the cops."

"You've just been looking for an excuse to fire me!"

"And you gave it to me." Dean bowed, his stomach jiggling. "On a silver platter. Now, since you won't leave, I'm calling the cops." He turned his back.

Robert stepped forward, not planning to fight. Not planning to do anything, just keep talking. But Dean jerked around, drawing his fist back, and hammered Robert's left eye with a single blow.

Robert's vision blinked like a dying light bulb. He stumbled against the door, slamming it shut, shock waves cascading through his body.

"Step to me again, and you'll regret it." Dean turned to grab his phone from the kitchen counter. Robert launched himself off the door, shoving Dean with both hands. Dean tripped on his own feet and fell, smacking his head against the countertop. He groaned, sinking to the floor.

Blood dripped from the counter's edge, where his head made contact.

Robert stared at the scene, thinking maybe he could prove Dean started the fight, but he doubted it. Not with Dean's blood on his own kitchen counter.

Robert looked around, suddenly afraid someone was in the apartment with them. Dean lived alone, and by the looks of his apartment, he wasn't used to company. Robert checked the bathroom and bedroom anyway, finding the apartment empty and in need of a deep clean.

Then the front door opened on slow, squeaky hinges.

Robert crept back into the kitchen, wondering who else would visit Dean at this hour. He leaned against the cabinets and peered around the corner. The front door stood wide open, and the living room was empty.

Dean was gone.

Oh no.

Robert raced into the hallway, finding Dean crawling away on his hands and knees, blood spilling from his forehead, disappearing into the red carpet.

Shit shit shit.

Robert grabbed Dean's ankles and jerked him back. Dean fell to his stomach, slurring his words. Despite Dean's weight, Robert managed to drag his boss back inside the apartment. Robert shut the door and locked it, running through his short list of bleak options. Right now, he had to keep Dean from leaving the apartment. If they could talk and reach an understanding, then maybe calling the police would be avoided. Robert could deal with losing a job, but criminal charges? Not a chance.

He found a belt in the bedroom closet and tied it around Dean's wrists. It wasn't the best precursor to a peaceful conversation, but Robert needed assurance this wouldn't get out of control any more than it already had.

Robert slumped against the front door and checked the baby monitor on his phone. Nathan and Layla slept soundly. He turned the volume up and set the phone beside him, his eyes growing heavy.

His head felt like a volcano had exploded inside it. He felt the bruise forming on his face, his left eye pulsing like a frightened heart. Dean knew how to throw a punch. Robert's skull reverberated like a church bell. Sweat rolled down his temples. He shivered, his vision failing.

Lying his head against the smelly carpet, Robert watched the baby monitor and closed his eyes.

I can fix this, he thought. *Once Dean wakes up, I'm going to fix everything.*

Chapter 24

The hidden door swung inward, revealing the narrow wooden stairs leading into the dark passageway. Florence had been careless earlier. Not only did she make too much noise and attract the unsettling attention of her upstairs neighbor, but she didn't stop to consider the forensic evidence she could accidentally destroy.

She pulled her hood up, tucked her hair inside, and climbed over the piano.

Turning on her phone's flashlight, she tiptoed up the staircase. The corridor was exactly as she left it.

"Alyssa," Florence whispered. "Are you here?"

Silence.

Florence began checking every corner, crossbeam, and cobweb. It was impossible to do this without building a narrative inside her head. Hopefully, Alyssa would soon confirm or deny her suspicions.

The resort started as a Victorian mansion. When John and Lori Walter knew they were onto something, they used family money to fund the resort's expansion. The mansion was swallowed up, and they built the resort over it. The lobby's balcony was a confirmed piece of the original "hotel" as the old-timers called it.

Adding multiple floors and wings required extra help. No one knew where Alyssa came from, or if the Walters knew her before she joined the staff. After she started, the narratives blurred together. Every public detail about the construction phase came only from personal testimonies, and very few concrete events.

Florence wondered how they managed the isolation out here, in the middle of nowhere. What did it do to them?

In 1985, the new resort was unveiled and instantly became heaven on earth for literature enthusiasts. Famous writers visited, and world leaders applied for personalized rooms. Within two years, it had cemented itself as a world-renowned attraction, and coming into 1988, The Reader's Resort seemed impenetrable.

Most critics raved about John Walter's vision and happily ignored the heavy investments from his wife's family and the outspoken claim that he'd built the whole thing for Lori. Those who knew better were quick to dethrone John as the sole visionary for this place. They claimed that John, Lori, and Alyssa were a codependent trio, and only when all three of them were in sync did everything start to make progress.

Florence swept her flashlight across the walls, now halfway through searching the corridor. She tried to imagine life here in 1988. Everyone living and working together, acting like a family.

According to sources, Lori was the dreamer of the group. She designed all the rooms, founded the curating department, and worked day and night to bring this resort to life. John managed the financials, logistics, and labor departments. Between John and Lori, they were either too busy dreaming or too busy planning. Alyssa became the doer. She knew every employee's name, every contractor's strength and weakness. When John and Lori argued themselves into a corner, they would turn to Alyssa and ask, "Can it be done?"

Florence paused a few feet from the opposite wall and slowly scanned it with her light. If a hidden door was there, she couldn't find it, and she wasn't about to start tapping on the wood.

"So, who did you piss off?" Florence whispered to Alyssa. "John, or Lori?"

In the spring of 1988, Alyssa was let go from her position, and she shortly left the resort altogether. This was the story Lori and John later repeated to the press, although contradictory dates were given.

Florence pressed her ear against the opposite wall. Was it in her head, or could she hear breathing on the other side?

Checking the ceiling one more time, Florence noticed a rectangular object wedged in the corner where the crossbeam connected to the wall. It blended into the wood, and Florence thought it was part of the structure until she stepped back and saw it sitting four feet above her head.

A suitcase.

Florence rubbed her eyes and wished she could've been fully sober for this. Or was the alcohol making her unusually confident?

Setting her phone on the floor, the light pointing up, she tugged her rain jacket sleeves over her hands. The thin material didn't hinder her, so she grabbed the crossbeam with both hands and pulled herself up, kicking her feet until she crawled on the crossbeam and reached for the suitcase. Using her sleeve as a glove, she lifted it by the handle. She shimmied down the crossbeam and hopped gently to the floor.

Throwing a quick glance at the opposite wall, Florence hurried down the stairs, over the piano, and shut the hidden door. She put the suitcase on her bed, realized she forgot her phone in the passageway, and had to trigger the mechanism again to retrieve it.

The hidden door swung open, and because she'd left her flashlight on, the stairs and corridor were washed in white light.

Florence started to climb over the piano when she noticed a strange shadow being cast over the stairs. It was small, misshapen, and so perfectly still, Florence almost didn't think anything of it. But the piano made a sound beneath her, and the shadow grew tall and lanky before bolting away. A wooden *click* echoed through the corridor.

She slid over the piano, flew up the stairs on her hands and feet, and snatched her phone from the floor. She barely paused to look at the opposite wall, but she could've sworn a pair of eyes were watching her from a sliver of darkness. She heard laughter in her mind, the shrill cackle of the mad wife upstairs.

It took thirty minutes, maybe more, for Florence to stop shaking after she was back in her room, the hidden door closed, and the suitcase still unopened on her bed. She kept staring at the door and waiting for someone to knock. Sometimes the chandelier seemed to sway, but maybe that was her mind again. It kept playing tricks.

Her back to the wall, facing the piano, Florence sat on her bed and opened the suitcase. "I hope you were worth it," she said, some part of her wishing she hadn't broken things off with Logan and how comforting it would be to have another human in this room with her.

Inside the suitcase, she found a well-worn wristwatch that didn't tick and had a small crack in the glass. She also found a hairbrush with dark hair woven through the bristles, folded clothes, and a dead flower pressed between the pages of an old, folded newspaper, dating back to 1983. A gift, no doubt, from one lover to another.

One of the items of clothing looked familiar. Still keeping her sleeves over her hands to avoid leaving fingerprints, she pulled the item out and let it unfurl.

It's the nightgown, she thought. Not the exact same one, but a cleaner version of the nightgown Alyssa currently wore.

Which made her think: if Alyssa died in her nightgown, then it occurred at night, possibly in her bed, while she was defenseless. That was an assumption, but it made Florence further believe Alyssa had been brutally murdered, and no one had come close to catching the killer.

The rest of the clothes included a single sunflower dress, two pairs of slacks, and button-up shirts. This suitcase belonged to a couple, packing lightly, either for an overnight somewhere or...

"Or you were running away," Florence whispered to the room. "Who were you running from, Alyssa? And who was planning to go with you?"

Florence decided to give Alyssa a chance. If she reappeared and told her story, Florence would have a clearer picture of how to present this to the police. If Alyssa never showed up, Florence would turn the suitcase in to the police and wash her hands of it.

And still, none of this helped her find Chloe. She needed Alyssa to come back.

"I'll try again tomorrow," Florence said. "Can you hear me? Alyssa?"

In the morning, she'd try the summoning again and hope for the best. But for tonight, she'd had enough.

Setting the suitcase on the floor, with Alyssa's folded nightgown inside, Florence showered and changed into her pajamas. She then took the stack of vinyl records from underneath the record player and lined them up on the piano, leaning each against the bookshelf. If someone opened the hidden door, the records would topple down and hopefully wake her up.

Finally in bed, Florence rested her head on the pillow and stared at the bookshelf. "I'm trying to find you," she said, thinking back to every sleepover, every dumb joke, and every slap-happy night together. "I love you, girl. I hope you can see me trying."

She fell asleep in a sea of darkness, where the good memories floated like islands and blossomed into dreams.

Chapter 25

Something nudged Robert's foot. He opened his eyes to a dark room he did not immediately recognize.

He focused his eyes. Dean was twisting on the floor, wiggling his hands free of the belt. Before Robert could open his mouth, the belt loosened and fell from Dean's hands.

Robert tried to stand, but Dean was already on his knees, holding the belt with both hands. Dean lunged forward, pressed the belt to Robert's neck, and pinned him against the door.

Dean snarled, his face a mask of blood and fury. The belt dug into Robert's neck, cutting off his air. His chest expanded; his head pulsed with alarms.

He started to flail, but Dean sat on Robert's legs and threw his upper body weight against Robert's neck.

Everything dimmed, and Robert's throat stopped working. Why did he let Dean live? He should have bashed his brains in.

Darkness flooded his eyes. He couldn't breathe or see, but he wasn't dead yet. He could still flex his fingers. Seconds passed; his head felt like a balloon on the verge of bursting.

Robert reached inside his pocket and withdrew the nutcracker. He'd forgotten about it.

He groped for Dean's fists, peeling back the meaty pinky finger on Dean's left hand. Either Dean missed the nutcracker, or he was betting on Robert passing out first, because he didn't react. Robert lifted the nutcracker and set it around Dean's pinky.

Dean should've been more afraid. Robert had been practicing.

Robert clenched the nutcracker, hearing that satisfying *split*, like exploding walnuts.

Dean sucked in a breath, as if about to scream, but he stayed frozen. He loosened his grip, his left hand trembling, dripping hot blood. Robert's vision returned, blurry and shadow-filled, but better than nothing.

He shoved Dean with both hands, knocking him to the floor. Robert jumped onto Dean and pinned his left arm down. He bent Dean's fingers back, trying to slip the nutcracker around the pinky, and got the ring finger instead. Much thicker, but worth a shot.

Robert threw his whole weight against it, squeezing with both hands.

Crack!

Dean sharply inhaled and started to scream. Robert threw Dean's head against the floor, silencing his voice and breaking his nose. Dean bucked Robert off, and Robert dropped the bloody nutcracker. His hands closed around the discarded belt, and when Dean spun around, spit and blood flying from his lips, Robert looped the belt through the buckle and slung it around Dean's neck like a noose, a trick he'd performed on Layla many times, in a much different context.

Dean swung his fists and clipped Robert on the chin. Robert fell, but he didn't let go of the belt. The noose pulled Dean to the ground, and Robert scrambled to his knees, gripped the leather with his shaking, bloodied hands, and jerked it upward.

Dean's neck hung suspended above the floor. He clawed at the belt, scratching his own flesh with his fingernails. Robert wrapped the belt around his own wrists to keep from slipping, rolled onto Dean's back, and yanked.

The snap was so loud, Robert thought someone must've heard it. He released the belt, letting Dean's head thump on the floor.

Breathless, Robert managed to stand. He leaned against the door and checked the peephole. No one in the hallway. So far, so good. Someone probably heard something, regardless of the hour. But would they know which room the noises came from? Not unless the apartment next door woke up and called security for a wellness check.

The hallway remained empty. For five minutes, Robert waited for someone to appear, but no one did.

I killed him, he thought, his one eye glued to the peephole. *I killed him even though it was self-defense. They'd want to know why I came to his apartment, why we fought, and how he ended up with a lacerated forehead and a broken neck.*

There were texts between them—texts between Dean and Charlie about Robert. And cameras! Cameras in the hallways and lobby; footage of Robert going near Dean's apartment.

"No, no, no, no." It fully dawned on him. He wasn't getting away with it. He had just murdered his boss in a bustling resort and left a long trail of evidence behind. How much microscopic DNA did he shed in his short time in this apartment?

Robert looked around. The world suddenly crawled with loose hair, germs, and saliva. Every forensic scene from every cop show sprang to his mind. This was it, buddy. The end of the story. The part where the good guy gets caught doing a bad thing, except it wasn't actually bad. Not a soul would miss Dean. Robert did the world a favor, but the law wouldn't see things that way, no, sir. They would only see a bad man doing bad things.

His phone had been knocked over. He straightened it, looking at the baby monitor, at Nathan turning in his crib, at Layla sleeping with her mouth open.

5:45 a.m.

He needed to get back to the room because Nathan usually woke up by 6:30. Deep sleeper, early riser. Layla also woke up around then and would wonder where Robert had been all night.

Pull yourself together, Robert thought. *You can't afford to melt into the floor, dammit, you have to do something.*

Robert limped into the kitchen. After a minute of searching, he found Dean's keys hanging on the wall and his phone on the counter. He limped over to Dean's body. There was so much blood in Dean's eyes, Robert doubted it would work. He held up Dean's phone, hoping the Face ID would unlock it. It didn't take. Robert spat on Dean's face and scrubbed some blood off. He peeled Dean's eyelids back and tried again. Face ID worked, and the phone unlocked. Modern technology.

Robert changed the settings so the screen would never turn off on its own. This way, he wouldn't need to unlock the phone again. He could impersonate Dean and text people. It would buy him a little time.

With Dean's phone and keys in hand, Robert pocketed his nutcracker and left the apartment. He ran toward the stairwell, making eye contact with the camera in the corner of the lobby, praying he didn't run into anyone while looking like he'd just been mugged. And in a way, he had. Dean would still be alive if he hadn't attacked Robert like that. Robert had no choice but to fight back. His heart still thundered in his chest, and not from the fight, no, though his blood felt like a living thing beneath his skin; his heart ached from the moment of blacking out, belt to his neck, when Dean had the upper hand. Robert, on the edge of death, thought, *I'm seconds away from losing Florence. This is how it feels to lose something dear to you.*

Robert unlocked Layla's apartment, trying to calm his terrified heart. That feeling of losing her scared him more than anything. He would never let it happen again.

He would make sure of it.

Chapter 26

Florence awoke to dawn's early glow seeping through the curtains. She rubbed her eyes and saw the stack of vinyl records still propped against the hidden door. She'd dreamt all night of the shadow in the corridor, but it turned out she had nothing to fear.

For now.

The suitcase was open on the floor, with Alyssa's nightgown spread across it. Florence had left it folded before falling asleep.

She bolted upright, her arm colliding with a warm body in the bed beside her.

Florence's heart stopped. Without turning to look, she slid off the bed, banging her knees on the hard floor.

Alyssa was tucked under the blanket, watching Florence with bright, shiny eyes, as if she'd just finished a good cry. Her pink lips were pinched together, blood trailing down the corners of her mouth and into her dark hair. She looked so young.

"Wow," Florence said, adrenaline rushing through her. "Sorry, you scared me. I'm actually really glad you're here."

Alyssa smiled with her eyes, but her face twisted in pain. How long had it been since someone treated her like a human?

"It's okay, it's okay." Florence reached across the bed and held Alyssa's hand. "You need help, right? That's why you came to me?"

Alyssa shook her head, pointed at Florence's heart, then pointed at herself.

"I called you, didn't I? When you first appeared?"

A short nod.

"Were you... asleep?"

Alyssa shook her head.

"Trapped?"

Another short nod. Alyssa peeled the blanket back, grabbed the hem of her nightgown, and pulled it up to her neck.

Florence's heart clenched in her chest.

Alyssa's body was scarred from her thighs to her breasts. Someone had carved small symbols, like runes, into her skin. The runes were sporadic and uneven. They looked like the little tracks birds leave in fresh snow, but there was nothing picturesque about the scars. Someone tortured her. They cut into her skin while she struggled, resulting in a convoluted map of some ancient language.

Alyssa didn't lower her nightgown. She kept it bunched between her shaking hands, refusing to look away with shame or self-pity.

Take a good look, she seemed to be saying. *Can you begin to understand?*

Florence blinked away tears. What if the symbols trapped Alyssa in a dark place somewhere in the resort? A place she couldn't escape from. "Did I break the spell?" Florence asked.

Alyssa nodded slowly, straightening her nightgown.

Florence had a million questions, but for some reason, Alyssa wasn't talking. Everything had to be yes or no.

Florence sat on the bed, leaning against the headboard. She crossed her arms and tried to appear non-threatening and friendly, but it was hard to think straight after being asleep two seconds ago.

"Can I ask you some questions?"

Alyssa nodded.

"Was this your room?"

A nod, yes.

"You wanted me to find the hidden passageway, right?"

Another nod.

"Did you share that secret with someone? Was it John?"

Alyssa nodded again, smiling sadly.

Oh no, Florence thought, *we were all wrong*. But she still had to ask. "Did John ever hurt you?"

Alyssa shook her head sharply.

"Did you love him?"

A quick nod, nothing more. The sad smile was gone.

So John didn't kill her, Florence thought. *There goes that theory.*

"You wrote on my mirror that you wanted my help. Is that true?"

She nodded.

Florence smiled. "But how can I help? What do you want me to do?"

Alyssa sat up and scanned the room.

"Would it help if you wrote it down? We could write to each other."

Alyssa ignored her. She stepped down from the bed, her nightgown swishing around her ankles, and walked over to the mirror. Smearing her finger against her bloody lips, she wrote above her last message: *They kill me.*

They, Florence thought. *More than one killer. Now we're getting somewhere.* But Alyssa wasn't finished.

Dipping her finger in blood, she wrote: *I kill them.*

Florence scooted to the edge of the bed. *I shouldn't be surprised she wants revenge, and I can't say I blame her*, she thought, *but this is not what I expected.* "How can I help?" she asked.

Alyssa wrote on the mirror. *Tell my story.*

Florence exhaled. She was about to express her doubts, her inability to help anyone, especially with something of this magnitude. But through the sheer material of Alyssa's nightgown, Florence could make out the trails of scars on her legs and stomach.

"I'll do whatever I can," Florence said. "Is whoever hurt you still at the resort?"

Alyssa froze, then slowly nodded.

Oh God, I'm in the same building as a killer, she thought. "I know you want to hurt them back, and I don't blame you. But if you want me to tell your story, should we try to prove who did it first?"

Alyssa nodded.

"Okay, I'll do it. Just tell me where to start."

Alyssa pointed at the ceiling.

"Does Lori live up there?"

Yes.

Florence knew it. "Is she the one?"

Instead of answering, Alyssa offered a thin smile, pointed at the ceiling again, and started to turn away.

"Wait!" Florence had to try. "Are there other...ghosts here, at the resort?"

Alyssa nodded.

Hope blossomed inside Florence's chest. "A lot of ghosts?"

Alyssa nodded again.

"Are they all..." She almost said, *Like you.* "Are they all wanting something? Is that why they stay?"

Alyssa frowned. No, it couldn't be that simple, could it?

"Have you met anyone named Chloe?"

Alyssa looked confused again.

Florence blinked, not wanting to cry in front of this woman who'd suffered so much. "She's uh, seventeen, and has brown hair down to here." She gestured to her shoulders. "She loves to read. She loves books more than anything. She likes to talk about the characters and what they'd be like in real life."

Alyssa's eyes deepened, telling Florence that life wasn't going to work out the way she thought it would.

You poor thing, those eyes said. Florence stopped talking and bit her lip to keep from crying. She'd even used the present tense, as if words alone could keep Chloe alive.

She might never find Chloe, no matter how hard she tried, and that truth stuck in her heart like a bitter splinter.

"Does it hurt?" she asked Alyssa. "Does it hurt when you die?"

Not a fair question, (assuming) Chloe and Alyssa died in different ways. Chloe didn't feel pain, did she? Or did she wake up and know the end was coming? Did she reach for Florence's hand? Was she afraid of the next adventure?

Alyssa lifted a finger to her lips, nodding. *Yes, of course it hurts.*

Florence didn't want to ask anything more of Alyssa. Even pushing her to reveal the killer's name could backfire. If she forced Alyssa to do something, it could trigger a reaction neither of them wanted. This was a woman who had spent the last thirty-eight years thinking about her own murder. Surely, she carried a hint of madness. And who would blame her? Only the Count of Monte Cristo could spend that much time alone and walk away with a suave personality and a devious revenge plot.

Whatever her reasons, Alyssa would reveal more to Florence in due time. Until then, Florence had plenty to do. And it started with meeting Lori Walter. How hard could *that* be?

Apparently, Logan was right about her. She had a better shot than anyone, but she had to hurry. Alyssa didn't return to make amends; she came back to make things right in her own eyes. Whether Florence found proof of Alyssa's murder or not, there may be no stopping what Alyssa did next.

But Florence had to try. For the first time in nine years, she desperately needed to do something meaningful. Someone in this resort murdered

Alyssa Larkin and got away with it, and Alyssa's family deserved to know the truth.

Her family deserved to know the truth.

Does that sound familiar, Flo?

Florence ignored those thoughts. *I promise I'm going to find you, Chloe. If I help Alyssa, will you hear me? Can you see how hard I'm trying to reach you?*

She changed into jeans and a long-sleeved shirt, throwing on her rain jacket in case she needed to go outside. She slung her purse and backpack over her shoulders, thinking that if she was going to do this, she had to do it right.

And she knew exactly where to start.

Chapter 27

Logan sipped black coffee from a borrowed thermos and followed Angel through the maze-like guts of the resort's lower level. Luckily, he didn't have to borrow Angel's phone and call his grandparents to inform them he wouldn't be coming back last night. Mimi and Papi were okay without daily updates, as if they knew he was embarrassed about his situation and tried not to treat him like a teenager. Still, he should've called them. He hoped they didn't wait up last night or fall asleep listening for the landline. After all, they were still parents, and far better ones than his own had ever been.

Angel drained the last of his own coffee, sighing loudly. "I hope you're ready for a stellar day today, Logan."

"You know, if I didn't stay up until three playing games, I'd feel a lot better." Somehow, Angel wasn't tired. He had *bounce* in his step at eight in the morning.

Angel turned around, walking backward. "Don't tell me it wasn't worth it."

"I lost every single game."

"I got lucky in *Catan*. You didn't stand a chance against the king of sixes."

Logan sipped his coffee, grimacing. "I'm too old for this."

Angel rolled his eyes. "Man, we're in our prime. You just had a tough night, that's all. You'll bounce back tonight."

"Oh no. I don't think I can stay up that late again."

Angel laughed. "What? I thought we were gonna play *Risk*!"

"How about *Call of Duty*? Betcha I'd kick your ass."

"If that means you'll stay up and party later, then I'm down. We could invite Mia, if you don't care."

They turned a corner and approached the stacks. "She likes video games?" Logan asked.

"You should see her play *GTA*," Angel said, swiping his badge.

They entered the dimly lit stacks, and in Logan's mind, he could still hear the printer chittering and spitting out a receipt. He prayed his coffee would kick in soon.

"Thanks again for letting me crash at your place. For the record, you have an amazing couch. Easily one of the best I've ever stayed on."

"No *problema*. Who needs a whole resort when you've got my place? I'll be making you mojitos tonight. My treat."

"You make it sound like I'm staying over again."

"Open invite, my friend."

This time, Logan would inform his grandparents. They deserved to know.

"It's no big deal, seriously," Angel said, clocking in and looking around the stacks. "Let's see what we've got going on today."

They left the stacks through the side entrance and followed the hallway to the busy dock. Angel walked slower compared to everyone else and had to stop every thirty seconds to greet a dockworker.

Bay doors flew open, casting early morning sunlight and a cool breeze across the dock. On the far end, a forklift driver was unloading a box truck full of pallets.

Angel paused in front of three pallets, each filled with gray, hard plastic totes stacked above Logan's head and held together with plastic wrap.

"Yo Mike!" Angel yelled, pointing. "These good to go?"

From his office, Mike gave them a thumbs-up. "Take those for now!"

Angel grabbed a pallet jack. "There's another jack over there," he told Logan. "You get one, I'll get one."

They wheeled the pallets down the hallway and into the stacks, parking them beside the long table near the dumbwaiter.

Angel left to grab the third pallet while Logan cut through the plastic wrap with a box cutter. He hauled one gray tote off the stack, set it on the table, and opened it, revealing a cache of books inside.

Angel dropped off the third pallet and moved his golf cart next to the table. "Okay, Logan, you can empty all the totes, load the cart's bookcase up, and then shelve the books. That'll be the hustle today, since we got our new shipments in. Mia and I will be helping you while we take orders and other random BS. You got questions?"

"Don't think so."

"You need golf cart training?"

"I think I got it."

Angel grabbed a radio, clipped it to his belt, and swung the earpiece around his neck.

"There's a radio on this table. Call me if you need me."

"Aye aye, captain." Logan emptied the tote, finding cookbooks, self-help, and military history.

Mia walked through the doors, holding a coffee that looked more for show than anything else.

"Morning," she said. "Let me guess, you stayed at Angel's."

"How can you tell?"

"Your face." She laughed.

How did everyone here have so much energy?

Logan looked around. "You didn't hear it from me, but I think Angel wants to invite you over tonight. To play games."

Mia cocked her head. "And you'll stay up late again?"

"Yes. That seems inevitable now that Angel has someone to play games with."

"I'll think about it." She didn't seem like the think-about-it type. She had made her decision within seconds and would find the right time to share it. She held her fox necklace between two fingers, her nails freshly painted black.

Around the corner, Angel's voice boomed. "Mia! 'Bout time you showed up. Logan was here early, 'cause he's a professional."

Mia flipped him off, and they fell into a conversation about to-do items for the day, so Logan stopped listening. He worked on filling up the cart's bookcase with strategically sorted books.

When the golf cart was full, he slid behind the wheel and turned it on. He hadn't driven a golf cart in years, and when he pressed the pedal, it jerked forward. This baby was made to *run*. To avoid killing or maiming himself, Logan took it slow, afraid he'd tip it or crash into a ladder. He drove to the other end of the stacks and parked in the cooking section. Scanning the shelves, he found the right spot a few feet above his head. He climbed a ladder, shelved the book, and scrambled down. On to the next one.

He improved over time. Finding the right section took forever, especially in nonfiction. The aisle names helped, even though numbers would be far more practical. He had to somehow remember that cooking was in the Winterfell aisle. Well, Arya Stark could bake a pie.

Easy enough.

He shelved all the books and started over again at the sorting table. Angel brought more pallets in while Logan emptied the totes.

Anime, graphic novels, religion, mystery, western, every genre was dissected, organized, and delivered. Logan acclimated to the golf cart's speed. He drove a little faster and climbed a little quicker, pushing off the shelves and riding the ladder halfway down the aisles; that was key:

knowing precisely where the book belonged and finding the fastest way to get there.

He wished things had ended differently with Florence last night. He liked her. And he might've been too blunt about her working on the cold case. Out of everything they discussed, the mystery was the only thing she seemed to care about. She had a point: how could she solve a thirty-eight-year-old case in four days? He also couldn't shake the feeling she'd kept something from him. Some aspects of the story didn't feel genuine, though he couldn't say what. Florence went to her room, saw a ghost, and immediately pursued the case of Alyssa Larkin. She didn't even mention her books, her room, or anything else a normal guest would've talked about. If she wasn't there for the books, why come at all?

It felt like she'd been *looking* for ghosts, and when it worked, she played it off as a random accident. He wished she had been honest with him. He wouldn't have cared if she were hunting Bigfoot.

The double doors swung open, and voices filled the room—voices that didn't belong in the stacks. Their tones were serious, their sentences clipped and official. Logan's hair stood on end, and he felt the room itself change, as if the stacks had raised its hackles against the intruders.

Ridiculous, maybe, but the air shifted; Logan felt it.

Logan jumped off the ladder and peered around the corner. A man and a woman walked toward the sorting table. They had badges, clipboards, and dress shoes. Not a good sign. Logan jogged back to the golf cart and drove down the center aisle.

Angel stood by the table, waving Logan over, his face grim. Mia stood beside him, tucking receipts and stapled inventory logs under her arms, looking even more unimpressed than normal.

He parked the golf cart. The newcomers waited by the sorting table, the woman crossing and uncrossing her arms. The man smiled, wrinkling his nose. His tight, high-water pants were spotless and absent from real-life scruff. He wore a shiny watch with a puffy vest over his button-up.

"I don't think you guys have met yet," Angel said, waving to the woman. "Logan, this is Amanda, our supervisor."

Ah, so this was Crusty, the TV-watcher. "Hi, nice to meet you."

"You too," Amanda said, looking through him. Her hair was a tad too shiny, and the more Logan looked at her, the more *Crusty* came to mind.

Amanda cleared her throat. "Everyone, this is *Neil*, he's a production analyst. Did I get that right?" She gave an awkward, shrill laugh and shifted from foot to foot, looking uncomfortable in her clothes. Her pointed heels were tight and made her feet seem pinched and blotchy. "He's here to assess operational issues in different departments and identify any problems."

Logan hated the sound of that. He wanted to go back to climbing ladders and shelving books and feeling like Belle from *Beauty and the Beast*. Anything was better than this.

"Hi, everyone." Neil flexed his hands, as if he was about to make the sales pitch of a lifetime. "So you guys like, shelve books, keep stock, all that?"

Angel shrugged. "All that."

"Huh." Neil turned in slow circles, looking disturbed and confused. "And you send the books up to the rooms?"

"Yeah." Angel pointed behind Neil. "There's a dumbwaiter over there, plus we have carts that can go up the elevators."

"A *dumbwaiter*?" Neil squinted at Angel, then turned to see for himself. "Wow!"

Mia sighed.

Neil looked at Amanda, who held her hands behind her back, probably sweating the potential outcome of a tour like this.

Neil cleared his throat, looking at them again, before turning back to Amanda. "So, there's like, no way to automate this, right? All the shelving and moving books to the rooms has to be done with bodies?"

The three of them stared.

Amanda shook her head. "They've considered a few ideas in the past, but there's not really a clear-cut way to pull it off."

"Wow, okay." Neil spun in a slower, lazier circle, examining the tall aisles, ladders, and carts as though they needed scrubbing. "I have some ideas already. Ways we can cut back on all this unnecessary book storage. We could cut it down to a quarter, maybe less. There's a lot of wasted space here." He smiled at them. "So great to meet you."

Angel said nothing.

Amanda and Neil walked away, Amanda asking questions about *operational efficiency* as if that would hopefully make her sound smart.

Mia flipped through the stapled papers in her hands and got back to work.

Angel leaned against the sorting table, crossing his arms. "Assholes."

"Is there a lot of that?" Logan asked, sitting behind the wheel of his golf cart. "Restructuring?"

Angel nodded. "It's happening all over the resort. They recently brought new chefs in and changed the menu. They basically fired the whole kitchen staff."

"What would you do if they let you go?"

"I'm not going to tell you. You'll make fun of me."

"I would *never* do that."

"You're doing it right now!"

Logan laughed. "I'm serious, really, what would you do? You got dreams, don't you? I know you do. You seem like a dreamer, so let's hear it."

Angel rolled his eyes. "All right. I wanna open my own bookstore in a few years, once I get a little more saved up."

"Seriously? A bookstore?"

"What did I say, man?"

"I'm just surprised, you know? People our age don't often... set out to own bookstores."

"People our age don't work in underground libraries, either. Yes, I want my very own bookstore. I have it all planned out. I won't even need to work the front counter because Mia said she'd come work for me. I can just sit in the back, open up new shipments, and read books that aren't on sale yet."

"Are you sure that won't turn into an alcoholic-owning-a-bar kind of situation?"

"I don't know what you're talking about." Angel grinned. "I'll give you a job. The more people working under me, the more reading I can get done."

Logan whistled. "Sounds like the dream, all right. If you get this bookstore up and running, give me a call. I'll need to see it with my own eyes."

He patted the passenger seat and Angel jumped in. The shelves blurred together as they cruised down the center aisle.

"Drive down by the hangout, I gotta show you something."

Logan turned the corner and parked by the old diner booth.

"I think we're going to lose this place," Angel whispered.

Logan shook his head. "Come on. They need you. How could they deliver books without people? They won't do it. Same reason they pay all those fancy curators instead of using an algorithm."

Angel smiled. "You said the A-word. I know, you're right, but if they get their way, they will cut this place in half. Downsize, until there's just a corner of books left, and they'll trade those out to keep from storing everything. It won't be the same."

Angel stepped out and grabbed something from the shelf: a stack of notecards. He sat back in the golf cart. "These are Mia's, for nursing school." He flipped through the cards, pulling out one with a drawing.

The picture showed a little bookstore called Angel's Books. It had a large front window and a stick-figure woman working the front computer.

Angel smiled. "I drew this for Mia. It's her, working at my future bookstore. I know she's going to be a nurse and won't have time for a measly bookstore job, but it makes her laugh when she sees it, so I leave it mixed in with her study cards. I put myself in the background, see? I'm reading a book."

Logan almost hugged Angel. "I think you should do it," he said. "Give it everything you got. You're smart, you love books, I mean, why not open the store now?"

"It's not that simple."

"That's why you should do it," Logan argued, but Angel acted as if he didn't hear him.

Logan had to try something else, something non-verbal. "Wanna help me sort the rest of this cart?" If the work itself wouldn't distract Angel, nothing would.

Angel took a deep breath and held it. He exhaled. It sounded painful. "Yeah, let's do it." He carefully put the bookstore drawing back in the middle of Mia's notecards and set the stack on the shelf.

They glided in and out of the aisles. Logan drove, Angel shelved, moving faster than usual, sprinting up the ladders just to slide down, not touching a single rung. He worked hard even though no bigwigs were here to see it. Just Logan, the new guy.

"They can't replace you," Logan said as Angel slid beside him, and they took off again. "You know that. They can't replace *people* in a job like this."

Angel shrugged. "We're all replaceable, man."

Logan was about to refute that when Angel's radio crackled in his earpiece. Angel frowned, pressing the talk button. "This is Angel. I'm with Logan. Can you repeat that?"

Angel listened. He turned to Logan, eyebrows bent in bewilderment. "Do you know someone here named Florence? 'Cause apparently she's looking for you."

Chapter 28

Robert wondered if he'd ever return to normal. Even after making breakfast, changing Nathan's diaper, and feeding the little guy some eggs and toast, Robert stayed in a thick, unending fog.

After his unfortunate altercation with Dean, he should've run to the police immediately. It might've earned him a little credibility.

But the clock kept ticking, and he did nothing. He fed his son breakfast and waited for the S.W.A.T. team to come through the door.

Because of Dean, he would lose Florence, Nathan, and everything good in his life.

No, he'd *already* lost them. He was living on borrowed time now.

It was half past eight in the morning, and well after his usual start time, but who would care? Dean read the tardy reports, and his report-reading days were thankfully over. Robert sent Margo a quick text, and she agreed to pick Nathan up at the resort.

While he waited, Layla changed into her ugly black cargo pants and a gray long-sleeved shirt printed with *Reader's Resort* in obnoxious, flowy script.

Layla laced up her boots. "Where'd you go last night?"

Robert threw on a fresh set of clothes since his bloodied jeans and shirt were currently stuffed in the bottom of Layla's trash can. "For a walk."

"What about your eye? There's a bruise."

"Banged it on the dresser trying to get around Nathan's bed. I'm surprised I didn't wake you both up." Robert balanced Nathan on his hip. "You better go. You'll be late."

She patted his chest, keeping a safe distance from Nathan. If she possessed any maternal instincts, they weren't obvious. Maybe that was Robert's type: awkward girls scared of children, even their own. Thinking about it, the similarities between Layla and his ex-wife were uncanny. What did Florence think of children?

Did she want any? She would make a terrific mother one day.

Thinking of Florence only made his head fog worse. He had to stop daydreaming and focus on what to do about his Dean problem.

Forty-five minutes later, he met Margo in the parking lot and kissed Nathan's beautiful little head goodbye.

With his son taken care of, Robert could really consider his next steps. Until he decided, he would at least make a show of going to work. Technically, Dean fired him last night. But did anyone *else* know that?

The kitchen was an absolute joke. With prep half-done and the breakfast rush crashing down, the chefs were managing a sinking ship without Captain Dean to save the day. Instead, the general manager on duty had taken the helm, barking pointless orders and getting in everyone's way. No one asked for Robert's help, and he didn't volunteer. He had a new job now, and those nuts weren't going to crack themselves.

Robert sauntered down the basement steps, feeling more optimistic. More like himself. He'd spent his whole life trying to be like everyone else, trying to fit in. It was all a charade, of course. He understood now, at least partially, why people related to Bateman from *American Psycho*. Robert crossed a line last night when he snapped Dean's neck, and he knew—he wasn't delusional—he *knew* he'd never be the same because of it, and that was a good thing. Ordinary people were actors playing out the roles expected of them, but Robert wasn't going to play those games anymore.

He saw through it now. Ending a man's life put things in perspective, a point of view that had evaded Robert for so long. Experience truly was the greatest of teachers.

The basement looked the same as always. Some boxes had been placed at the foot of the stairs, for the new *inventory clerk/nutcracker* to take care of. Robert would oblige. He'd fought to keep his job for one more day; he might as well do it while he considered his options.

He brought Dean's phone and a phone charger with him. He plugged it into the wall, the home screen still on, and checked for notifications.

Dean had thirteen missed calls and eight texts, all from the general manager upstairs, wondering why the kitchen manager wasn't answering his phone.

Robert sat in his round wooden chair and started typing on Dean's phone. He texted the general manager, explaining how he, Dean, got nasty food poisoning and couldn't stop barfing.

OK, the manager responded. Just **OK**. He was upset, and understandably so, because now he would take the heat for the kitchen's shortcomings.

We're eighty-six Dean! Robert wanted to yell up the stairs. He was about to set Dean's phone down when it buzzed in his hand.

Charlie texted Dean:

Robert came to my place last night and begged for his job. I hope you take care of this before it becomes a bigger problem.

Robert stared at the text, dumbfounded. He'd assumed his problems had ended with Dean. Clearly not.

He looked at the pet door and the slanted black rubber with the dark eyes blinking in a pitch-black void. This time, he ignored the creature, considering the last time he'd interacted with that thing, he had hallucinated a gravelly voice and teeth biting his arm. No thanks, once was enough.

He set up a bag of walnuts and took the nutcracker out of his pocket. "Whoops, didn't clean this."

The nutcracker, still caked in Dean's blood, moved stiffly at first. Robert went to work on the walnuts, knocking flecks of blood loose with every deep *crack*! Such a sweet sound, like a tree limb breaking.

The creature watched the process, eyes moving slowly. Robert, though convinced it wasn't real, liked the idea of having something to talk to.

"I have to do something about Charlie," he told the creature.

He checked the earlier messages between Charlie and Dean.

Yesterday, Charlie texted Dean and asked if Robert was an okay worker. This was after Robert's pitch and before Charlie discovered Florence's altered bookshelf. Dean replied: **He's one of my worst employees. I hope he quits.**

Charming guy.

Robert smiled and cracked a walnut, flinching, looking down at the split shell in his hands and remembering Dean's finger.

"Do I seem different?" Robert asked the creature in the cellar. Since this hallucination was going to continue, might as well have fun with it.

Eyes blinked. No response.

"I'm not sorry about what I did," he said, the words sticking in his chest.

It was wrong to say that.

No, society wants you to think it's wrong. You had every right to do what you did.

Robert glanced at the creature. "I liked it," he said, a massive weight falling from his chest. "I liked it a lot. I'd do it again."

Dean's phone vibrated. A text from Charlie:

I know you're busy. Text me when you're on lunch. We need to talk.

Robert texted back, ignoring the earlier message about himself. He told the same story, impersonating Dean perfectly: I'm sick and can't hold anything down blah blah too bad.

Charlie was going to be a problem, maybe one Robert didn't have time for. Florence needed a few more days to finish her books. How was Robert supposed to wait around for *days* without anyone finding out about Dean?

He didn't have days, he had hours. Unless Charlie could back off for a while, Robert would have no choice but to protect himself again.

Robert could check in on Florence and make sure her old-soul eyes were tied to a book. If she were reading, she'd fall in love with his books. No question about it. For the moment, he would ignore his problem and hope it went away. A lot could happen in one day, and he needed time to *think*.

He stood and began brushing crumbs from his pants when the pet door opened. A small, bony hand slowly stuck out, palm-up, shaking. The dirty, broken fingernails made Robert sad. He mourned his poor, misfiring brain. The basement air, a tumor, the Devil... did it really matter what was causing these hallucinations? A short break would help. He couldn't keep staring at those dark eyes.

He jogged up the stairs, feeling good about the day. And if he found Florence curled up with one of his books, he'd feel just about perfect.

Chapter 29

Florence waited for Logan in the cafeteria, which quickly filled with hungry readers who stayed in their pajamas and brought their books with them. Conversations were scattered; the introverts ate early. The groups of friends would likely come next, slightly hungover, taking all the big tables.

Florence occupied a small two-person table with two coffees and a half-eaten omelet pushed to the side. Her open laptop was the centerpiece, with three dozen bookmarked tabs at the ready, everything the internet had to offer about Alyssa Larkin and Lori Walter.

She felt bad about disrupting Logan's workday, but she needed a second opinion. She wouldn't think about their time on the balcony, or the way he listened and let her talk; the way he told her to go after this case, or his fingertips on her shoulder.

Florence smiled and checked the front entrance, hoping to see him there.

Instead, someone else stood by the open doors. A pale man in long sleeves and jeans, staring at her.

It was the same man from yesterday who had watched her in the reader room.

She remembered his messy hair and the soft, almost sexual gaze that made her insides squeeze. Focusing on her laptop, she forced herself to read an article, word by word, until a minute had passed. Then she looked at the doorway.

The man now stood beside an empty table, slowly orbiting it, and pretending to look anywhere else.

He's coming closer, Florence thought. Sure enough, he started toward her. He cleared his throat, maneuvering through chairs.

Florence didn't know what to do. He looked anxious, like he was scared to talk to her but didn't have a choice.

He bumped into a few people and whispered apologies, not paying attention, his eyes unable to leave her. His lips moved without sound, as if talking to himself or rehearsing something to say. His left eye was badly bruised. Florence stared at him, silently daring him to keep walking.

It didn't work because he approached her table with a little grin, like he'd witnessed a puppy doing a neat trick.

"Florence, right?"

She waited a beat too long, and his energy changed.

"I'm sorry," he said. "I don't want to make you uncomfortable. I think I met you at a coffee shop in Sharonville, right? Two months ago? I thought I recognized you!"

She searched his face, but nothing came to mind. "Sorry, I don't remember."

"Oh, that's okay." He slipped his hands inside his pockets and pretended to be at ease. "I just had to say hello. I'm Robert, I'm actually your curator, and I know we're not supposed to meet our readers, but we have a connection, so I had to ask! How are your books?"

"Oh." Florence stared at her open laptop, not a book in sight. She actually had one book in her backpack, and it was the one Logan gave her. "Good. It's been good."

She saw Logan enter the café and tried not to look overly pleased, but she welcomed the diversion.

The guy followed her sightline and crossed his arms. Logan approached the table slowly, giving the curator a curt nod. "Hi." Then he turned to Florence. "You called?"

The man backed away. "It was nice to see you again," he mumbled, now in a hurry to get away from them.

Florence hated every second of that interaction. Why did he make it so weird? Of course, she hadn't known he was her curator; *that* would be a problem if they ran into each other again, and please God, hopefully that wouldn't happen.

"Sorry it took me so long," Logan said. He pulled the other chair back and sat down. "I had to finish up some stuff so I could take a break."

Logan looked at Florence expectantly, but she didn't break eye contact with the man standing ten feet away from their table.

"What are you looking at?" Logan twisted in his seat as the man abruptly left the room. He stopped in the hallway and looked at them, a frown creating deep rivets in his round face.

"Someone you know?" Logan asked, pointing at the second coffee mug on the table. "And is this mine?"

"All yours." Florence waited for the man to leave. "Sorry. I don't know him. He was... I don't know what he wanted."

Logan turned to the entrance, then back at her. "Just some random guy?"

"Yeah, I have no idea who he is."

Logan sipped his coffee instead of saying what he was thinking.

Both times, the guy hadn't casually been in the room, working, or with other people. Both times he showed up like he'd been looking for her. But why? What did he want from her? Florence shoved the thought away, feeling sick.

"Well." Logan sighed, setting his coffee down. "I'm sure you can take care of yourself. But if he bothers you again, and you need backup, you obviously know how to find me. And I know taekwondo, so that helps."

"Do you really?"

Logan nodded. "I got bored on YouTube one day, so I'm basically a professional now."

Florence smiled. "If he turns out to be a weirdo, I can always punch him in the face without breaking my hand. I watched a video on that once."

He stirred sugar into his black coffee. "I guess we're both fans of hand-to-hand combat. Why am I not surprised?" He laughed. "But what's up? You needed to talk?"

Florence took a deep breath. "It's about last night, all that stuff I told you." She waited for the blow: *Look, I was buzzed and bored and liked talking to you, and went along with the ghost stuff because how could I laugh in your face?*

But Logan straightened. "You saw her again? Please tell me she came back."

"Uh, *yeah*, she came back."

"Holy—"

"And she showed me a secret passageway in my room."

Logan nearly jumped out of his seat. He looked around, embarrassed to be this excited in public, and leaned over the table, glowing with pride. He wore the same clothes as yesterday, and looked tired as hell, but that did nothing to diminish his enthusiasm.

"Literally tell me everything." He smiled, as if hoping she'd get the reference.

And she did, of course she did. For ten minutes, they were the only people in the entire world, and it felt different than before. This time, she *wanted* his opinion on the secret passageway and the flood of information Alyssa had given her.

Like last night, he didn't interrupt her. He waited for her to finish, sipping his coffee at first, then letting it grow cold and stale.

Florence finished her story, searching his eyes for disbelief and finding none. "So, you still believe me, right? About all this? I *know* it sounds insane."

Logan ran one hand through his hair. "According to Alyssa, Lori knows what happened? She knows about the murder, but she didn't kill Alyssa?"

"Right. That's why I need to meet Lori. It's the only way forward."

Logan squinted at her. "So, you're doing this? Actually doing this?"

For some reason, she hadn't expected this question, this line in the sand. She could read his thoughts: *Cross this line, and there's no going back. You might start something you won't want to finish.*

Florence nodded. "I'm doing it. Alyssa needs someone to tell her story, and she picked me. I won't run from this."

Logan watched her closely. "I bet there's a way I can help. If you're okay with me sharing a few details with some people I know."

She did need help; that was the whole reason for contacting Logan. The *only* reason. "Do you trust them?"

"Mostly, but I know they can help us."

"How?"

"I need your phone number." He patted his pockets. "And I don't have my phone. Can you write it down?"

"Okay, but why?"

"I'll call you in ten minutes." He gave her a devious smile that she both hated and loved. A smile that promised he wouldn't tell her until he was ready. "I think I can help get this investigation rolling. Trust me here."

He pulled a Sharpie from his pocket and patted his right arm, the one without Poppy the Owl and the mysterious phone number.

"Are you serious?" Florence pointed at his arms. "Is this a thing you do?"

"Not usually. It's been a weird few days."

"Is this other number here someone you need to call?"

"I hope not."

She held his wrist against the table and wrote her number on his forearm. The Sharpie point swirled across his soft skin. Under the number, she wrote *Florence*. "That's so you remember which one is mine."

Logan brushed a finger across her name. "Okay, I'll tell you. The number is part of a stupid bet I made. It's embarrassing."

"You don't have to tell me."

Logan hesitated. "But we're swapping ghost stories, right?"

She nodded and sipped her coffee.

"I moved back to the country last year after living in Europe for five years, and I've had a hard time adjusting."

Now it was her turn to listen. He smiled and played it off, but his words came from somewhere deep inside him.

"I've made a lot of poor choices, and my brother thinks I can't take care of myself, and yes... he has some good reasons to think that. But he raised me, you know? He acts like my parent, because our parents were addicts, so of course, he thinks I could be doing better for myself, and this," he tapped the fading number on his left arm, "I have to call this when I fail, which my brother knows I'm inevitably going to do."

Florence uncapped the Sharpie, pressed it against the number on his left arm, and retraced it. She used her free hand to hold his wrist steady, her fingertips grazing his skin, and suddenly, she wanted to touch more of him; she wanted to sit there and trace old scars and fill in the parts he held back.

She handed him the Sharpie. "So how do you win this bet and prove your brother wrong?"

"I have to keep this job for a year," he said with a slight groan. "I have to get my shit together, and if I don't, I'll go work for my brother in his *office*."

"Eww?"

"I know."

"You just have to stick with this job, that's it?"

He nodded, avoiding her eyes. "Yeah, that's it."

It didn't feel like the full truth, but she was impressed he'd said what he did. Most guys pretended their shit was all the way together just to flex in front of her, as if she cared about their resumes above everything else. "Thanks for telling me, Logan, I mean it. Keep his number on your arm, maybe it'll motivate you. And if you need someone to talk to, my friends say I'm an average listener."

That earned a smile, a real one. "Deal."

"So you'll call me in ten minutes?"

"Max." He left his seat, not bothering to say goodbye, not when they'd talk again so soon. She watched him leave, a strange emotion shifting inside her. It would be a long ten minutes.

She checked the cafeteria, hoping for the best.

Sure enough, the strange man was nowhere to be seen.

Chapter 30

Robert stormed through the kitchen, embarrassed and a little pissed off. Speaking to Florence had been a mistake, yes, because regardless of how much he longed to sit at her table and hear her voice, it was stupid to approach her openly like that.

But even worse, she wasn't reading.

That was painfully obvious. In a cafeteria brimming with silence, flipping pages, and clinking silverware, Florence had her *laptop* out.

Sure, there was a small chance she was using it to read, but Robert knew that wasn't the case. At a resort, where every format of reading was available, no sane person would choose to read on a laptop.

Something was going on that he didn't know about, and Robert knew every single detail of Florence's life.

Like the young man who came to her table. She had a second cup of coffee waiting for him. She *called* him. And who was he? Florence came to the resort alone. Either she coincidentally ran into an old friend, or the young man worked at the resort. A fellow employee.

Robert jogged down the basement stairs and walked to the pet door. "She's not reading," he said, crouching. "Someone's distracting her."

The young man was good-looking, the type who liked distracting beautiful women, who flirted and seduced and left them pregnant, heartbroken, or both.

Robert flipped open the pet door, seeing darkness. "Is that why she won't read? Is he *bothering* her?"

His throat burned. "It's not a problem with the books."

His picks were pure perfection. Mysteries, coming-of-age adventures, inspirational memoirs, he hit the mark with her list, and all he wanted was a little affirmation, a little thank you. Was that so hard?

No noise came from the old cellar. The imaginary creature wasn't in a social mood, and that was fine. It could still listen.

Robert sat on the wooden chair, clacking the nutcracker's teeth together in his palm. "Florence *is* reading, I just haven't seen it yet. She's a good girl. She'll read them."

Before falling asleep at night, Robert liked to picture Florence reading. He imagined her reading all the time: on a break at the coffee shop, in the park on a breezy day, in the bath or in bed, wearing her favorite matching pajamas; her eyes full of heavy concentration, her lips parted, her cheeks flushed like a pink sunset.

Robert closed his eyes and smiled at that image. If only he could *see* it.

Dean's phone went off in his pocket.

A text from Charlie: **Call me please. It's about Robert.**

Why would no one give Robert time to think?

"What should I do?" he asked the pet door. "How can I make Charlie leave me alone?"

The pet door didn't move.

"You know what." Robert knelt on the bottom shelf. "Where are you today?"

Despite the creature only existing in his mind, he liked the company in such a lonely place. He activated the flashlight on his phone and looked inside. The creature wasn't there. The deadbolt was still locked. Robert hit the deadbolt a few times with the nutcracker, jarring it loose. He unlocked it, twisted the handle, and pushed the door inward.

The creature wasn't in the cellar because it didn't exist, like he thought.

"You're gone," he whispered, smiling like a fool. "Is anyone there?"

He sat on the floor and started to laugh. He was cured! Whatever innermost part of him the creature represented had fundamentally changed.

What changed?

Robert flexed his hand, clicking the nutcracker's teeth together like a hungry little biter. *Crack* goes Dean's pinky finger, *crack* goes his ring finger, *crack* goes his neck.

The true self wasn't caged anymore, no sir. Robert let it out last night, when he ended a man's life and made this world a better place.

Dean's phone chimed again and again—more texts from Charlie, desperate to talk about Robert.

Something had to be done about Charlie. Robert inspected the cellar again, ideas flowing through his active mind. The creature had escaped, like Robert's true self.

Such symbolism was reserved for works of excellent fiction. Robert knew them; he knew their power. His life, for all its roadblocks and delays, had all the qualities of a Hero's Journey. It made a lot of sense when he framed it like that.

He leaned against the pet door, pushing it open with his forehead like a good doggy returning home. He stuck his head inside the cellar and inhaled the grimy, earthy scent. Ideas flowed from the cellar and out into the basement, filtering through and around his brain like a strong rock in a warm stream. He felt a breeze on his face, the feeling of freedom; such sweet, savory freedom.

He knew what he had to do with Charlie and Florence and that young man. He knew what to do with all of them, and he didn't have to be careful, no, because he was already on camera, his DNA already exposed. In a way, that made things simpler. He didn't have to worry about little details; he just had to be careful enough until it came time to leave, and he would be long gone before anyone realized what happened.

And good luck finding him.

Dean's phone went off again, delivering yet another spiteful text. Charlie couldn't shut up.

Sitting in his little wooden chair, Robert lifted a walnut from the bag and cradled it in his palm. "What do you want, Charlie?" he whispered.

He gently placed the walnut between the nutcracker's teeth. It looked like a bulging wooden eye.

Crack.

The pieces fell on the cold cement floor.

Robert set another walnut.

He needed the cover of darkness, if he could wait that long. Survive the day, don't let anyone find Dean. Keep Charlie away.

Crack. The walnut's little bones slipped through his fingers.

His eyes drifted shut. He took another walnut and rolled it into the teeth. "I'll save you, Florence." Her name on his tongue made him shudder.

"No one will keep us apart."

Crack.

Chapter 31

Logan waved his arms, bringing Angel's golf cart to a stop.

"Hop in, my dude. Let's finish this rack."

The new arrivals were half done, the empty totes stacked neatly inside each other. The only thing left on the sorting table was a leaning tower of damaged books, which would be returned to the distributor. Earlier, Logan opened one book to find a massive boot print on the title page. That bothered even him, a lowly non-reader.

"How'd it go with Florence?" Angel asked, driving down The Shire. "Do you know her?"

"We met last night."

Angel arched his eyebrows. "My man! Just don't go telling people you got down with a guest, 'cause that's kinda frowned upon."

"What? No—"

"I mean, it happens." Angel grimaced. "You hear stories, you know? But the readers really should be off-limits. Honestly, if you want a good time, just hang out with housekeeping. They have no boundaries."

"It's not like that! We met last night, and she told me this huge secret about her room. She wants my help, but what we really need is you and Mia."

"What secret?"

No way around this. Logan braced himself. "It's about a ghost."

Angel slowly turned his head. "Florence saw one?"

"Yeah, and none other than Alyssa Larkin, that girl who disappeared."

Angel slammed on the brakes. "Fill me in, dude, what are you waiting for?"

Logan rehashed his discussions with Florence. Surprisingly, Angel didn't seem perturbed by the ghost. If anything, it was the passageway that startled him.

"A secret room?"

"That's what she told me." Logan jumped out of the cart and scanned the bookcase on the back. He picked *Station Eleven* by Emily St. John and climbed the ladder.

"Like, no one knows about it?"

Logan shelved the book. "I guess so. It connects to the room upstairs, which is apparently where Lori Walter lives." He sat in the golf cart and held the overhead handle. "Florence has questions about Lori. That's why we need you."

Angel was silent.

"You barely asked about the ghost, though," Logan said. "You're not impressed by a ghost?"

"No, I am." Angel turned down the center aisle and picked up speed, the wind blowing in their faces, the golden lights above them turning into blurry shooting stars. "I know this place is haunted. Everyone knows it, and people talk, you know? We all hear about it when a reader goes viral for some 'incident' in their room. But most of it *is* BS. Most people just get a feeling, and that's the scary part."

"Why is that?"

Angel parked in another aisle. "Because you can't see it. If Florence saw a ghost, if she's interacted with Alyssa, that's a good sign, I think. It's the ones you can't see you should run from."

"Never thought of that before," Logan said. "Thanks for ruining my day."

Angel grinned. "If Alyssa is here and you want to help her, you've got bigger problems, *amigo*." Angel collected a stack of books. He kicked a ladder, watched it roll to a stop, then climbed it without using his hands. "Tell me. Why are you helping a stranger work on a cold case the police couldn't solve? Why get involved in that? It's probably a dead end, ghost or no ghost. It's Florence, right? She's hot, isn't she?"

Logan's face reddened; he couldn't help it. "I don't know."

"You *don't* know?"

"Come on, man. Yes, she's beautiful. But it's more than that. It might be a dead end, but she found a hidden passageway!"

"It's an old building with old secrets," Angel said. "Rooms were sometimes designed to engage with the reader. This could be that very thing. Just another fancy trick to make the readers think they're someone special, when in reality, just about every good or bad thing imaginable has happened in those rooms. This place has a history, you know? Secret rooms don't go unnoticed by everyone for decades. It just doesn't happen."

His words clicked inside Logan's chest, the logic undeniable. "I know it's a long shot," Logan said. "I wouldn't blame you or Mia for doubting Florence's story. I've done plenty of that myself but at least wait and hear what she has to say. I bet she'll convince you."

"Love is a powerful drug, Logan, and it can also be a bitch."

"Dude."

Angel saluted him. "I commit to being your wingman."

"Dude, that's not—"

"I'll do whatever I can to help."

"Okay, seriously, thank you, but—"

"But don't you dare say she's not hot." Angel smiled.

Logan shut his mouth.

"You can't fool me, fool." They drove to another aisle. "Hey, listen though, we need to be strategic about this. What's the plan?"

"If you let me borrow your phone, I'll call Florence." Logan held up his right arm. "I got her number right here."

Angel stared at Logan, at both arms. "What is up with you? I know, I know, you don't have a phone." Angel held up his cell phone. "Let me see that number, and I'll explain the plan to her. We do this on speaker, conference call, style."

Logan lifted his arm, waving Mia over from the other side of the room. She joined them as Angel dialed Florence's phone number.

On speaker, the phone trilled in the quiet stacks. Angel sat in the cart, his arms crossed over the wheel. Mia leaned against the shelves, her body leaving a slight imprint on the books. Logan paced, hands in his pockets, hoping this was the right call to make, hoping that like Florence, he had the guts to finish whatever they were about to start.

And finally, Florence answered.

Chapter 32

True to his word, Logan called Florence ten minutes later from his coworker's phone.

She was introduced to Angel and Mia, and although they seemed friendly, Florence hoped she'd made the right choice. Telling Logan about her investigation was difficult enough, and now all four of them were in on it. And somehow, Angel and Mia didn't just believe her story about Alyssa, but they wanted to help her. She almost refused. She almost stubbornly hung up and committed to doing this alone, but she couldn't ignore the warm gratitude bubbling inside her. They were her best chance of meeting Lori face-to-face.

They planned a 1:00 p.m. lunch break to brainstorm ways to kickstart the investigation. With time to kill, Florence packed her backpack and left the cafeteria. She walked to the elevators and was considering trying them again when the stairwell door across the hall cracked open. Alyssa's thin frame stood in the gap, a finger pressed to her bloody lips.

Florence ran inside the stairwell, shutting the door behind her. It was deathly quiet, but a reader could enter at any moment.

"What's going on?" Florence asked. "Are you all right?"

Alyssa grabbed Florence's hand and led her down to the lower level.

"Won't someone see us?"

Alyssa made a *shushing* sound, spilling two fresh trails of blood from the corners of her mouth, like a vampire. Florence pushed the thought away. Alyssa wasn't a monster.

At the bottom of the stairs, Alyssa opened the door and peered down a long, plain hallway.

In fiction, ghosts were commonly portrayed as partially invisible, where only certain people (and the main characters) could see them, while others couldn't. Florence realized this was not the case. Even though Alyssa could travel to and from the spirit world, when on this side, she was all here. Otherwise, why would she worry about being seen?

Alyssa stepped into the hallway, and Florence followed, torn between excitement and fear.

They walked through two sets of doors and stopped at an intersection of hallways. This side of the lower level seemed almost vacant.

Could Florence find her way back? What if Alyssa disappeared again? Florence would be trapped inside a maze.

Alyssa turned down the hallway and froze. At the far end, a pair of doors swung shut. Through a small, round window on the right side, a stooped shadow disappeared into the room beyond.

Florence tapped Alyssa's arm and whispered, "Why are we down here?"

Alyssa stared at the double doors. She looked back at Florence, tears in her eyes.

"Alyssa, why are we here?"

But Alyssa ignored her and walked to the doors, her bare feet silently padding the linoleum. Above the doorframe, letters had been removed, leaving an outline in the white paint: LAUNDRY.

Florence peered through the round window, but it was too dark to see anything. "What should we do?"

Alyssa quietly pushed through the door and craned her neck around the corner. She waved Florence inside.

Florence glanced behind her, expecting someone to catch them, but the hallway was empty. She followed Alyssa into the resort's old laundry room and let the door shut behind her.

The fluorescent lights above them were burned out, keeping them in the shadows. The walls closest to Florence were bare, with double-stacked water hookups meant for industrial washing machines. Dryer hookups were on the other side. In the middle was a long, wide table, made of wood and painted white. Someone had written 'The Altar' on the side of it with a red marker.

At the far end of the room, worktables and tool carts lined the perimeter, and boxes of spare parts and cleaning supplies littered the floor. It looked like a tool shop for a handyman.

The pit in Florence's stomach deepened. Somewhere close, a toilet flushed. A sink turned on, then back off. A door opened.

Alyssa grabbed Florence's hand and squeezed it, trembling.

What was she scared of?

Florence knew the answer and immediately stopped herself. She wouldn't panic. She wouldn't scream, but she knew what Alyssa had done, and why she'd done it.

An older man emerged from the bathroom, adjusting his jeans. He wore his T-shirt tucked in across the front, showing off a chrome cowboy belt buckle. He was tall, stocky, and wore a battered ballcap loosely over his balding head.

He faced his worktable and hummed softly to himself. Florence couldn't see his face, but she was too scared to move closer.

The man turned to his right, spit into his trash can, and started tinkering with a handheld radio on his workbench.

Florence bumped against the swinging doors and pulled Alyssa's hand, but the woman refused to acknowledge her. She couldn't take her eyes off him. They were seconds away from making an irreversible mistake.

Florence tried again. She pulled on Alyssa's hand, and this time Alyssa looked at her.

Florence tilted her head back, toward the swinging door. She wanted nothing more than to get away from this room, the man inside, and the table they called The Altar.

"Please," she whispered.

The man coughed loudly, making Florence jump. He didn't turn around.

Tears spilled down Alyssa's cheeks. She cupped a hand over her bloody mouth.

"Alyssa, *please*."

Alyssa finally complied. Florence led her through the swinging doors and gently shut them with her fingertips.

Then they ran down the long hallway. Florence kept looking back and picturing the man's head in the little glass window, watching them run.

They turned the corner and Florence dropped Alyssa's hand. "Why did you do that?" she said, breathless.

Alyssa kept walking down the hallway, her back to Florence.

"Alyssa! Was he...? Was he the one?"

Alyssa didn't turn around.

Florence jogged forward. "You needed to tell me that!"

Alyssa's eyes were so bright and haunted that Florence almost missed the anger hiding beneath them. It wasn't the same rage she saw in Alyssa this morning, writing bloody messages on the mirror. This might've been the first time in thirty-eight years that Alyssa saw the face of her killer, and it gave her a panic attack.

"What were you thinking?" Florence demanded. "He could've seen us! What would happen then? What would I do? He can't—"

She almost said, *He can't hurt you again,* but something finally kicked in. Maybe it was the look in Alyssa's eyes, or the shame finding its way to her heart, but Florence shut her mouth. Her words fell between them, dripping with poison.

Alyssa leaned against the wall, sobbing, blood gushing from her pinched lips.

Florence wiped her eyes with her sleeve. "Alyssa, I'm—"

But Alyssa was gone, leaving Florence alone in the resort's basement with a killer one hallway over. And Florence couldn't blame her.

She almost peered down the hallway to make sure the man hadn't crept up behind them, but she didn't have the backbone for that.

Instead, she ran back to her room. Safely inside with the door locked, she sank into the bed and let herself cry while the chandelier swayed above her.

The way Alyssa acted in the tool shop went beyond trauma and fear. It was helplessness. She wanted to kill that man. She seemed so determined this morning, and yet what did it matter if they couldn't prove it? Alyssa knew who killed her, and now, so did Florence.

But the truth was just another dead end.

Chapter 33

Robert's fingers were sore and tired from squeezing the nutcracker. He'd crushed half of everything he touched and sat in the center of a blast radius, surrounded by splintered shells, walnut dust, and the lumpy ridges of mangled castaways.

Time spun like bands of light inside Robert's head. His daydreams of Florence were starting to not be enough. He kept waiting for Charlie to find him with security in tow and decided he would not let that happen without being prepared.

He abruptly stood and saw the pet door in the corner of his eye, but nothing moved. The hallucination was gone for good. Still, he needed a break from this stifled coffin air.

When he left the basement and stepped outside, Ohio's countryside greeted him with rich colors and scents. The sky looked bluer and deeper than before, and he smiled at it with gratitude.

He walked through the parking lot and opened the trunk to his car, where he kept spare clothes and tools. He picked up the stainless-steel machete he'd bought himself ten years ago, during an outdoors phase that lasted six months. He'd bought a tent, a lantern, a sleeping bag, and a machete, and never used any of them.

He pulled the machete from its sheath. The black, eleven-inch blade had a serrated top and a dark green rubber handle. Easing the machete back in the sheath, he grabbed a thin rope he'd purchased for carrying it. He looped the rope inside the sheath's outer handle, tied the rope off, and slung it around his neck, then down one shoulder. The machete hung across his torso. He slipped it inside his shirt, pulling the rope tight so the machete nestled against his side, practically invisible. He threw a light jacket over himself and took a few steps to test it. It wasn't too uncomfortable, and it would stay concealed until he could hide it in the basement.

A giddiness set in, starting in his lower stomach and churning upward, making him laugh. Was he really about to murder the resort's prince? When the kingdom was rotting from the inside out, he might be doing the people a great service; a chance for new leadership at the resort, while also removing an obstacle from Robert's path. Win-win.

Robert cut through the parking lot and the freshly cut green lawns. He crossed the sidewalk that circled the resort and went for the side door, but it opened before he got there.

Charlie stepped out, blinking in the sun. He held a hand over his face, staring at Robert with little rat eyes. They faced each other. Charlie let the door shut behind him, not bothering to move out of the way.

The machete shifted against Robert's side as he cleared his throat. "Hey, Charlie."

Like an idiot, he'd completely forgotten the time. Charlie's daily lunch-hour walk.

Charlie didn't move. "Two days in a row? Are you serious?"

"I'm going back inside. I'm not trying to bother you."

"Have you seen Dean?"

Robert shook his head, staring at the cracked concrete beneath his feet. "No. I heard he was sick or something."

"He hasn't called you?" Charlie sighed, pulling his phone from his pocket. "I honestly don't think anyone would give two shits if I fired you right now. But I've been reprimanded before for 'abusing' my position, which is a joke because I own this place."

"Your mom owns it." Robert couldn't stop himself. He felt like using the machete now and opening Charlie up from end to end under this ocean-blue sky.

Charlie ignored him, lifting the phone to his ear. "Nice knowing you, Robert." He stomped down the sidewalk like an angry little kid. Robert felt some inward satisfaction, knowing he'd ruined Charlie's precious ME-time.

"Dean! Call me back!" Down the path, Charlie glared at his phone, thrusting it back inside his pocket.

Yep. Charlie was going to be a big problem.

Dean's phone was charging in the basement with no one there to answer it, but Charlie wouldn't tolerate the silence for long. Soon, he'd go *looking* for Dean. Big problem indeed.

Robert watched Charlie stomp away, feeling a stupid smile on his face.

Enjoy your last walk, Charlie.

Chapter 34

Logan had lost all sense of time. Something about not having his phone made him less curious about what went on in the world. Working in the stacks, he didn't just lose track of time; he lost track of *everything*.

Angel had to remind him to eat lunch before they met up with Florence. Logan wasn't hungry, but he took the elevators to the second floor and ate at the taco bar anyway. One swipe and his paycheck shrank a little. He inhaled his meal and returned to the underground realm before surface dwellers could ask him where the pool was.

Going back inside the stacks felt like stepping onto a stage without an audience. Even with no one watching or appreciating what they did every day, Logan believed he had a purpose here. The room itself had accepted him, and it seemed to hold a spell over everyone who entered.

Everyone except Neil, the statistician or whatever the hell he was. No one had mentioned him again, and maybe that was the real reason his job had meaning: he knew they were running out of time. And the room knew it too, somehow. Something this good couldn't last forever.

After a quick sort and tote stacking, Angel and Mia were ready to go. They would wait in Angel's apartment while Logan escorted Florence through the lower level.

Logan stood between the elevators and the stairs, although he knew which way she'd take. A few employees he didn't recognize walked past him and took the elevators up. The doors closed again, and for a few minutes, nothing happened. Logan wondered if she'd changed her mind.

But then she came through the stairwell as he predicted, wearing the same jeans and black rain jacket from earlier.

Down the hallway, the elevators dinged, and the doors opened. No one got in, no one got out.

Florence stayed far away from them.

"I think you were right about those," Logan said.

"They followed me all the way down here," she said. "I heard them on every floor I walked past."

Logan laughed. "If I were you, I'd be in a panic right now."

Florence stood beside him, staring blankly at the warm elevator light spilling into the hallway floor. "I don't know. Some things are worse."

She wouldn't meet his eyes. Her hands were stuffed inside her jacket pockets, and she kept glancing up and down the hallway.

"You okay?"

"No. Something happened."

"Like what?"

She shook her head. "Let's go meet your friends. I don't want to tell it twice."

Logan led her to Angel's apartment, failing to come up with anything smart to say. Florence kept looking over her shoulder. Did she think they were being followed?

They stopped at Angel's door. The *Star Wars* welcome mat made it easy to spot.

Logan knocked. "Angel's a little... you'll get used to him."

Florence pointed at the floor. "Never saw *Star Wars*."

"Geez, don't tell him that."

The door opened, and Angel stood in the gap. "Welcome to the crib."

He retreated into the kitchen and turned off the sink, dabbing his wet shirt with a towel, apologizing for the messy condition of his *crib*. He introduced himself again to Florence, along with Mia, who sat cross-legged and barefoot on the couch in the living room. Florence said it was nice to meet them, even though her eyes told a different story.

Logan knew Florence could handle herself, but she stood so rigid and tense, as if expecting an attack. It made Logan want to give her a hug, but he didn't want to cross a line and make things worse.

Meanwhile, Angel gave Florence a boisterous tour of his apartment. He started with his tiny galley kitchen and extensive foreign alcohol collection on the counter. In the living room, cheap artwork covered the walls, mostly done with a Sharpie. Angel told Logan last night about a little antique store in Lebanon that sold local art, usually from anonymous artists. The store owner sold them in the back, like an illegal art auction, because some of it was violent and disturbing, and he didn't want that hanging where anyone could scoff at it.

Angel didn't like the extreme stuff, just the unusual—a UFO crashing in the woods, a cave with shapes crouched inside, a fairy bathing in a river.

The living room had one couch and one recliner, with a large coffee table between them, littered with beach-themed coasters and empty mugs, a cigar humidor, and old beer bottle condensation stains. Four bookcases lined the left wall, the books organized by genre, with tabs separating each section. In the corner, a leaning tower of board games and playing cards.

Angel offered Florence the recliner, where she sat down and waited uncomfortably.

Angel plopped down beside Mia, leaving enough room on the couch for Logan, but he preferred to stand. The three of them looked his way. After all, he was the link between them, and the reason they'd called this meeting.

"Um. Thanks for coming," he said, putting his hands in his pockets. "Uh, as we know, Florence is looking into the disappearance of Alyssa

Larkin, from thirty-eight years ago. And so far, the strongest lead is Alyssa's ghost, which... is wild. How many times has she...?"

Florence held up three fingers.

"Three times." Why was he leading this? "She's shown up three times, and Florence found a hidden passageway attached to her room, which apparently belonged to Alyssa."

Angel held up a hand.

"You know you don't have to do that," Logan said. "Are you making fun of me?"

"I would *never* do that."

"Stop it."

Angel smiled and addressed Florence. "First of all, yes, we believe you. I know I said that on the phone earlier, and trust me, although I've never personally seen a ghost, every old-timer here has a story. Too many to count. So throw everything you got at us, and we'll do what we can."

Mia clicked her nails together. "Whatever you need. Our job is flexible, so we're here to help."

Florence pulled her jacket sleeves over her hands. "You really believe me?" She said this with a sigh of relief, and for a moment, the tension inside her body seemed to relax.

"We work at a haunted resort," Angel said. "Of course we believe you. And we trust Logan, sort of. I'm sure he vetted you. You know, no offense, we do get some weirdos coming through here."

Florence smiled a little, but the conversation died.

Logan cleared his throat. "So, Florence, what's the next move?"

"It can be anything!" Mia said. "We got like, almost all our work done."

"I mean, we're still on break," Angel said, checking his watch. "We have to go back at some point."

Mia shrugged. "Mostly just you. Me and Logan will work on this."

Angel threw his hands up.

"I know who killed her," Florence whispered.

They all froze, staring at her.

Florence hugged herself, moving closer to the edge of her seat. "Alyssa brought me down here a little bit ago, to this floor. Not on this side, where the apartments are. It must've been the other half. I don't really know."

They waited for her to continue. Outside, voices echoed down the hallway.

Florence glanced at the door, then at Angel. "Is there a handyman here? Someone who works in a tool shop on this level." Her voice was deadpan, but her eyes were dark, murky pools.

Angel's voice had gone dry. "Frederick. He works on the carts we use."

"Has he been here a long time?"

Angel nodded slowly. "Since the beginning."

They let that soak in. Finally, Logan spoke up. "Is Alyssa positive?"

"She started shaking when we saw him," Florence said. "I watched her cry quietly so he wouldn't hear us. You tell me."

Logan couldn't fathom what that must've been like. "I mean, this is good, right? She led us to the killer. Isn't that progress?"

"It doesn't matter if we can't prove it." Florence glanced at the door again. "We can't tip him off and let him know we're involved. He'll..."

"He'll kill you," Angel said. "He'll kill *us*."

"Look." Florence stood up. "I'm really sorry I dragged you guys into this. I didn't know about him when we talked earlier. I kept this meeting, but I can't ask you for favors. You know that, right? There's a murderer at this resort. If we can't prove he killed Alyssa, he's going to still be here, working right down the hall. This isn't fair of me to put on you, when I get to leave in a few days, and you don't."

No one responded. Logan felt an ache in his chest. He wasn't ready to say goodbye.

"So thank you again for believing me, seriously." Florence moved closer to the door. "Most people wouldn't."

Logan cleared his throat. "Florence?"

She paused, her eyes red and exhausted. "I don't think you want this."

He shook his head. She was wrong, couldn't she see that?

Finally, Angel stood up. "Hold on. We don't want to give this up."

Florence frowned. "Why?"

Mia straightened up and waved Florence back over. "Florence, listen to me. Frederick is a major asshole."

"Yeah, you didn't give us a chance!" Angel said. "He's so creepy."

"So creepy." Mia shivered.

"When you were like, 'Frederick's a killer,' I thought, 'well duh!' He is not normal." Angel sat close to Mia. "No, seriously, we can actually help you with this. No one has to know we're involved. No one. If you want to take the downfall, it's yours. But at least let us help."

Logan didn't know what was happening, but he loved every second of it. From the look in Florence's eyes, she wasn't used to someone fighting to keep her around.

She moved from the door and sat down, perched on the edge of the recliner.

"We need to find her bones," she said. "Or something to link Frederick to her death. Far as I can tell, that's how we win. Alyssa told me that Lori Walter knows something, so we start with her."

Angel snapped his fingers. "If Alyssa shows you where her body is, the case breaks wide open. Maybe Frederick is tied to it, maybe not. But now the police are back in, there's new evidence, new technology, and something might resurface. Also, Alyssa's family will finally know what happened."

Florence flinched a little. Something about that struck a chord. And if Logan were a betting man, he'd bet it had something to do with the many,

many things she wasn't telling him. He would support her all the way, but he wasn't stupid. Florence was not the average reader. He didn't know why, but she jumped into this thing way too eagerly. For now, he'd trust she had a good reason for not telling him the full truth.

Mia tapped Angel's shoulder. "The weekly book."

"I was getting there!"

Mia turned to Florence and stared deeply into her eyes. "How brave are you?"

Florence frowned. "Not very."

Mia shook her head. "You saw a ghost, and you stayed. You saw a killer, and here you are, talking to complete strangers. You're very brave, Florence. We can get you in a room with Lori Walter. Can you handle it from there?"

"How? I thought no one saw her."

Angel raised his hand.

"Dude," Logan sighed, "cut that out."

"No, I'm saying it's *me*, I see her. And it's unfortunate because she's really scary."

"Can you guys just explain something from start to finish?" Logan said. "Our break is about to end."

"Okay, okay." Mia tucked her legs under her and looked at Florence. "Once a week, Charlie, Lori's son, puts in a request. He reads a lot, and he always sends his mom a book delivery through us."

"He can't take it himself?" Florence asked.

"A lot of times, he does," Angel added. "But when he's busy, he has us do it. Since we got the books and all."

"I just realized I don't know what you all do here."

Mia nodded. "We keep track of all the books, including the ones sent directly to Lori Walter's room on the fourth floor. She always answers. If you take a book up there, you'll see her. That's your chance."

"Fourth floor is kind of a weird spot for the owner to be living, right?"

Angel shrugged. "Well, the roof wasn't originally a reader lounge, it was a hangout for employees only. John and Lori built their room on the edge of the fourth floor so they could be close to the roof. They spent a lot of time up there, I guess. When they let readers use it, years later, maybe Lori didn't want to move. So she hides in her room."

Logan hated every part of this plan. Too many things could go wrong. "If Lori knows what happened to Alyssa, what will stop her from telling Frederick that someone's asking questions?"

Florence looked at him, her eyes still shimmering. "I'll have to be careful and not give too much away."

"What about cameras?" Logan asked.

"They don't have them in the hallways," Angel said. "This place wants to be cozy, and with how secretive they are about the room themes, they only keep cameras in the lobby and stairwells, and most of the lower level."

"My room is at the end of the third hallway," Florence said. "But I can't get back there without being seen."

"Don't look at the cameras," Mia said. "Your hair can hide your face."

"That's not very reassuring." Logan shook his head. "What if Lori knows you don't work here?"

"Logan," Florence said softly, making his stomach twist. "They've gotten away with it for thirty-eight years. I think it's been long enough."

He wanted to ask her why she cared this much; why she'd risk her safety and well-being for a ghost she just met, but he kept his mouth shut. She'd already made up her mind.

She held his gaze for a long time. "Her family deserves to know. I feel like I owe it to them."

Logan disagreed. She didn't owe Alyssa's family anything. Why was she putting so much pressure on herself? But once again, he held his tongue. Maybe she would eventually tell him the full truth once she was ready. If it wasn't too late by then.

Florence stood up and smoothed out her jacket, looking at Angel. "You got a uniform I can wear?"

Chapter 35

Despite Mia's gentle reassurance, Florence didn't feel brave. She forced herself to walk down the fourth-floor hallway, moving aside for a small group of readers who, thankfully, didn't ask for help. The collar of Angel's work shirt kept irritating her neck. If a real employee spotted her, the plan would fall apart. She held a book from Angel's bookshelf, a biography on Steve Jobs, and hurried down the hallway.

Every step filled her with dread. She wanted to turn around and give up, but that meant no justice for Alyssa. No consequences for Frederick.

No chance of seeing Chloe again.

How proud would Chloe be if she saw this foolhardy mission? She'd think all those detective stories had gone to Florence's head.

With the hallway clear, she slipped inside the blood-red curtains leading to the unmarked door. She never imagined herself doing something this stupid. Clearly, this broke the law in some way, so she could attempt to pry information from a woman famous for her silence.

Normal people didn't do this. Normal people read their books until they passed out from booze and exhaustion. Oh, to be normal. It sounded so serene.

Florence stared at Lori's apartment, almost dropping Steve Jobs on his face. She clutched the paperback with both hands, thinking it would make a decent weapon if necessary. Should she ring the little bell? Dropping off the book would defeat the purpose; she had to get inside the room.

She approached the door, the peephole glaring at her. She knocked, too softly at first, then tried again, much harder, like she belonged there.

The deadbolt slid back, the door cracked open, and Florence's first view of Lori consisted of spindly white hair, a wrinkled face, and deep blue eyes.

Florence blurted the first thing in her mind. "Here's your new book, Miss Walter, from your son." She shoved the book through the door.

Lori caught it like a football, too shocked to speak.

Florence clenched her hand against her chest. "I'm so sorry to bother you, but do you have a Band-Aid?"

Lori licked her lips, looking at the book in her hands.

"Please, I just need a small one." Florence frowned, convinced she was the worst liar in history.

"One moment," Lori muttered, slipping away.

Florence pushed through the door and entered Lori's private suite, the place readers constantly theorized about.

How did Lori live? What books did she like? Was she disfigured, like in a fairy tale? Was she a monster?

If monsters preferred charcuterie boards and copious amounts of red wine, then maybe.

The living room had a tall ceiling with a gorgeous brick fireplace. Exquisite paintings hung on the walls, accompanied by placards citing dates, titles, and the artists. The painting near Florence was a lighthouse, titled *Aurora*, and made Florence think of all the back-alley lowbrow art in Angel's apartment.

Beside Florence, the entire right wall was a built-in, color-coded bookshelf. A vintage typewriter was tucked away in the corner of the top shelf. A sheet of paper stuck out of it, with small lines of prose typed neatly down the center, too small for Florence to read.

Lori didn't seem like the color-coding type, but the sweeping rainbow on her shelf provided the only source of life in the room. Florence didn't know anything about Charlie Walter, aside from his infamous addiction to work. She could picture him fussing over these shelves, matching colors, chiding his mother for her disorganization.

The furniture was expensive, the kitchen spotless aside from empty wine bottles and discarded corks.

The living room featured a U-shaped leather couch with cup holders and a coffee table with two glass ashtrays on either end. A wine bottle sat crookedly on the couch, only a sip remaining. Past the living room, through a half-closed door, Florence could see the edge of a large bed, the covers rumpled, and the blackout curtains beyond, hiding everything except a sliver of light and a breathtaking view of the valley.

Candles decorated the mantle above the fireplace. Three were lit, sending little spirals of smoke and flame upward. The room smelled like lavender and fresh laundry, masking the stench of sweat and wine and death.

Yes, death. Lori was slowly dying, day by day, from some unknown, maybe unseen illness. Her room was little more than a rich woman's coffin.

Lori emerged from the bathroom, a box of Band-Aids in hand. When she saw Florence inside her apartment, she stopped short and dropped both Steve Jobs and the Band-Aids.

"Oh, thanks so much. Sorry to bother you." Florence knelt, keeping her arm stiff, and scooped up the box. "I'll be out of here in a minute." She fumbled with the lid, her scalp already lined with sweat. Lori's hazy eyes burned through her. The woman looked so angry, she couldn't form words.

"Oops." Florence dropped the box, lid open. Band-Aids fluttered to the floor like tiny pamphlets.

"What's your name?" Lori whispered.

Florence tried picking them up, scraping her fingernails against the wood floor. For some reason, she couldn't look Lori in the eye. She now wished, far too late, that she hadn't agreed to this insane plan. Lori twitched like a cat. She swayed on her feet, more than a little drunk.

"Abby," Florence said. "Sorry again, I'm new here."

She managed to gather the loose Band-Aids and sweep them back inside the box. Lori did not offer help. Florence forced herself to really look at the woman who founded The Reader's Resort. The woman who outlived her husband, her husband's mistress, and decades of gossip and slander.

Lori was shorter than Florence, with a ragged mop of curly white hair. She wore a stained black dress and reminded Florence of the mad wife upstairs in *Jane Eyre*. A normal person would be utterly ashamed to appear like this in front of strangers, but Lori was uncaring, as if she hadn't removed the dress in a long time and had forgotten what it looked like.

"Thank you again, really." Florence stood, fitting a small Band-Aid on her palm. She had one chance to connect with Lori, so she used the only thing she could think of: the wristwatch from the suitcase. She'd picked it up before coming here. She needed a neutral way to get on Lori's side, even though she wasn't fully positive the watch had belonged to John.

"Is this yours? I found it, and someone said it might belong to you." Florence slipped the wristwatch from her pocket. She held it out, a peace offering, and prayed Lori wouldn't kill her in a drunken rage. She felt like Bilbo in the dragon's lair.

At the sight of the watch, the old woman deflated. She plucked it from Florence's hand, her skeletal fingers encapsulating it.

"John," she whispered. "My John."

Lori collapsed on the leather couch, her bones thin and knobby beneath her dress. "I forgot all about this watch. Isn't that something? The things we forget."

"I read about what happened to him," Florence said. "I can't begin to understand what you've gone through." *Empathy works, lay it on thick.* "Sorry if the watch brings back some bad memories."

"Mostly good ones." Lori set the watch on her wrist. "John loved this old thing. I bought it for him on our one-year anniversary, and I promised to love him 'till the end of *time*. Clever, huh?"

"Do you love him still?"

Lori nodded, sniffing. "'Till the end of time."

She offered nothing else, but Florence had to keep trying. Maybe she could discard the rumor that Lori killed John because of his affair. "I'm sure you miss him. Did one of you love books more than the other?"

Lori smiled. "He built this place for me. John read, of course, but not like I did. I... devoured."

"Was it hard to read after he passed?"

"Oh yes, I thought books would dull some of the pain, but it didn't work. Not like other things."

Like wine, Florence thought, standing up and setting the box of Band-Aids on the couch. "Is it hard hearing what people say about him, about this place being haunted? I imagine it drives you crazy, all those stories."

Lori glanced at her, the watch's face casting an eerie glow over her eyes. "Where did you say you found this?"

"Someone brought it to the lost and found."

"How did someone find this?" Lori asked no one.

Get out, Flo.

Florence stuttered, wondering if the watch had been a bad idea. "I don't know."

"This watch has been gone for over thirty years, so how did *you* get it?"

Get out, right now.

"The lost and found—"

"Oh, right." Lori nodded, picking up her cell phone. "Abby?"

Get out, Flo, right now. You stayed too long.

Florence momentarily forgot her fake name. "Um, yes?"

Lori held her phone to her ear. "Pat? You there?" She set the phone against her leg. "Please take these, dear, in case you need them." Lori grabbed the box of Band-Aids and held them out.

Go, just go.

Florence reached for the box right as Lori dropped it and wrapped her long fingers tightly around Florence's wrist. Lori brought the phone back to her ear. "Pat, there's someone in my room. She doesn't work here, and I don't know who she is."

Security.

Florence jerked her arm back, but Lori held on. "Please help, Pat!" Lori dropped the phone, heels digging against the floor.

"Let me go!" Florence tried pulling her arm back, but Lori clutched it tighter.

"*Who are you?*" Lori growled, her face twisting into an ugly mask of hatred. "And why are you asking about my husband!? Can I not live a single day without someone *accusing me of murder!?*"

"Let me go, please." Florence threw her weight backward, dragging Lori off the couch.

Lori slammed into the coffee table, knocking the ashtrays onto the floor. Her fingers loosened, letting Florence slip away.

Falling, scrambling on her hands and feet, Florence turned to face the old woman.

"I've seen Alyssa's ghost."

Lori turned to stone. Her jaw set. She didn't even blink.

Florence swallowed. How much time did she have? "She found a way back."

Still, nothing.

"Lori, I can help you. You already know Alyssa's back, don't you? I heard you yesterday, you were yelling at someone."

Florence remembered the voice in the dark passageway. *I know you're there.*

"She's upset with you, but you didn't kill her," Florence said. "Let me help you. Just tell me what happened, and Alyssa will go away. She just wants her family to know the truth. I'll believe you, Lori. If you tell me how Alyssa died."

Lori's face finally broke. She looked troubled. "Is she still insane?"

Insane? Florence paused. She wanted to say Alyssa was perfectly sane, but was that true?

Lori gave her a sad smile. "Oh, you poor thing, you have no clue what's going on, do you?"

Then Lori's cell phone rang—Pat from security.

Time's up, Flo.

Florence tore through the front door, accidentally kicking the little bell once again, and sending it straight into the wall, a blaring alarm through the entire fourth floor.

"Please!" Lori wailed. "Someone help!"

Florence sprinted down the plush carpet. The elevators dinged up ahead, and three men rushed out, pointing at her.

She veered into the stairwell door, taking one last look behind her.

Lori had edged into the hallway like a vampire afraid of daylight. She peered around the corner, only showing half her face. One bloodshot eye settled on Florence, and Lori's half-frown slowly curved into a smile.

Florence jumped down the stairs, skipping four or five steps at a time, her bones jarring with every landing. She kept her face down and her eyes away from the cameras.

The door flew open above her. "Stop!"

She came to the third floor and sprinted toward her room, her shoes imprinting a perfect black trail on the maroon carpet. Skipping to the side, she hugged the wall and avoided the light fixtures, anything to prevent leaving the tracks.

Her sweaty palm stuck to her jeans as she fumbled with the skeleton key. She unlocked her door, slid inside, and quietly shut it, locking the deadbolt. Curling up on the floor, she tried to breathe again. Her heart battered her ribcage; her lungs begged for air.

Voices neared her door, carried by squawking radios and curses. Then they faded away.

Florence crawled away from the door, finally breathing again, then rolled to her back and stared at the chandelier. She almost called Alyssa's name.

She almost closed her eyes and reached for her, but Lori's words rang endlessly inside her head.

You have no clue what's going on, do you?

The chandelier remained perfectly still. Did Lori already know who'd been sneaking around the secret passageway? Was Lori standing above her right now, staring down at Florence through the floor?

Chapter 36

Florence's phone kept buzzing inside her pocket. When her breathing returned to normal, she checked her notifications, seeing a dozen missed calls from Angel. They probably thought she'd been caught.

She called him back, and they put her on speaker phone.

"Are you okay?" Logan asked.

Florence sat up on the floor. "I think so. I made it back to my room."

"Security's been quiet the last few minutes," Angel said. "They don't know who you are, or Lori isn't pressing them to keep looking."

Florence feared it was the last one. She'd guessed correctly about Alyssa visiting Lori, maybe even taunting her, and for what? To get her confession? As unstable as Lori looked, Florence couldn't shake the feeling that the old woman was right: Florence didn't have a clue. And that needed to change.

"Florence?"

"Sorry," she whispered into the phone, now afraid Lori could somehow hear her. "You guys still there?"

"We're here," Logan said, sending a warm rush through her heart.

"Thank you. Okay, I don't know if Alyssa's going to talk to me anytime soon, and Lori confirmed that she's seeing Alyssa, too, so it's not just me."

"Holy shit," Angel said.

"Can we get into Frederick's room?" Florence asked.

The line was silent.

"Hello?"

"Yeah, sorry," Angel said, and Florence could almost picture his worried glances at the others. "You think we can find a link between him and Alyssa?"

Florence stood up, lowering her voice and keeping an eye on the hidden door behind the piano. "We have to try. Lori knows Alyssa's back, and I expected her to be afraid when I said that, because she has to know Alyssa could tell me things that would damage her, right?"

"How much do you trust Alyssa?" Mia asked. "Are we making a mistake?"

Florence thought of the scars carved into Alyssa's flesh. "No. Frederick killed her, and I think Lori knows about it. Maybe she's not worried because she knows we can't prove it."

No one knew what to say.

"Alyssa spent the last thirty-eight years dreaming of this chance," Florence said. "I don't know what she's going to do, but if we can't find anything proving her murder, she'll finish this herself, and I'm scared she won't care about the resort or who gets in her way."

On the other line, they broke into a string of whispers.

"Hold on," Logan was saying, "Angel!"

"Angel!" Mia shouted. "We have to talk about this!"

Angel's voice finally came through the phone. "I just called for a cart check on the radio. We have ten minutes, maybe fifteen, until Frederick shows up here. That's how we guarantee his room will be empty. This is by far our best chance. If we wait any longer, his shift will end, and we have to wait until tomorrow."

Florence sat on her bed. "How do we get into his room?"

"No, that's too dangerous," Logan said. "What if he finds out?"

"I need your help, Logan," she said. They didn't have time to keep weighing the risks. "Will you help me?"

He paused for so long, Florence was afraid he'd finally had enough.

"How do we get into his room?" Logan asked.

Angel chuckled. "Remember that janitor who keeps our private break area a secret?"

Logan sighed. "Dude."

"I owe him a few favors," Angel said.

Florence changed out of the resort uniform and threw on her rain jacket.

"But does he owe *you* any favors?" Logan demanded.

"Well, no, the point is, if he's willing to keep secrets, he'll keep one more. I just need to call him."

Florence stared at the hidden door. "Logan, Mia, if you're positive, absolutely positive you want to do this, meet me in the lobby in ten minutes, then we'll go downstairs. Angel, text me when we have an open door, and we'll need a room number."

"Ten minutes," Logan said, a hint of nervousness in his voice. "I'll be there."

"Me too," Mia said.

They hung up the phone, and Florence left her room. She stood outside her door for a minute, half-anticipating security to be waiting for her, but nothing happened. A few readers were waiting for the elevators.

She ducked into the stairwell and ran down to the first floor. The lobby was mostly empty, so Florence sat on the balcony steps and tried to hide behind the railing. She had no idea if security was still looking for her, but a man in a black T-shirt was addressing the workers at reception, and through the wooden bars, Florence could see him holding out his phone.

The stairwell door opened, and Logan and Mia quickly filed out. They waved to Florence, so she met them by the elevators, keeping her head down.

"We can go the long way to his room," Mia said. "I'll show you. We can get close and wait for Angel's signal."

She took off down the hallway. Florence and Logan fell in behind her.

"Thank you," Florence said. "For believing me."

Logan gently bumped into her shoulder. "I thought you weren't into this stuff?"

Florence knew he had questions, but that wasn't her concern right now. "It's been a long day."

"And plenty left to go." Logan smiled. He was dead wrong if he thought she'd give up answers that easily. But to his credit, he was starting to deserve some.

Mia opened a door to a different stairwell, marked EMPLOYEES ONLY. "This goes straight to the apartments," she explained, rushing down the steps. "Anything from Angel?"

Florence checked her phone. "He said room 62. Freddie Krueger in sight. Be safe."

They counted the numbers down the hallway and stopped in front of 62.

"If you have any doubts at all," Florence said, staring at the door, "now's the time to leave."

Mia twisted the doorknob and barged inside.

"We got your back," Logan said, "let's do this."

Florence entered the apartment, and Logan closed the door behind them.

The living room was a blur of 90s furniture, six pairs of work boots, a bicycle, and stacks of books on architecture and world history.

"Where do we start?" Mia asked, circling the kitchen.

Florence needed to slow down and think. They couldn't afford to waste time. She crouched in the living room and covered her eyes with her palms. Her heart was trying to race out of her chest.

Logan tapped her shoulder. "You okay?"

"One sec." She drifted in the darkness, bringing everything inside her brain down to a single point. Even Chloe, who lived inside her head, had nothing to say.

"We're looking for a souvenir," she said, keeping her eyes covered. "We can touch stuff only if we put it back. No light switches. We won't remember what it looked like before." She opened her eyes, seeing spots. "He wouldn't keep anything in the open. We stick to the bedroom and anywhere you'd hide something. Files, safes, lock boxes, even plastic containers. Anywhere you'd keep something precious."

Logan and Florence moved into the bedroom while Mia searched the closets.

The bedroom was mostly bare. Plain walls, two lamps. A VHS and DVD player, a large TV, and a nightstand covered in orange, white-capped prescription bottles.

"His closet," Logan said, pointing to the door in the corner. "Guy like this keeps it in his closet."

They opened the door, and a black-barreled shotgun fell to the floor.

Logan jumped back. "Sorry, that scared me."

Florence stepped over the gun and knelt. The closet shelves were filled with stacks of papers, mostly old tax forms. Clothes hung from the rack, a mix of T-shirts and old button-ups. A weathered pair of work boots was shoved in the corner, and beside them, baby clothes in plastic totes.

"We don't know anything about him," Florence said. "He could've had a kid, or these clothes were his when he was little."

Logan opened a shoe box, finding knick-knacks and random power cords inside. "What about this?"

"Dump it out," Florence said. "That's a good place to look."

She pushed clothes aside and found a black backpack hanging from a hook. She pulled it down and unzipped it. A boxy laptop was stuffed inside, along with a history textbook.

"There's nothing here," Florence said, returning the bag to the hook. "How are we supposed to find something this fast?" She stood up and scanned the bedroom again. "Anything yet, Mia?"

"Not yet!" Mia called. "Living room and kitchen are almost done."

"Shit." Florence spun in a circle. "Come on, where would you put it?" She left the bedroom and stood in front of the dark bathroom. Using her phone, she shined a flashlight inside.

The shower curtain was striped white and navy blue, with fabric on one side and a plastic liner on the other.

It's been almost forty years, Florence thought. *You don't have to hide your souvenir unless it's something obvious. What if you want to display it where only you can see?*

She moved into the bathroom, closer to the striped curtain.

"Not finding anything," Logan said from the bedroom. "Florence?"

She peeled the shower curtain back and shined her light inside.

On the tiled wall, facing the showerhead, a stained-glass picture hung from a hook. It was a woman in a white dress, jet-black hair covering her eyes, standing in a red ocean.

"What the hell?" Logan said over Florence's shoulder. "Why is that in here?"

Florence imagined Frederick standing in the shower, the hot water rinsing down his neck and back, his eyes glossing over the picture he'd seen thousands of times.

A woman in a sea of blood.

Florence handed her phone to Logan and carefully removed the picture from the wall. "We need to take this."

"He'll know," Logan said.

"We can't leave it."

"We have to! Florence, he'll know we were here!"

Florence took her phone back from Logan and walked into the hallway. "Look at the colors in this glass." She tapped the picture with her finger. "Why is the red color so dark? Why would he hang this picture in his *shower* if it didn't mean something very important to him?"

Logan nodded. "I'll admit, it's super weird and creepy, but what are we going to do once he finds out?"

"Working on it." Florence called Angel, who immediately answered.

"You guys got anything?"

Florence held the stained-glass in the light. "I think so. Where is he?"

"Over by the carts," Angel said. "It's weird though. He's been staring at his phone for five straight minutes."

Florence froze. The glass felt heavy in her hand. "What do you mean?"

"Like I said, he's watching something on his phone."

"Guys," Florence breathed. "Mia, Logan."

They were in the kitchen, having a hushed conversation of their own.

"Guys!"

They turned to look at her.

Florence peeked into the living room and spotted a compact video camera mounted in the corner above the front door. Florence stared at the small, dark eye and blinking red light.

"What?" Angel said over the phone.

"Angel, is there anyone else there with you?"

"Nah, but Frederick's looking at me right now, why?"

Florence couldn't take her eyes off the camera. She knew Logan and Mia had seen it too. They were caught.

"He left."

Florence adjusted the phone on her ear. "What?"

"He just left. What's wrong? Where are you guys?"

Florence hung up the phone and rushed out of the apartment with Logan and Mia, the glass image firmly in her hand.

Mia turned around. "What the hell do we do?"

Logan checked the hallway. "He can't report it, right? He wouldn't want anyone seeing that picture."

"That's what I'm hoping," Florence said, searching her brain for options. They were out of time.

"Or, Frederick will try to kill us," Logan said. "We need to leave the resort."

Florence paused. She knew how to fix this. In her heart, she knew the way out.

"Hide," she said, digging out her room key from her pocket and tossing it to Logan. "Meet me in 350, third floor. Understand?"

Logan frowned. "What are you doing?"

"Trust me, please. I'll meet you." She walked back inside Frederick's apartment and shut the door on her friends.

Feeling the camera on her, she ran into his bedroom and shut the door, blocking his ability to see or hear her.

"I found it," she said aloud. "Alyssa! I'm sorry about earlier! Can you hear me?"

Nothing happened.

If this didn't work, Florence had better figure out how to use the shotgun in the closet.

"Alyssa!"

The room shifted. A breeze fell over Florence's face, and Alyssa stood in the corner of the bedroom, her nightgown swaying in the unnatural wind.

"What about this?" Florence held up the stained-glass. "Have you seen it?"

Alyssa shook her head, her dark hair falling across her face.

"Look at the color." Florence handed the picture to Alyssa. "What if... what if he used your blood? Killers like that, don't they? They keep trophies and mementos. What if he took your blood?"

Alyssa's eyes widened. She pursed her lips, spilling blood down her chin, and slowly nodded her head.

Florence waited for the apartment door to open. "You're positive? He took blood from you?"

Alyssa nodded again, more eagerly this time. It was perfectly believable, given the amount of torture Alyssa sustained.

"If this can prove it, I'll take it to the police," Florence said. "Everyone, especially your family, will know he murdered you."

Alyssa handed the stained-glass back to Florence and pointed at the bedroom door.

Florence felt a knot form in her stomach. She hoped they were right about this. "He knows I'm here, Alyssa. He knows I found it."

Alyssa knew what she was asking. It wasn't fair, but hadn't this been Alyssa's plan all along?

"I'll tell them," Florence said, clutching the stained-glass picture to her chest. "Everyone will know."

Alyssa nodded and lightly pressed her palm against Florence's cheek. *Thank you*, she mouthed, sending a fresh wave of blood down her lips and throat. *Now go.*

Florence knew it might be wrong, but in the end, she didn't care. "He deserves it," she said, leaving the bedroom.

With a small smile, Alyssa gently nudged Florence toward the front door. She then walked into the kitchen. Florence left the apartment and shut the door, catching a glimpse of Alyssa standing barefoot in the kitchen, removing a grilling fork from the drawer.

Florence heard footsteps down the hall. She scrambled in the opposite direction, slipping into a narrow hallway and sinking to the ground.

She heard Frederick's apartment door open and slam shut. Before doubt crept in, before the hallway echoed with the sound of a dying man, Florence ran to the stairwell.

Chapter 37

Robert would no longer whisper his feelings through the pet door. The basement had no empathy for his thoughts; it was a cold, dark room created for things without beating hearts. It never wanted him down here, so it sent monsters to intimidate him; it tried to squeeze him out like skin refusing a splinter, and he'd happily leave and never return once he completed this final chore.

He checked the time. It was 9:00 p.m., and the resort had begun its shift changeover. The daytime people were heading home or locking themselves inside their apartments to shoot up or drink until they crashed into a black wall of nothingness (typical daytimers). Flushing their potential down the toilet with their vodka-soaked vomit. The night shift would take over, showing up to work already blitzed, because how else do you stay up all night?

No one worked in the main kitchen after dinner. The second-floor taco bar ran 24/7, but if you wanted a Cobb salad in the middle of the night, too bad.

Layla was in her apartment, doing a half-decent job of playing with Nathan. Robert kept checking the baby monitor on his phone, hoping Layla wouldn't notice the camera moving. He didn't completely trust her with his kid, but so far, she kept him entertained. Robert promised her he'd be back soon, but this would take as long as it needed to.

Earlier, Margo had dropped Nathan off with another remark about Nathan's safety at the resort.

Robert told her one problem at a time, and said it again to himself, standing in the basement, dangling the machete from his fingertips.

One problem at a time.

If everything went okay, Robert could finish the week here and keep a watchful eye on Florence's progress.

If not, then Robert would improvise.

He waited until the final footsteps receded from the kitchen above him. With the kitchen wrapped up, no one would be on this side of the main floor. Funny, not one chef closed the basement door or turned the light off. They knew he was down here; they saw him come through thirty minutes ago. He hadn't known them for long, but he'd still been their supervisor, and a damn good one at that. He knew about their families, their pets, and their past jobs.

No one cared to check on him. They left without saying goodbye.

Robert hid the machete on the shelf, beneath a bag of almonds. He picked up Dean's phone and found Charlie's name in his messages. He crafted a text.

Sorry, I've been sick and sleeping all day and couldn't call you back. I found something in the basement, and it concerns your parents. Come down here and see what I mean. You won't believe this.

Robert took a deep breath. The kitchen had gone completely quiet upstairs—no creaky footsteps, no conversations or little mop bucket wheels.

He sent the text with no doubt in his mind that Charlie would show up. Despite Robert's respect for the man, Charlie didn't have a clean view of reality. He grew up in a resort and never had the risk of losing everything.

He didn't have to spend thousands of hours honing a skill because he'd inherited the job.

Some people had to give up everything to chase their dreams.

Robert sat on the wooden chair and stared at the pet door. Fifteen minutes passed.

The ceiling groaned above him; footsteps crossed the kitchen floor.

"Dean?" Charlie called from the stairs. "You down there?"

Robert held his breath, reminding himself that this was necessary. If he wanted to keep Florence close, Charlie had to disappear. It was all part of the Journey.

"Dean?" Charlie descended cautiously. He wasn't entirely stupid. He stopped at the last step, glaring at Robert. "Where's Dean?"

"We found something," Robert said, reading from the script in his mind. "Dean and I were going through the shelves down here, reorganizing for the chefs, you know? And we found this." He waited for Charlie to relax a little. "Did you know there was a secret cellar down here?"

Charlie looked like someone had slapped him. He didn't know, and he knew *everything* about the hotel.

"It's right here." Robert pointed at the door behind the shelves. "It's unlocked. And empty, but it looks like someone might've lived in there once."

Charlie crossed the basement for a closer look, his better judgment nowhere in sight. Seriously, no one with an ounce of common sense would buy into this.

Charlie gawked at the door. "If I didn't know about this, I doubt anyone else does."

Yeah, yeah, you ignorant asshole, Robert thought. He nearly lunged for the machete right then, just to preserve his ears from another self-serving compliment, but the cellar was the goal here. No cleanup required in a secret room no one knew about. Easy-peasy.

Robert pulled the shelf out, creating enough space for Charlie to slip behind it. "Take a look. I think it could've been part of the original house, right? The one your parents built around?"

Charlie's eyes lit up, childlike. "That has to be it. This basement belonged to the old mansion."

Still, he didn't go behind the shelf. His better judgment was slowly waking up.

Robert quickly pulled his cell phone from his pocket. "Hey, it's Dean." He turned away from Charlie, pretending to answer his phone.

"Okay? Yeah, he's here." Robert glanced at Charlie, smiling.

Charlie edged behind the shelf, examining the cellar door.

Go on, walk inside, Robert thought. "Okay, yeah, okay, see you in a sec."

Robert put his phone back. "Dean's coming. He had to take a bathroom break... cause, you know..."

Charlie stared at the deadbolt and the rubber pet flap, yet he still opened the door. The dark cellar let out a sigh of putrid breath. Charlie activated the flashlight on his phone, then paused, finally getting smart. "Where's Dean?"

"He's almost here."

Charlie stood in the doorway, one foot in, one foot out. He understood something was wrong but couldn't fathom how or why something bad could ever happen to someone like him. Charlie blinked twice with the pale eyes of a cornered animal.

He had instincts. Good for him.

Charlie tried to move back out, away from the doorway, right as Robert stepped into the gap between the shelf and the door and shoved Charlie backward.

Charlie tripped over the doorway and staggered inside the cellar.

Too easy.

Robert grabbed the machete's handle and yanked it out, the blade screeching beautifully against the metal shelf and slicing open the bag of almonds. He ran to the doorway as Charlie kicked the door shut. It slammed in Robert's face. He twisted the doorknob and pushed, meeting resistance.

Charlie was using his body as a barricade.

Okay, not good.

Robert dropped to his knees, pushed the pet door back, and stabbed the machete through, feeling the blade sink into something soft. Probably Charlie's right leg. Charlie gasped, dropping his cell phone. Robert reached inside, found Charlie's ankle, and tripped him. Charlie's head ricocheted off the door on the way down, then finished with a muted thump on the dirt floor. Migraine material.

Charlie went limp, twitching. Lights out, but far from dead.

Robert rammed his body into the door, making a gap. The door was slowly pushing Charlie back. After a few attempts, Robert squeezed through the doorway. Charlie's phone, still lit up, showed 911 typed in, with CALL waiting to be pressed. If Charlie had been a split second quicker, he might've forced Robert to run. This was not, however, Charlie's day.

Robert dropped Charlie's phone in his pocket and looked down.

Charlie's eyes were open and blinking. "What is that?" he whispered, staring at something in the room.

Robert looked across the cellar, at the figure balled up in the corner, something with dirty pale arms and legs all twisted and curled like a dead spider. The thing moved. White eyes flashed at them.

The real world, as Robert understood it, abruptly halted.

The creature was real. It had been real this whole time, even though it never actually bit Robert's arm. Seeing it now, through Charlie's horrified expression, was like watching a nightmare come to life while you're wide awake. And you realize the nightmare's not playing by your rules because it doesn't belong in your world.

Robert dropped back, shoving himself through the narrow doorway, tossing the machete ahead of him so he didn't fall on it and cut himself to ribbons.

"Go, go, go," Charlie shrieked, his inner child bleeding through his voice. "Move!"

Robert wiggled backward and was almost clear of the doorway when the creature unfurled its arms and legs and crawled toward them. Once out of the cellar, Robert spun around, caught the square opening for the pet door with both hands, and slammed the door shut.

Charlie, still on the other side, was trying to stand on his injured leg. He jiggled the doorknob, his voice breaking, and pleaded for Robert's help.

Robert braced his feet against the wall and pulled, his hands keeping the pet door propped open, and allowing him to see the other side. Charlie fought to move the door, but it made no difference.

"Help!" Charlie screamed, punching the door.

Someone would hear them. Robert reached back, grabbed the machete, and aimed for the pet door.

The creature crawled closer—not a creature, a woman. She saw the machete in Robert's hand and tried to scream; nothing but a hoarse growl came out.

Robert stabbed Charlie's leg again, withdrew the blade, and as Charlie fell to the ground, Robert slashed through the pet door, finding the mark, the serrated steel catching on its way out.

Charlie couldn't speak. He pawed at his chest as if trying to brush off a bug. In the dim light, blood escaped Charlie like a water balloon with multiple leaks. The machete had snagged his throat.

The creature-woman knelt beside Charlie and cradled him in her arms, rocking him back and forth with a gurgle in her throat. Like she wanted to cry but had forgotten how.

All right then, not the response Robert had expected.

The woman wept, and how sweet it sounded! It meant Robert wasn't crazy. How afraid he'd been of losing his mind down here!

Crack goes the nutcracker; another one split, shattered, ground into dust. The basement tried to split his mind like a walnut, but he had a hard shell.

Should he lock the cellar door? Would it keep the disturbed woman stuck inside? He set the machete down and began reaching through the shelf when the door opened.

The woman stood eye-to-eye with him, caked in dirt and blood, fresh tear-trails on her dirty face. In the basement light, big, dark eyes filled those wide, malnourished sockets.

She looked familiar; someone he had seen around the resort, or in a picture somewhere.

Robert backed away. The woman stared at him, opening the door wider. Charlie's blood dripped from the hem of her old-fashioned nightgown. She looked at him with fiery pain.

He scooped up the machete and slashed the air behind him, but she hadn't pursued. She shut the cellar door, crying softly.

Chapter 38

Florence wanted to be alone. When she'd returned to her room, Logan and Mia peppered her with questions. All she could say was, "It's over." Even though Lori was still a loose end, one half of the mystery had been resolved.

After realizing she wasn't going to talk, Logan and Mia finished their shift with Angel.

Now, night had fallen, and Florence hadn't eaten or left her room. She'd called for Alyssa several times without an answer. The stained-glass image rested on her pillow, and looking at the dark red hues of the bloody sea made her stomach churn.

The resort was surprisingly unchanged. Whatever Alyssa did to Frederick made no impact on anyone else, and no one except her knew the truth. The others had guessed it, and Florence would tell them what happened, but for now, she had to find a way to live with it.

Logan knocked on the door. She opened it, expecting to see the others around the corner, but he'd come alone.

"Are you okay?" he asked.

The last few hours of waiting for Alyssa, talking to Chloe, and sitting alone had broken every defense Florence had ever built. She wrapped her arms around his neck and hugged him in the doorway, and when his arms encircled her waist and held her, it stirred a longing she didn't think existed.

"I'm sorry," Florence said, reluctantly letting him go. She shuffled to her bed and sat down. "I know I shut down earlier. That must've been jarring."

Logan sat beside her, their shoulders brushing. "I was terrified for you."

"Why?"

"Honestly, I thought maybe you killed him," he said. "But it was Alyssa, wasn't it?"

Florence nodded. "We think he used her blood in the stained-glass. We can get it tested, if we can also find her bones or other DNA. It's still a long shot, and even if we can never legally prove anything, we know Frederick did it, and I think the world will believe us."

Logan stared at his hands like he didn't know what to do with them. Maybe it was an exercise of self-control, but she didn't care; she wished he'd just be himself.

"Do you regret it?" he asked. "Do you regret anything we did today?"

"No."

"Why not?"

"Some people deserve to suffer, don't you think? For the things they've done?" His eyes burned through her, and she wondered if he'd known the truth from that first conversation.

He chuckled. "Florence, this would be a lot easier if you told me why you're here."

Florence didn't know where to begin, so she started with the worst of it. If she got past that, she could fight through the rest. She hoped he wouldn't run away after this because she was really starting to like him, and she didn't want to hide that anymore.

"My best friend overdosed when we were seventeen," she said. "We'd tried different drugs, you know, because when you're a teenager, you feel left out. I think that's the worst part. We weren't addicted to anything, we were just trying to fit in with people around us, like Chloe's friends."

Logan held her hand, his warm fingers gently resting between hers.

"I brought some Xanax over one night for a sleepover," she said, forging ahead. Trying to be brave. "Chloe's parents had no idea I was sleeping over because I came through her window, and it was a school night. We eventually passed out, or I did, at least. But Chloe mixed her pills with something her friends had given her."

She thought, *I woke up early in the morning and looked at her. There was vomit on her face and in her hair, and she was staring at me with dry eyes. The sheets were wet. When I moved, pills shifted on the bed, following me as I climbed off and cried on the floor.*

"Holy shit," Logan whispered, looking like he wanted to wrap her up in the warmest hug imaginable. She wouldn't complain if he did. These memories made her feel like the loneliest person alive.

"Did she kill herself?"

"No, it was an accident." Florence thought she might be sick, but she tried to keep talking because this was it: the weight, the dam breaking. She could feel the walls crumbling—walls she'd carefully built, brick by brick, to keep from falling apart.

"But she died alone, and no one deserves that. I was there, but I wasn't awake. And even when I woke up, I could've cleaned her face, I could've done anything to make it better. But I didn't." Tears dripped from her cheeks. "I left through the window and let her parents find her. How horrible is that? I went to the funeral, and her mom, Stephanie, asked me if Chloe had been unhappy. I didn't know what to say, I mean, I was a mess, I was broken. I couldn't look her in the eyes because she had no idea I'd been there and given her Xanax. To this day, she still believes Chloe killed herself. And this whole time I could've told her I was there, and that it was an accident. And that Chloe and I talked about our dreams, about coming here. And here's this woman who treated me like a daughter, who thought Chloe killed herself because she hated her family, and I've let Stephanie believe that lie for *nine* years."

Logan finally hugged her. "I'm so sorry, Florence," he said softly.

"What's wrong with me? How could I do that to her? How could I let her think Chloe hated her mom, and hated her own life enough to kill herself? I mean, it destroyed Stephanie's marriage. She fell apart, and I did *nothing* to help her."

"Come on, Florence, you were seventeen. If you went back in time as the person you are now, you would tell her, wouldn't you? You would do it differently. You were young and scared, and that makes you human. It doesn't make you a monster."

She didn't want to be defended. She wanted him to back away with disgust; to confirm that she deserved to suffer.

"This resort was Chloe's dream? Is that why you're here?"

Florence nodded. "Yeah, I came here to find her and tell her how sorry I am. For everything."

Eventually, after searching for the words, he looked at her with those endless dark eyes. "If you want my opinion, I think you're a beautiful, wonderful human being. And when we solve this case and become heroes, maybe I can get to know you better."

"Weren't you listening to what I just told you?"

"I heard every word. None of it changes my opinion of you."

She pressed her forehead to his shoulder, feeling his muscles tense.

"I don't want to be alone," she said. "Not tonight."

"Can I show you something?"

"Like what?"

"Like something." He held out his hand, waiting for her to take it.

If she took it, there would be no going back. She wanted more of him, all of him, hoping he could fix these broken pieces inside her. She knew it didn't work like that, but she'd stubbornly try. She'd do anything to feel whole again, so she took his hand.

"I don't want to get your hopes up," he said. "But if Chloe loved books, I might know where to look."

Her heart skipped. "Where?"

He smiled. "Come on. I'll show you."

Chapter 39

Robert had rocked Nathan to sleep while Layla watched a show on her phone. He felt Nathan's tiny heart beating against his chest and hugged him tighter, whispering how much he loved him.

He set Nathan inside the pack 'n play, helping him roll over, so his small fist rested against his chin. Robert brushed Nathan's hair off his forehead. How had it already been a year since his birth?

Killing a man makes you appreciate life's fragile nature. Humans are infinite until you see their blood run and their skin turn ashen gray. In addition, the proven demon in the cellar made Robert's head ache. He couldn't start down that path—he didn't have the time or brain capacity to understand the thing in the cellar. He never wanted to see it again.

While laying Nathan down, Charlie's phone had been comfortably resting in Robert's right pocket and was lighting up with notifications non-stop. Robert fished Charlie's phone out and scanned the texts and missed calls, all from his mother, Lori.

Who else would care about Charlie this much?

Accessing Dean's phone and texting people a bunch of excuses had mostly worked, and he'd been hoping to repeat the trick with Charlie. Now, he couldn't unlock the phone and had no way to deter Lori Walter. She would keep calling and texting until she went looking for her son. Or sent someone else. Either way, every new text felt like sand through an hourglass.

Where are you?

We need to talk NOW

Call me please

Charlie?

Call me back

More texts followed. Robert put the phone on the dresser, thinking. Had he been reckless, removing Charlie from the picture? Maybe he underestimated Charlie's importance to his mother. Maybe applying the old 'it worked with Dean' logic had been a huge misstep.

Even if the police didn't investigate Charlie's disappearance immediately, there was no telling what lengths Lori would take in the meantime. She'd want her son found, and not in twenty-four hours, but right NOW. And there was evidence. Two bodies, however discreetly tucked away, were still going to rot and smell. Robert had two phones currently in his possession—two traceable devices that would lead police straight to Layla's apartment.

The texts kept coming. Lori was having an emergency at the worst time imaginable.

He couldn't leave the resort and leave Florence behind, but he couldn't stay at the resort and wait to get caught. He couldn't kill Lori, either. Killing everyone wasn't the answer.

The lake house.

Robert smiled in the darkness. His life was already forfeit, but for a brief time, he could have everything he wanted.

He couldn't hide here any longer. He had an inkling of an answer, and it started with Layla, who was curled up in bed and still on her phone. With her AirPods in, the black and blue light slashed across her dull-eyed, expressionless face. Layla was always absorbed in her own little world. She didn't notice Robert staring at a phone that wasn't his, or that he left the phone on the dresser while it rang and rang.

She didn't notice anything.

Robert glanced at the phone, then back at Layla. The machete hung from his neck, with the sheath scratching against his side and the thin rope cutting into his skin. He crossed the room without tripping and stood over the bed.

"Scoot over."

Layla turned her back to him, rolled toward the wall, and continued with her phone.

He lifted the machete out from under his shirt and set it on the floor beside the bed, though he doubted he would need it. He bent down, quietly unsheathed it, and set the blade on the floor, tossing a few clothes over it. Sitting on the bed, he tapped Layla's shoulder.

She turned, removing one AirPod. "What?"

He briefly wondered if this part would be difficult, if forcing Layla to do what he wanted would take a toll on him. The old Robert might've thought that, but whoever resided inside his skull now hungered for it.

"I need the keys," he said.

"What?"

"The keys, the ones you carry around. Where do you keep them?"

Layla frowned. "Why do you need room keys?"

"So I can get inside Florence's room."

Layla shook her head. "You can't sneak into her room—what if someone catches you? Why would you even go there? What's *wrong* with you?"

Robert grabbed her wrists and pinned them to the mattress. "Just tell me where they are—"

"Robert, let go."

He tightened his hold. "I'm sorry, okay? I'm sorry to put you through this, but you know this means everything to me. Listen, I just want to see if she's reading. That's it. I won't talk to her—I won't do anything. Just observe. Is that wrong?"

"What if you get caught and fired? It's not worth it."

"Yes, it is."

"Is losing him worth it?" Layla glanced at Nathan, asleep in his pack 'n play.

Robert slapped her face. She cried out, which made him angrier. What if she woke Nathan up?

"Don't look at him. Look at me." He gripped her face, forcing her terrified eyes to focus on him. "I need the keys, babe. If I get caught, I'll say I stole them. This won't come back on you."

"It's wrong," she whispered pathetically.

His hand trembled against her face; his fingers kept trying to form a fist. "Is it worth saying no to me?"

A simple question for a simple woman, and boy, did it work.

"The front counter," she said. "There's a p-pink key on my keychain. It opens a drawer in the front counter. The backup keys are all there. One set for each floor."

Robert released her face. "See? That wasn't hard."

He rolled off and walked over to the dresser, where her keychain was. He wasn't worried she'd call security. She didn't have the courage for that because she'd have to admit her involvement in editing Florence's resort application.

Robert threw the keys in his pocket and turned around.

Layla sat on the edge of the bed, her small, bare feet on the floor. She held the machete in one hand. She must've stepped on it through the clothes.

"Whose blood is this, Robert?"

She showed him the blade, and even in the dim light of her phone he could see the crusty stains of Charlie's blood.

He said nothing. She should've stayed in bed.

She gripped the handle, pointing it at him. "What did you do?" Her voice wavered.

"I'm doing what I have to," he said because that was the truth, wasn't it? This all started with Dean punching him in the face. All this because of some bully's ego.

Layla shook her head, tears spilling down her face. Robert realized the look in her eyes wasn't fear, but acceptance. Even though she held the weapon, she knew she was already dead.

Robert crossed the distance between them in two strides. Layla jabbed at him quicker and harder than he would've thought. The blade raked along his side, scraping him through his shirt. Robert snatched her wrist and squeezed, throwing his other hand over her mouth to muffle her screams.

She was going to wake Nathan up.

The machete fell to the floor. Robert shoved her back, grabbed a pillow, and flipped it over her face. He climbed on top of her, pressing her limbs against the bed.

She thrashed beneath him, clawing his arms. He held the pillow firmly, using his weight to keep it sealed over her. She kicked and sobbed into the pillow, the muted cries of a trapped animal. Her nails cut his wrists, but he barely felt it. He was twice her weight; she never stood a chance.

After a while, the kicking turned to twitching. She'd soiled herself—the bed growing wet beneath his knees. Disgusting.

He rolled off, removed the pillow, and checked for a pulse, finding none. His eyeballs pulsed with adrenaline. He'd never felt so alive, so capable of anything.

Robert checked the pack 'n play, but Nathan slept soundly. Layla stared at the ceiling, mouth open, so he grabbed heaps of her clothes from the floor and dumped them on top of her. Maybe her clothes would bury the smell.

Charlie's phone kept ringing; Mommy dear needed her son.

No time to waste.

He checked himself in the mirror. Aside from scratches on his hands and one on his side, nothing was out of the ordinary. Just a regular guy finding his place in the world.

For you, he thought. *I did all this for you, Florence. Can't you see my devotion?*

He left the apartment, locked the door, and checked the baby monitor on his phone. The night was young, and he had plenty of work to do.

Chapter 40

Logan loved the feeling of Florence's fingers intertwined with his. He led her down to the lower level, into a hallway dimly lit by a flickering fluorescent light and the red glow of the badge scanner.

"We told you we shelve books, right?"

Florence nodded. "Book inventory? Book storage? Something like that."

"We made it sound boring." Logan scanned his badge. "I don't think you'll feel that way."

"Will you get in trouble for bringing me down here? You can't lose your bet!"

"I won't lose it. No one will know."

He held the door and let her walk inside first. She made it three steps before pausing and cupping her hands over her mouth. She gazed at the tall shelves with pure, unburdened wonder. Why did she hide this version of herself? Logan wished he could say or do the right thing to permanently unlock this part of her.

The stringed lights reflected in her eyes. "Logan…"

"I know, we really undersold this earlier."

She walked into the nearest aisle and brushed her hand along the smooth ladder rungs. "She would've loved this, Logan. I mean, she would've given anything to be right here."

His heart ached for her. "She's not here, is she?"

"Maybe not." Florence sniffed, wiping her eyes on her rain jacket sleeve. "But I'll tell her about it when I see her. If she's already in Heaven, I hope it looks like this."

Logan nodded, words failing him.

Florence grabbed his hand, smiling. "Can you push me?"

"What?"

Florence jumped onto the ladder and climbed halfway up. "Push me!"

Logan looked up at her. "Like a small push?"

"Just push it!" She held the rungs with both hands, hugging the ladder with her body.

Logan shoved it and watched her glide away before losing momentum.

"Push it again!" Florence climbed a little higher.

Logan had an idea that she would either love or hate, so he decided to go for it. Like with Angel earlier—if the work didn't save you, even for a day, then nothing would. Florence didn't need saving; she needed peace, a small dose to keep her going.

But his face gave him away.

"Why are you smiling like that? I don't trust that face you're making."

He started walking with the ladder in hand. She clutched the rungs and laughed. "What are you doing?"

"Hang on." Switching to a jog, the ladder rolled smoothly alongside him.

Florence stared at the end of the aisle. "Logan, it's going to knock me off!"

He gave the ladder one final shove. As the ladder left his fingertips, he realized he'd made a horrific mistake and was about to get her killed.

The ladder swung around the bend, taking Florence with it and disappearing to the other side.

Logan followed the steel rails around the corner. The ladder was empty.

Florence jumped at him, punching his arm. "You jerk!"

"It was all under control." He laughed, climbing the ladder. "My turn. You can get me back now."

Shaking her head—but still smiling!—Florence took off running with both hands on the ladder. Logan's hair rippled in the wind. He wrapped one arm around the ladder and let his other arm hang free, feeling a rush of magic as real as the golden light slipping through his fingers. There was nowhere else on earth he'd rather be, and no one he'd rather be with.

He drifted farther from the rungs, feeling a little like flying.

But Florence didn't let go. Running at full speed, she jumped onto the ladder with him and climbed the rungs, stepping on his toes. She grabbed his shoulders and clung to him. He wrapped his free arm around her waist, taking in her flushed cheeks, her warm body, and that same golden magic in her eyes.

Before he could move, she stood on her toes and kissed him. They rode the ladder like stowaways on a train, and everything inside Logan melted. Sliding her arms around his neck, she kissed him again, holding him captive. He wished she'd hold him here forever.

She hugged him, her cheek against his wild heart, as the ladder finally stopped.

"Thank you," she said.

"For what?"

"You know what." She jumped off the ladder. "I can't believe you work here!"

"Honestly, same here." He climbed down, took her hand, and walked to the golf carts. "You won't believe this, either."

"They have bookcases on them!" Florence gawked at the carts. "You *drive* these around here?"

"Yes, and they are even more dangerous than they look. Wanna take a ride?"

"Are you serious? Logan, you're going to get fired."

"Come on." He patted the seat beside him. "No one will care."

She sat down and held onto his arm.

He drove through the center aisle, surrounded by endless books and ladders, and had to keep his eyes forward (which was hard—he loved her reactions). Driving down The Shire, he explained how they organized the books, but Florence had stopped listening. She held the handle grip for balance and leaned out of the cart. Logan maneuvered closer to the wall of books, her fingertips gliding across the spines. She didn't want an explanation of how things worked; she wanted to be lost.

"Whoa, what the hell?"

Logan hit the brakes and nearly sent Florence flying off the cart. She managed to pull herself back inside, pale with shock.

Angel stood at the far side of the aisle, arms crossed. "This is what you guys have been doing instead of coming to my place for drinks?"

Logan shrugged. Of all people, *Angel* couldn't be mad at this. "I'm giving her a tour."

"Bro, that's my job. Get the hell out of my cart."

"Sorry, man." Logan jumped out, rolling his eyes. Florence smiled at him.

Angel slid into the driver's seat, nodding at Florence. "I'm sorry about him. He's a little misguided."

"Hey—"

"Furthermore!" Angel held up a finger. "Logan, you owe me for ditching us. Mia's at my place with the drinks. Go help her bring them back, and we'll meet at the hangout. I'll finish this."

Logan grinned and walked away, even though he didn't want to leave Florence's side. He left the stacks and carried the magic with him, on his lips and in his heart.

Please never end, he thought. *Why can't this last forever?*

Chapter 41

Robert checked his phone. The baby monitor showed Nathan peacefully asleep with a mountain of clothes on the bed behind him. Robert should have felt bad about leaving his son in the same room as a corpse, but what choice did he have? He'd get Nathan soon enough, pack up the car, and never come back.

He walked into the empty lobby. Zachery, the laziest reception clerk Robert had ever seen, watched Netflix on his phone. The sounds of a party echoed through the halls. The ballroom was always lively this time of night.

Zachery glanced his way. "'Sup Robert?"

"Slow night?"

"I'm so bored." Zachery sighed, pausing the show he'd been watching.

"Don't mind me." Robert moved behind the counter, scanning the drawers. "I left something here earlier, and I can't remember which drawer I put it in."

"Need help?"

"Nah, man, do your thing." Robert flipped open a few unlocked drawers, playing the part.

"I'll find it, don't worry about me. Thank you, though."

"No problem." Zachery continued watching TV, the sound bleeding through his AirPods. He had it turned up loud. Kids like Layla and Zachery were part of a distracted generation. Sure, millennials owned their fair share of the blame, with phones and computers and all, but good God, Robert could at least pay attention to his surroundings.

He withdrew Layla's pink key, found a locked drawer, and turned the lock quietly. Zachery looked at his phone, his eyelids half-shut. Receptionist of the year, ladies and gentlemen. Whatever little they were paying him, it was too much.

Robert opened the drawer, finding large key rings with tags. F1 to F4. He thumbed across the tags, found F3, and lifted the key ring out. Ironically, Layla kept an organized key system. You had to in this place.

He closed the drawer and locked it, stuffing the keys in his pocket as he walked away.

Zachery didn't notice. He glanced up and waved to Robert.

Robert waved back, slipping inside the stairwell and walking to the third floor.

Now for the big question: was Florence in her room?

If so, then she must be reading. Robert knew she wasn't at the ballroom party like the other girls—laughing and smiling and begging for attention—no, she wasn't like those other girls at all.

She was reading his books, snuggled up in bed with a drink.

Following the hallway down, he stopped at her door for a quick wellness check.

He knocked three times. "Housekeeping!" Then he ran around the bend, waiting to hear the deadbolt click.

Housekeeping never came this late, but Florence wouldn't suspect a thing. Only, nothing happened.

He waited two minutes before going back to the door and leaning against it; silence on the other side. No calling out, running shower, or footsteps. Not even the sliding balcony door.

Where was she? He knocked again. "Housekeeping!"

Was she ignoring him? He knelt, his face against the plush carpet, and tried to see through the tiny gap beneath her door. No light whatsoever.

He unlocked the deadbolt naturally, like he belonged there. If she called out, he'd apologize for the misunderstanding and leave. No harm done.

Robert slipped inside the room and flipped on the light. He was greeted by a gust of warm air and perfume.

No sign of Florence, but her suitcase and backpack were slumped over on the floor. Her purse, which she had at the café this morning, was gone. Robert forced himself to breathe. Whenever he'd looked for her, she was never in her room. Why was that?

This was Alyssa Larkin's old room. They had remodeled it two years ago and added a 1940s-style room to the roster. At Robert's request, Layla edited Florence's room selection—something even Charlie didn't catch.

Robert picked this room for two reasons: Florence was an old-fashioned girl, *and* she loved mysteries. What better mystery than a thirty-eight-year-old disappearance? A rumored murder/suicide with decades of built-in theories, misinformation, and ghost stories attached to it? Did Florence have any clue as to the significance of this room? No. The room itself held no secrets, just memories buried in the small dents in the walls and scrapes on the wood floors. Florence would never know the nuanced approach he took to curating her bookshelf. Once he explained it to her, she'd understand his level of commitment.

He checked the bookshelf, but the books were in perfect order, lined up, and untouched. No replacements. Maybe she had read one of the books already and put it back on the shelf, but he knew that wasn't true. He'd seen her twice now out in the resort, and she wasn't reading either time.

Robert tried to get his heart rate down before he threw something. There could be a million explanations for why she wasn't reading, and none of them had anything to do with his book list.

For example, it could be related to the creepy messages written on the mirror. What was *that* about? Or, the guy from earlier was still bothering her. Not good, either way, but fixable.

Robert fell on her bed and filled his lungs with her smell.

Not long now. He had to be patient if he wanted this to work. Unfortunately, the resort had failed Florence and only provided endless distractions instead of the perfect reading atmosphere.

Robert would soon rectify that.

He rolled off the bed, left the room, and locked the door.

Only one thing bothered him: If she wasn't in her room, then where was she?

Chapter 42

Florence got to experience *The Tour*, where Angel put on his best theater and managed to thoroughly entertain her. But aside from the part on the mechanical dumbwaiters (those were fascinating), she struggled to pay attention. The aisles seemed to go on forever. The ladders, polished and regimented, glowed with a dark, inviting aura.

The stacks stole her heart. She'd never seen anything so beautifully mesmerizing.

Angel stopped the cart. "Got any questions?"

Where to even start? "I just can't get over it. I couldn't work here. I'd be looking at books the entire time."

"I get distracted bad, especially by new releases. Speaking of books, what's your bookshelf like? I know you've got your hands full with this case, but did you start reading before that?"

"To be honest, the books didn't interest me. But my best friend died when I was a teenager, and I came here for her. So, my expectations were a little unrealistic." What happened to her? When did she become so honest with strangers?

Angel nodded. "I get it. This place is magic. It's easy to forget that books are just books."

"I thought you were obsessed with books!"

"I am, but there's a difference."

"What difference?"

Angel leaned over the steering wheel, looking at the shelves. "Most people are wrong about reading. They think books are for escaping, like the reader is going somewhere for a while."

"Is that not true?"

"It is true, but not to the extent people hope for. See, books are not destinations. Books are keys, and keys unlock doors, you see?"

"Maybe?"

"You can't live inside a book, no matter how hard you try. You can't live inside a dream, either. You wake up eventually."

"Sure."

"Books are keys, right. They get you from point A to point B. It's a magical, dream-like roller-coaster, yes, but it's fleeting. The book ends, you throw it on the shelf, and you read the next thing. Another key, another open door, another adventure. The real question is not 'What book can I escape into?' The real question is 'Where is this book taking me? Who will I be when it's over? How will my life look different after this?'"

"Are you saying it's not about the book?"

"Bingo. Even some authors will admit it. It's really not about the book. It's about the reader."

Florence thought she knew what he meant. "So, what does that change?"

Angel started driving again. "You're the reader, you tell me. Where are you trying to go?"

She didn't know, but she had a feeling. The last nine years had been leading her somewhere, even though she'd taken the long route to get there. She could feel the magnetic pull, the gut-feeling that she needed to do something incredibly hard, something that terrified her. Not just to find Chloe, but something more.

"Reconciliation," she said.

Angel smiled, like he expected nothing less. "I got just the thing."

He drove three aisles over, pulling into Arrakis. He parked, walked along the shelf, and stared at the books. He plucked a small paperback from the bottom shelf and handed it to her.

"Keep it. I can mark out a book once a quarter. Employee perk. This one's all yours. I got too many books anyways."

Florence read the title. "*The Heart is a Lonely Hunter.*"

"By Carson McCullers. You read it?"

She shook her head.

"Read it."

"Where will it take me?"

"It's a key, remember? It'll open the right door at the right time."

When Florence thought back to her relationship with Chloe, Angel's words finally clicked. Their relationship changed after *Jane Eyre*. The book and movie nights built a stronger friendship than either of them had experienced before. *Jane Eyre* was the key. And as much time as Florence spent dreaming of Thornfield, she never wanted to live in that world, but only pass through, in a dream or as a ghost.

"Thank you for this, and the tour, and the philosophy lesson."

Angel beamed. "No problem. Just promise me you'll read it and remember that it's only a key."

"I will."

Mia and Logan came through the double doors with a drink in each hand, cheering.

"Rum and Coke, right?" Logan handed Florence an ice-filled glass and raised his beer bottle to Angel. "You're the best, man."

Mia sipped something the color of pineapple. Angel took a dry whiskey. He lifted his glass to them. "To us. To solving this."

Florence drank, secretly hoping they'd all stop thinking about the case and enjoy their night. Part of her felt guilty about Frederick's death. Lori's warning hadn't left the back of her mind. What if she'd gotten this all wrong? Tomorrow, she'd take the stained-glass image to the police and make up a story about how she found it. She would contact Alyssa's family and confirm what they already knew: Alyssa Larkin had been murdered.

But for now, Florence would leave it alone. She wanted everyone to enjoy this morbid victory.

They migrated over to the secret hangout and sat in the old diner booth. Florence and Logan on one side, Angel and Mia on the other. Logan kept bumping into Florence 'by accident.' Not that she minded. She loved having him close. She wanted to hold his hand, kiss him again, and let herself believe that fairy tales are real and good things last forever.

Florence took it all in: this weird club, this guy who kept stealing her attention, this room; the books, the gold light. Chloe could not have imagined a more radiant paradise.

I miss you, Florence thought, bringing herself back to the people in front of her.

"I need to eat," Mia said. "We need snacks."

Angel sipped his drink. "Screw that. We need food. We could order pizza or something. I think they deliver out here."

"I'd go for tacos again," Logan said.

Mia nodded. "Yes please."

"Who's gonna drive?" Angel took a long swig of his glass, followed by a sigh. "Not me."

"I got it," Florence said, the perfect idea forming in her head. "Listen, I'll be right back. Trust me." She tossed her new book inside her purse, picked up her drink, and left the stacks.

In the hallway, the elevators waited with their doors open.

No thank you.

She took the stairs to the second floor, the faint thump of music bleeding through the walls.

The nightly parties seemed like fun, but she wasn't much of a party person. She'd rather be in the stacks, directly beneath the party, with the people she was starting to care about.

Florence walked down the second-floor hallway, finding one of the closets Angel mentioned on the tour. He said they had one on every floor. She opened the door and found the dumbwaiter system, the closed outer doors marked with EMPLOYEES ONLY.

Now that she knew where to find it, she took a drink and set her rum and Coke on the floor. She walked to the end of the hallway, where a small kitchen and cafeteria served a 24/7 taco bar. After digging through her purse and scanning her badge, she collected four plastic plates and loaded them up with tacos. She asked the worker on duty if she could borrow a tray, and the worker gave her one, no questions asked.

Florence filled the tray with the four plates and carried it down the hallway. Placing the tray inside the dumbwaiter, she hit the S button. The dumbwaiter rumbled down. She closed the outer doors, picked up her drink, and left the closet, nearly colliding with a man in the hallway. He'd been checking his phone, and he dropped it when he saw her, visibly shaking.

"Sorry, didn't mean to scare you." She picked up his phone, the screen showing what looked like a crib inside a messy room. She handed it back to him.

The phone quickly disappeared inside his pocket. "Hey, Florence."

It was him. The man from the café this morning, her curator. What was his name? Robert?

Had he been looking for her? "Can I help you?"

Robert smiled. "I'm sorry to spring this on you. But I wanted to know what you think of your books. I'm new here, so I'm a little insecure about my picks."

"I like them," was all she could say. She wanted to get away from him. He stared too intently. For too long. Like he knew everything about her. And he probably did.

"Good, good."

Why was he sweating?

"Have you read any yet? You haven't updated the app."

The app? The resort's reading tracker?

"I need to use it more," she said, moving around him.

"Are you at the party downstairs?" He pointed at the drink in her hand. "Or sneaking off for a little reading time?"

Her skin crawled. She glanced at the drink. "Yeah, I was at the party."

"Oh, I'm surprised."

Why would that surprise him? She kept moving away. "I might read a little now, though. So."

He glanced at the book inside her open purse, his eyes glazing over. "Where did you get that?"

"What do you mean?"

"That's not one of your books."

"Someone gave it to me," she said, starting to rush her sentences. "He recommended it."

Robert gazed at the book, stunned. She realized now how awkward it would be, seeing a reader choose something other than the twenty books diligently researched and poured over.

"I have to go." She turned around.

"Do you like your room?"

She paused. How much did he know about her? What information could he access? "It's fine."

"It's old-fashioned." He followed her, his shoes swishing on the carpet. "You like old-fashioned."

She didn't have a response to that, other than running away.

"I thought you'd like *Rules of Civility*. You remind me so much of Katey."

Her stomach lurched. She needed him to leave.

"I hope you'll read it, and if you want, you can tell me what you think of it." He was standing behind her now. His shadow over hers. "We like a lot of the same books. Maybe we can talk about them sometime."

"I really have to go." She rushed toward the elevators, both of which had been waiting for her. She ducked inside, pressed the LL button, and the doors began to close.

A hand appeared in the gap, and the doors retracted. Robert stepped inside, saying nothing. Florence couldn't breathe properly. She pushed the buttons again with an unsteady hand, wishing she could shove him out of the elevator.

Robert stared through the glass walls as the elevator sank through the floors.

She stepped out on the lower level, realizing her mistake. Guests didn't belong down here, and now Robert knew what she was up to. She sent Angel a quick text to let her back inside the stacks. The hallway was too short and narrow and reminded her of how she ran through here earlier, afraid Frederick was following her.

The double doors were a dead end unless Angel opened them. Florence heard Robert's shoes behind her. She wanted him to leave, but she didn't trust turning her back to him. Leaning against the wall, she pretended to ignore him.

"It was great seeing you again," Robert whispered. "Goodnight, Florence." He slowly shuffled away from her.

The double doors opened, and Logan came through, holding an empty beer bottle with the label half-peeled off.

"Hey, I was getting worried." He stopped short. "That was amazing, by the way, sending the tacos down the dumbwaiter. I'm pretty sure you made everyone's night." He followed her eyes down the hallway.

Robert turned briefly, looking them over, then disappeared around the corner.

"Is that the guy from this morning?"

"Yeah, my curator. He keeps wanting to know what I think of the books."

Logan cocked his head to the side. "Again? Well, that's not okay. We should tell someone. Report it to the GM or something."

"Yeah, maybe." She grabbed his hand. She didn't want to think about it anymore. He was just a creepy guy. "I'm ready for tacos, though."

Logan smiled, his worries melting away. "They love you, you know. I think they want you to work in the stacks."

"And what would you think of that?"

"I'd say it's a terrible idea," he said.

"Why?"

"Because I'd never get any work done." He tugged on her hand, leading her into the stacks. "Then they'd have to fire me."

"You're getting fired for letting me in here anyways."

He laughed. "That's probably true. But you impersonated an employee earlier, so they'll kick us both out."

"That doesn't sound so bad." She looked back at the hallway as the doors shut.

Maybe it was her imagination, but she thought she heard someone walking and imagined Robert just around the corner, listening.

Chapter 43

Robert waited in the hallway as the doors swung shut, locking him out of the stacks. He pressed his ear to the door, catching numerous voices, mostly Angel, who was always obnoxiously loud.

An employee party in the stacks, with a resort guest? The same guy from the café was in there. He showed her the stacks, didn't he? She *would* be impressed by that. Of course she would love an old-fashioned library.

Robert wished he had thought of it himself.

These employees were stealing her time, getting her drunk, and giving her books not on her bookshelf.

It was the *book* that made him fume with rage. Who the hell was Carson McCullers? Florence would never focus on reading, on changing her life, if people like Angel and the new guy kept distracting her.

If Florence couldn't focus in the world's most intensive reading environment, then Robert would remove every single distraction until she could read in peace.

He entered Layla's apartment, gagging at the smell of feces and piss seeping through the mattress, ruining a perfectly good bed.

Then he sat beside Nathan and watched his chest rise and fall.

Seeing Florence with the stackers confirmed everything. His plan would fix Florence. He wasn't just a curator, but a guardian, and what better addition to his Hero's Journey than a damsel in distress?

He would take Florence somewhere quiet. The Reader's Resort worked for a lot of people, but its glamour had proved too enticing this time.

"It's for your own good," he whispered.

His old co-worker had a lake house in Maine, and although Robert never accepted the numerous invites to vacation up there, he knew its location. The house stayed empty through the winter, and winter was nearly here. It was the perfect hiding place—an isolated, rugged getaway.

The whole country would be looking for them. Nathan would come along, of course, and Florence could help with him. Was she good with children? Would she make a good mother?

Naturally, she'd likely resist this plan. It would have to be forced, at first. Once they reached the lake house, he could set up a baby monitor in a locked room and give her instructions on what to read. A little schedule to help her along. He could keep a close eye on her. No distractions.

Once she was far away from the resort and her new friends were silenced, everything would align. She'd read. She'd fall in love with his books, and maybe even fall in love with him.

His stomach fluttering, Robert smiled, leaned inside the pack 'n play, and kissed Nathan's soft forehead. He had the key. He would wait in her bedroom for her to stumble in, drunk, that other guy not far behind. Robert fit the machete inside the sheath and wore it under his shirt, against his side.

He was going to need it.

Chapter 44

They lounged in chairs and hammocks, drinking round two and eating the tacos. Logan barely touched his food; his stomach gnawed at a bad feeling. Like when you have a dream someone is chasing you, and no matter where you go, you feel them close behind. Even worse, Florence wasn't fully relaxed either. She didn't want to leave them for a second taco run. She kept looking down the aisles, toward the entrance, as if waiting for that man to return.

Logan finished his third beer, his own mind preoccupied for similar reasons. Did Florence see the slow anger building inside him? Maybe it was an overreaction because he liked Florence a lot but seeing that brief flash of fear on her face gave him borderline psychopathic thoughts about protecting her.

Even when they were discussing theories about Lori and Alyssa, Logan wanted to participate, but his thoughts wouldn't leave him alone. Something was very, very wrong with Florence's curator. What if he'd been following her ever since she arrived? Stalking her from room to room? It almost sounded absurd, but not after everything Logan had gone through today.

They stacked the plates beside the empty glasses and beer bottles.

"I think Florence is, hands down, no competition, the coolest guest we've ever let in here." Angel gave a little bow.

Florence blushed. "You invite people down here often?"

"No." Angel smiled. "Almost never. I *did* say there was no competition."

"Rude." Mia swatted his arm. "I think you're one of us, Florence. Come visit all the time, please."

"I think Mia gets bored of us simpletons," Logan said.

"We just can't compete with her peers at school." Angel swiped one of her notecards, not even trying to pronounce the term written on it. "She's surrounded by fellow geniuses there, then has to come here and deal with *us*."

"I'm no genius," Mia said. "I have a bad grade in cardiology. Fail test, bye-bye degree."

The room quieted.

"You didn't tell me that." Angel frowned. "When's the test?"

"Two days."

"Well shit, you gotta study. What the hell are we still doing here?" Angel looked at the notecard in his hands, lips moving, trying to sound it out.

"Angel, stop."

He glared at Mia. "No, you're not failing that test. Are you serious? You've worked your ass off for this. This is your way out of here. Come on, this place is cool, and I'll be depressed when you leave, but you don't want to be here forever. This," he said and tapped the notecard, "this is what you want."

"We don't always get what we want." She clenched her jaw, daring him to deny it.

He didn't. He smoothed the notecard over in his hand.

"I don't know what I want, Angel."

"We'll run through the cards right now, then again in the morning."

"I'll help," Logan said. "I'll even pronounce them correctly."

Surprisingly, Angel ignored the insult. He stood up, stretching. "This has been a total blast, guys, but we got work to do."

"*Angel*."

Everyone paused at Mia's tone. "I don't know what I want."

Angel blinked at her, totally clueless. Logan wondered if these two had ever had a serious conversation, or if this was their first.

Angel held out the notecard. "Can I help you study, for now? Until you figure it out?"

Mia nodded, her eyes slightly red from emotion or alcohol or both.

"I should try Alyssa one more time," Florence said, standing. "She might meet me in the room."

Logan stood with her. He collected his beer bottles while Florence grabbed her empty glasses.

"Thanks again for what you all did today," Florence said. "You helped Alyssa as much as I did."

"Nah, we got more to do." Angel gestured to the space around them. "We'll pick it up tomorrow. Whatever you need, Florence. We got your back."

Logan nodded. "Goodnight, guys."

Angel sat back down, swiping the entire stack of notecards from Mia's hands.

Logan and Florence walked to the double doors.

"Will you walk me to my room?" she asked, tilting her head a little, as if he needed any help remembering last night.

He pictured them together in her bed, a little drunk, a little timid, until they would laugh and kiss and treat each other's bodies like rare, precious terrain. Yes, he wanted to see her without her clothes. He wanted to unzip that rain jacket and kiss her neck and know what her hands felt like on his body. He wanted that wholeheartedly, and his hesitation was already driving a wedge between them. Florence started to look embarrassed.

"Florence, I owe you an apology."

Her face fell, betrayal setting in.

Logan thought of what she confessed to him earlier about Chloe, and how it must've felt like removing a splinter from her soul. "I told my brother I'd do two things for one year: work this job and stay single. Two rules, not one. I agreed to it because I was in a serious relationship a year ago, and it nearly killed me. I'm trying to do things right, for once. The point is, I like you, and I don't want to mess this up. So, I'm coming clean."

Her mouth twitched. "Are there more secrets?"

"No, this is it. Now you know where I stand."

"What did she do to you?" Florence asked softly.

He sighed, biting his lip. "She cheated."

She embraced him so quickly, it knocked him back. Her hair was in his face, her cheek against his heart. "I'm sorry, Logan."

"It's okay. I didn't handle it well."

"Does anyone?"

They broke apart. Logan leaned in, kissing her lips. "I know I just said all that, but I still want to come up with you."

"Are you sure?"

"Yes."

"What about your bet?" She kissed him again, harder. "I don't want you to blame me for your soul-destroying office job."

He laughed. "Okay, okay, I get it. I'm overreacting about the job."

"I'm just saying."

"I want to come up," he said again. "Give me your glass, thank you. And one more kiss, and I'll drop these off at Angel's and catch up with you. Just... give me a few minutes. Deal?"

Florence kissed his cheek, no suspicion in her eyes. "See you there."

Logan watched her walk away, unable to shake that small voice. *This is a mistake, buddy. You're stuck in a summer camp fantasy.*

I know, he thought. *But right now, I don't care.*

He hoped she wouldn't be angry with him when he showed up late.

He had something to do first.

Chapter 45

Florence entered her room and noticed the chandelier was on. She thought she'd flipped the switch on her way out, but now she couldn't remember. It was all a blur anyway—her conversation with Logan, the stacks, the kiss, the drinking, and finally the alarming curator she was trying hard to forget.

She flopped on the bed and stared at the ceiling, slightly giddy from that last kiss. She wanted Logan here, on the lumpy mattress, but she should try Alyssa one more time.

The chandelier didn't even flinch. Lori was either sleeping or dead after all the stress Florence had caused her today. It all amounted to nothing anyway because Lori still refused to talk.

"How can I get Lori to tell me her side?" Florence asked. "Alyssa? You there?"

The room stayed the same.

"Chloe? Can you hear me?"

No sound. Even the hallway outside was perfectly silent. Florence thought the footsteps were in her head at first, but they continued in small, hesitating batches. *Step step* pause. *Step step* pause.

The chandelier remained perfectly still.

It's the passageway, Florence thought. *Someone's inside it.*

Florence slid to the floor, crawled under her bed, and triggered the secret door. It swung backward, and she saw a flash of bare feet pounding up the wooden steps.

Without thinking, Florence climbed over the piano and plunged into the passageway. She entered the corridor as the door on the opposite wall slammed shut.

Florence felt the wall for a handle, finding a small latch she'd missed earlier. She pulled it, pushed the door open, and came face-to-face with Lori Walter for the second time that day.

Lori skittered away from the door, jabbing a finger at Florence. "Where is she?" Lori wore a fluffy coat over her wine-stained dress.

Florence stepped inside the apartment, raising her hands. "Why were you outside my room?"

Lori stumbled around to the other side of the couch. "I heard noises in there yesterday. I thought it was her, but she showed you how to get in, didn't she?"

Florence edged around the couch, trying to stand tall. She had six inches on Lori and would use every bit of it. "How many times has Alyssa been here?"

"I keep seeing her," Lori muttered. "Always the same, always smiling at me like she used to."

Alyssa wasn't going to stop until she got what she wanted. If she'd spent the last two days toying with Lori's psyche, a part of her probably enjoyed it. She wanted Lori to snap.

Florence pointed to the secret passageway. "After I came here earlier, did you know I was staying in Alyssa's old room?"

"I had a hunch."

"Why didn't you tell security?"

"Because you told me you were seeing Alyssa, and I didn't know what she would do or say to you. I was afraid of what she'd do if I tried to kick you out."

"Lori." Florence was close enough to grab her, as if that would help anything. What was she going to do, beat Lori until she talked? This had been a particularly stressful day, and the thought of getting this close and walking away empty-handed made her blood boil. "Alyssa's family has waited decades to find out what happened to their daughter."

Lori shook her head like a stubborn child.

"Her parents are dead. Did you know that? They died young. They died heartbroken. How do you think her mother felt, knowing she'd never find her daughter? Could you have prevented that?"

Lori slowly backpedaled, and Florence followed her through the apartment.

"She has siblings who still want to find her. All these years later." Florence almost cried with rage. She pursued Lori into the kitchen, telling herself to stop—stop now, before she made a horrible mistake. "How can you live with yourself? How could you do that to them?"

Lori collapsed on the tile floor and crawled into the corner by a white trash can. She held her hands up in self-defense. Tears marked her face. "I told you." Her voice shuddered. "I already told you, Alyssa was unstable. Y-You should've never trusted her. You don't know what you're talking about—you weren't there, you didn't see her. She knew what she was doing. She wanted to take this place from me, piece by piece, and she started with my husband! Do you really think I was sad when she disappeared? She would've torn this place apart." Lori hugged herself, sobbing.

"She didn't deserve to be murdered for it," Florence said.

"You don't know anything," Lori spat.

Florence's anger dissipated, turning to shame. Was she completely wrong about this? Lori looked like a victim in her grimy dress with her hands trembling and paper-white skinny legs exposing her cracked and dirty soles.

What was wrong with Florence? Why couldn't she control herself?

You know why, Flo. You know perfectly well.

Florence almost apologized. She looked at the kitchen, at the dust and food stains on the counters, the knife block, and the closed cookbook. She looked at the dirty dishes, the smelly washcloths, the old tea bags, then back at the reclusive woman sitting in her own filth, when another thought came to her.

"Lori. Why did John kill himself?"

Lori gritted her teeth, finally showing a little spark. "I don't owe you an explanation. Who are you?"

"I'm nobody."

"That's what I thought. You don't belong here. You don't know what you're doing, you don't know anything. You're a child." Lori smiled a little, dry lips parting over wet teeth.

Florence slowly knelt on the kitchen tile, trying to appear relaxed despite the tension throughout her body. "Tell me the truth, and I'll get you out of here. Alyssa listens to me. She'll trust me on this. You were planning to leave, right? That's why you have your coat?"

Lori shifted uncomfortably. "I haven't left this resort since the 2000s, I think. I keep calling Charlie to come get me, but he won't answer, and he always, always answers for me."

"I'll take you," Florence said. "Tell me where Alyssa was buried, and I'll drive you wherever you want to go."

Lori snickered. "She won't let you, stupid girl. You don't know a thing about her."

"I know she hates you, and I believe she has a good reason. But that doesn't mean you have to pay the price. I'll drop you off somewhere, give you a head start. That's all I can do."

Lori shook her head again. "Foolish, foolish."

"Frederick's dead." Florence had no idea if saying that would work, but the look on Lori's face made it clear she didn't know. "Alyssa killed him because I found his sick little art project. Did you know about that?"

Lori's eyes shimmered with tears. "She'll kill me."

"So let me protect you! Just show me where she is."

Lori withdrew her phone from her coat pocket. "I need to call Charlie. We have to leave."

"I agree, Lori, one way or another, this is happening, and the story is going to come out now whether you like it or not."

"He's not answering," Lori cried, her voice breaking. "*Why isn't he answering me!*"

"Lori, please, let me help."

"No, no, no, not Charlie; she wouldn't hurt Charlie. She wouldn't touch him."

Florence opened her mouth, but nothing came out. She was starting to believe Lori now; she really didn't have a clue. "Why would Alyssa go after Charlie? To hurt you?"

"I couldn't have kids," Lori said.

"But Charlie—"

Lori nodded. "Alyssa's baby. Or so I believe. She went missing in August. Two months later, John walked off the roof because he couldn't live without her. No one saw Alyssa leave. But months later, a baby was left on my doorstep. Little Charlie. He had John's features. He had some of hers as well. But I raised him, and I never told him the truth."

What if Alyssa had been Frederick's captive? It could explain the continuous torture and eventually, the runes carved into her body to keep her soul from haunting the resort. If he'd kept her alive long enough to give birth to Charlie, it could've been somewhere here, at the resort. A secret room where no one would find her. But how did he keep her quiet? Florence thought of the blood dripping through Alyssa's lips, and any lingering guilt she'd felt about Frederick's death melted away.

"Why didn't you tell the police?" she asked Lori.

"Charlie didn't need to know. I was his mother. Alyssa had long been gone, and I was all he had." Lori swallowed, finally calming down. "Alyssa didn't deserve John's baby," she whispered.

Is this what keeping secrets does to someone? Florence thought. *Is this the price you pay?*

"He built that room for the two of them. As if I wouldn't find out eventually. I think he did it out of spite. He built the whole place for me and reserved a little corner for himself. They carried on for a long time. People knew about it. I knew about it. We were all young and stupid back then. Just kids with big dreams, too much family money, and too much time together. It was a season of life unlike anything I've experienced. Building this place took everything we had. We were sleepwalking every night, counting measurements in our heads, counting the rooms, the floors, the books. I basically slept with a tape measure in one hand—I'd never been so consumed by anything. John went to Alyssa when he was stressed. Then it was all the time. We couldn't have children, and he eventually saw me for what I was: a dead end."

She looked at Florence, defiant. "I finally confronted John. He was miserable about it. He told me that divorce was the only option. We'd have to sell the hotel, try and make some money back, and part ways. That was before the roof, before Alyssa vanished. Before the baby."

"How did no one know Charlie was adopted?"

"Some did, of course. But most of them are gone. Only a few left, now, and they won't tell a soul."

Like Frederick, Florence thought. *He kept all Lori's secrets, didn't he? Did Lori implore him to take action? Did she have an affair of her own and use Frederick to deal with her Alyssa problem?*

Lori looked at Florence with stricken, ash-colored eyes. "I poured everything I had into this place. It took my marriage. It ruined my family. I had nothing left, just this. Just this place and my baby boy."

Florence felt the tug on her heartstrings, but she wouldn't fall for it. She knew Lori was guilty.

Lori tapped her phone. The screen illuminated her pale, gaunt cheeks. "He should be in his room. He should've answered by now."

She tried Charlie's number. No answer. She dialed again, looking at Florence strangely. "Come on, Charlie, pick up the phone." And still, nothing. She stood up, brushed past Florence, and marched into the living room. "I've tried him a hundred times. God, what if she took him? Is that why she's taunting me? What if she took my baby?"

Lori plucked her keys from the mantel above the fireplace, tossed her phone inside her coat pocket, and opened her apartment door.

"Where are you going?"

Lori paused in the doorway. "To find my son. You can come if you want. Maybe you'll finally see who Alyssa really is."

Florence followed her out. As she closed the apartment door, she noticed the dusty knife block on the kitchen counter had one missing slot, where a small, sharp knife should've been.

Was the block full when they were both in the kitchen? Or had one always been missing?

Florence followed Lori down the hallway and into the stairwell. She called Angel but he didn't answer. And she couldn't call Logan because he wouldn't unlock his stupid car and get his stupid phone. God, what was wrong with him?

She texted Angel, jogging down the stairs, thinking about that missing slot in the knife block.

If you don't hear from me in fifteen minutes, CALL THE POLICE.

Chapter 46

Hopefully, Nathan wouldn't wake up while Robert waited in Florence's room. If he did, Robert would have to let his little boy cry. No telling how long it would take for Florence to return, or what methods Robert would use to get her from the third floor, down to the parking lot, and into his car.

Robert made his way up the stairs and stepped into the third-floor hallway. A few drunk ladies brushed past him, laughing at some incident in the ballroom. Robert walked away from them.

He checked the baby monitor and felt a pang of guilt. Margo would miss Nathan. The police would interrogate her about what she knew. How did she not see this coming? Were there warning signs?

Even still, Robert was making everyone's lives better. Margo could go back to work instead of babysitting. Florence would be hurt *at first*, but she'd come around. Nothing like quality time in a winterized lake house, surrounded by books.

A noise came from the baby monitor on Robert's phone. Nathan abruptly sat up in his pack 'n play and started crying.

Great, what terrific timing.

Robert stopped in the hallway, twenty feet from Florence's door. Getting Nathan back down would lose time. If Robert hurried, he could still beat Florence back to her room. The element of surprise was much safer than unlocking her door while she was already inside.

He went back into the stairwell when Nathan's cries suddenly stopped. The baby monitor flickered as someone walked past the camera. Robert stared at it, shaking. Who would be in Layla's apartment?

The shape of a woman hovered on the edge of the screen, slowly approaching Nathan's pack 'n play. She wore a tattered nightgown, her skin covered in dirt and blood. It was the woman from the cellar, the one who had sobbed over Charlie's lifeless body, the woman Robert only now recognized. How did he miss it? He knew she had looked familiar. It was Alyssa Larkin, the resort's famous missing girl.

She leaned over the pack 'n play, observing Nathan as he sat there and stared at her. She smiled at him, eyes glistening, and with jagged nails, gently plucked Nathan from his bed and cradled him in her arms. Nathan did not cry. She rocked him back and forth like any caring mother.

Alyssa stared at the camera with dark eyes, sending Robert a perfectly clear message, and then carried Nathan away.

Robert gazed at the screen, at the empty pack 'n play, his brain malfunctioning. His body had shut down. He kept staring, holding his breath and blinking, hoping this wasn't real. This was not real.

But Alyssa did not come back. Nathan was gone.

Robert sprinted down the stairwell, stumbling around every corner until he reached the lower level. He recalled the way Alyssa cried over Charlie's body. Was this her retaliation? A life for a life. A child for a child. That made absolutely no sense, but the message in her eyes was unmistakable: *This child is mine.*

He ran through the hallway and tried to open Layla's door. It was locked. How could that woman have locked it? How did she get in?

Hands shaking too much to work properly, he jabbed the key in the lock and twisted, slamming one palm against the door, grinding his teeth.

He fell inside the empty apartment. They were gone.

They could've gone to the basement, but why would she take Nathan there? It didn't matter why; he needed to find his boy. *If anything happens… no, stop thinking. Just move.*

He took off again and ran to the main floor, through the kitchen, and thundered down the basement steps.

"Alyssa!"

His body hurt. He couldn't breathe. A ghost had stolen his baby, and for what? What would she do to him? *Help me.* Those were her only words, spoken through the pet door yesterday morning. And what did Robert do? Well, nothing. He thought he'd been hallucinating.

The basement was empty, the cellar door still closed. He dropped to his knees and opened the pet door, greeted by the smell of death—a scent Robert was starting to identify. Alyssa's wild eyes flashed in the darkness. She sat on her bottom, legs crossed, with Nathan in her arms, somehow asleep and still so beautiful.

Asleep… or dead?

He pulled out his phone's flashlight and aimed it through the pet door. Her eyes glowed like an animal's, and Nathan's chest rose and fell in gentle waves.

"You bitch!" Robert reached through the pet door to grab her, but she backed away, Nathan stirring in her arms.

Robert tried the door handle. It turned, but the door wouldn't open. Charlie's body was shoved against it, his head bent at an unnatural angle.

She held Nathan close, kissing his forehead. Then she smiled at Robert.

"Don't touch him!" Robert punched the door. "Give him back!"

Nathan started to cry. The woman rocked him, shushing his worries. What was her endgame? Why take Nathan just to hold him in the cellar?

"Please." Robert swallowed his anger, his pride, everything. He had to reason with this monster. "Please, please, give him back to me."

On the cellar's right wall, a black circle appeared. No, not a circle. A black hole, a pool-like substance. A breeze came through it, and the wind slithered across Robert's arms and face, thick as smoke and smelling like the sea.

The black pool was a portal, or a door, to someplace normal people couldn't go.

The woman looked at Robert with determination. Nothing he could say would stop her from doing what she wanted.

"Please." Robert extended a hand. "Please bring him back to me."

Alyssa shook her head. She kissed Nathan's forehead and crawled toward the hole in the wall.

"Stop! Stop, please! Stop!" Robert tried to squeeze through the pet door. Tears streamed down his face. He could kick the door until he shoved Charlie's body backward, but that would consume precious time, and he couldn't take his eyes off Nathan. The woman took one final glance at Robert, clutched Nathan to her chest, and shuffled through the black pool. Nathan cried in her arms, crying out for his daddy.

They both vanished.

Robert held his breath, expecting the black pool to disappear, but it stayed shimmering on the wall. If he could get the door open, he could follow them. If Nathan were allowed on the other side, then normal humans could cross over to their world. He just had to kick the door hard enough.

But then the pool rippled, and a pair of hands came through, followed by a shiny bald head. A man crawled through the portal, a thick, syrupy liquid dripping from his arms. He sat in the cellar, sniffing the air. He wore no clothes and only had one leg. His yellow eyes fixed on Robert, and he grinned, his mouth black with rot, his teeth long gone. Only his tongue remained, which he used to lick his glossy lips.

Robert, too terrified to speak, slowly edged away from the door.

The man crawled over to Charlie, seized him with both hands, and dragged him across the dirty cellar floor.

The man slipped through the black pool and pulled Charlie through with him.

The wind swept through the cellar with a final puff, and the hole vanished. The wall returned to normal. The portal had closed.

Robert sank, resting his cheek on the concrete. He couldn't even follow them. It didn't matter where Alyssa took Nathan. It didn't matter what universe or supernatural realm they entered, Robert would've followed without a second thought. He would've followed them anywhere. But the door was gone, leaving him stuck on the wrong side.

Chapter 47

Logan approached the front counter in the lobby. What he was about to do didn't quite reach the level of impersonating an employee, but it was close, and getting caught could result in termination. *I'm losing this bet anyway*, he thought, remembering Florence's lips against his mouth.

The kid behind the counter peeled his eyes away from his phone. "Help you?"

"Yeah, I work here. Just started yesterday." Yesterday, approximately one million years ago. "Name's Logan."

The kid put the phone down. "What's up Logan? Where you working at?"

"The stacks."

"Ah," he said sourly.

"Do you know Mike, the dock supervisor?" Logan asked.

"I think so. Why?"

"I need to talk to him. Can you tell me what apartment he's in?"

"I don't know, man. It's kinda late."

"Mike knows me. He told me if I had any issues, I should go straight to him."

The kid frowned. "Even when he's not working?"

Logan took a deep breath, smiling. "Can you call him, please? I wouldn't bother him if it wasn't important."

"All right, all right, let me find his number."

The kid dialed Mike's phone and waited. "Hey Mike, sorry to bother you, it's Zach, from reception. I got a new hire here, Logan? Says he needs to talk to you. Awesome, thanks." Zach hung up, nodded down the hall. "Room 13A."

Logan followed the hallway, forcing himself to slow down and think this through. How much did he want to involve Mike? Mike obviously knew Charlie and the curators, but did he know them all by name? Logan didn't even remember the curator's name who had cornered Florence downstairs. Did she mention it? Logan had a vague description, and that was all.

It was also entirely possible he'd overreacted to this whole thing, and it was only a misunderstanding. Perhaps the curator was simply quirky and broke protocol by speaking with Florence.

That didn't make him a stalker.

Still, Florence saw the same guy three times in two days. No chance in hell that was a coincidence.

Logan needed to rule out the possibility of something bad happening. Maybe the guy was harmless, but maybe not.

He made sure his badge was hidden inside his pocket and then knocked on the door at the end of the hall.

After a minute, the door cracked open. Mike stared at him, wearing nothing but pajama pants and a wall of chest hair. "Hey, Logan? What's going on, man?"

"I'm so sorry to bother you." Logan was a terrible liar and hoped Mike's grogginess would dull his observation skills. "I locked myself out of the stacks. My badge, my keys. I didn't want to bother anyone, and the kid at the front desk was not helpful."

Mike wheezed with laughter. "You mean Zach? Kid's a joke, man. No wonder you gotta wake my ass up. Hang on."

Mike returned a few minutes later and handed him a badge. "This is mine. Don't use it on anything other than the stacks. They monitor that shit. They don't like people going where they don't belong."

Logan nodded, feeling guilty. "I understand. I'll bring it right back."

"Slip it under the door, man. I'll see you tomorrow." Mike yawned and shut the door.

Logan ran back the way he came, turned around a few times, backtracked, got lost, then, after wasting fifteen minutes, eventually found the hallway he'd traveled down once before, a million years ago.

He scanned Mike's badge, unlocking the curator's office. This was going to land him in hot water, but he didn't care anymore. If Logan were asked about it tomorrow, he'd say he was searching for the break room. An honest mistake. Hopefully, they wouldn't check the cameras and see him rifling through the office like a thief.

He flipped the lights on and quickly ran by each little cubicle, reading off every name. He then sat at a random desk, grabbed the dusty corded phone, and dialed Florence's number off his arm.

Chapter 48

Lori left the stairwell on the second floor and turned left, her bare feet leaving black streaks on the carpet.

Florence followed from a safe distance, saying nothing and asking no questions. She kept thinking about the missing slot from the knife block and Lori's winter coat, with all those pockets. Florence didn't buy any of it. Maybe Frederick acted alone. Out of devotion to Lori and this resort, he held Alyssa captive, took her newborn baby, and murdered her. Lori got the baby she always wanted, the Walter family kept the resort, and Frederick was able to satiate his desire for cruelty. What if there were others after Alyssa? What if more young women disappeared out here, and no one knew about it?

Lori stopped in front of an unmarked door, sifted through her keys, and unlocked it. She disappeared inside, leaving the door open. From the hallway, Florence saw a leather couch like Lori's and the edge of a beautiful, sprawling, built-in bookshelf.

"Charlie!"

Inside the apartment, Lori slammed doors, calling her son's name over and over, as if he was in there somewhere and choosing to ignore her.

Charlie wasn't home. While there could be a reasonable explanations for this, Florence wondered if Alyssa had paid him a visit. But what would she do? Kidnap her own son? Convince him that she was his birth mother?

Lori stumbled from the apartment. "She took him. He would never leave me."

"She wouldn't hurt him."

"You don't know that!" Lori turned and rushed off.

Florence followed Lori back into the stairwell, to the first floor, down a hallway, and through double swinging doors. The kitchen lights were on, but the place was vacant. Everything had been scrubbed clean and put away. Lori maneuvered through the kitchen and stopped at an open doorway with wooden steps leading down. Maybe a basement. The lights were already on down there.

"Where are you going?"

Lori paused. "Why did Alyssa appear to you?"

There was no point in telling Lori that Alyssa's entire revenge campaign was thanks to Florence summoning her and breaking the spell. Lori already had a few good reasons to hate Florence; why add more?

Lori looked at her, annoyed. "Why you? Of all people?"

"I was staying in her room."

"Other people have stayed in that room. They didn't find a secret passageway. They didn't find a fucking ghost. So don't lie to me."

"Why are you checking down here?"

Lori clicked her tongue. "It's the only place I can think of where Alyssa might be."

Florence felt her heart pick up. Were they close to Alyssa's remains? "I thought you didn't know what happened to her."

"I don't," Lori said, descending the stairs. "But Alyssa had many secrets, and this was one of them."

Florence waited at the top, holding her phone at the ready. She could call the police now and tell them a senile woman with a knife was threatening people, just so they'd send someone.

"Who the hell are you?" Lori was on the last step, talking to someone Florence couldn't see.

Florence rushed down the stairs. What was her curator doing in the basement?

Robert stood beside a round, wooden chair, surrounded by spilled bags of walnuts and almonds. His eyes were puffy and red, and when he saw Florence, his face split into a painful smile. Like she'd just brightened his dark and lonely evening.

Robert was facing a rack of shelves laden with kitchen supplies, but it wasn't until Florence saw the pet door behind it that she *knew*, without a doubt, this was the place.

She believed that Lori asked Frederick to keep Alyssa in the cellar and to cut out her tongue to keep her quiet. He kept her alive until she gave birth and then murdered her. Florence could picture Alyssa's bloody hands lifting little baby Charlie through the pet door and surrendering him to Lori. Frederick knew how to keep Alyssa's ghost from roaming. If this place had been a thin spot from the beginning, Florence could only guess what darkness seeped into Frederick's mind from the other side.

Lori saw the pet door and gasped. "Did you go in there?"

Robert didn't reply. He seemed shellshocked.

"Where is she?" Lori asked, scanning the room.

Robert and Florence stared at each other, an unwelcome but necessary alliance forming between them. Seeing Robert again made Florence want to sprint back upstairs, but for the moment, she'd take him over Lori. Right now, he looked perfectly sane compared to the skinny woman in the oversized coat.

"Alyssa!" Lori yelled, turning in circles. "*Where... is... my... son?!*"

Robert twitched slightly. Lori didn't notice, but Florence wondered if Robert being here was no accident.

Florence's hand shook, and she dropped her phone. It fell on the ground and lit up with an incoming call from an unknown number. She ignored it.

"He's gone. I know he's gone; I know he's gone."

Lori couldn't breathe. She looked at the two of them as if they had the solution to her problem. No one could do anything. No one *wanted* to do anything. Lori's panic was exactly what Alyssa had planned. Whatever remained of Lori's sanity was slowly disappearing, like water turning to steam. Soon, there would be nothing left but an empty husk of an old and bitter woman.

"Where are you?" Lori called to the room. "Or are you still afraid of me? You know, John didn't stick around after he fell, did he? Funny, he had a chance to haunt this resort with you forever, and where is he? I guess he had nothing to stay for."

The pet door cracked open. Bright eyes peered through the opening, dirty fingers holding the rubber flap steady.

Lori walked to the shelves and squatted. "Thirty years didn't change you one bit. All this time, and you're still the same pathetic whore."

The pet door swung shut. Seconds passed.

Lori smiled. "That's what I thought. I guess dying taught you nothing."

"What did you do to her?" Florence had to ask again, one last time.

But Lori stood up and faced Florence. She removed a small knife from her coat pocket, the one from the knife block in her apartment.

"I don't know who killed Alyssa. You have to believe me, Florence. I never knew. I was just so happy she was gone that I didn't care who did it. You don't know what she was like, or what she was doing to my resort. You never saw her—"

Lori didn't get to finish. Alyssa appeared behind her, snatched the knife from her hand, and sliced open Lori's throat.

Lori stared at Florence with bright eyes. She made a choking sound and crumbled on the floor.

The cellar door opened. The same dirty fingers from before curled through the gap and beckoned for Alyssa to come back inside. Alyssa smiled at Florence. She threw the knife behind her, inside the cellar, before taking Lori by the arms and dragging her through the open doorway. After a moment of shuffling, the cellar door closed, and the room was quiet.

Florence knew there would be no body, no weapon. Lori wasn't in the cellar; she was *gone*.

But she didn't have time to think about it, because Robert wrapped his arm around Florence, his chest pressing against her shoulder, smelling like sweat and old clothes.

"Are you okay?" he asked, his attention solely on her. No reaction to the ghosts or anything else. Just her.

Florence jerked away from him. Her phone, still on the floor where she'd dropped it, started ringing again, a call from the same unknown number. She hated Robert's touch. She hated how close he got to her. Robert looked morose, offended that she hadn't melted inside his warm arms. Florence picked up her phone and quickly answered it.

"Florence? Finally! It's Logan! Listen, what was the guy's name, the curator who talked to you?"

Florence stared at Robert, her mouth dry. "Robert," she said.

Robert frowned.

"Okay, I'm sorry I didn't tell you I was doing this. I'm not trying to be weird or overprotective or freak you out, but I knew something was wrong, and I was right! I'm in the curator's office right now, and no one named Robert works here."

Robert watched her with big, bird-like eyes.

"Whoever he is," Logan continued, "he's not a curator. He either lied to you or stole your file somehow. He's stalking you."

Florence couldn't pretend they weren't talking about Robert. She nodded, backing away. "Can I see you?"

Robert stepped toward her.

"Is something wrong?" Logan paused. "Where are you?"

Florence bolted up the stairs and through the kitchen, glancing back.

Robert wasn't following her.

"See you in the stacks, two minutes."

"Two minutes." Logan hung up.

Florence ran down the stairwell to the lower level, her mind spiraling out of control. Robert was a problem, but right now, the police needed to get here. Someone had to start sorting through this mess.

She dialed 911, fully unprepared to tell them the most unbelievable true story.

Chapter 49

Robert let Florence walk up the stairs, her phone glued to her ear. Everything in him wanted to take her right now, but the mysterious caller got in the way. How did they know Robert wasn't a curator?

Florence's next call would be to the police. Considering the walnuts on the floor were soaking in a pool of Lori's blood, Robert maybe had less than an hour before the cops would lock the resort down.

He heard Florence at the top of the stairs making plans to meet in the stacks. Robert would find her there, with her new friends, and do what had to be done. He'd need a distraction to buy additional time; enough for him to get halfway to Maine before the authorities realized Florence was missing.

An idea was coming to mind at the same time the cellar door swung open. Alyssa stood in the gap like a terrifying movie villain. The pet door rustled from the wind swirling behind her. The portal was open again.

"Where's Nathan?"

Was it his imagination, or could he hear his son's whimper in the breeze?

This time, Alyssa did not look angry. Killing Lori had put her in a better mood. She nodded behind her, toward the wall with the black pool.

"Is he safe?"

She nodded.

"Can I see him?"

She nodded again, giving him a second chance to protect his son. She wasn't giving Nathan back, just allowing Robert to verify his son's health, as if some part of her twisted soul had found a little compassion for him. Maybe she knew how it felt to lose a child.

"Will you send me back here after I see him?"

Alyssa frowned and shook her head.

"I'd be trapped there?"

Another nod.

Stuck in another world, forever, all so this insane woman could have an infant. What a price to pay to keep his son.

Alyssa gestured like, *You coming or what?*

Robert looked at the stairs, wondering if Florence had already reached the stacks. If he hesitated, he'd lose his opportunity. The police were on the way.

His Journey didn't end here, playing games with a ghost. If she said Nathan was safe, he believed her. But... he couldn't leave Florence. He had no future without her.

"Please take care of him," Robert said.

Alyssa smirked and turned away, the wind following her.

Robert jogged up the basement stairs, his heart heavy. He'd made an irreversible choice—he knew that. But was it the wrong one?

He started to run. *I'm so sorry, Nathan, but my story doesn't end here. I'll find you one day, I promise.*

He cut through the lower level and came out on the dock. He pushed through the back door and into the night, pausing briefly for the sound of sirens.

The maintenance crew kept supplies in a large shed right outside the dock doors. It had a padlock, but it was never locked. An obvious camera lingered above it.

Robert smiled at the camera, opened the shed doors, and turned on the light.

First, he gathered a handful of zip ties and shoved them into his pocket with the nutcracker. He took one lighter and then picked up two five-gallon cans of diesel fuel. One in each hand, he took them inside the resort to Layla's room.

He set one can in the hallway outside her door, uncapped the other one, and started sprinkling diesel over the mess of clothes on the floor. After months of tripping over her things, he was finally cleaning up. He dumped a little on the bed. One of her hands stuck out from the pile of clothes, her nails shiny and soaked in diesel. Robert splashed a little more on the clothes, grinning.

He turned to the pack 'n play, a brief stab of pain in his chest, and prayed Nathan would understand.

Robert backed out of the room, slowly spilling more fuel on the carpet. In the hallway, he lit the damp trail, slipped the lighter back inside his pocket, and grabbed the two cans. Layla's room slowly filled with fire. He chose diesel over gasoline to avoid blowing up the place. He wanted to cripple it, not burn everyone alive.

No going back now. The fire would keep the police far too busy to worry about Florence.

Robert carried the diesel cans over to the stacks, hearing voices down the hall. Any minute now, this place would slip into chaos.

The stacks had two exits. The primary double doors and a side door.

He leaned against the double doors, hearing their muffled voices.

Since he couldn't lock them inside, he had to block their exits. Using whatever remained of the first can, he dumped the fuel on the double doors. Robert loved the smell of diesel. It reminded him of summers at his uncle's farm. He emptied the can and tossed it aside. Kneeling, he used the lighter on the doors, and they were soon engulfed in flames.

Taking the second can, he ran up to the main floor. He popped off the lid and started pouring. He threw diesel on the walls and in the carpet, turning it from red to black.

He walked back to the stairwell, the carpet squelching under his shoes.

No innocent people deserved to die. He just wanted Florence. It really was that simple. The best he could do was give everyone a head start.

Robert set the carpet on fire, then tossed the lighter into the flames.

He walked back into the stairwell, pulling the fire alarm on his way out.

Chapter 50

Florence reached the stacks before Logan, banged on the door, and waited for Angel.

She looked back at the elevator beckoning her, doors open and panting like a hungry beast. She expected Robert to show up because he'd already found her three times in two days and clearly didn't intend to stop. How much time had he spent wandering the resort, hoping fate would bring them together?

The door opened. Angel raised his eyebrows. "You okay?"

Florence rushed inside, shutting the door behind her. "Where's Mia?"

"At the hangout." Angel started walking that way, shuffling notecards in his hands.

The double doors opened behind them. Florence's heart skipped; she spun, braced for Robert. Instead, Logan jogged through. She waited, the tension tight between her shoulders. Mia and Angel sat across the booth, oddly silent.

"Guys, guys." Logan leaned over the booth. "We have a problem."

"We have a few problems," Florence said. She recounted the events of the last hour and her phone call to the police.

"What did you tell them?" Angel asked.

"That there's a hidden cellar in the resort's basement, and the owner of the resort told me Alyssa's bones were in there. Someone's on the way."

Mia and Angel sat in shocked silence. "So, that's it, Lori's gone?" Mia asked.

Florence checked the double doors. "I think so. If the police can find Alyssa's remains, and we give them the stained-glass, hopefully everything will come out. They'll somehow piece it together."

"And you'll tell them," Logan said. "Alyssa wants that, right? She doesn't want justice or proof; she wants someone to share her story. And now you can. Even if you can't prove all of it, I bet people will believe you."

Florence knew he was right, but she hadn't expected Alyssa to kill Lori so quickly. It felt like she didn't care about proof anymore, only revenge. But Florence had to save that thought for later. "Okay, what do we do about Robert?"

"Report him to the GM," Angel said. "They'll suspend him, at least, and do an investigation. But he technically hasn't broken any laws. He could claim running into you multiple times was an accident. The police wouldn't do anything, but the resort would, especially if a guest filed a complaint."

"How can we do that?" Florence asked.

"Let's talk to the GM. There's always one on duty, even overnight."

"I should be waiting for the police to show up," Florence said, looking at the doors again. "I guess Robert can wait."

Logan sighed, clearly irritated. Florence understood his frustration because Robert's true intentions made her feel sick. Why would someone go through the trouble of stealing a reader's profile and pretending to be their curator?

They'd only do it if they were dangerously obsessed.

The police were conveniently on the way. Whatever Robert wanted, he wouldn't get it.

Second, Florence couldn't stop seeing the other pair of hands dragging Lori's body into the cellar. Earlier, Alyssa confirmed that other ghosts lived at the resort, but she never elaborated.

Now that Florence had seen another ghost, Chloe felt so much closer.

Florence stepped away from the group and stared down the center aisle. She looked at the ladders and books and wondered how far she'd have to go to reach Chloe. She felt a noticeable shift in the air.

Come on, Chloe, where are you?

There was nowhere else to go. If Chloe wasn't at The Reader's Resort, this all would be for nothing.

Chloe, please talk to me. I need to see you.

Florence paused and listened, aware that the group was no longer talking but watching her instead.

Something smelled bad, like burnt food.

The air shifted again.

"Chloe? Can you hear me?"

A loud blaring sound tore through the stacks, making Florence jump. White lights flashed on the walls, matching the fire alarm as it rang on a short loop.

"Uh-oh." Angel collected Mia's notecards and set them on the floor with her textbooks. "We better go. It's probably just an accident or some moron smoking in their room. It happens every now and then."

The others headed for the double doors, but Florence stayed still, overcome with a premonition that something horrible was about to happen. Dread settled in her stomach, even before Angel called out.

"Guys!"

Florence ran down the aisle and caught up with them, covering her nose with her sleeve. Smoke drifted beneath the double doors; fire crackled on the other side, growing louder, filling the air with heat and the smell of burnt carpet and plastic.

"Okay, shit, this is real." Angel pointed across the room. "Other door, let's go!"

Logan kept looking at the double doors like he couldn't believe it. Florence grabbed his hand and they sprinted together, smoke turning the stacks' golden light into a hazy, apocalyptic sunset.

The side door was closed. The EXIT sign and fire alarm glowed white and red above it, ringing loud enough to hurt Florence's eardrums.

Angel grabbed the door handle and pushed, but it wouldn't move. He tried again, moving the door slightly, before it was shoved back in place.

Something scraped against the other side. A sharp metal object tapped the door three times. Three hollow knocks.

"Florence?" Robert's muffled voice came through the door. "We need to talk, if you can hear me."

Angel stared at them, his usual confidence gone. The fear in his eyes scared her more than Robert.

Footsteps shuffled from behind the door. A woman's voice grew close and frantic, calling Robert's name repeatedly until he yelled in return. A scream followed, then something heavy thumped against the door. The sharp metal object clattered on the floor.

A dark pool of blood seeped beneath the door and into the stacks.

Angel looked at them, speechless and wide-eyed.

Unintentionally, she'd planned on Angel knowing exactly what to do. From the looks on Logan's and Mia's faces, they'd thought the same thing. Angel's loss for words incapacitated them. Robert just killed someone on the other side of that door.

Florence's phone vibrated. She pulled it out, saw an unknown number, and showed it to the others.

Logan raised his voice above the fire alarm. "Put it on speaker."

Chapter 51

Robert waited by the side door, trembling with excitement, his palms and fingers sticky with blood.

Poor, stupid Sherrie surprised him by coming from the dockside of the hallway; following the tradition of many resort employees who would slip out the dock doors late at night and smoke weed by the dumpsters. She recognized Robert. He knew her from his early days in the kitchen. She'd been a good friend.

For some reason, she wouldn't leave him alone. Maybe she didn't see the machete or she knew he was guarding the door to the stacks and thought a confrontation would scare him off, but she was wrong.

"Why did you make me do that?" he asked, pulling her body away from the door, his shoes slipping on the bloody floor. He picked up the machete.

The next part would be a challenge because Robert didn't have time to rehearse. He'd have to wing it. A dangerous thing.

He called Florence's number (which he stole from her resort application and swore he'd never use), to talk one-on-one, away from her nosy friends.

The phone rang a few times before connecting.

"Hello?" She sounded nervous.

"Florence?"

"Yeah."

He took a deep breath, wishing he'd prepared something. "It's Robert. Your curator."

Silence on the other end. The fire alarms inside the stacks echoed through her phone, a beat behind the ones in the hallway.

"What do you want?" Florence sounded frightened, making his stomach twist uncomfortably.

"I don't want you to be scared," he said, having to shout over the noise. "I put everything I had into your book list. I wanted to change your life! I wanted to change both our lives. That's all I want, Florence. I just want you to read those books."

A pause. "I'll read them, Robert. Of course I'll read them."

Warmth flooded his chest and stomach at the sound of his name. "I know you will. Look, my car is in the parking lot. I'm going to take you somewhere quiet. We can grab your books, or I'll buy you new ones. I realized this place isn't the best for true readers. There's too much going on, and you can get so distracted. I can do better. I promise you. I'll build you a room you'll love, not some 1940s rip-off. But something *made* for you."

"That's nice of you to want that."

"I just want you to love your books because I know you will." He almost teared up. He could feel her understanding him through the phone. "I know there are a few people with you. I don't want them to get hurt. No one's getting hurt, okay? But the fire's spreading fast."

The fire had left Layla's apartment by now. The lower level would soon be consumed.

"We don't have a lot of time. You can all get outside safely. I just need you to come with me, Florence. It won't be forever, obviously." He chuckled, picturing her lying in his bed in a short nightgown, smiling, reading, telling him about a new book she loved.

"Unless you want to stay with me. But we can talk about it later, okay? Will you come with me?"

It was no speech for the ages, but he could feel it working on her. The silence on the other end was killing him.

Someone laughed in the background. A harsh, mocking laugh.

"He's such a freak," someone said.

"Were they listening that whole time?" he asked Florence. Embarrassment swelled inside him. He was too caught up in the moment, and he hadn't considered speaker phone.

"Obviously, you psycho!" Definitely the new guy. Trying to sound tough, yet unable to fully shake the fear from his voice. "She's not going anywhere with you, you f—"

"Logan!" Florence hissed. "Robert, listen to me. I want to read your books. I really, really do. And maybe we can talk about it outside. But right now, we all have to leave this building."

He heard it now—the gentle padding in her voice, like when you're talking a toddler out of a tantrum. He'd been such a fool, trusting her like this, when she let her new friends listen while he gave her his weak, bleeding heart.

"Robert?"

"Yes or no, Florence. Are you coming with me?"

A long pause this time, with broken whispers. "No."

No? The edge in her voice flustered him. "Fine. You have two minutes to change your mind and save your friends, otherwise I'm coming in and carrying you out. Let me know what you decide." He hung up, clenching his phone.

It didn't have to be this way.

He heard their bullish laughter through the door, mocking him the same way Dean and Charlie used to.

Whether Florence agreed to his conditions or not, the other three would not leave the stacks alive.

Chapter 52

They stood around Florence's phone as the call ended. No one said a word.

How did Robert sound so sincere? He just murdered someone and then talked to her like a child he didn't want to disappoint.

"What if we're wrong? What if I go with him and he lets us leave?"

"He has a weapon. He'll kill you," Logan said. "We should call the police! He just murdered someone!"

"He doesn't want to kill me, Logan. If I go with him, maybe he'll let us all walk out, like he said. What else should we do?"

"He's lying," Mia said. "We know him. How could he let us go?"

Angel nodded. "She's right. Mia, can you call the police? It might not make a difference, but we have to try."

Mia turned away, phone to her ear.

Logan grunted, his face red. "Okay, but we have to do something. Or he's going to come in here, and then what? We can't fight him!"

"Yes, we can, it's four to one," Angel said. "If he doesn't have a gun, we have a chance."

Florence's phone buzzed. She opened a text from Robert. **You coming?**

Angel took the phone from her hands and typed, **Yes, be right there.**

Florence waved her phone. "I thought you said we shouldn't do that!"

"Go to the door! Talk to him. Then get out of the way." Angel disappeared between the aisles.

Florence dropped her phone inside her purse and approached the side door, hoping she could give Angel enough time for whatever he had planned.

"Robert?" she yelled.

"Are they with you?" His voice was timid and non-threatening. If she hadn't seen the blood leaking under the door, she would have believed he didn't mean to harm anyone.

"They're moving to the other end of the room," she replied.

The door barely cracked open. Robert didn't trust her. His eyes glowed through the gap. "They have to give us a head start."

Somewhere in the stacks, Logan yelled something. Florence glanced behind her, wondering what Angel meant about getting out of the way.

Logan began running toward Florence, waving his arms. But he wasn't screaming at her; he was trying to stop Angel.

A golf cart drifted into the center aisle. Angel sat behind the wheel, punching the accelerator. He was going to drive it into the door, right where Florence stood.

Logan was too far behind it. He jumped and hollered.

"Angel! Stop! You're going to *kill* yourself!"

Florence smiled at Robert, reached through the crack in the door, and gripped his arm. "We can go right now." She forced herself to look at Robert even as the golf cart drew closer.

Robert frowned. "What's happening in there?" The fire alarm drowned out their voices, but Florence could still hear the golf cart flying directly at her.

Despite Logan's efforts, Angel neared the side door with no intention of slowing down. "Move!" he yelled.

Florence dropped Robert's arm and bolted along the wall.

Confused, Robert opened the door a little more as Angel jumped from the cart and sprawled on the floor. The cart rammed into the side door, snapping its hinges and sending chunks of plastic splintering against the door frame. The cart bounced back, losing the left front wheel, and tipped on its side. The cart's roof came down on Angel's foot as he tried to crawl away, crushing his ankle.

Angel screamed and clawed at the floor, dragging his twisted, bleeding foot behind him. Florence and Logan made it to him first, and they helped him stand on his one good foot with his arms around their shoulders.

"Did it work?" Angel groaned.

A shadow crouched in the doorway, holding a long, serrated blade, silhouetted by the white fire alarms flashing in the black smoke.

They carried Angel away from the door and deeper into the stacks, into a dead end.

Robert limped through the broken doorway, peering around before stepping, as if expecting another golf cart to fly at him. Smoke followed him inside the stacks.

Logan, Angel, and Florence reached the opposite end of the stacks. Mia joined them, hugging Angel as Logan gently set him on the ground. She told them the police were on their way, and they knew about the attacker, as if that helped anything right now. She had also tried calling over the radio on the sorting table, but nobody answered.

At the other end, Robert faced them, his machete swinging lightly.

Florence stood in the center aisle. Maybe she could talk to him. If they could agree on something, on *anything*, everyone would get out alive. They were almost out of time.

A noise stopped her. A quiet hissing, growing louder.

"No," Angel said, his voice choked with emotion. "No, no, no!"

At first, she thought he was talking about Robert. But he meant the hissing sound.

Florence looked up as the sprinkler system came to life, spraying silver streams of water across the entire warehouse. A last defense against the growing fire.

The water fell like rain—catching her eyelashes, dripping on her cheeks, and rolling down her black rain jacket. Water spilled down the shelves, soaking into the books. She turned to the aisles around her, to all the books growing soggy and heavy, their thin pages falling apart. The air changed, and despite the storm raging inside the stacks, Florence noticed a breeze flowing over her hands and into the aisles, fighting to push the smoke back.

Robert didn't seem bothered by the water. He closed his eyes, tilted his head up, and smiled at the sprinklers like they were an answer to prayer.

Angel cried on the ground, gripping his hair, his foot bent unnaturally. Logan and Mia stared at the water, at Robert, utterly hopeless.

Robert opened his eyes, his face grim. He walked through the rainfall, the rivers of black smoke, and the flashing white lights. The machete hung at his side, the blood rinsing off of it and leaving a long trail of red behind him.

Chapter 53

Logan wiped the sprinkler water from his face, counting the seconds until Robert would reach their group. The main entrance was engulfed in fire, and the side door was guarded by a maniac with a black, serrated machete.

They would find a way out of this. Logan would kill Robert if he had to.

Part of Logan *wanted* to kill him.

Think, think, think! What can I use?

"Take Angel and run." Logan looked at Florence and Mia. "Please, run!"

They grabbed Angel's arms, hoisted him up, and helped him limp away on one foot.

Logan watched them turn the corner and cut through the secret hangout. Robert approached him slowly, craning his neck to see which direction they went.

"You can't have her," Logan said, standing his ground. "The police are already here now. You can't get away."

"I can if she agrees to go." Robert grinned.

It was the smug little smile that made Logan's vision turn into a black tunnel. His brain switched off, his body took over—two hundred pounds of adrenaline and muscle.

Logan charged him, catching Robert off guard. Robert tried to swing his arm up, but Logan caught his elbow, keeping the machete pointed at the floor. Robert jerked back, flustered, and swung the machete. Logan had already backpedaled out of reach. Water droplets flung from the blade.

He couldn't beat Robert hand-to-hand, so he sprinted down an aisle and ran to the golf carts. He wasn't as proficient a driver as Angel, but that was fine. How hard could it be to run someone over?

He jumped in the seat, snatched the keys, and brought the cart to life. Stomping the pedal, he drifted around the corner until he swerved down the center aisle. Robert was looking for the others, checking each aisle with increasing anxiety.

Logan floored it. The golf cart revved toward Robert, hydroplaning and nearly losing control. By the time Logan straightened out, Robert had spotted him and ducked down Arrakis. Logan swerved into the aisle, pushing the cart faster and praying he wouldn't spin out. Robert ran toward the other side, looked back, and realized he wouldn't clear the aisle before Logan caught up to him. Logan aimed the cart at Robert's back, hoping the hit would either knock him out or kill him. Didn't matter at this point. Robert wasn't fast enough, and he had nowhere to go.

Logan gripped the wheel, imagining the sound of bones snapping. But Robert jumped on a rolling ladder and started to climb.

Logan drifted alongside the shelves and hit the ladder at full speed. As he made contact, Robert grabbed onto the shelves, knocking books off, somehow still holding the machete.

The ladder snapped off its rollers, crunched against the golf cart's hood, and cartwheeled down the aisle, crashing against the far wall.

Robert climbed to the top of the shelves, knocking more books down. They splashed on the floor like wet laundry. Stepping out of the cart, Logan looked up, blocking the water from his eyes. On the edge of the shelves, Robert fixed his gaze across the room. He'd spotted the others.

Logan jumped back in the golf cart as Robert ran along the aisle above him, looking for a way to climb back down.

The others were limping along the wall, not making enough progress. He drove back to the center aisle and checked the side door, only to see it swirling with smoke and flames, blocking off their only exit. Angel's golf cart lay off to the side like a fallen stallion.

They had no way out.

Chapter 54

Florence struggled to keep Angel upright. He was trying to help with one good foot, but his entire body shivered from the cold sprinkler water and the pain of his crushed ankle. His head rolled to the side as he faded in and out of consciousness.

On Angel's other side, Mia persevered, also struggling but refusing to let go of Angel. They would've carried him for miles.

Florence paused. "We're too slow. He'll catch us before we make it to the door."

A loud clang echoed through the stacks. Behind them, a ladder flew through the air.

Mia looked around, suddenly excited. "We don't need that door."

"What are you talking about?"

Mia shook her head. "It's crazy. And stupid. But there's another way. Right down here."

They carried Angel another twenty feet and set him on the ground, his back to the wall. Mia opened the outer doors to the dumbwaiter.

Florence shook her head. "No way."

"It'll hold you! I'll send you up one floor so you can get out of here!"

"That's not right. What about all of you? I can't leave you guys here! This is only happening because of me!"

Mia blinked, eyes wet. "Exactly. He wants *you*, Florence. He won't stop."

A golf cart pulled up, and Logan jumped out.

Florence looked down the aisle. "Where's Robert?"

"Climbing down a shelf. He'll be here any minute. And the side door is on fire, but we can try and run through it."

Mia snatched Florence's wrist. "Florence! Get in!"

"No, I'm not leaving you guys!"

Logan knelt and scooped Angel into his arms. "We'll try the side door. I can drive him over there. If the fire's too bad, I'll drive us around. I'll do whatever I have to."

"That won't work—this place is burning down!"

"He's coming." Logan looked at her, and Florence knew his thoughts in a single heartbeat. He was wondering if they'd see each other again. "Florence, you need to go. Maybe he'll leave us alone if he realizes you're gone. Maybe you'll lead him out of here, but if you don't go now, you're not getting another chance."

They were trying to save her, Florence understood that. But if any of them got hurt protecting her, she couldn't live with it.

Mia shoved her with both hands. "Please, go! Just go! Bring help."

I'm not running away; I'm going to save them, Florence thought.

So save them.

Florence crawled into the dumbwaiter, pulling her legs against her chest. She'd never panicked in tight spaces before, but this was different. It felt like a coffin. And she should've left her purse behind because the strap was strangling her. She adjusted, resting the purse on her stomach, inwardly laughing at how she'd originally brought it along in case she found time to contact Chloe and read her confession again. All that seemed so pointless now.

Logan set Angel in the golf cart's passenger seat, slid behind the wheel, and waited for Mia.

Mia leaned inside the dumbwaiter, one hand on the outer doors. "I'll stay here with them. We'll run circles around that guy. Just get us help, please."

Florence swallowed. She didn't want to leave them. This wasn't their fight. "What if he doesn't come after me?"

"He will. I'll see you soon." Mia shut the doors and pressed the button for the main floor. The dumbwaiter was cold and pitch black, aside from a sliver of light leaking through the outer doors.

Florence tried to relax her muscles and not think about all the ways this could go wrong. Logan's muffled voice shouted at Mia to hurry up.

The dumbwaiter hummed with life. It rattled upward, moving faster than she'd anticipated. Her stomach lurched.

It stopped abruptly, and she could see again. Not a sliver of light this time, but a warm, golden glow. Smoke spilled inside the dumbwaiter, filling her mouth and nostrils and lungs. The main level was on fire, and the flames had reached the dumbwaiter.

She punched the metal wall over and over again, screaming—the fire on the outer doors hot enough to make her skin tighten, so she cried and screamed and inhaled smoke and broke down, coughing, gagging, hitting the wall again and again, kicking her feet, trying to make as much noise as possible. The smoke kept pouring in and the dumbwaiter didn't move. Her friends were gone. Her eyes stung so badly, she clenched them shut, sending tears down her cheeks.

She was going to die.

Chapter 55

"You're killing her!" Robert's voice cut through the fire alarm.

Logan stood frozen at the terror in Florence's voice. They heard the pounding from inside the small dumbwaiter shaft. Florence was trapped in the fire on the main floor.

Horrified, Mia hit the Level 4 button, probably to get Florence as far away as possible. The dumbwaiter whirled and carried Florence up—maybe to someplace worse. Mia hit the button until the pounding disappeared, and the dumbwaiter stopped on the fourth floor.

Logan clenched the wheel, hoping Florence wasn't hurt. *"Mia,* come on."

Mia ran to the golf cart, passing directly in front of Robert, but he ignored her. He flung the outer doors open and looked up the dumbwaiter shaft. The Level 4 button glowed red. Robert stared at it.

Mia sat on the edge of the passenger seat beside Angel. "Logan, just drive."

"What about Florence? What if she's trapped up there?"

"We can't help unless we get out of here!"

Logan looked back at Robert, who waited patiently. The dumbwaiter rumbled back down, delivering an empty box.

"She made it out," Mia said. "She'll be okay."

Robert turned to them, but not with anger. He looked perfectly calm. He was past angry.

"Logan." Mia held onto the seat. "Go!"

Logan accelerated too quickly, causing the golf cart to jerk forward and throw him off balance. He tried to brake and turn down the center aisle, but the tires spun on the wet floor. The cart veered, clipping the edge of a shelf and spiraling.

It crashed on its side, throwing all three of them.

Robert approached the wreckage, shoes splashing through the growing puddles.

Logan wiped water from his eyes, checking if everyone was okay. He'd collided with a shelf, and his vision tilted as if drifting in an ocean. Blood trickled down his face, and he tasted metal on his tongue.

Mia held Angel's hands, blood spilling from her mouth. Angel struggled to stand, but Mia dragged him to his feet, and together they limped toward the side door.

Robert followed them, the machete swinging by his side, his posture that of a man perfectly at peace with the world.

"Leave me, Mia. Just go." Angel pushed her away, leaning on his good leg. "I'm not worth dying for."

Mia's eyes blazed. She clutched Angel's shirt and pulled him forward, his useless foot dragging through the water.

"*Mia!*" Angel's voice broke. "*Please, leave.*"

Logan started running, too unbalanced and too slow. It wouldn't make a difference. Angel's frightened voice punctured his heart.

Robert caught up with them, still calm, only doing what had to be done. Someone helped Florence escape, and they had to pay the price for that. He raised the machete above his head and brought it down toward Mia.

At the same time, Angel shoved Mia aside, stepping into the path of the machete. The long, serrated blade lodged in his neck and shoulder, spraying blood.

Mia screamed.

Logan tackled Robert, and they crashed on the floor. He reached for Robert's throat, his hands slipping.

Robert grabbed Logan's shirt and yanked him sideways, throwing him off. Logan scrambled for the machete. It was still in Angel, and his heart and stomach clenched when he pulled the machete out of his friend. But Angel didn't feel a thing. He was already dead.

Logan turned, machete raised, but Robert was already on him and knocked him over. His head smacked against the floor, the machete sliding through puddles.

Robert ran after it.

Mia grabbed Logan's arm, yanking him up, even though his eyes were unfocused. Fury boiled inside of him, and he saw Robert as nothing but an animal—a skeleton wrapped in flesh and bone, all soft and mushy, able to be broken, stripped, and left to dry in the sun.

Mia pulled him away from Robert, away from Angel.

"Stop it!" Logan brushed her off. He'd kill that motherfucker. He wasn't leaving this place until Robert's guts were rinsing off in the sprinkler water.

Mia slapped his face and pulled his arm. She wanted to say things, but she couldn't speak and sob at the same time.

Robert picked up the machete, smiling.

Mia hit Logan again. "*Don't.* He'll kill you!" She let go and yelled for him to follow.

Logan waited five seconds, his anger sharp and knife-like inside his soul. He then turned and ran after Mia, seeing Robert's blurry shape standing in the stacks, looking up at the falling water.

They reached the side door. The hallway was engulfed in flames, but mostly to the left. The sprinklers were making a difference. Logan and Mia sank to their stomachs and crawled to the right, beneath the smoke and the fire.

Logan's arm hair sizzled. He kept moving, nose to the floor, until the heat above him died down. They jumped to their feet and ran toward the dock, coughing out the black smoke in their lungs. Robert hadn't followed them. Why would he stay in the stacks?

Crossing the dock, Logan pushed through the exit, taking a deep, fitful breath of country night air.

The surrounding fields and woods glowed with flashing lights. Emergency vehicles were parked by the front entrance. Logan had to tell someone about Florence. About Angel. Even if they were too late.

But his knees hit the concrete. He bent over, his forehead on the ground, and tried to breathe. Mia collapsed next to him, holding her palms against her cheeks, catching her own silver tears.

They let a precious minute slip by on the concrete lot behind the resort, right where a long, jagged crack had let a few resilient weeds grow through.

Logan then stood up, extending a hand to Mia. He couldn't lose Florence, too. They had to get help.

Mia took his hand, her fingers slick with Angel's blood. He helped her stand, and they ran together.

Chapter 56

Killing Angel did nothing to solve his problem, but it gave Robert butterflies all the same.

He considered hunting down the other two cowards, but they were slipping away, and he didn't have time to chase them. Florence was the goal, despite the pleasure he would feel watching Logan bleed out in the raging fire.

Robert sent the dumbwaiter back up to the fourth floor and watched it ascend, then he climbed inside the empty shaft. He didn't have the sheath for the machete anymore, and he couldn't carry it with him, so he dropped it on the ground. He wouldn't need it anyway. He would never, ever hurt Florence. Did she understand that?

He gripped the small wooden ledges lining the inside of the square shaft. If he could climb to the second floor, he'd find another way up to the fourth. Even with adrenaline, he doubted he had the strength to climb higher than two stories. Already, only ten feet up, his fingers and arms trembled with weakness.

Smoke filled the dumbwaiter shaft like a chimney. Robert held his breath in intervals, which made everything harder. He passed the outer doors on the main level, which were on fire and melting. Florence nearly died in this spot. Robert moved up, past those doors, and tried to focus. The shaft was narrow, allowing him to use his back and knees to push against the walls and give his arms a break. Still, he trembled.

Up ahead, light reflected on the wall. Not far now, but he couldn't stop and rest, otherwise he'd suffocate. He didn't look down—he climbed. He'd never been athletic, but this was something else; raw energy coaxed from deep wells within his soul. He had no idea he possessed such strength and dexterity.

Fighting for every inch, shaking with every handhold, he finally reached the second level, forced the outer doors open, and clung to the ledge. Fresh air washed over him, and he laughed at the bright, white, fluorescent lights. Never had they looked so comforting.

Climbing out, he landed quietly on his feet. He cut through the hallway—the air already filling with smoke. He ran into the stairwell, into a pillar of black smoke coming from the first floor, when footsteps echoed on the stairs above him.

Florence.

She'd tried using the stairs to get down, only to find them blocked on the main floor. He realized this would be an obstacle when trying to leave with her, but he'd deal with that when the time came.

Covering his nose and mouth, he rushed through the smoke, the flickering bursts of fire, and ran up the next flight. He leaned over the railing and looked up.

One level up, Florence looked down, her slender hand on the railing, her rain jacket fading into the black smoke. She had nowhere to go.

"Florence!" He started up the stairs, pushing his body to run faster. He called for her again, but she didn't answer.

Her footsteps disappeared, and the stairwell door swung shut above him. She was running through the fourth floor, still with nowhere to go.

He finally made it. He crashed through the doorway, his legs nearing the point of surrender. The fire alarms wailed, and white lightning flashed through the hallway.

On either side of him, doors were left open. Dozens of options for Florence to hide.

Robert looked at the carpet, the fluffy material smeared in the direction of the stairs. Dark footprints led in the opposite direction, away from him, the color slowly fading as the carpet fought to regain shape. He followed the dark patches, spaced far apart. She was sprinting.

Robert followed the footprints down the hallway, expecting them to veer off into a room, but they disappeared at the roof's entrance.

He sighed, wishing he could predict that beautiful mind of hers. There was nothing on the roof but a long way down. All this trouble just to end in a corner.

Robert opened the door and walked out, hands in his pockets, like the place wasn't literally burning down beneath them.

Florence stood in the corner, exactly where any trapped animal would be. That bright fear in her eyes tugged at his heart. She clutched her purse with both hands, thinking of her phone, no doubt, knowing it didn't matter. No one was rescuing her from this. Her friends (what friends remained) had run away.

It was only the two of them.

"Florence, why are you running?" Robert picked his way through the tables and chairs, arms open, showing no threat. "I'm not going to hurt you. This whole time, I've been trying to get to know you better."

She didn't believe him. He had to win her over.

"Come with me." He stopped a few feet away, offering one hand. "Come on. I'll take care of you. There's a place we can go. A quiet, gentle place. No noise. No stupid parties, just books! All the books you could ever want. I'll get them for you, I swear. If I can explain my vision for you, you'll see why I did all of this. You're so special, don't you see that?"

Florence said nothing, but her expression changed. "Why did you start the fire?"

"To give us a head start," he said. "It's just a resort. They can build another."

Her face scrunched up like she wanted to cry, but then it changed again, something *inexpressible*, something like fury.

He was losing her—he had to win her back.

"I know you better than you know yourself," he said. "Can't you trust me? Everything I've done, I did for you. Don't you see that?"

Florence slowly shook her head. "You don't get it, Robert. I'm not who you think I am."

He smiled; she was cute like this, all spitfire and tough. "I know you."

"*No, you don't.*" She lifted her phone from her purse, as if that would save her.

Robert closed in to take her phone away. Getting a head start on the road was crucial, and a 911 call could ruin that.

"You don't understand," he said. "I get it; you don't know what I went through to be your curator. You don't understand how important this is, and that's okay! I'll show you. It's not your fault, but please give me the phone."

He was closer now, close enough to smell her perfume.

Florence pouted, handing over her phone.

He took it, their fingers brushing, shivers dancing down his spine.

"I know you worked hard, Robert," she said, a tremor in her voice, "but you missed something."

Robert blinked. "What do you mean? What did I miss?"

Florence exhaled slowly. "I didn't come here for me."

She dropped her purse. In her other hand, she held a knife. No, not a knife—a small handheld shovel.

She drove the shovel into his neck. Robert sputtered, his mouth incapable of screaming or forming words. She yanked the shovel out and stabbed him in the stomach over and over, as if digging something up.

He sank to his knees, his thoughts like weightless little clouds floating away. He couldn't breathe air, only blood. He rolled on his side, his body falling apart.

What did she mean, she didn't come here for herself? Who did she come here for?

The shovel clattered beside him, covered in things that should've stayed inside his body. He tried to say her name, but she was already walking away.

"Please," he whispered, his eyes closing on their own, his body becoming an alien thing he had no control over. "Come back."

"No." Her footsteps receded. "You deserve to die alone."

Robert shuddered, his soul sinking into a dark, endless pool, the water warm and smothering.

Chapter 57

Florence stood in the fourth-floor hallway, blood dripping from her hair to her shoes. She looked down, watching the drops disappear into a carpet almost designed to hide blood.

Her hand hurt from gripping the shovel too tightly, even though carving into Robert's stomach felt like digging in soft ground. She clenched her fists together and pried them back open, the blood making her fingers stick together. She smelled like death.

Alyssa stood in the hallway in front of her. With their broken nails and bloody clothes, they resembled each other. Florence wondered if she now carried the same feral glint in her eyes.

Alyssa must've noticed something unraveling inside her, because she opened her arms to Florence and without hesitation, Florence stumbled into them.

Florence couldn't breathe. Her quest to find Chloe had miserably failed. She'd never get to see her again, or make her laugh, or return the necklace, or give back a small portion of life, of which Florence had too much and Chloe far too little.

Their embrace ended, and she wanted to plead one last time, *Can you help me find Chloe?*

But before she could ask, Alyssa moved her lips without speaking.

"What did you say?"

Alyssa held Florence's head with both hands, mouthing the words, *She's not here.*

"But Chloe has to be here—I thought I could find her, and now I don't know where—"

Alyssa held a finger to Florence's lips and silently said, *No, she's not here. Do you understand? She's not angry or bitter. There was nothing for her to cling to. She's gone, Florence. She let go.*

Florence rested her forehead on Alyssa's shoulder, fighting to stay on her feet. All this time, Florence told herself she wanted to find her best friend and apologize, while inwardly dreading what she would find. Would Chloe appear as Alyssa had? In the exact state of how she died?

She wanted Chloe to show up and prove Florence's life was a wreck, that she wasn't worth anything, that she deserved every guilt-ridden night she spent with air in her lungs.

But Chloe didn't stay. She didn't cling to this world like Alyssa, dreaming of revenge for thirty-eight years. She didn't blame Florence for what happened, so she let go. Her life had ended in tragedy, but the same didn't have to be true for Florence.

Alyssa smiled and took Florence's hand and pressed it against her stained nightgown, right over her chest.

At first, Florence didn't get it. Then Alyssa moved Florence's hand and placed it over her own wildly beating heart.

Go on, Florence. You still have a life to live.

Message received. Florence forced herself into the stairwell, taking one last glance at Alyssa.

"Thank you."

Alyssa bowed slightly, placing a hand over her lifeless heart. *Go on now.*

Florence ran down the smoke-filled stairwell to the second floor. She crawled along the carpet, her eyes aching, and managed to see one room on the left side with an open door.

She army-crawled inside the room, pausing to check the bathroom and closet in case someone was trapped. She shoved open the balcony door and inhaled the fresh air, feeling the starry night sky above and the roaring fire below.

Coughing, she stood tall, waving her arms at the group of emergency vehicles, and farther out, the army of readers who silently watched the resort burn. They sat on the hillside, in their pajamas, under the protection of the towering tree with its outstretched branches and giant dying leaves.

The readers noticed her before the police, and a great cry swept through the crowd. People pointed and jumped and yelled.

Firefighters jumped in their ladder truck and maneuvered through the grass until they were parked in front of her balcony.

Florence leaned over the railing as a ladder extended toward her. A young firefighter climbed the rungs and held his gloved hand out to her.

Come on, Florence.

Just reach.

She grabbed his hand and stepped onto the ladder. Glancing at the resort, Florence didn't look for shadows in the windows or ghosts on the battlement. Instead, she held the ladder and listened to the firefighter's instructions. The crowd cheered for her. Not because she was anyone they knew or cared about, but because she was alive.

See you soon, Florence thought. *I love you, goodnight.*

Chapter 58

Robert opened his eyes, surprised to be alive. But he was alone on the roof; Florence had long gone.

He sat up, pleased to find his body moved like it used to. He could tell his legs to stand up, and they obeyed. It felt like old times. Of course, he'd only been passed out for a minute, maybe less. He wasn't dead, not even close, just badly injured.

Fine. He'd get rescued and hospitalized and could pay the price later. Right now, he wanted to live. Florence really did shock him. He never imagined her being capable of doing what she did.

How did he get it so wrong?

Robert staggered across the roof, his insides on fire. He was in bad shape all right; nothing worked properly. He felt like a puppet independently trying to walk for the first time. His bladder let go all on its own—how humiliating.

He'd been reduced to a frail, dying sack of meat and bones. Pitiful. He refused to die like this.

He made it to the hallway. Impressive. Time to crawl on his hands and knees and pray they had the fire under control.

The hallway was dark. Aside from the fire alarms, the electricity had gone out. He reached the stairs, thinking about how rolling down them would finish him off, but what other choice did he have?

There! Up ahead!

The elevators. The one closest to him was lit up with a warm, golden light. It looked like a lighthouse in a storm.

He crawled toward it, hoping it would take him to safety. He could almost feel the ticking clock inside his heart, counting the seconds until everything self-destructed.

The doors were already open for him. How courteous. Elevators were not recommended for escaping fires, even a child knew that, but he would die without it, so he crawled inside. The air was warm and relaxing. The hazy light made him think of a fairground at night, when you're sitting on the bleachers waiting for the show to start, with your best girl beside you, and her warm hand on your thigh.

The elevator moved. It was going down to the lobby. There were flashing ambulance lights right outside the front doors! He knew he was going to be fine.

The lobby was on fire, and the stained-glass window was smeared with black smoke. Firefighters worked to catch stragglers and move them outside.

"Thank you, thank you," Robert whispered as the elevator lowered to the main floor.

Only... it didn't stop. It kept descending. The elevator sank below the main floor, down to the lower level.

"No, no, no!" He tried to stand, but everything felt so wrong. How did he ever manage to walk? He fell on his back as the elevator stopped with a *thud*.

The warm, golden light vanished, and the elevator became his coffin because maybe he deserved to die like this. Was this the resort's way of paying him back for starting the fire?

The elevator doors opened, light poured in, and Robert stared into a sea of fire. Alyssa stood in the flames, and she wasn't alone.

The bald, one-legged man was crouched beside her. Behind them, shadows watched, waited. How many ghosts lived at the resort?

"Please," he cried, his throat too mangled to speak clearly. "Please don't touch me."

Alyssa smiled and made a *tsking* sound. She reached into his pocket, removed the nutcracker, and raised it into the light.

"No," Robert wept.

The one-legged man grabbed Robert by the shirt and dragged him into the fire; into the company of ghosts who called this resort their home; into their arms, their hungry hands and teeth.

Before his death, Robert understood that his son, his beautiful boy, would be raised by ghosts, by a mother who would never return to the resort or the world of the living.

Alyssa watched dispassionately as the fire consumed him and his soul slipped through the cracks of the earth, into a place far from their ridge, a place where souls are lost and not given a second chance. He would be in good company there.

As he fell, Alyssa carefully collected Nathan, swaddled and sleeping. She now had everything she needed right there asleep in her arms.

Chapter 59

Logan hiked through the dark woods, shining his flashlight on the ground to avoid tree roots. Florence walked beside him, and next to her, Mia swept her flashlight from shadow to shadow, startling the occasional nocturnal animal.

They broke from the tree line and faced a long, sloping hill with a tall tree at the top, its leaves nearly gone.

Two weeks ago, the night of Angel's death, The Reader's Resort almost burned to the ground. The sprinklers fought the fire until the firefighters took over. Despite their combined efforts, and the fact that much of the structure was still standing, the bastion of literature-themed destinations was declared a total loss.

After Angel's funeral, Mia called Logan and Florence and asked if they wanted to go back. While discussing it, Florence made a remark that Logan found chilling. She said, "We don't know what's there."

In the end, they agreed to make the trip. They didn't say it—such things were impossible to articulate. But Logan knew they all felt like they'd left something there. Angel's funeral didn't bring closure; it felt like a story cut off in the middle.

They hiked up the long, sloping hill and rested under the tall tree and stared at the ruins.

The Reader's Resort was dark. With missing windows, blackened stone, and yellow crime scene tape, it looked like an abandoned, haunted landmark. Something to dare your friends to sneak into. A light fog shrouded the cliff and glowed under the moon, swirling at the slightest breeze.

They silently found their way to the front and ducked under the tape. The lobby was mostly gone, and the stained-glass window remained intact but covered in ash. The stairs and balcony were husks, the bookshelf a hollow black cave. The elevators were shattered and frozen on the main floor, their doors open like dead, slackened jaws.

They picked their way through the rubble and down to the lower level, where the hallways were partially collapsed. Thanks to Robert, the stacks had no doors. They walked in; no badge required.

Logan entered the underground library he'd so briefly known, feeling like a trespasser in a stranger's dream.

The floor was damp and littered with soggy, moldy books. The shelves towered above him like blacked-out skyscrapers; a city gone quiet. He found the golf cart he'd wrecked and felt his composure falling apart.

If he'd done one thing differently, Angel would be alive.

Just one thing.

I'm sorry, buddy. I had a chance to save you and I messed it up.

He squatted beside the cart, tears hitting the damp floor.

How are you gonna open your bookstore now?

Logan sat, his heart and mind and limbs going so numb, he felt dead inside.

"No, stop." Florence knelt beside him. She held his face with two soft hands and made him look at her. "You do not get to blame yourself, got it? You didn't kill Angel."

"If I'd changed one thing—"

"Logan, you didn't kill him. Robert did. He killed him, not you—do not ever take what Robert did and put it on yourself. *Robert* did this, and he paid for it."

Logan swallowed. "One thing… just one thing."

She hugged him, kissing his head. "You can go back through it a million times. You can think about all the things you'd change, knowing what you know now, but it won't make a single difference, and you can't live like that."

She was right; she would know.

But Logan knew he'd see Angel's death again and again in his nightmares because some things never go away. Some things linger. Florence left him and followed Mia to the other side of the room.

Logan looked around, wondering if the resort's ghosts were still there, or if everyone had left. His guess? They were gone. The resort didn't exist anymore, like the stacks. It was no longer a place for the living or the dead.

Angel didn't stay. He was gone with the rest of them.

Logan walked to the back wall and found Florence and Mia at the hangout.

They were picking up Mia's notecards, and Logan helped peel them off the floor, collecting their soggy, ink-smeared remnants in his palm. They were scraps now, but Mia gathered them carefully. Preserving history.

After a few minutes, they had the notecards in a pile and tears on their cheeks. Their hands were cold and wet.

Mia sat at the old diner booth. She cradled a notecard in her palm, the one with the drawing of Angel's bookstore and those goofy stick figures saying everything that was never said.

Florence sat beside Mia and hugged her while Mia cried.

Logan stared at the ceiling, an ache deep in his chest. They stayed like that for a long time. Maybe hours. Logan felt things change inside all of them; a shift so visceral, you could feel it like the growing pains you felt as a kid, like the bones were about to burst through your skin. They realized none of them would go on living like they used to; they knew too much now.

And they knew, once and for all, the resort was empty. There was nothing left to save.

Eventually, they agreed to leave. Logan dried his eyes as Florence leaned against him. "You all right?"

He nodded. "Gonna be. You?"

"I hope so." Florence held his hand for the first time since Angel's funeral. "Can you help me with something?"

Chapter 60

Florence knocked on the dark green door, hoping no one would answer, so she wouldn't have to go through with this.

She looked behind her. Logan was parked by the curb, in the driver's seat, giving her a reassuring smile. Like any good moral supporter, he was ready to drive off and leave her if she tried to back down.

She'd made up her mind to do this when they went back to the stacks. That was two weeks ago, and she still didn't feel ready.

The door opened and Florence stood face-to-face with an older version of Chloe.

Stephanie Lang.

"Florence?" Stephanie smiled, scrunching her face at the sunny day. "What on earth are you doing here?"

Despite her apprehension, Florence's fears began to melt away. "I'm sorry. I know I'm going to rush this, but if I don't say it now, I never will. I just want to say I'm sorry I wasn't around after Chloe died."

Stephanie's face fell, her old pain resurfacing. The question rose in her eyes: *How could you bring this up?*

"I couldn't face you at the funeral because I was there the night she died. I came over, we took something, and when I woke up, she was gone."

Stephanie went so pale, Florence thought she was about to faint.

"You were there?"

"Yes. I don't know what happened, or why I lived, or if someone else was involved in whatever she was taking, but I was there, and I left, and part of me still wishes I'd gone with her."

Shame tried to cripple her, but she pushed on. "I stopped seeing you guys because I couldn't tell you the truth. I was so terrified you'd hate me that I wasted those years because of it. We could've been friends still, and I could've kept coming over for Saturday morning breakfast, and instead I just ran away. And I fell apart, and I let you down."

Stephanie closed her eyes and exhaled. "Why now?"

"Because you need to know. Chloe didn't kill herself; it was just a horrible accident. She never meant to leave you."

Stephanie leaned against the doorway, the pain inside her so visible, she looked sick.

"Chloe loved you. We talked about our dreams, about places we'd visit and books we'd read and never once did Chloe say she was unhappy. You guys loved her, and she knew that. Even I knew it, all those days I spent at your house because I didn't want to go home. Chloe brought me into your family, and she never wanted to give that up."

Stephanie stared at the welcome mat, mouth slightly open, almost catatonic. "People think they see you coming apart," she said. "At the funeral, right? I cried the whole time. No one knew that was the tip of the iceberg. The real falling apart happens at night when you're by yourself and you can't stop shaking. It's the loneliest feeling in the world."

Stephanie crumbled. She fell into Florence's arms, and Florence held her, her own tears dampening Stephanie's shirt.

Eventually, Florence let her go. "She loved you. She loved you so much. So do I, and I'm sorry I haven't shown it." She removed the raven necklace from around her neck and gently placed it inside Stephanie's hand.

Stephanie nodded, clenching the necklace, and retreated inside her dim house. "Thank you for telling me. It was good to see you." She shut the door, still crying, and locked the deadbolt.

Florence felt like her heart had fallen out. What did she expect? That her words would heal Stephanie's crippled soul? Saying those things didn't bring Chloe back. It didn't help with the years of self-harm, divorce, and depression.

But this was *something*. A narrow way forward. If Florence kept checking on Stephanie, things could improve. It had to start somewhere, and it started here, on this porch, on a sunny but cold November day.

She walked back to the car and slid in the passenger seat.

"Went okay?"

Florence wiped her eyes. "I guess. I'm not sure I helped."

"You helped. She knows you're thinking about her. That goes a long way."

"I was hoping for... something more."

"Maybe she just needs time."

He started driving back to her apartment, the silence between them obvious but not awkward.

It had been four weeks since Angel's death. Since then, Florence and Logan hadn't gone on any dates or even kissed. It felt wrong, somehow. Not just because of Angel or Robert or all the people that died. But because their relationship flourished in a carnival of excitement, wonder, and tragedy, and neither of them wanted to test it against the cold light of reality.

Robert's son, Nathan, was plastered all over the internet in a national attempt to find him. Robert's sister, Margo, pleaded with the public for their help. Four weeks now, and no one had found Nathan.

Since the fire, the police had released a variety of reports.

Lori and Charlie Walter, and longtime handyman, Frederick, were all missing and wanted for questioning.

Dean Winksy and Layla Thomas were found dead in their rooms. The police claimed Robert killed them, although evidence of Layla's death had been severely damaged in the fire. They found Robert's remains in the lower level, of all places.

Florence didn't know what to think of that, but she had an idea.

Once the narrative started forming, many of the loose ends connected. Robert's goal and movements in those final days, the people he killed, the way he stalked Florence.

And ultimately, Florence stabbed him and left him on the roof. The public accepted this and praised Florence for stopping a rising serial killer, credited with at least four deaths, including Angel's.

The police found Alyssa's bones in the cellar, along with patches of blood from both Charlie and Lori. The police tested the stained-glass and confirmed the red paint was indeed blood, and shortly after, Frederick was publicly wanted for the murder of Alyssa Larkin. Lori hadn't been tied to any crimes, but Florence would always wonder if John actually stepped off that roof on his own volition or not. She may never know.

Florence went to Alyssa's siblings directly. She sat with them, told them the story, and described Alyssa's ghost in detail. They listened politely and didn't believe her at first, but by the end of it, they were convinced Florence was telling the truth. It was the closest they got to resolution. She didn't mention Alyssa's scars or her involvement with Lori and Frederick, but she assured them that Frederick was dead, and even though the police wouldn't take her word for it, he was never, ever coming back.

Alyssa was finally mourned, and that was what mattered. Her family could let go.

Logan drove to her apartment, a little three-story brick box beside the Sharonville rail yard. Two trains slithered by while a third was parked, waiting for something. Florence could never figure out why trains sat for such a long time. When she was little, she liked to think they were napping.

They walked to the third floor. "Got a text from Mia the other day. She passed her test," Logan said, leaning against the wall, hands in his pockets. "They let her reschedule it, 'cause, you know."

Florence unlocked the door, and they walked inside. "I don't think she was ever worried about failing."

Logan shrugged. "I don't know. I didn't pay close enough attention at the time."

He waited by the front door. If he thought being with her would end his nightmares, he was wrong. She'd only remind him of those days at the resort. Those beautiful, tragic days.

She knew that, but did he? Or would she have to break his heart? *I don't want to hurt you*, she thought. *But look at us. We can't fix this.*

Real life didn't feel real anymore. Florence looked around her apartment, thinking of all the things that needed to get done. All the bills and chores she'd neglected the last few weeks. Just sitting down to budget her groceries felt like a dream. She walked to the window in her living room, opened it, and breathed in the city air. The stopped train was still there. The other two trains were long gone, off to faraway places.

Logan stood beside her. "I like the railroad in your backyard."

"It's actually a rail yard."

"My bad. You pay extra for this view?"

"Shut up."

He chuckled, letting the moment fade.

Please, Logan, don't make me break your heart.

He cleared his throat. He couldn't say it.

Florence leaned her head against his shoulder. "I'm sorry."

"For what?"

"You know what."

Logan hugged her, kissing the top of her head. "I know. Things are weird. They can't be normal, not with everything we went through."

Florence nodded, taking a deep breath.

"But I think there's a way, if we want to try."

"What do you mean?"

Logan smiled. He let go, reached into his pocket, and pulled out a Sharpie.

"Are you serious!"

"Listen, listen." Logan held her hand. "Florence, I don't want to lose you. I really don't. You're brilliant, and kind, and you hunt ghosts and solve crimes—"

"Stop that!"

"I'm serious. I'm serious." He uncapped the Sharpie. "I lost the bet with my brother. Though he's cutting me slack for losing my job, for obvious reasons, so I'm starting another job that is *not* at an office. It's actually at a glass-blowing shop, which is kinda wild. But still, I lost the bet because I fell in love. Even though he was right. I'm not ready. But, with a little time, and starting a new job, and trying to get on my feet and move out on my own, I think I'll be ready."

"What about—"

"Time heals," he said, kissing her hand. "We met too early. So I'll wait for you, if you'll wait for me too. Just a little time, Florence, and I know we can give each other our best."

He was right, and also somehow describing everything she'd been feeling. "How long?"

He held her arm steady, brought the Sharpie down, and wrote: Oct. 4, 2027. "There. That was the one-year mark for the bet. I'm going to hold up my end of the deal." He looked at her with such resolve, she wondered how long he'd been thinking about this. "I'll wait for you, I mean it. And!"

He put the Sharpie away and pulled a paperback novel from his back pocket. "I've been reading."

"You *what*?"

"I'm a reader now." Logan grinned, handing her the book. "I started *The Shining*, and it was a little too much, too soon, which... I should've seen coming. So I read *Misery* instead. You read it?"

"I did a long time ago. What did you think?"

"I took notes." Logan tapped the book.

Florence opened the pages, finding his scribbles in the margins. Little comments and jokes and reactions to the story.

Logan beamed. "I wanted to write you a letter, and thought, why not put it inside a book? So there you have it, my letter to you."

"Logan." She flipped through the book. "This is incredible."

"You have my address already. I thought... since we'll be waiting for that magical date next October, maybe in the meantime, we send each other books? Whatever you read next, write me something inside the pages, and send it to me so I can read it."

She jumped into his arms, dropping *Misery* on the floor. He spun her around, like in the movies, and they kissed for the first time since that night, and it didn't feel strange at all.

"I'll write you a letter inside a book," Florence said. "I promise."

"I'll be waiting."

Logan kissed her cheek. "Don't take too long. I need another book to read."

"I'll hurry. I promise."

With that, Logan left her apartment, shutting the door gently behind him.

Florence picked up *Misery*, dusted it off, and thought, *I think you were right, Angel. I can see it now.*

Her phone chimed.

A text from Stephanie, who still had her number saved after all these years.

Thank you for what you said earlier. I'm sorry I ran away. If you're free Saturday morning, I'll make breakfast and coffee. I hope you'll come over.

Florence smiled. Some things can't be fixed, and that's okay. They can be improved over time. Little by little, over eggs and coffee, over letters written inside of books

Chloe was gone, and nothing, not even Florence's best efforts, could've brought her back. Unlike Alyssa, Chloe didn't have unfinished business. She had forgiven Florence a long time ago. And it was time for Florence to do the same.

Florence picked up her copy of *The Heart is a Lonely Hunter*. Having finished it, she grabbed a pen, opened the book to the title page, and wrote:

Stephanie,

I think you should read this. It will be difficult, and parts of it might hurt. But a friend gave it to me, and he believed books can heal people. I believe it, too.

Love, Florence

She put the book on her dresser, for Saturday's breakfast, and moved back to the open window.

The last train had finally left and moved on, and for the first time in her life, she didn't want to follow it.

She turned to her bookshelf, picked up a new novel, grabbed her favorite pen, and sat beside the window. She began her letter to Logan, listening to the city noise and the soft scratch of her pen with the faint beating of her heart.

And that was enough.

ACKNOWLEDGEMENTS

Writing this novel was an act of endurance. I won't pretend it was easy, because it was by far the hardest story I've ever written. If I didn't believe that this is what God wants me to do, I would've quit a long time ago, and I thank God for making this adventure possible.

My first drafts were a mess. I wanted to dive endlessly into the mundane and technical aspects of how the resort functioned, and eventually (some of you will not be pleased by this) I decided to cut entire chapters that focused solely on the world and lore inside the resort. But after rewriting, I absolutely fell in love with these characters, and their place in this world of readers and ghosts.

Even as the story improved, it took many drafts and changes before I was satisfied with it. I'm amazed it's here for you to read! It shouldn't have survived the long, grueling rewrites or the dark nights of doubt. This story could've died a thousand deaths, but it somehow prevailed.

Whether it's Logan and Angel driving the golf cart, Florence standing under the sprinklers in her rain jacket, or her final hug with Alyssa amidst the fire, something about this story refused to let go of me, and I hope, in a beautiful way, that it refuses to let go of you, too.

I would've given up without my editor, Erin Healy. Her insight in the early drafts led to a major rewrite, and this story became more satisfying and rewarding than either of us imagined. Thank you again, Erin. Tiffany

Avery is my terrific copy editor. Every chapter of this book benefitted from her incredible work, and it would be worse off without her.

Any errors and mistakes in this story are mine, and I take full responsibility for them. My editors and early readers are impeccable, but I have the final say for every word in this manuscript. That being said, elements of this story are intentionally fantastical. The Reader's Resort is a magical place, and I think myself, and many readers, would love to get lost in it for a long time.

Early readers like my wife, Caitlin, and Aaron Bogan, Bayleigh Horn, and my sisters, Anna, Katie, and Martha, were all endlessly patient, helpful, and instrumental in making the story better. Jesy Boals and Kennedy King were phenomenal readers, their notes helped raise the bar on the manuscript and get it one step closer to completion. They were both difference makers for this story.

Huge thanks to the staff of the Mason Public Library, Ohio. They gave me a tour of the library's closed stacks and inspired many aspects of this novel.

Eternal thanks to my wife, the other half of our family life balancing act. Without her, this book and dream of mine never would've come to pass.

And finally, special thanks to the two primary inspirations behind this story:

I once eavesdropped on my former coworker, Zane, telling someone, "They turned the hotel into a bookstore." Or... the bookstore turned into a hotel, something along those lines.

(Either way, I spent the rest of my shift outlining a concept idea of a library hotel. There actually is a real Library Hotel in New York City, that I discovered well after writing this book).

And for the second inspiration: Years ago, I stood outside a restaurant with my coworker, Timmy, while he smoked and told me he'd applied for a job at a pub across the street. The pub offered him a position: he could crack nuts in the basement for minimum wage.

I asked him what he thought of that.

He threw his head back and laughed. "I told them, HELL NO."

em jones